PAINTED DEVILS

PAINTED DEVILS

WORDS AND INTERIOR ILLUSTRATIONS

MARGARET OWEN

HENRY HOLT AND COMPANY
NEW YORK

If you made it through *Little Thieves*, you ought to be fine with this one.
That said, this story contains the following potential triggers: verbal and physical abuse,
abandonment, anxiety and panic attacks, blood and gore, mention of animal death
(off-page), misuse of animal carcass, cults, mention of death of a parent (off-page), body
image issues, and sexual situations. Oh, and for one unfortunate prefect: horses.

Henry Holt and Company, *Publishers since 1866*
Henry Holt® is a registered trademark of Macmillan Publishing Group, LLC
120 Broadway, New York, NY 10271 • fiercereads.com

Our books may be purchased in bulk for promotional, educational, or business use. Please
contact your local bookseller or the Macmillan Corporate and Premium Sales Department at
(800) 221-7945 ext. 5442 or by email at MacmillanSpecialMarkets@macmillan.com.

Library of Congress Cataloging-in-Publication Data is available.

First edition, 2023
Book design by Rich Deas and Maria Williams
Printed in the United States of America

ISBN 978-1-250-83116-3
1   3   5   7   9   10   8   6   4   2

To the wicked girls,
The hard truth about shooting for the moon is,
when you miss, you don't always land among the stars.
Sometimes all that slows the fall are the thorns.
The good news is:
The sun won't see you coming.

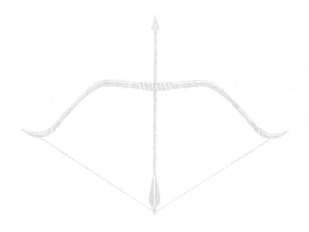

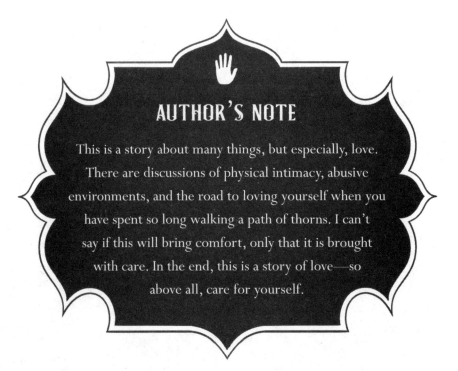

AUTHOR'S NOTE

This is a story about many things, but especially, love. There are discussions of physical intimacy, abusive environments, and the road to loving yourself when you have spent so long walking a path of thorns. I can't say if this will bring comfort, only that it is brought with care. In the end, this is a story of love—so above all, care for yourself.

A child's eye fears the painted devil,
but an elder wields the brush.
—Almanic proverb

PART ONE:

RED
PROPHETS

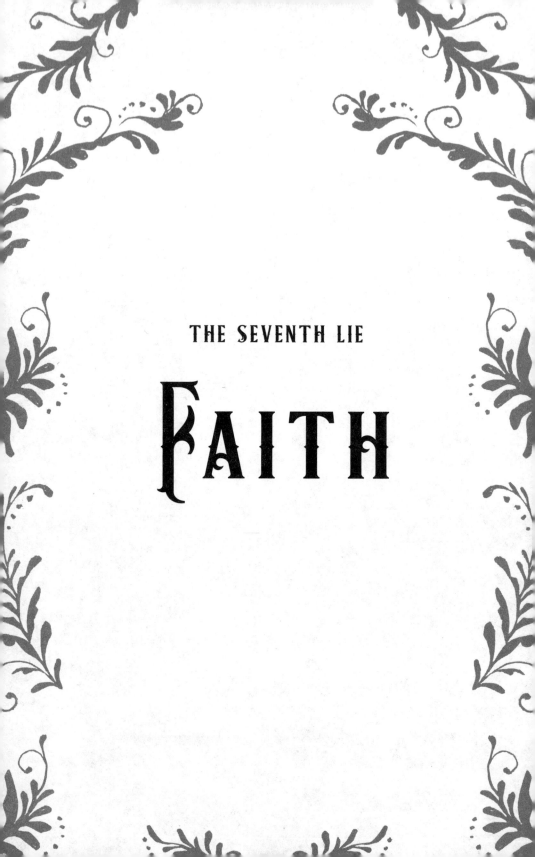

THE SEVENTH LIE

FAITH

ONCE UPON A TIME, A BRIDE FLED INTO THE NIGHT ON A STEED SPUN from starlight. The clouds were her road, and her veil tangled in the constellations, tearing away until her golden bridal crown tumbled into the chasm below.

The bride watched it fall, and she told herself she was free.

༄ৎৡ৸৯

Once upon a time, a princess made a desperate and terrible oath. She would marry no one, she swore, until they conquered the terrors of the deep and brought her a lost golden crown.

The princess spoke the words as a wall between herself and the world. And she told herself no one would be foolish enough to die trying to climb it.

༄ৎৡ৸৯

Once upon a time, a wicked maid came to a village in the hawthorn-dark hills.

It was a frosty night, not in the full clutch of winter's jaws but with the fangs of that cold beast still gnawing at tree and stone. Only a mere slip of moon remained to wink slyly at the wicked maid as she stumbled down the rocky road. Bright crimson glistened through fingers pressed to her shuddering chest.

You see, the wicked maid was most atrociously drunk.

Three weeks had passed since she'd left the march of Bóern at the start of the new year, bound for her lover's home city of Helligbrücke.

It had been two weeks since she'd reached the outskirts of a town called Quedling in the principality of Lüdheid, only a few days' travel from Helligbrücke, and stopped there.

When her party went on, her message went with them, a folded parchment addressed, in shaky hand, to one *Emeric Conrad.*

The wicked maid's message went on to Helligbrücke. The wicked maid did not.

Instead, she had wandered into the rolling wheat-velveted hills of the Haarzlands. And for the past two weeks, she had kept wandering.

By now, the letter surely would have reached her lover. He would know she wasn't coming to Helligbrücke. Not yet. Not . . . like this.

Not when she wasn't enough.

She told herself she had to be more than a thief and a liar, more than a faithless servant, more than a wayward daughter. That she could *make* herself something more.

Two weeks before tonight, the wicked maid had said as much in her letter.

One week, six days, thirteen hours, and forty-three minutes before tonight, she had realized she'd made a tremendous mistake. But the carriage had already left, the letter was gone, and the cold truth remained: She was not enough.

And since then, she had wandered all 'round the Haarzlands, searching in vain like a mournful ghost and learning the hard way that there are few honest trades for a thief.

Tonight, she'd had quite a lot to drink, for she had quite a lot to drown. It was not long before she became soused well past the point of belligerence and sallied boldly into insensibility. She had already been evicted from the nearest inn after first scathingly denouncing the tavern minstrel's performance, then putting on her own show of how many meals she could vomit onto the stage. She had attempted to pay off the innkeeper in rubies, but the man had no use for her "bits of red glass." She had threatened to bring the wrath of Death and Fortune down upon the town in revenge. (Her godmothers, still acclimating to their daughter's newest flavor of bullshit, politely declined to visit their wrath upon the town.)

And so the wicked maid found herself staggering into the neighboring village well after midnight, clutching a rucksack full of rubies and looking for somewhere to lay her head. To encourage the townsfolk to open their doors to her, she was bawling the tragic ballad that she'd previously roasted the tavern minstrel for at the top of her lungs. It was not particularly effective.

Like many, many things that had befallen her, what happened next was preventable to the point of being self-inflicted.

"*Red-handed maid, red-blooded maaaaid, red was the maid o' the river,*" the horrible girl sang, like a cat in a territory dispute. She reached a plain wooden bridge over a brook that ran sluggish and frigid, little more than a trickle of slush this time of year. "*Lost was your hoooome, lost was your looooooooooove, lost was . . . was . . .* Oh, *scheit*, what rhymes with—"

The wicked maid, preoccupied as she was with her quest for one of myriad words that rhymes with *river*, found herself abruptly ambushed by the planks of the bridge. She was not certain how they had managed to get the drop on her, only that one moment she was maintaining a respectful and professional distance from the ground, and the next she was intimately acquainted with the woodgrain.

The fall knocked the wind out of her. It took a moment to register a brittle *skitter-patter* of something spilling over wooden planks, and by the time she did, it was far too late.

Her gutted bag of rubies lay before her, only a meager blood splatter remaining on the bridge; the rest were rolling merrily over the edges of the planks. As she watched, one fell with a self-satisfied *plink* into the water below.

For a long moment, all the wicked maid did was stare at the carnage of her fortune. She was sober enough to fathom the measure of what she'd just lost; she was drunk enough to tap into that special booze-fueled kind of despair.

So she did what any rational person would do, having cut herself off from her loved ones, failed to find gainful employ after two straight weeks of searching, and then drunkenly ejected most of her personal wealth into a river in the wee hours of what could generously be called the butthole of winter.

She gave up.

She lay facedown on the dung-stained boards of the bridge and cried. She cried like a routed general. She cried like a jilted bride. She cried like a two-year-old who has been told they cannot eat rocks.

This was, admittedly, not her proudest moment. But can you blame her?

(I mean, you can, and you should. Saints and martyrs, I certainly do. Brace yourself: It's only going to get worse from here.)

When she had cried herself out, she didn't get up, not for a while. At first, she was just marinating in her own miserable failures; it's mandatory with these kinds of things. But eventually, she made a decision.

The whole "honest living" idea was a noble goal. And maybe it would work later, somewhere else. But those rubies were her safety net. Her easy way out if things went bad. She *had* to get them back.

More critically, she had to do it without freezing to death in the river or being apprehended by villagers, who almost certainly would claim the rubies for their own.

She gathered up the handful of stones she had left, then stole into the nearest available barn, sneaking around drowsy sheep to curl up in the straw for warmth. She tried not to think of two months ago, when she'd had a soft, cozy bed in Castle Reigenbach. It was even harder not to think of one month ago, when she'd had a bed in an inn, friends who would laugh with her at her own folly, and a boy who might have shared that bed if she'd asked. It was impossible not to think of Emeric now, of where she might be if only she'd kept her word.

If Emeric were here, he could have pulled her rubies out of the icy water with a splash of witch-ash oil and a wry smile. If Ragne were here, she would have done something horrifying and helpful, like turn herself into a fish, swallow all the rubies, then horf them back up for the wicked maid onshore.

But the maid had to do this herself. She had to be more than who she was.

The chill kept her awake as she plotted a lie that could save her. Then, when the dark beyond the clapboards began to ease, she tiptoed out again.

Later, she would learn that she'd stowed away in the barn of the man who, at the grudging crack of dawn, found her wading in the frigid creek. He was a sheep farmer named Udo Ros, come to fetch water for his flock.

"Strange girl," he said, setting his wooden pails on the bank, "whatever you lost, it's not worth the chill you'll catch."

The wicked maid shook her head, donning a look of wide-eyed wonder. "I had a vision in my dream last night," she announced. "A beautiful maiden dressed all in scarlet, spinning thread on this very bridge. She pricked her finger on her spindle and blood fell into the water. She said if every drop was gathered and returned before sunset, she'd bring blessings on us all."

The man gave her a narrow look. That was good; better to win over a skeptic than a known dupe. That would give her more credibility later.

"Might you lend me a pail, good sir? I would hate to drop any."

The girl lifted her cupped palms, in which she'd pooled all her remaining rubies.

Udo Ros's eyes nearly fell out of his head. Unlike the innkeeper, *he* knew precious stones when he saw them.

It was the inverse of the game the terrible girl had played in Minkja, masquerading as the princess Gisele to hide her jewel heists. That game had worked because she'd shown people what they expected to see: a princess or her maid.

This, on the other hand, was the opposite: credible because it was impossible. Even a mere handful of rubies was still far, far too many for a bedraggled traveler to carry. It could only be a miracle.

Udo held out a bucket. "You saw a maid in red?"

She nodded, taking care to let the rubies sparkle bewitchingly in the morning light as she tipped them in. "She said she lost something long ago." (I'll be honest: I didn't remember much else from the ballad, only that the man playing it should have been charged with murdering a lute.) "Do you know of her, the scarlet maiden?"

The rubies skated across the bottom of the bucket as he handed it to her. "There's a song," the shepherd said shortly, frowning in thought. "How many stones did you see in the brook?"

The girl made a show of rubbing her stiff red fingers for warmth. "Dozens. Hundreds, maybe. But the blessing—"

"Yes, yes," he interrupted, waving a hand. "I don't know much about visions and dreams, strange girl, but it's clear there's a Low God's summons here, and I know better than to shirk it."

Within the hour, the horrible girl had a steaming mug of broth between her mitts and a nice view from the bank as the hardier towns-folk took shifts fishing for her rubies. It was too early in the year for snowmelt, so the waters were no higher than Udo's knees, but the bitter cold drove each villager out before too long. That was no matter; others splashed in to take their place while the previous scavengers warmed by a fire. Udo had gathered enough of the town to make much quicker work than if the girl had tried to find every stone herself.

As for the maid, she just stationed herself by the bucket and answered questions as she collected rubies: She was but a poor wood-cutter's daughter from Bóern who'd set off to seek her fortune after her parents died. She had dreamed of a noble maiden in a fine red gown who promised blessings on the village, and no more could she say. (You have to keep these lies simple. They'll catch you in the details.) She did not know how many rubies there were, so they would need to be diligent and try to find every last one.

She did not know why the Scarlet Maiden chose her.

By early afternoon, the village—Hagendorn, she was told—had salvaged enough rubies to satisfy the terrible girl. When twenty minutes went by without anyone finding another, she decided the next would be the last, clutching the bucket to her chest.

Udo was the one to find it, splashing back to pass the stone to her. What the people of Hagendorn saw next was fairly typical for a minor miracle and about the best the wicked maid could do with the kind of hangover she was nursing.

She dropped the ruby into the bucket. (It was not the ruby.) There was a small bang and a puff of crimson smoke. (Joniza Ardîm, the bard of Castle Reigenbach, gave me some of her flash powders before I left.) When the villagers crowded around to look, the rubies had all van-ished. (Of course they had; I'd been skimming them into my rucksack all along.)

"Surely," the wicked maid cried, "the Scarlet Maiden's favor is upon this town!"

She had to give Hagendorn credit: There were plenty of gaping yokels but also plenty of doubtful looks. Not that it mattered. She had every intention of blessing herself right out of this village posthaste, then finding a real bed in a place with a population, at minimum, in the triple digits.

Then someone let out a shout of alarm, pointing to the nearby roof of Udo's house. An ember had escaped the smoking chimney and fallen to the thatch. A tongue of flame licked up from the straw, coy and deadly.

Udo took the bucket from the wicked maid, scrambling into the shallow brook, but everyone on the shore knew it would not be enough. Nothing would. The thatch was good as tinder, the timbers of his walls kindling and firewood. The best they could hope for would be to save the barn.

Udo was about to lose everything, and they could only watch.

Then—

A bough bent on a great fir tree beside Udo's house. A heap of watery snow plopped onto the thatch in just the right spot, dousing the fire in a trice and leaving naught but a crooked finger of steam.

That alone might not have been enough to do it. Enough to let the wicked maid leave Hagendorn unscathed, probably, but not enough for . . . what followed.

What *really* sold it was a young boy running up to one of the women only a moment later, calling, "Mami, come quick! The milch-cow's had twins!"

Every eye turned to the wicked maid, each glittering with the same wonder as Udo's when she'd first held up the fistful of impossible rubies.

She did a surreptitious check for the glimmers of Godmother Fortune's handiwork but saw none. This was all pure chance.

"The Scarlet Maiden's blessing!"

"The Scarlet Maiden!"

The girl didn't know who started the cheer, but it rose faster and more ferociously than the flame in the thatch. Udo's hand landed on her shoulder. She looked up.

"Would you like to stay for dinner?" he asked.

At the time, it seemed a simple enough of a lie. There was no harm in giving Hagendorn that bit of comfort, the illusion of a benevolent god in hard country. I saw the light in their faces, I saw hope.

I knew I was lying when I told myself: It would not matter who, or what, they believed.

CHAPTER ONE

THE MIRACLE OF THE BRIDGE

LET ME STATE ONE THING UP FRONT: I WASN'T *TRYING* TO START A CULT.

I know that may be hard to buy. Especially given that I'm currently squinting into a tin mirror and painting stark red diamonds onto my face, robed head to toe in equally stark red, and hurrying to finish before the last dregs of sunset swirl down the drain.

And given that the minute I exit my little half hut, I'll see pilgrims and penitents and devotees all decked in red, chanting around the shabby wooden bridge now festooned in garlands of anything that blooms crimson.

And given that, when they see me, everyone in Hagendorn will hail me as the Scarlet Maiden's prophet.

But the important thing is that I didn't do any of that on *purpose*, so technically none of it's my fault.

It's been a strange two months since the Miracle of the Bridge. (That's what they're calling it now.) And you have to understand, I stayed only because they asked.

At first, Udo Ros just wanted to make sure I had somewhere safe and dry to spend the night before I went on my way. But the next morning, Leni's little girl toddled off while Leni was boiling ashes for lye. There were two sets of footprints in the snow: Leni's daughter's and those of a *waldskrot*, one of the nastier Mossfolk of the forest. When *waldskrotchen* lead a child away, the child rarely makes it back. Well . . . not in one piece.

Yet Leni's girl was found safe and sound at the edge of the woods, giggling under a rare holly thicket. *Waldskrot* blood was splashed new-leaf green on the snow and on the spiked fronds; its trail vanished under the hedge. Just above, dangling like a bribe, hung plump clusters of shockingly scarlet berries.

After that, the villagers of Hagendorn would not hear of my leaving. Not when I'd brought the blessing of a prodigal Low God, and not when there was a chance it might follow me out. Never mind that we all know *waldskrotchen* are stupid enough to run right into a holly bush, or that the red berries were in season.

What mattered wasn't whether the Scarlet Maiden was real, but only that they didn't lose her favor.

And . . . I'll admit, it was nice to be wanted again. To know I could still be wanted. Even if it was for a lie.

So Udo Ros and his grumpy weaverwitch brother, Jakob, made over the lean-to behind their house for me, putting up rough timber walls and laying straw over the hard-packed dirt. Their chimney runs up the wall I share with the house, and if the chimney stones themselves don't warm my teeny half hut enough, there's a little iron door I can crack open to let in heat.

It was no Castle Reigenbach. It wasn't even mine, not really. But it was made for me, and for a time, that was enough.

Slowly, it filled. Leni collected cloth scraps from around town, enough to make me a warm quilt to spread over my pallet, then a pillow stuffed with dried clover. The pallet was traded for a straw tick. Sonja periodically brought me fresh milk from her cow that had twins. The Ros brothers called me in for breakfast each morning, and in turn I helped Udo with the sheep or Jakob with his witch-work.

And, day by day, each welcome coincidence was chalked up to the Scarlet Maiden's hand.

I was asked to bless crops, flocks, babies. To choose which lamb teeth to bind into a protection charm. To read ash and bone and speak for the Scarlet Maiden. As you can guess, I made up *literally* all of it. And that's when my conscience, fragile in its infancy though it was, started wailing in my ear.

I tried to get out at the end of February, after a crudely hammered iron statue was erected in the town square and the first pilgrims started filling the small inn. I staged a maudlin miracle involving a bonfire, more flash powders, and a goat. (Don't ask.) Suffice to say it didn't work (I blame the goat), and instead of vanishing in a pillar of flame, by all accounts, Hagendorn saw me call on the Scarlet Maiden, then walk through fire unscathed.

The town got an uncomfortable number of pilgrims after that.

Which is why I'm embracing this whole prophet thing, at least for one more month. Tonight's the Vigil of the Weeping Saint, which needs a modest miracle, and then, by the time we get to the May-Saint Feast, Hagendorn and all its pilgrims will be primed for something big. I figure I'll spend the month hinting about being called to the Scarlet Maiden's side while rigging more bombastic miracles—you can apply red dye to an astonishing number of uses—and then, after the grand finale of the May-Saint Feast, I'll vanish into the wind once again.

And it all starts after sundown. The Vigil of the Weeping Saint is an old custom in these hills, always a week after the spring equinox. Most families get ready for bed within the hour after sundown, but we're all wide-awake tonight. It's typical for a house to have rough-carved idols of Low Gods and saints for protection. For the vigil, you're supposed to put them by your doorstep, then stay up with them. If any shed tears, it's supposed to be a sign of divine favor.

Which is why I've hidden balls of red wax behind the eyes of the Scarlet Maiden statues. (Yeah, that's statues, *plural*, now.) And why I said she appeared to me wearing a wreath of burning roses; wrought iron roses are above the Hagendorn smith's pay grade, but a crude iron head with a basin in the crown is not. On festival days, the basin is filled with oil and set alight. It won't take too long for the wax to melt and run from her eyes, and since it's a nightlong vigil, by the time the fires go cold, all traces of wax will have burned off.

Minor miracles: easier than you think.

I finish my face paint just as it gets too dark to continue without a candle, and not a moment too soon. There's a knock at the door.

"Prophet?" Leni's voice chisels through the oak, pointed in a way that means something's amiss.

I stand with a dull tin drizzle from the bells around my wrists, then open the door. "I had a vision there might be trouble," I say. (All right, maybe I'm embracing the prophet thing a little more than necessary.) "What's wrong?"

"A heretic," she breathes, wide-eyed, clutching the end of her flaxen braid. "Followed the pilgrims in, asking questions. He said the Scarlet Maiden isn't a real god. What if she heard and turns her face from the Red Blesséd?"

I hide a wince. I forget who came up with that name, which is for the best, as I'd make them feel a lot less blessed otherwise. But the newly minted devotees of the Scarlet Maiden wanted to call themselves *something*, and for lack of other options (turns out *red* tends to be popular in melodramatic names) the absolutely dismal "Red Blessed" caught on. The worst part is, no one can agree if it's *Blessed* or *Blesséd*, and neither party will concede.

"I'll handle it," I say firmly, pulling up my robe's hood as I step outside. Hagendorn is in a hilly part of the Haarzlands, and when night falls, the cold is no joke. "Where is he now?"

"We shut him in Udo's barn. He kept saying he needs to speak to the head of Hagendorn, but . . ."

There is no head of Hagendorn. None but the Scarlet Maiden. I stifle a groan. "I'll speak some sense into him."

If you've been wondering how an entire town could so easily tumble under the sway of a seventeen-year-old girl, the answer is depressingly simple: The headwoman died around midwinter, and Hagendorn's been waiting for the Imperial Abbey of Welkenrode, the principality's administrative center, to appoint a new one. They have no authority figure, no one to mediate squabbles or make decisions for the town. People are accustomed to off-loading certain choices on someone else, so when those choices suddenly become their responsibility, they get jittery.

Then, one day, in walks a girl, and a god that speaks through her, and that's all the authority they need.

Jump ahead two months, and that girl is striding across the farmyard to Udo's barn through the settling twilight, bells chiming, robes billowing, waving to the flock of chanting pilgrims. The Imperial Abbey still hasn't appointed a new village head, and this isn't the first "heretic" I've rescued from overzealous Red Bless(é)d and gently shooed out the back door. I do wish they'd have shut this one up somewhere a bit farther from the pilgrims' earshot, though I suspect Udo's sheep will help in that regard.

"Make sure everyone stays well clear of the barn," I say ominously nonetheless. Leni nods and retreats to the crowd of people draped in prickle-poppy, viper's head, spur valerian, wild roses—all red flowers they would swear bloomed early. Drums start punctuating the pilgrims' chants. I make a show of gathering myself before the doors of the barn; really I'm making sure my boot knife is ready if I need it.

Then I push the doors open and step inside.

Immediately there's a chorus of bleats from ewes and their lambs, punctuated by a bone-chilling scream from a goat. The doors swing shut behind me.

"Hello?" I call out, pushing through the huddled sheep as my eyes grudgingly adjust to the thicker dark inside the barn. A glut of hay, dung, and unwashed wool sticks in my nose. There's no answer. I try again. "Hello?"

A soft rustle, then silence.

Someone's here.

I let out a sigh and lower my voice. "Look, whoever you are, don't make this harder than it needs to be. All we have to do is walk out together and talk up how amazing you think the Scarlet Maiden is, and then you can sneak off once we start the vigil—"

Cold, colorless light blooms behind me. And hot on its heels follows the last thing I want to hear:

"*Vanja?*"

It feels like someone just dropped a stack of books on my heart.

Nope. I refuse. This can't be happening.

See, it's not that someone in Hagendorn knows my name—unlike in Minkja, they all know me as Vanja here. I hadn't planned on sticking around long enough to need another identity.

It's that I know this voice, I know this light, and, if I look back, I know exactly who I'll find.

Still I turn, because there's no running now. Not from the boy I asked to catch me.

(Junior?) Prefect Emeric Conrad stands near the barn doors, a pewter coin shining in his hand like a pale beacon, looking almost exactly the same as when I last saw him nearly three months ago. Well, not quite the same. His dark hair's as close-trimmed and tidily combed as the day he left Minkja, his round spectacles just as ludicrously large on his narrow face, and he still looks like a soothsayer stood over his crib and heralded the birth of an accounting ledger made flesh. But instead of watching me wistfully as his carriage rolled away, now he looks just about as floored as I feel.

I was really hoping that when I saw Emeric again, I could lead the conversation with something like *Hello, dear, thank you for your patience; while I was on my journey of self-discovery, I solved poverty.* Or *I discovered a cure for a plague.* Or *I invented something so incredible, the printing press was embarrassed for itself.*

But you know that feeling? The one where your entire brain melts out through your earholes because your head is on fire, and the rest of your body overcompensates by freezing on the spot, and the only thing left in your skull is a ghost marching in a circle and banging two pots together? That's about where I'm at.

So the best I can muster is an utterly clotheslined "*Scheit.*"

Somewhere behind me, another goats lets out a scream, I can only imagine in solidarity.

"You—" Emeric's voice falters as his eyes rove over me, taking in the robes, the paint, the tinny chimes. A full opera of emotions plays out over his face, overture to curtains in record time. His next words come out strangled: "*You started a cult?*"

"No! I mean . . . a little?" My hands ball up in my billowing sleeves. "It's cult-adjacent? Cult-ish?"

"Cult-ish," he repeats, like each syllable is a personal grievance. Then Emeric carefully removes his spectacles, places them just above his hairline, and runs his free hand down his face so hard, he's in danger of crumpling his own nose. "Cult-ish. *Cult-ish.*"

"Hi to you too," I say peevishly. "I'm doing all right, thank you for asking—"

"I gathered that, since it appears you've spent the past three months starting a cult, and furthermore, *cultish* is *already a word*," he seethes. "One that specifically means '*emblematic of a cult*,' Vanja, such as the one *congregating outside*! *This*! *Barn*! *Vanja*!"

I mutter, "I'm going to make you put a *sjilling* in a jar every time you say *cult*."

"*Åååååååå*," seconds a goat.

"Fine, yes, I may have been creative with a local legend and things got weird," I continue in a hideously ungainly pivot, "but that's enough about me, what have you been up to?"

Emeric stares at me with the kind of wordless, whiplashed outrage of someone presented with a buffet of indignities and overwhelmed by their options.

"What brings you to Hagendorn?" I try again.

Emeric presses his hands together in front of his face, closes his eyes, and inhales through his nose. Even his windpipe sounds angry with me. And . . . we both know he has every right to be. All I can do is brace for it.

Then a goat stretches its neck out and bites his elbow.

"*GAH.*" Emeric yanks his sleeve away only to dodge another attempted chomp for his forearm. "No—get *off*—"

In response, the goat opens its mouth and emits one more

bloodcurdling "*ÅÅÅÅÅÅÅÅ*" before tottering off to gnaw on a support beam.

Emeric shakes his arm, scowling, but some of the wind has left his angry sails. "I'm here," he snips, "because the Helligbrücke First Office received word of a new Low God potentially emerging in Hagendorn. Verifying and registering new gods falls under the jurisdiction of the prefects."

"Huh," I say, cleverly. Of course it does. They're Prefects of the Godly Courts, investigators for the Low Gods themselves.

"This case is open-and-shut, to say the least." There's a bitter note in his voice. He looks away. "I . . . thought you weren't doing this anymore. It *can't* be the easiest way to make a living."

"Oh no, you'd be amazed, cults are wildly profitable," I blurt out, then cut myself off at his flinch. "I mean, I'm not—this isn't what it looks like."

There's a tug at my skirt. I look down and find an ewe, with a mouthful of red linen, making direct eye contact as she chews.

"How, exactly, *isn't* this what it looks like?" Irritation creeps back into Emeric's tone. "Did the cult spring into existence fully formed, just waiting for a prophet when you came along?"

"No," I grunt as I try to pry the sheep off my skirt. "I—"

"Did the Scarlet Maiden descend to you in a vision and say you'd die in a cart accident if you didn't tell five friends about her by midnight?"

"Now you're just being ridiculous." I drag at the fabric. The ewe digs in her hooves.

"Then what *is* all this?" He sweeps the glowing coin through the air as the shadows of the barn squirm. His voice sharpens to a thorn, but I can hear it draw blood from him, too, on its way out. "What . . . what happened, Vanja?"

We both know he isn't asking about just the Scarlet Maiden.

I've had three months to think about what I wanted our reunion to be like. I'd arrive in Helligbrücke, wealthy and successful and wildly attractive. We would see each other from opposite ends of a bridge on a sunny spring day, flower petals sailing on the gentle breeze, and rush to meet in a passionate embrace sure to gross out the local nine-year-olds.

Instead, there's a rip of linen, and then the ewe retreats with a significant portion of my skirt. Not enough to be indecent, but enough to be a bold fashion choice.

I let my head hang a moment, feeling the pinnacle of pathetic. Maybe it was stupid, thinking he'd be happy to see me. I didn't expect things to be the same after I all but ran screaming from the plans we'd made, but . . . I'd hoped his feelings wouldn't change. Maybe I was wrong.

If we're going to break things off, it's not going to be in a barn. I ask, "Can we do this someplace else?"

". . . Fine." There's a taut resignation in Emeric's shoulders.

I try not to dwell on that, pushing past him as I head for the doors. "I'll come up with some excuse to get away once the vigil's started. Just play along."

"Wait—" Emeric sputters.

I don't wait. I plaster a wide, jubilant smile over my face and throw open the barn doors.

"Friends!" I call to the crowd waiting for us in the torch-spangled night. Leni's done her job well, keeping them far enough at bay that I don't think they could catch a single word over the drumming. "It was all a misunderstanding! Rejoice, for a new soul joins the Blessed!"

There are cheers, of course, as I expected.

Then there is something I didn't expect: an unearthly hiss that jangles in my very teeth.

"*Yes,*" it whispers. "*Rejoice.*"

Shouts and gasps sweep the crowd. They scatter away from the bridge as a brilliant crimson glow wells up beneath it, spreading through the water until the whole stream is an incandescent vein burning from within. Red mist rolls up from the banks. Green shoots pierce the ground wherever it touches, exploding into crimson blooms.

Emeric draws up beside me, brow furrowed. "Please tell me this is you," he says under his breath. I shake my head.

The crimson haze winds up, like it's tethered to a giant lazy spindle over the bridge—then, with a damp pulse, it's no longer a haze but near-tangible carven light.

An ethereal woman floats over the bridge, too tall to be human. Long cascades of crimson hair drift in an unseen breeze, her ice-pale face the vicious kind of beautiful, stinging like a nettle when you look her in the eye. She wears a gown of scarlet and rubies, a pattern of red diamonds dancing over her cheeks just as it does mine. One hand holds an ivory spindle; the other spills rubies from a wound in the palm.

On her brow rests a wreath of golden leaves and burning ruby roses.

The Scarlet Maiden surveys the crowd. Her carnelian eyes find me, pin me to the spot like an insect. A razor smile slices through the blood-less flesh of her face.

That jangling, hissing voice returns. And this time, it says: "*My prophet.*"

"Uh," I stumble, "hi?"

"*Are you not overjoyed to see me?*" The Scarlet Maiden's voice slithers through the night with the barest flash of fangs.

"Totally! Totally overjoyed!" I try to muster a convincing degree of jubilation. Internally, of course, the ghost in my skull has ditched the two pots and opted instead for the goat scream. "What, uh, brings you to Hagendorn?"

Emeric makes an annoyed noise until I jab him with my elbow.

The Scarlet Maiden's head tilts, regarding me a long moment before she answers. "*I have always been here, my prophet. Long have I slumbered* beneath the Broken Peak, but the prayers of your congregation have roused and renewed me."

"Ah." Someone explained to me long ago that Low Gods and their believers have a . . . mutually symbiotic relationship, let's put it that way. But I've never heard of a *dormant* god, nor one woken with a surplus of faith.

This is what I get for appropriating a tragic ballad.

"Hail the Scarlet Maiden!" Leni shouts from the crowd. It echoes through the pilgrims in a chorus of "*Hail! Hail! Hail!*"

The Scarlet Maiden burns brighter, pleased. "*Yes, my children, be merry! My blessings are upon you, and a time of great prosperity!*"

The cheers grow louder. Emeric and I trade furtive looks.

Before we can say anything, though, the Scarlet Maiden swells with ferocious, bloody light. "*But take heed! We must first have a proper celebration, as in the days of old. A feast for midsummer!*"

"Two months from now? I think we can pull a feast together," I venture. "How do you feel about lamb?"

"*No, little prophet, I speak of the* old *ways,*" she says with a laugh like shattered glass. Then she draws herself up even further. "*Is there one unclaimed among you who will be the servant of my sacred feast?*"

"Your what?" My question goes ignored as the Scarlet Maiden's head swivels about, peering among the crowd.

Then her gaze passes over me—and halts.

She glides closer, smiling. "*You. You are unclaimed, are you not?*"

That hits my gut in a way I don't expect. "I don't . . . have a family," I admit, "if that's—"

"*Not you, Prophet.*" The Scarlet Maiden stops in front of Emeric. "*Him.*"

"Er," Emeric says.

"*Did you not say he is among my blessed?*" the Scarlet Maiden coos.

Emeric clears his throat. "I am honored, your divinity, but there's been a misunderstanding. I'm Prefect Aspirant Emeric Conrad of the Helligbrücke—"

"*You will do,*" she purrs.

"—Helligbrücke First Office . . ." He falters as she extends a hand, then soldiers on. "Of the Order of Prefects of the Godly Courts. If you don't mind, I have a few questions—"

"*I make my claim.*" The Scarlet Maiden plants her hand flat on his chest. There's another throb of red light, one so bright my eyes water—

And then she's gone.

"*Keep watch over my chosen servant, little prophet.*" Her spectral voice slashes through the crowd as luminous crimson mist coils around us. "*And remember, my blessing is ever with you.*"

My eyes aren't just watering. Something hot spills down my face. There are cries from the worshippers, then a sudden grip on my shoulder.

"Are you all right?" Emeric sounds strangely alarmed.

I blink up at him. "I'm not the one she just claimed. How are *you?*"

"I think—I'm fine. But you . . ." There's another jolt in my belly as he touches my cheek. Then he shows me.

Fresh, unmistakable blood glistens wet on his fingertips.

"Oh," I say, a bit dizzily.

Shouts of wonder are still ricocheting around town. I look for the cause and find an even more unsettling answer.

Every idol set out tonight, from the statue in the square to the Ros brothers' oaken Brunne the Huntress, is weeping blood.

CHAPTER TWO

THE GOOD PROCTOR

THE GRAVITY OF THIS BEGINS TO SINK IN. THE SCARLET MAIDEN STARTED as a lie, one I could control. I don't know what exactly has manifested tonight, but one thing is clear:

This is rapidly spiraling out of my control.

"Hail the servant!" Leni calls. "Hail the prophet!" That, too, starts echoing through the throng. The Red Blessed press closer before Emeric and I can duck away.

"No—please, give us some room—" I can barely hear myself over the sudden crush of bodies. Hands reach for us, catching at sleeves, hems, locks of hair, even as I try to evade them.

Emeric's voice rises, a strange sizzling current to his words. "Everyone, please *step back.*"

There's a shift like someone smoothing out a bump in a rug, and the crowd is suddenly back by the bridge, as if they were picked up and gently returned to where they'd stood before.

"*The might of the gods!*" someone cries out. Emeric pinches his nose and sighs.

"That's a new trick," I observe. "So you passed your second initiation?"

When last we spoke, he'd been on his way to Helligbrücke to begin the process of graduating from junior prefect to, well, standard-issue prefect. The promotion also meant he'd be able to call upon higher powers, literally and figuratively. Prefects of the Godly Courts can tap into the powers of the Low Gods in addition to wielding more potent magic than the average hedgewitch.

But, to my surprise, he grimaces. "Not quite. It's—"

"Was that truly necessary, Aspirant?"

Emeric's face drops further as a tall, steely rail of a woman steps out of the crowd. Her silver-streaked walnut hair is pulled into a severe bun, her icy-blue gaze boring from a once-pale face long since windburned to ruddy tan. She methodically removes a small notebook from a pocket in her black woolen coat—a coat almost identical to Emeric's but for bands of rank on the sleeves and a gold ring around the insignia of the Godly Courts.

Emeric stands straighter. I don't know if he even realizes he's linked his hands behind his back like an eager cadet. "P-Proctor Kirkling. I thought my instructions were to begin the preliminary investigation myself."

"They were," the woman—Proctor Kirkling, I guess—says stonily. "But *you* made the assumption that you'd go unsupervised." She produces a small, neat charcoal stick, cracks open the notebook, and reads aloud as she writes, "'Needless . . . use . . . of force.'"

"That's a stretch," I object.

Proctor Kirkling doesn't look up. "'Reckless . . . assumption . . . Lack of . . . oversight.'"

Emeric opens his mouth, then closes it, staring at the ground. His ears are turning red.

Some tinder in my bones catches at that. "I don't know who you are, and I don't care," I say. "In case you missed it, we have bigger problems than—"

The woman snaps her notebook shut and fixes her glacial gaze on me. "Elske Kirkling. Prefect Emeritus of the Godly Courts and designated proctor for the journeyman trial of Prefect Aspirant Emeric Conrad."

I refuse to be impressed. "Could you repeat that? All I got was *Prefect Emeric Emeritus Proctor Prefect.*"

"Proctor Kirkling will determine if I pass the second initiation," Emeric translates hastily. "Proctor, this is Vanja . . ." He hesitates, looking to me. It's not exactly a secret, but he's the only person I've told outright that I don't know my birth family's real name.

"Schmidt," Kirkling finishes curtly before I can answer. "From the Minkja case. I've read the file."

"Let us speak to him!" someone cries from the throng. "We want to hear from the Scarlet Maiden's servant!"

"Let him speak!"

Kirkling frowns at me. "Take us somewhere we can talk privately."

I almost tell her a *please* wouldn't hurt but abstain for Emeric's sake. Instead I weave around her and call to the throng, "Friends, we are going to pay our respects in the chapel! Please let us pass in peace. Celebrate the end of the Vigil of the Weeping Saint as you wish!" Then I tell Kirkling and Emeric, "Follow me."

I lead them over the bridge and across the Hagendorn town square, up to a small wooden stave chapel that still smells of new timber. The iron Scarlet Maiden statue in the square seems to watch us as we pass, her spindle held aloft. Something's off, but I don't realize until I see her statue in the chapel too: Both bleed not just from the eyes, but also from the tip of the spindle and the wounded palm of her empty hand.

Once the empty chapel's doors close behind us, Kirkling says briskly, "Much better. No interference here. Vanja Schmidt, by the authority of the Godly Courts, I am arresting you for profane fraud."

"*What?*" Emeric and I both burst out, voices ringing off the raw timber walls.

"You falsified the existence of a Low God and exploited that belief for your own gain, at the expense of the town of Hagendorn and various citizens of the empire. Conrad, put her in irons."

My heart jumps to my throat as Emeric looks between the two of us, wide-eyed. He's been training to be a prefect since he was eight; at eighteen, he's spent more of his life working for that goal than not. I remember the pained edge in his words when he told me of the bailiff who murdered his father, how the officer abused his station to cover his crime. And I remember his fire when he spoke of being able to hold the powerful to account, despite their wealth or rank.

I don't know what he still feels for me, if anything. I don't know if he cares for me more than that dream. But I would never ask him to choose.

Which is why I'm stunned when he says, "I can't do that."

So is Proctor Kirkling. After an excruciatingly drawn-out pause, she extracts her notebook and her charcoal stick again, saying thinly, "'Forgot routine equipment . . .'"

"No, I have my manacles—" Emeric holds them up as Kirkling narrows her eyes. "But procedurally and ethically, this is all wrong."

Kirkling's nostrils flare.

"Procedurally, as a retired prefect, you no longer have the authority to arrest or detain citizens, or to order an arrest," Emeric rushes on, knuckles tightening on the manacles. "Charter of the Prefect, Article Nine, Subsection Three states that a prefect permanently surrenders that authority upon being decommissioned, even should they assist the Order at a later date. And the ethics . . . the Scarlet Maiden is *demonstrably* real. Plenty of clergies make their living off donations from worshippers. Unless we intend to charge them with exploiting piety as well?"

Kirkling's charcoal stick dangles like a dagger over the throat of her page. Then she carefully folds it away with her notebook, a paper-thin humorless smile unfolding across her face. "That was a test. I find your determination adequate, Aspirant. You may proceed."

As a professional scammer, I smell crap, and it's not because we tracked in sheep dung from Udo's barn. But before I succumb to the urge to say so, the chapel door creaks open. Udo himself slips inside.

"Apologies for the interruption," he says, removing his woolen hat with a quick bow of his head to the statue of the Scarlet Maiden. "It's about accommodations."

That's a wrinkle I hadn't quite considered yet. Pilgrims have already started packing in for the vigil, and it's only going to get busier with the May-Saint Feast five weeks from now. And, you know, with *the actual god* showing up to dispense miracles. We have one longhouse already built for visitors, but the other is still under construction.

The hat twists in Udo's hands. "We've freed up a bed in the pilgrims' lodge, but that's all we have. Madame Prefect, Jakob and I can escort you to the nearest inn—"

"You may call me Proctor Kirkling, and I will take the bed in the lodge," she says in the sort of tone that renders *may* functionally indistinguishable from *will*. "You may accompany Aspirant Conrad back to our inn in Glockenberg."

Udo bobs his head again. "No disrespect, Ma—Proctor Kirkling, but I don't think the Red Blessed will abide him leaving Hagendorn. Might anger the Scarlet Maiden."

"Then they will learn what happens when they try to detain a prefect of the Godly Courts," Kirkling returns.

"Oh, so now we're all for needless use of force," I scoff.

She glares at me, unsurprisingly. "I will not be lectured by the likes of *you*."

"Don't speak to Vanja like that." Udo draws himself up to his full height, and I'm reminded abruptly that Udo Ros is a patient, gentle man up until the moment something prowls too close to his flock.

But Emeric holds up his hands. "Everyone, please. It's getting late, and we're all too tired to be doing this right now. Let's just sort out the sleeping arrangements, then we'll figure out a plan of action in the morning."

"I'm staying in Hagendorn." Kirkling's frosty tone says she will not be persuaded otherwise. "And I want assurance that Schmidt will not cut and run overnight. An assurance I think *you* ought to understand, Conrad."

I feel that sucker punch in my teeth. Emeric goes pale, save for two spots of bright red in his cheeks.

A tide of hot anger rushes up my every vein as an absolutely unhinged idea bubbles to the surface. My voice comes out the fluty, cheery kind of furious. "He'll stay with me. The Scarlet Maiden herself told me to keep an eye on him, after all, so that solves both our problems."

"If you're sure?" Udo says hesitantly, glancing from me to Emeric.

"Quite," I say before Kirkling can object. "Udo, could you please show the doctor to her accommodations?"

"Proctor," Kirkling corrects.

I give her a scrunch-mouthed smile like I *haven't* made it my life's mission to call her by the wrong title from now on. "How careless of me. We can reconvene in the morning, after we've all had some rest. Emeric, my quarters are this way."

Then I pull the same trick as in the barn, bolting for the door and leaving no room for argument. I find the Red Blessed have pooled in the town square outside, but they make way at my request. I follow it up with another request for privacy until the morning. I'm less confident in that; they certainly stare as I lead Emeric to the Ros brothers' house.

Jakob is sponging blood off the oaken idol of Brunne the Huntress by the door. A battered old lantern lights his work. He grunts in greeting. "We're sending for Helga in the morning. Maybe she'll know more about this sleeping-god business."

Helga Ros is Jakob and Udo's sister, and she normally resides in the forest with Hagendorn's ancient hedgewitch midwife, Auntie Gerke. She's training to take up the trade, which calls on older, more-regional magic than Jakob's methodical textile witchery. That means there's sure to be one of the fiery debates they're so fond of tomorrow . . . and that things must be serious if Jakob's willing to summon his sister for help.

"I appreciate it," I say.

Jakob gives an awkward shrug and eyes Emeric. "You had dinner, lad?"

"Yes, thank you," Emeric says quickly, his coin light throwing his face into sharp relief as it kindles. "I apologize for the intrusion."

"Intrusion?"

I shift my weight. "He's . . . staying with me. Do you want help cleaning up?"

Jakob drops his rag into a bucket, scowling at the idol, and shakes his head. "Won't stop bleeding. No use wasting your time."

You'd think, after spending the better part of three months missing Emeric, I'd be less nervous about being alone with him as I head to the back of the Ros brothers' home. "Privy's there if you need it," I say, pointing to a little closet attached to the house. The coin light spills onto my lean-to around the corner. I reach for the door. "It's not much, but it'll beat sleeping in the chapel."

Emeric doesn't say anything. He *has* to be mad at me, I'm sure of it. We were already on shaky ground, and that was before I let him be claimed by a god I made up and then declared a blood feud with his boss.

But once we're inside the lean-to and I'm fumbling for the lantern so he can put the coin away, he musters words after all: "There's only one bed."

"Well, yes, I don't know what I'd do with two," I say, flustered. "Sleep with my head on one and my feet on the other?"

"Right. Of course." He sounds unexpectedly fuddled. I look over my shoulder. He's leaning against the door, a hand to his brow.

"What's wrong?"

"Nothing. I'm just tired."

I don't believe him, but there's little point in prying. I crack open the chimney's iron door and hold a piece of straw to the embers inside. "So, Kirkling's awful."

"She's just . . ." Emeric pauses. "She came out of retirement for this, said it ought to be her. She used to be Hubert's partner."

"Oh." No wonder she knows who I am. I'm no longer surprised she's so eager to have me arrested and rather more surprised she didn't just throttle me on sight. Hubert Klemens, Emeric's mentor, was killed in Minkja—and found with my signature red penny in his mouth. The prefects officially (and correctly) determined that I'd been framed, but we all learned that day that grief seldom listens to reason. I can't say for certain, but I have a hunch which of the two governs Kirkling now. "How long do you have to put up with her?"

"Until I pass or fail a Finding." He rubs his brow again. "Sorry, er.

A Finding is a test case I'll have to resolve, either by proving no crime was committed or by successfully arguing it before a Godly Court. The proctor assigns it when they decide their aspirant is ready."

"I thought Justice told Helligbrücke to promote you back in December."

"She did. I completed most of the second initiation by the end of January. The Finding is all that's left."

I shoot a look over my shoulder. "Does it normally take two months for a proctor to assign a Finding?"

Emeric presses his lips together, looking away, and I know the answer before he tersely says, "No."

There's a knock at the door that makes both of us leap out of our skins. Emeric answers.

It's Udo, peering over a heap of fabric. "Jakob thought you'd need extra blankets. If he asks, I said it was my idea."

"Thank you, sir." Emeric takes them, then adds uneasily, "Your sheep are very . . . . healthy."

Udo beams. "Let me know if you need anything."

He's gone by the time I get the lantern lit. I stand, pulling off the elaborate red robe and tossing it in a corner. The shift and the plain wool dress I was wearing under the robe will keep me warm enough, especially with two people in this tiny space. "You can have the bed. I still need to wash off all . . . this." I gesture vaguely at the mess of blood and paint on my face.

"I'm not kicking you out of your own bed. I'll take the floor."

"You're my guest!" I protest. Emeric's mouth twists mulishly. "Fine. We'll both take the bed." I yank a quilt for myself out of his arms as sheer panic floods his face. "Just two people, fully clothed with separate blankets, sharing a mattress. That's all. We don't have to make it weird."

"Sure," he rattles, as if the words I just uttered did not breach bold new frontiers, *plural*, of physical and emotional weirdness.

"Then go lie down. You look like you're two feet from the grave."

"Vanja." His voice hitches. "We . . . need to talk."

I've planted myself at my washstand under the pretense of soaking clean rags. "I know," I admit, not looking at him. "But we're going to yell a lot more if we do it now. Can we wait until morning?"

Maybe I'm just delaying the inevitable. Maybe Emeric just wants that, too, because all he says is "Promise?"

"Promise."

It isn't until I hear the rustle of the straw tick that I understand why he wants a promise. It's not just my saying we *will* finally face this in the morning.

It's my saying I'll be here when the sun comes up.

When I'm done washing my face and wrapping myself up in the quilt, Emeric's already in bed, his back to me, lying on the far side so I won't have to climb over him. He doesn't stir as I stiffly sink onto the mattress.

For a moment, all I can think of is the first and last time we shared a bed, the night before he left Minkja. We were both a little tipsy on *glohwein*, and more than a little emotional, and there were hands under shirts and bodices—and dangerously near waistbands—but that was it. Neither of us was ready to go further after being together for only a few weeks, and we passed out in a wine-drowsy heap instead.

Neither of us knew three months would pass before we were in the same town, the same room, again.

I would give anything to go back to that night.

I swallow the knot in my throat, then roll onto my side and blow out the lantern. I think, for a moment, I hear my name whispered in the dark. But nothing follows, and I decide I've imagined it.

As my eyes slide shut, I think I imagine, too, the dim pulse of arterial scarlet light.

❧

"Vanja."

This time I can't deny the quiet murmur. My eyes crack open only to find the dark has yielded to soft gray. No, not gray—just the white linen I've mashed my face into—*no*, not just linen—

There is a choked beat as I quickly audit how, precisely, I've arranged myself in my sleep, and come up with a wealth of embarrassing answers. Somehow one arm is tangled loosely around Emeric's neck, it appears I've had my face buried in his chest, the separate-blankets strategy has failed spectacularly, and the crowning indignity of indignities: My leg is fully flung, perpendicular, over his hips, my foot almost flat to the wall. The only consolation is that his arms are wound around me as well.

At least until I let out an ungainly squawk and all but leap to the edge of the bed. "Sorry—I didn't mean—"

"Sorry," he's babbling at the same time, scooting away. "I woke up and tried to let go, but you just made—*angry noises*—and I didn't want you to—to be upset about waking up like this."

I rub the crust from my eyes. Judging by the meager light seeping through the cracks in the boards, it's barely past sunrise. Then my sleep-fogged mind catches up to what Emeric just said, and I squint at him. "Upset? Why would I be upset?"

Emeric props himself up on an elbow. Whatever haze plagued him last night has seemingly passed; his brown eyes are sharp and bright as he unfolds his spectacles and returns them to his face. He takes a deep breath, steeling himself. "Is it time to talk now?"

I shrivel a little, but . . . "We're probably not going to have another chance for a while."

"Then first"—he swallows—"I swear, whatever you have to say, it won't affect what happens with this case. I don't want you to feel like you won't be safe unless you lie about what you want."

I stare at him, bewildered and more than a little preoccupied with what bedhead has done to his hair. "Why would I lie about that?"

Emeric stares back. "Because I've been getting the acute impression that you, er, reconsidered our relationship. And have been trying to let me down gently. But—"

"No, I told you in the letter!" I say helplessly. "I need to figure out what to *actually* do with my life."

"You said you wanted to find a real way to make a living," he agrees, "and then left me with no way to reach you and didn't contact me again. And then three months later I discover you've been less than a week's travel from Helligbrücke this whole time, starting a cult."

I wilt a little. "Right. I see it now."

Emeric's voice softens. "Vanja, if this was just about looking for honest work . . . you wouldn't still be in Hagendorn. What happened?"

I forgot how casually he sees through my nonsense, sometimes even when I refuse to see it myself. A childish part of me still tries to dodge. "I got drunk and dropped my rubies off the bridge, then made up a story so the villagers would help me fish them out. Then they—"

"Before that."

My throat tightens. But it's long past time to stop running from this. I owe him that much.

I roll onto my back, staring at the rafters and gathering my words.

"I kept thinking," I start hoarsely, "about being in Helligbrücke, or . . . if we went looking for my family, like we planned. And I know this sounds ridiculous, but I couldn't stop thinking about being introduced. What were you supposed to say? 'Hi, I'm Emeric Conrad, the youngest prefect in history—'"

"Prefect aspirant," he whispers.

"'—who also just took down a margrave and saved the empire, oh and this is Vanja, no surname, she's basically a feral maid who used to steal until she was cursed so bad she died. Kind of.'" I blow a strand of hair away from my face. "It wouldn't be fair to either of us. And I was scared that I'd . . . get complacent. Never make more of myself. At least, not before we tried to find my family. And you know the rest."

Emeric lays a hand on my arm, and I turn my head to look at him. His expression is so intensely open, so serious, I feel even smaller for trying to dance around the truth before. "To be *absolutely* clear, you weren't trying to break things off? You still want . . . us?"

I manage a wordless nod.

Then the tension passes as he throws an arm over his face and starts laughing.

I shove him, my cheeks burning as I scowl at the ceiling. "This isn't funny."

"No, I mean, I understand, I really do, it's just—" Emeric presses closer, propping himself up again until he can look me in the eye. There's a relieved mirth in his eyes, a pardon at the gallows. One of his hands alights on my cheek, and it feels as right as a key turning in a lock.

I catch my breath, terrified to let myself hope this—*we*—could be salvageable.

"You absolute *goose*," Emeric says, softening the words with a chagrined smile. "You know how I would introduce you? I would say, 'This is Vanja, the bravest person I've ever met.' Or 'This is Vanja; there's a *statue* of her in Minkja.' Or 'This is Vanja; there's a statue of her in Minkja because a *god* put it there.'" He pushes his spectacles back as they threaten to slide off his face. "Or something better that I'll come up with later, because half my brain has spent the past three months occupied solely by how much I've wanted to kiss you."

Giddy elation swells in my chest. I shoot a tentative grin up to him. "I sincerely doubt it was half your brain."

"Maybe closer to a third," he allows. "Diminished capacity regardless. *Three months*, Vanja." A fingertip traces a careful circle at the corner of my mouth, and my heart all but stops.

Around Winterfast, when we were first venturing into the exciting world of getting handsy, we also established a . . . system of sorts. Considering I panicked and pulled a knife on Emeric the first time we kissed, we decided to take certain precautions; neither of us wanted to trigger another reaction. If he wasn't sure, or just wanted to ask, he would trace a circle near where he wanted to touch me and wait for an answer.

Just as he's doing now, his smile yielding to something more sober, more intent.

"Yes," I breathe, and reach up to pull him to me.

I'm almost painfully aware of my body and his: the mattress shifting with him as he eases himself over me, a startling shudder below my belly as a knee settles between mine, the exquisite pull of fingers curling into my hair. I feel the warmth of his breath on my lips first, then the softest brush of—

The door rattles with a knock.

We both jump, banging our foreheads together. There's a quiet flurry of mutual cursing.

"Breakfast," Jakob calls from outside. "And the proctor's here."

I make a noise like an angrily deflating cushion as Emeric hides his face in my shoulder, shaking with silent laughter again. Trust Kirkling to ruin the moment. "We'll be right there."

Jakob grunts in acknowledgment. His footsteps crunch away.

Emeric starts to pull back, and I grab a handful of his shirt, a little more desperate than I'd like to admit. "No, we'll be fast——"

Laughter lingers in his smile as he stills my lips with his fingertips, shaking his head. A familiar, heady heat saturates his words, flush with promise. "Three. *Months.* When I kiss you, Vanja, we are going to take our time."

There's that jolt in my belly again. Damn his knack for getting under my skin. Damn *me* for liking it so much. I tug on his shirt once more anyway, prepared to sulk prolifically. "But what if we did that *now.*"

Then—something below his collarbone catches my eye. My stomach lurches in a way that has nothing to do with kissing.

Emeric looks down, flustered, as I start yanking at his shirt buttons. "Vanja. This is, in fact, the opposite of . . ."

Then he trails off as he sees it too.

Across the dead center of his chest blazes a vivid blood-red handprint.

CHAPTER THREE

ᴅISTRACTIONS

"IT'S CLEARLY DYE."

"Jakob jumping to conclusions, *there's* a surprise. If it were dye, I'd sense pigment in the skin."

"Perhaps your senses aren't as acute as you'd like to think, *Helga*."

"Can I button my shirt now?" Emeric asks a bit plaintively from the bench where he's been wedged between a neat stack of folded green broadcloth and a bushel of carded wool. His shirt's open to expose the handprint, though he's wrung the hems like dishrags from the moment he sat down. Jakob, Jakob's sister Helga, Kirkling, and I are all crowded in Jakob's little workroom with him, and while the press of bodies helps offset the chill, it's not exactly balmy.

Jakob and Helga are nearby, preoccupied with their catfight. "Perhaps the explanation isn't alchemy and head games for once," Helga fumes, wiping her hands on her breeches before starting to braid her russet hair back from a pale narrow face. In her early twenties, Helga is Jakob's junior by something like four years, but they're equal height, a fact he seems to resent on principle. "I know you'd rather sleep in the barn than admit I'm right, but that"—she points to the handprint on Emeric's chest—"is too bright, too precise, and too *weird* to be just a dye transfer."

I scoot over to stand by Emeric. "They're going to be at it a while," I tell him quietly, and start working on his buttons. (It's only fair, since I undid them in the first place.) "It really doesn't hurt?"

"I didn't even know it was there." A little of his tension wanes as he slips an apprehensive smile up to me. I return it the best I can, a knot in my belly.

I don't know what the Scarlet Maiden did when she claimed him as her servant. I thought it would be like me being her "prophet," but . . . clearly there's more to it. And if I woke her up like she said, it's all my fault.

The back of my neck prickles. Out of the corner of my eye, I see Kirkling watching me fuss with the buttons.

"It's not a Low God," she declares, like she's issuing a sentence.

Jakob and Helga's debate pauses. "Pardon?" Jakob says.

Kirkling pushes off from the wall she's been haunting. "That *thing*, it's no god. The prefects have no records of a Scarlet Maiden, and Section Seven of the Accord of Prefectorial and Godly Alliance forbids the Low Gods from claiming a prefect for their rituals in such a way. A true god, even a new one, would be bound to that."

Helga gives Kirkling a long look. Then she turns to Jakob and asks flatly, "Who is this again?"

"Emeric's boss," I answer, then, as Emeric opens his mouth, I clarify, "or supervisor, kind of. It's complicated."

After a pause, Helga asks, just as cold, "And why is she still here?"

Kirkling draws herself up, bristling. "As Prefect Emeritus, I am currently the ranking authority in Hagendorn, and I have the right to know about the well-being of the prefect aspirant I oversee."

Helga, for reasons beyond me—perhaps an abundance of insight—has never taken a shine to me. Yet as her lip curls, she is rapidly becoming my second-favorite person in the room. She produces a plain knotted cord from her practical brown tunic and begins winding her braid into a bun at the back of her head, steely blue eyes glinting. "The Scarlet Maiden wouldn't be in *your* records. The Haarzlands are full of old gods"—she cinches the cord brutally tight around her bun—"who mind their own business. Boderad's Gorge alone is littered with ritual sites and shrines centuries older than your accords."

"The Scarlet Maiden said she'd been sleeping beneath the Broken Peak," Emeric says. "That's part of the gorge, yes?"

Helga nods. "The stream outside starts as a river in the gorge as well. There are legends of a Low God in that area who faded away long ago, originally called the Maid Painted Red, or—"

"The Red Maid of the River," I finish. I really, *really* should have known better than to appropriate the tragic ballad, then. "So she could have been dormant when the accords were set, but . . . I called her back."

"That would be absurd," Kirkling snaps. "That's not how it works."

Helga rolls her eyes. "Just because it's beyond *your* comprehension doesn't mean it's impossible."

Jakob and I trade looks as he runs a hand over his short beard. For his part, Jakob seems delighted his little sister has a new person to harry, even if a brawl is brewing in his workroom.

Udo pokes his head around the doorframe. "Breakfast's getting cold."

"We're not solving anything letting it get colder," Jakob sighs. "If—"

Kirkling doesn't move, but her voice cuts across the room. "Aspirant Conrad." Emeric scrambles to his feet. "As the proctor of your journeyman trial, I hereby assign this case as your Finding. You are to investigate the true nature of the being calling itself the Scarlet Maiden and to determine whether it is a true Low God with a valid claim to you."

Emeric stands a bit taller, curiosity sparking in his face. This is exactly the kind of puzzle he loves, even if the stakes are a bit personal.

But Kirkling isn't done. "As part of your investigation, you will also determine whether Vanja Schmidt has committed profane fraud by deceiving the town of Hagendorn into worshipping a counterfeit god for her own benefit. Do you understand your orders?"

Udo's face darkens. "That's not fair, making him investigate Vanja when they're . . ." His mouth twists with uncertainty, and he lands on "roommates."

"It will be a test of Aspirant Conrad's impartiality," Kirkling says coolly. "Prefects cannot allow any bias to stand between themselves and their duty to justice. Aspirant Conrad, *do you understand your orders?*"

Emeric swallows. Then, to my surprise, he takes my hand, lacing his fingers through mine. To everyone else, I'm sure it just looks like a casual, comforting gesture, but I hear exactly what he's telling me: Whatever we're facing, we're in it together.

"I understand," he answers with a clipped note in his voice that makes me stifle a cackle. I wonder if Kirkling knows exactly what manner of pedantic, punctilious, annotated-within-an-inch-of-its-life beast she's just unleashed. I know without a doubt that she is about to learn.

I'm not sure *where* Emeric was keeping the charcoal stick and his notebook, only that one moment he's letting go of me and the next, they're already in his hands. A playing card peeks out as a bookmark: the Queen of Roses, the one I left him in Minkja.

"I'd like to begin this investigation immediately, then, and if you don't mind, I'll have some questions over breakfast," Emeric says briskly. "Starting with . . . how far is it to Broken Peak?"

⚬⚬⚬

"I would just like to remind you," Helga grunts a few hours later, as she, Kirkling, Emeric, and I drag our way up a steep rocky trail, "that this would have been much easier on horseback."

"*No*," Emeric and I bark simultaneously. He's harbored a distrust of horses since long before we met, and while I'm mostly equine-neutral, I'd be lying if I said Adalbrecht von Reigenbach's creative and horrible application of horse monsters in Minkja hadn't put me off most ungulates for at least a few months after.

But there's no denying they'd help this hike. Emeric has decided to kick things off by going to the source—that is, the Scarlet Maiden herself. If we can find her, we can directly ask what she wants instead of speculating.

It did, unfortunately, only leave me with enough time to scarf down breakfast, wash up and change, then go reassure the Red Blessed that we're just heading out to commune with their god. Sonja the dairy farmer was already driving into Glockenberg to sell her cheeses, so she offered to collect Emeric's and Kirkling's belongings from the inn. Then we set off for Broken Peak.

It did *not* leave time for Emeric and me to have a private moment to ourselves to . . . revisit our prebreakfast activities. Which is fine. It's *fine*. I've only spent the past hour thinking about the way he rolled up his shirtsleeves, well, an hour ago. I'm pretty sure exposed forearms qualify as a personal attack.

At least it's still relatively shady and cool; the beeches of this forest hold their leaves long into spring instead of shedding in autumn. If we were under the full bore of the midday sun instead of what's filtering through the withered boughs, I'm sure there would be more sweating involved, and at that point I think I'd wind up staring like a letch until I walked into a tree.

"So, how long has *this* been happening?" Helga asks, waving vaguely at Emeric and me, as if compelled to increase the personal attacks. "Did you make some staggeringly good first impressions last night?"

We both blush furiously. "Uh, no, we . . . we met back in midwinter," I say, glancing at Emeric. We haven't had a chance to discuss this wrinkle either—we're not exactly hiding anything with the handholding and the button-fussing, but I can't imagine it's helping Kirkling's evaluation.

Sure enough, I see the proctor's expression sour again at the edge of my sight.

"Vanja was the reason I survived a major case in Minkja, which we won only because of her," Emeric says firmly, ducking under a gnarled branch. "If you think I'm exaggerating, Minkja has a statue of her now. One a Low God put there."

Oh, the bastard, I think my heart's going to explode. I seriously might tell Kirkling and Helga we'll catch up in an hour and haul him off into the bushes.

"Always figured you were holding out on us," Helga says a bit cryptically. Before I have a chance to ask what *that's* supposed to mean, we break through the tree cover and into sunlight.

Boderad's Gorge yawns before us. The swift-moving Ilsza River has cut seemingly down to the bone of the Haarzlands, leaving stark walls of spotted slate and hornfels striped fancy as a parlor, heaps of greenery collecting on ledges the way dust gathers on mantels. The last traces of morning mist cling to the water some sixty feet below, the divide spanned by an old sturdy rope bridge rising from our side to a higher cliff across the way. Another sixty feet to our right, the head of a waterfall nearly meets our eye level, spilling a pale curtain into the distant churning pool that feeds the river. A second bridge arches far below us, little more than a thread of ancient stone strung much closer to the pool's surface.

Towering beyond the opposite end of the rope bridge is Broken Peak itself. Unlike the other jagged spurs of milky feldspar or hawthorn-dulled hilltops, this is a great block of mostly barren granite with a summit that looks to have been sheared off like the tip of a broken tooth.

And unlike the timid fringes of buttercup and pale thimbleweed along the trail behind us, violent unbroken red blooms from every crevice at the peak's base, turning it into a massive bleeding gum.

"Promising," Emeric says mildly.

Helga steps off the trail, uncorking a small bottle of something sharp-smelling, and sprinkles a few drops over a small granite altar I hadn't noticed. I see little bundles of dried wildflowers, tallow stains, even what looks like the remains of a straw doll. "Thank you for the safe passage," she says to the air. Then she calls back to us, "Knock on the post as you pass."

That's about when I realize we're going over the rope bridge. I don't know why it didn't occur to me before. And it's not that heights bother me—at least, not the way they bothered Dame von Falbirg, who couldn't look down a staircase in Castle Falbirg without getting the shakes.

But there's a significant difference between a flight of stairs and a sixty-foot plunge.

Helga taps her knuckles to a rune-spangled bridge post and steps onto the planks. I take a deep breath, then rap the post and follow. The hempen guide ropes look ancient and weathered, but they barely give a creak at our weight, abuzz with old power.

"The story goes that, centuries ago, a giant named Boderad wanted to marry Princess Brunne from one of the old kingdoms, and her father was too afraid of the giants to refuse," Helga explains as she leads us up the rope bridge. I don't know if she's talking just to keep our minds off the drop. "Princess Brunne . . . did not appreciate it. She tricked Boderad into teaching her how to ride one of his horses—"

"Why is it always horses?" Emeric mutters behind me.

Helga clears her throat. "And then, the night before the wedding, when everyone was drunk, Brunne stole the horse and ran."

"No, actually, now I'm curious: What's the deal with horses?" I ask.

Helga makes an exasperated noise. "I don't know! It was a special giant horse or something! The point is, Boderad chased her, but when they got to this mountain"—she flaps a hand at Broken Peak—"Princess Brunne decided to jump it instead of going around. The force of the leap split the hills and made the gorge, and her horse's hoof clipped the mountaintop, snapping it off. Boderad couldn't stop in time and fell into the chasm, and his dying rage turned him into a hellhound. Brunne became Huntress of the Haarzlands, and Boderad still guards the basin where Brunne's bridal crown fell." Helga points to the tumultuous pool at the waterfall's base. "We call it the Kronenkessel."

There's a scoff from Kirkling.

Helga stops in her tracks, and since the rope bridge isn't very wide and I don't feel like rolling the dice, I stop, and so do Emeric and Kirkling.

"I get," Helga says slowly, "that to people who prefer their world neatly measured and registered and codified, this all sounds like superstitious peasant nonsense. But what *you* need to get is this."

Helga fishes a rye roll out of the lunch Udo packed for us, then pitches it with considerable effort toward the waterfall. I can barely see it by the time it hits the foaming water of the Kronenkessel.

I have no trouble whatsoever seeing the enormous gaping jaws that surge up from the froth a heartbeat later. They close with a thunder-clap we hear even through the roar of the waterfall, and I get a fleeting glimpse of algae-stained gray fur over a monstrous muzzle before the creature sinks below the surface once more.

"Just because it isn't in your records," Helga continues, glowering at Kirkling, "doesn't mean it won't bite you in the ass. And by the way, that was your lunch roll."

Neither Emeric nor I have to say a word; our hands latch together and stay that way until we're off the bridge.

Helga points out other details as we pass: a small rune-bedecked cabin to shelter anyone caught out too close to sundown, a distant ring of boulders called the Witches' Dance, toadstools marking an enormous beech claimed by the Mossfolk. The flowers grow larger and redder the closer we get to the base of Broken Peak, and I see they're not even the kinds that naturally grow crimson. Some, like vetch and hollowroot, aren't too far off from their usual magenta, but stems of toothwort and saxifrage, meant to be shell pink and green gold, are stabbing from the earth in the same vivid red as Emeric's handprint.

It's not long before we reach a path of worn, crooked stones that has long outgrown its time as a staircase and since lapsed into a noncom-mittal slope. It leads up to a crude archway hewn into a granite wall looming ahead. Red-blooming vines wreath the ingress.

"Is that Felsengruft?" I ask.

Helga nods. This was her suggestion; the Scarlet Maiden had said, after all, that she'd slept *below* Broken Peak. Felsengruft is an old shrine and a barrow cut out of the peak's cavern system—exactly where a god might nap for a few centuries. "Just remember, you go up the stairs for the shrine's rite hall, down for the crypts. I'd try the rite hall first, it's where they did any ceremonial business."

"You're not going with them?" Kirkling asks as we reach the entrance.

"Neither of us should," says Helga. "It's an old structure. If anything happens in there, someone needs to be ready to help here and the other to go get aid from Hagendorn. Besides, I hate caves."

Kirkling scowls, but she can't argue with that. "As long as Schmidt isn't going to be a distraction, Aspirant Conrad."

Saints and martyrs, I should have pushed her off the rope bridge. "I don't know," I simper, "nothing screams *romance* like rolling around on a sarcophagus. Is it weird if the skulls watch?"

"*And* we're going." Emeric loops his arm through mine and leads us under the vine-choked arch.

I ask loudly over my shoulder, "Do you think all the desiccated corpses might give it a certain, oh, ambience?"

"Please stop antagonizing her," Emeric says under his breath as the daylight fades.

"Maybe when she stops being such a—"

"Oh, and, children?" Helga calls after us (despite being, at most, four years Emeric's senior), "Don't forget, with all that stone, sound *carries.*"

"—dedicated . . . servant of . . . the people," I finish through my gritted teeth.

Emeric lights his prefect coin, then reaches for the well-worn lantern I borrowed from Jakob and Udo. "Here." He taps a pane, and the candle inside ignites.

Ordinarily, there are two ways for the average person to work magic in the Blessed Empire. One is as a warlock, bound to a spirit's immense power but usually for a terrible price. The other is the most human way of gaining power: eating it. Low Gods, spirits, they all shed bones, fur, scales, and so on. It can be burned down to what we call witch-ash and eaten by the pinch for its magic.

This is the second time I've seen Emeric work magic without it, though. Prefects have something like a warlock's bond with the Low Gods at large, but . . . I blink up at him. "I thought you wouldn't get new tricks until after you're fully ordained."

"That's what they told me. It turns out the second initiation's more incremental." He gestures to his upper back, where the mark binding him to the Low Gods' power is. "They add to the mark with every stage I pass, so mine's almost done."

Murals begin to unfold over the uneven stone walls the farther we go, each painted in faded chalky pigment. Lantern and coin light spill over Brunne, riding into the night. Another seems to depict a girl before a crowd in a castle, a story I don't know.

"Does that mean you don't need witch-ash anymore?" I ask, partially to take my mind off the eerie stillness of the passageway.

"Not unless it's been a very taxing day." He catches my muffled sigh. "Why? What's wrong?"

"Nothing, it's fine."

"I don't believe you," he says primly.

"It makes you smell like juniper," I mumble, sheepish. "It was nice."

"Oh." An equally sheepish grin creeps across his face. "I'll see what I can do."

I dart ahead like a flighty colt. I'm still not used to being around him like this again, dancing around each other. "Careful, wouldn't want the good proctor to think I'm distracting you."

"As long as I do my job, it shouldn't matter." He lingers at another mural. This one looks like the Witches' Dance henge. Then he shakes his head. "Our records on the Haarzlands are . . . woefully inadequate. I don't think there's been a prefect in these parts for forty years."

"Ominous."

"*Exciting.*" Emeric continues down the corridor. "Dormant gods, ancient hellhounds, unprecedented loopholes in prefectorial-godly regulations . . ."

"I don't feel like those belong on the same scale of exciting," I note.

"Agree to disagree."

"So when we find the Scarlet Maiden, we want to know . . ." I start ticking off fingers. "Why she was able to bypass the accords."

"Correct."

"What this whole sacred-feast thing entails."

"Yes."

"Why she wants *you* to be the servant."

"Right."

"And maybe her thoughts on the inherent seductive allure of a crypt." We reach a wider chamber, and I feign a swoon against one of its blocky columns.

"I would rather not," Emeric says, scanning the newest crop of murals. Rusted sconces are bolted to the stone, torch stems long since disintegrated. Matched brackets of stairs descend out of sight on either side of the chamber, and ahead, broad shallow steps rise.

"Helga did say to try the rite hall first. We could fool around in there." I jab a thumb at the central stair leading up, sarcastic. "Then again, we already got frisky on an altar in Minkja; maybe you want to change it up with the coffins."

There's a pause.

"I need to borrow this." Emeric abruptly plucks the lantern from my hand. I assume he's spotted something, but he just sets it on the floor.

Then he slides one hand around the nape of my neck, braces me against the column, and proceeds to kiss me like both our lives depend on it.

Oh.

I can't hold in a startled little gasp, but I catch up fast enough, marveling in the sweet heady rush, leaning into him with a kind of hunger I've tried and failed to forget these past few months. In the end, all I forgot was the way every little thing—every fingertip pressing into my hip, every pulse in his jaw beneath my palm, every feverish collision of lips, teeth, tongue—strikes new lightning down my every last bone.

Then Emeric draws back, running a shaking thumb over my bottom lip. "Will you *please*," he says, hoarsely enough to puncture the smugness in his voice, "stop distracting me."

"Absolutely not," I say with zero hesitation, pulling him to me again. A wicked smile flashes over his face before he veers off, pressing a kiss below my ear, then continuing down my throat. I shiver, making a horrendously undignified noise, and let my head tilt back.

Then, for the second time today, I go cold from head to toe.

"E-Emeric."

His eyes flash with concern as he immediately lets me go. "Sorry—are you—was that too much?"

"No—not you—" I catch his sleeve and point to the ceiling.

Another mural unfurls above us, this one unfaded by time.

A woman in a crimson cloak presides over three great circles; each circle holds an identical view of the waterfall and the unmistakable frothy, stone-fanged Kronenkessel. A golden crown lurks in the depths.

In the first circle, a crude human figure stands on a low stone bridge over the pool, a red handprint plain on their chest. In the second, the marked person leaps into the raging white water. And in the final image, the figure is gone. All that remain are the bridge and the pool, with one stark, terrible difference:

The waters of the Kronenkessel have turned a dark and bloody red.

"I don't think," I say slowly, "that it's dye."

CHAPTER FOUR

ᘓLAIMS

"HMM," HELGA HUMS, SWINGING HER OWN LANTERN TO STUDY A
mosaic in Felsengruft's rite hall. "Yeah, this definitely looks like
human sacrifice."

I have one rule for dealing with a bad situation. You may be familiar
with it, and with how anytime I break it, things have a nasty tendency to
go sideways. This rule, for the uninitiated, is: *Don't panic.*

Helga is not currently helping with that rule.

For the record, neither is Kirkling, lurking near the hall's entrance
like a disgruntled gargoyle. Unfortunately, when Emeric and I went to
get Helga to confirm our suspicions, the proctor insisted on seeing the
antechamber's murals for herself, then followed us up into the rite hall.

"It's against the accords," Kirkling snaps, busily scratching in her notebook yet again.

"We've been over this," Helga drawls back. Then she pivots in place, looking over to me. "Right? I didn't hallucinate this morning, when I specifically told her that Haarzlands gods probably predate whatever accords she's going on about?"

"Can we please focus?" I can't help squeezing Emeric's hand tighter. He returns it but stays silent as his eyes rove the walls. He hasn't said much since I spotted the sacrifice mural; I wish he would, even if it's just to blame me for bringing him into a mess that's getting worse by the second.

"You said the Scarlet Maiden called it a midsummer feast." Helga points to a niche, her words echoing off the walls. The rite hall is sparer than I expected and not much bigger than Hagendorn's new stave chapel, but every rustle feels louder than a stampede as it bangs around the vaulted ceilings and the simple hewn-rock benches. Even the main altar is a massive unornamented slab of granite, and the murals are either thin flaking paint like those in the antechamber, or the embedded tiles of mosaics. The niche Helga's highlighting is crowned with an inlaid sun of vivid yellow porcelain chips. "That sun should mark midsummer. And here's the ritual again."

Sure enough, the same three images from the antechamber's ceiling—figure stands on bridge, figure leaps into water, water turns into either a bloodbath or a very ambitious punch bowl—are repeated along the niche. This time, the jaws of the hellhound are also clearly visible.

"So was anyone going to tell me about the yearly sacrifice to the local hellhound, or was I just supposed to sort that one out on my own?" I ask, my voice rising to a squeak despite my best efforts.

"I am *telling* you, human sacrifice is forbidden—" Kirkling starts at the same time Helga says, "This whole 'feast' business is news to—Do you *mind?*"

Kirkling ignores her, scowling into her notes. "No Low God has the power to demand a human sacrifice. *Especially* not of a prefect."

"Incredible," Helga breathes. "Like bouncing a penny off a boulder. Not a single thing gets through." It's her turn to ignore Kirkling's scowl as she turns to Emeric and me. "Anyway, we don't know if it's a sacrifice to the hellhound or to the Scarlet Maiden, or if it's even necessary since it hasn't happened since the Scarlet Maiden's time . . ."

"If the Scarlet Maiden is even a real Low God," Kirkling interjects, detonating another round of squabbling with Helga.

I tune them out as I sneak another look at Emeric. His gaze is fixed on the final image in the niche: the hellhound's fangs in a pool of terminal red.

If the Scarlet Maiden is really some elaborate fraud, he'll have to bring me to trial before the Godly Courts himself. But if she is a true Low God . . .

No. I've defied Low Gods before; I'll do it again. I'll find us a way out.

There *has* to be a way out.

The argument between Helga and Kirkling is getting louder and louder, crashing off the granite walls as doubt starts welling up, fear deepening in its wake. All I can think is, *I did this, I did this, I did this.*

"Hey." The single word pops out of me. It doesn't so much as register with Helga and Kirkling (all I can hear is "*How many times do I have to tell you this, old woman?*"), but another, louder "*HEY*" stops them in their tracks.

But I'm not talking to them.

"*Scarlet Maiden,*" I half bellow as Emeric stares at me, "it's, uh, your prophet! Can you come out here for a minute?"

Helga plasters a hand over her face. "Does *no one* know how these things work?"

"What are you doing?" It's not accusation but intrigue in Emeric's voice.

"We came here for answers," I say under my breath, setting my lantern down by a pew, "so I'm getting them." Then I raise my voice again: "*SCARLET MAIDEN! CAN YOU GIVE US YOUR LOCATION? I JUST WANT TO TALK!*"

For a moment, the words rattle around the rite hall. Then every flame in the room goes out, plunging us into darkness. That familiar jangling whisper sweeps the room as Kirkling and Helga both jump.

"You called, my prophet?"

Red mist rolls across the floor, weaving into the too-sharp, too-bright vision of the Scarlet Maiden. This time she's suspended above the granite altar, her eyes glittering like broken glass.

A wire-thin smile flexes over her face. *"And you've brought my servant. To what end?"*

"Well, I'll be damned," Helga breathes.

Emeric is fixed in place, almost frozen, until I brush his knuckles with my thumb. Then he takes a deep breath and pulls out the prefect coin, lighting it once more. "We have questions about the, er, sacred feast, your divinity."

"Among other things." Kirkling rolls her charcoal stick between thin fingers. "How is it, precisely, you aren't bound by the same rules that govern every Low God regarding their prefects?"

The Scarlet Maiden tilts her head. *"Prefect? What is a prefect to me?"*

"'Claims . . . ignorance,'" Kirkling mutters into her notes, "'of basic knowledge.'"

"By the Accord of Prefectorial and Godly Alliance," Emeric says diplomatically, "a prefect is sworn to investigate crimes of extraordinary magnitude and harm, to gather the facts of the case to the fullest possible extent, and, if necessary, to call the Godly Court to present their findings. We are bound to the rules of conduct as established by the accords, and in exchange, we are granted limited use of the Low Gods' powers."

"I recall no accords."

Emeric purses his lips. "How long would you say you've been asleep?"

"Too long. The world is strange now to me." The Scarlet Maiden's mists coil tighter. *"Your questions do not concern the sacred feast."*

Emeric adjusts his spectacles. "I do apologize; this is an unusual situation and we're just trying to learn as much as we can. Do you know why you went dormant?"

"Have a minstrel sing you the song," the Scarlet Maiden says tersely. The mist twines into tendrils, almost like vines.

"I'm afraid I'm not familiar—"

The Scarlet Maiden's nostrils flare. Fast as a whipcrack, a needle-sharp red spine thrusts from the altar and spears Emeric through the throat.

There's a scream that I do not know as my own until much, much later.

Emeric's eyes, whites and all, burn with crimson light. So does the handprint on his chest, blazing even through the shirt. Somehow, he's still on his feet.

"Do not waste my time further, servant," snarls the Scarlet Maiden. *"I have brought great fortune to this town, but do not mistake my generosity for patience. Ask of the ritual, or leave me be."*

The vine dissolves into curling mist, and the blood-red light vanishes from Emeric's eyes. He lurches, but I'm already there to steady him, my own knuckles creaking from my grip.

There's not a mark on him beyond the handprint, no trace of broken skin on his throat. He's—he's breathing. He's alive.

I still can't make myself let go.

Emeric's jaw stiffens. Then, to my astonishment, he gently extracts his hand from mine and pulls out his own notebook and charcoal, his face a steely sort of unperturbed. "Could you please elaborate on this sacred feast?"

"Do you maybe . . . want to take a moment?" I nearly wheeze.

"I would like," he says, in the pleasantly stiff way of someone vexed beyond reason, "for the Scarlet Maiden to tell me about the sacred feast."

The Scarlet Maiden sighs. "*Perhaps this age does not remember, but once I made the river run silver with fish and the fields all but sink beneath the abundance of crops. Such was my blessing . . . but the beast of the Kronenkessel devoured the fish and drank my power from the soil.*"

"'. . . blessing . . . abundance . . .' Right." Emeric nods, jotting even faster than Kirkling. "And how does that involve me?"

"*In the days of old, well before midsummer, I chose one yet unclaimed among the people of the gorge and bestowed the honor of my mark, the same you bear now. It is their duty to either vanquish the hellhound or sate its hunger another year.*"

Emeric's charcoal stick goes still as he looks at her over his spectacles. "To vanquish . . . ? *Vanquish.* A hellhound? Did I hear that correctly?"

"*It has starved for too long,*" the Scarlet Maiden continues. "*I fear if it is neither fed nor defeated—*"

"Definitely fed," Emeric says under his breath.

"*—it will soon turn its wrath upon Hagendorn. I am not strong enough now to restrain the beast, but I, too, take strength from the sacred feast, as a sacrifice in my honor. So, live or die, my chosen servant will serve us all. But we must have a feast by midsummer, or it may be too late.*"

There's a knot in my belly growing heavier by the second. I'd strongly considered resolving this situation by hitting Emeric over the head with a rock and smuggling us out of Hagendorn before he woke up. That gets less . . . *ethically* viable if a hellhound will raze the town in our wake.

This feels too close to the December morning in Minkja, standing on the gallows, the noose a scratching torc resting on my collarbones, the hangman's hand at the ready.

I had a way out. I'll find one again.

"Why does it have to be Emeric?" I blurt out.

At that, the Scarlet Maiden tilts her head, and another serpentine smile bares its fangs. "*Because I chose him, Prophet. That is enough. Besides, it is always one unclaimed. Would it not be cruel to send someone claimed by another?*"

There it is again. *Claimed* and *unclaimed.* Maybe it's a loophole. "What does that mean?" I push. "What kind of claim?"

I really, truly, should have left it alone.

The Scarlet Maiden titters as she lifts a hand to her face, scattering phantasmal rubies from the wound in her palm. "*Why, the claim of a lover, of course; the one made by man and wife in a marriage bed. My servant must have never known such a claim.*"

It clicks.

The scratching of both charcoal sticks crashes to a halt, and a wretched, excruciating silence blasts through the rite hall. No one so much as moves a muscle; I feel all the blood drain from my face, only to come rushing back at once in a boiling flood.

Emeric snaps his notebook shut, saying faintly, "I have to go."

Then he turns on a heel and strides out of the room.

I start after him. "Emeric—"

A hand closes around my wrist. "Trust me, he doesn't want to talk to you right now," Helga hisses. "Give him some space."

She's right. I yank free anyway, scowling.

"*Teenagers,*" she mutters.

"*Do you have any further questions?*" the Scarlet Maiden prods, a bit testily.

I open my mouth to thank her for ruining both my love life *and* my everyday life, but Helga speaks first. "Actually, yes. Midsummer is two and a half months away, and"—she eyeballs me—"circumstances may change. What if your servant is, uh, claimed before then?"

The Scarlet Maiden's mists begin sharpening to thorns once more.

"*Then I would require,*" she says slowly, "*a greater sacrifice.*"

To my surprise, she reaches out and snaps a long, slender thorn from the mist. The color begins to bleed out, seeping into the air like dye.

"*You must not only answer for the insult of denying me my servant, but also grant me the strength to hold the beast of the Kronenkessel in check.*"

She slashes the pale thorn along a sleeve. A perfectly square section of fabric slices free and flutters onto the granite altar, also leaching red until there's nothing left but undyed cambric. The thorn is laid beside it, now so pale it looks to be an awl carved from bone.

"*The blood of seven brothers will suffice.*" The Scarlet Maiden's words slither and ring around the stones. "*Use my awl to collect a drop from each upon this cambric, and render this sacrifice unto me by midsummer. Then I will have no need for the servant, and Hagendorn will be spared my wrath and that of the beast.*" The mist begins to contract and fade. "*I have overexerted myself. I will rest now. Do not disturb me again before the feast.*"

"Hold on," Kirkling starts, raising her charcoal. "What kind of power—"

"*Farewell, Prophet. Watch over my servant.*"

As abruptly as she arrived, the Scarlet Maiden vanishes.

Another brutal silence frosts over the rite hall. I try to gather my thoughts, but that would require thoughts for me to gather in the first place; right now we're back to goat screams. I make myself take a long breath.

The awl. The hellhound. The god I made up. *Maybe* a way out.

I did this. I did this. I did this.

I have to fix it. Somehow.

I point at the altar, where the cambric and the awl lie in wait. "Nobody touch those. I'm going to find Emeric. He . . . needs to know his options."

"The proctor and I can take a closer look," Helga states more than suggests. "And, er." She coughs. "I *am* a trained midwife. If you have any questions—"

"*None,*" I snap. "No questions, thank you, goodbye." I start marching out, then stop to add, "Don't come after us. I'll bring him back here."

Kirkling's and Helga's voices fade behind me as I make my way out of Felsengruft. There's no sign of Emeric, but that's not too surprising. If I were in his shoes, I'd want to put plenty of distance between myself and, well, the rest of the world.

It isn't hard to guess where he went when I see it: the rune-covered hut a little ways from the rope bridge, the one meant to shelter people caught out after dark in lands overgrown with old magic. Private, but close enough that he'd hear the rest of us coming. Sure enough, when I push on the heavy door, it cracks open to show Emeric leaning against a sturdy dust-draped table, spectacles pushed up into his hair, hands plastered over his eyes.

The door judders to a noisy halt before I can slip in, though, sticking on a rut in the dirt floor. Emeric jolts to his feet and hurries over. "Oh—hold on, here—"

"No, I've got it—"

With a tortured squawk, the door grinds free and swings wider,

Emeric still clutching the handle and standing in the doorway. There's a pause.

"Can . . . can I come in?" I ask, tentative.

He ducks his head and steps aside. "Right. Yes. Of course."

It's cooler inside the little hut, not the mortal chill of Felsengruft but the relief of shade and stillness. A few small windows let in just enough sunlight to navigate by. There's a crude fireplace with a well-stocked pile of logs, a short stack of carved plates, an ancient pot, a chair beside the table, and a heap of blankets and furs that could suffice for a bed.

I'm not sure I want to think about beds right now.

No, this is silly. Just hours ago we were *sharing* a bed. But that was before we had to dissect exactly what might happen there.

The crackle in the air says we both know where this conversation is going. I still try a sideways approach. "How are you doing?"

Emeric wavers, then leans against the table's edge once again. "I mean . . ." He shakes his head. "It is what it is. What about you?"

I sit on the table next to him. "Fine enough," I say carefully, "except the human measuring stick I'm inexplicably fond of is dodging my question."

He gives me a sidelong glance, bitterness seeping into his attempt at a smile. "You really are worried. I know you can do better than 'human measuring stick.'" It's my turn to give him a pointed look, and he sighs, then turns his gaze away again. "How am I doing? Well, the god that's marked me for death just announced to a relative stranger, the proctor of my career-deciding trial, and the girl I'm trying to court that I'm a—that I haven't ever—" He throws up his hands. "And *that* apparently qualifies me to fight a hellhound to the death. *My* death, because between me and what we saw at the waterfall, my money is on the hellhound."

I brush his sleeve. "There may be another option. Helga asked what would happen if—if you were . . . disqualified." My face is burning, and my only consolation is the flush I see rising up his neck too. "The Scarlet Maiden said we can make it up to her by bringing her a drop of blood from each of seven brothers instead, by midsummer. That would be the sacrifice." I frown. "She said she wouldn't even need a servant that way, so nobody would have to . . ."

"*Claim* me," he says with a hoarse, humorless laugh, but his hands are knotting viciously in his lap.

There are moments when, as divergent as our lives are, I still see something in him so familiar, it might be cut from my own heart. I know this unease in him because it took root in me years ago, and I may never burn it out. It's defiance and humiliation in one: I haven't bedded anyone yet because I haven't desired it, and for much of the world, that means there must be something wrong with me. That the older I get, the more it becomes something to *get over with* instead of something to want for myself.

That the reason can't be because I rarely desire people that way; it must be that I'm undesirable.

I slip off the table and stand in front of Emeric, lay a hand on his face, wait until he meets my eyes. Half sitting as he is, we're nearly the same height.

"I knew I was your first kiss, and you knew you were mine," I tell him quietly. "And we're both smart enough to have figured out the implications. So yes, you're a virgin. Yes, so am I. And yes, this is miserable and awkward because we have to talk about it instead of just"—I flap my free hand—"letting *things* happen." Then I realize I've neglected one very critical point. "I'm assuming you want, er, things . . . with me."

"Yes," Emeric says, so swiftly I almost jump. Even he looks startled, his ears turning red. "I mean, at some point, yes, I—" His voice cracks. "I've . . . given it some thought."

"Oh," I say, cleverly. Even though that's the answer I was hoping for, hearing him say it still sends a giddy shock through my veins.

His mouth twists. "The thing is . . . Do you remember in Castle Reigenbach, when you said your first kiss would have mattered to you, but you could have faked it to save us?"

"Because I was used to all the choices being bad," I finish, nodding.

Emeric wraps his hand around mine and reaches for my other one, so our linked hands are strung between us like a bridge. "Vanja, I never want you to have to make that kind of choice for me. You deserve so much more than the least terrible of your choices. Especially with something like this." He swallows. "That is . . . if you want, er, *things* yourself."

"I do want," I blurt out, and suddenly understand how Emeric could answer with such immediate certainty before. I want him, pure and simple, in a way I haven't wanted anyone else. It's somewhere between hunger and curiosity and something else entirely, and it wakes in me even when he's not here, like a memory written in my bones.

But . . .

"But?" Emeric does not miss my hesitation.

And that nervous unease climbs back up my throat. I shift in place, trying to pick my words like a surgeon chooses instruments, only to become increasingly aware of how long it's taking me to answer. I panic and instead flip the metaphorical tray.

"It hasn't even been a day," I say in a rush, "since we've been together again. And I want this, I want you, I just . . . I don't know if I'm . . ." It's my turn to duck my head. This is the part that matters most, but it's funny how those parts are always hardest to say. "Have you ever wanted something, and you *knew* you wanted it, but you were still . . . scared of getting it?"

Emeric lets out a breath. A moment later, the air warms on my cheeks as he rests his forehead on mine.

The relief in his voice is almost palpable when he says, "I know *exactly* what you mean."

"Really?" I ask, a little stunned.

"Really. I don't think I'm, well, ready either. You said it yourself, this is all moving so fast—"

"*So* fast!"

He draws back to search my face. "And I don't want you to feel rushed *or* like I don't want—*things*—but this time yesterday, I thought I might never see you again. Now I'm just trying not to lose you."

"We don't have to figure it all out now," I say.

"Just . . . by midsummer."

I shake my head. "If we go straight for the blood sacrifice—oh, that doesn't sound good, does it?"

"It's not great," he says dryly.

"Then we don't have to worry about any timeline at all. Unless we want to be, er, cautious. Or . . . if it happens on its own."

He huffs another laugh, still bitter, but at least with a hint of humor this time. "We can barely get in a single kiss without being interrupted by bad omens and blood sacrifices. How are we supposed to, to do *more*?"

"I don't know," I admit. It's hard not to be overwhelmed with all that's been uprooted in the storm since I walked into the barn last night. If Emeric weren't here, I might have let myself be swept away entirely.

But he's still with me. Even after the Scarlet Maiden, even with Kirkling hounding us for any opening—despite everything, he's been with me. Just like in Minkja.

"Here's what I do know," I say softly, summoning his own words from a winter night months ago. "As long as we're in this, we're in it together."

Recognition sparks in his eyes, and the smile that follows breaks my heart in a way I never want to end. "Then 'drag this out as long as possible' is what you're telling me."

"Something like that." I return his smile, then sober. "So, how's this for a plan: We go along with the blood-of-seven-brothers thing to get you out of the sacrifice entirely. And in the meantime, it won't *hurt* if we, uh, disqualify you, but . . . only at our own pace. Is that better?"

"Yes—" His voice cracks, and he shakes his head. "Yes. When we're both ready." Then he frees a hand to lay on my face, thumb tracing my cheekbone, expression softening. "I'm so lucky it's you."

All these months and he still hasn't lost the trick of catching me in the throat. "You know . . . I told Helga and Kirkling to wait in Felsengruft. It's just you and me here, no interruptions. And this morning you said you wanted to take your time."

I step closer until our knees bump, our faces only a few inches apart. Emeric goes still as my fingers slide up the back of his neck, into his hair; something different ignites in his eyes.

"So take it," I whisper.

He does not need to be told twice.

I don't know how long we stay there, just that we don't leave until we're ready, still flushed and a bit rumpled but with at least three months' worth of lost kissing accounted for. When we return to the rite hall, I walk straight to the altar, where the cambric and the awl are waiting. Helga and Kirkling seem to have finally bickered themselves into silence; they're scowling at each other from opposite ends of the room.

"So," I say briskly, picking up the awl, "anyone know where we can find seven brothers?"

Helga opens her mouth, shuts it, thinks a moment. Then, with peculiar reluctance, she says, "Actually, yes."

CHAPTER FIVE

MISS SCHMIDT

GOLDEN EVENING SUNLIGHT SLANTS THROUGH THE WINDOWS OF THE Ros brothers' house, catching motes of dust as Jakob hovers over a cabbage-and-*wurst* stew simmering in the open hearth. Little by little, the light dims as Udo moves around the main room, pulling curtains shut. Too many faces are turning toward the house now, sneaking looks just a little too casually, and the weight in the air says none of us wants any more observers than we already have.

Not Helga, cutting thick slices of rye bread at the heavy dining table beside me; not Emeric, sitting across from me, his hands tangling again. And certainly not me, fidgeting just as badly.

Jakob and Udo, it turns out, have five more brothers. But before we even get into that, there is one thing they've asked of me: the truth. And not about the fact that I may have forgotten their lantern in Felsengruft.

They've already given me so much these two months, and now I have to tell them it was all because of a lie.

(I can't believe I actually feel bad about lying. Lying might be the *most*-legal thing I'm good at. If this is what being around Emeric does to me, by the end of the week Hagendorn'll be putting up churches in my name.

In retrospect, I need to make sure the Red Blessed don't get any ideas.)

Emeric reaches for a pocket. "Do you mind if I take notes?" he asks quietly. "It may save us some questions later on."

My stomach twists. It's not like I forgot he's supposed to be investigating me too; it's just an uncomfortable reminder that all my bad choices are going to be meticulously documented, starting with inventing the Scarlet Maiden.

I want him to leave out details for me, is the thing. Smudge out my failures until there's just the girl I want him to see.

But one of the many reasons I've let him in is because we both know he won't.

"I don't mind," I lie.

"Me either," Helga adds, frowning as a chunk of bread frays on a clumsy slice. "Your knives are terrible."

Jakob just grunts from the fireplace, but that seems to be an assent. All the curtains are drawn, and now Udo's rummaging in a hutch in the corner. He shuts a drawer and drags a chair over to my corner of the table.

The chair legs creak as Udo sits, brow furrowed. His dark beard is longer than Jakob's, but they have the same habit of running their fingers over it as they think, as he's doing presently. He only says, "All right, Vanja. We'll have the truth now."

"What do you want to know?" My voice fragments a bit.

Jakob, Udo, and Helga trade looks.

"Everything," Jakob says finally. "Where you really came from, why you came to Hagendorn, why you stayed."

"I'd say you owe us that much," Helga drawls.

Udo rumbles, "It's not about owing." Then he nods to me. "Go on, then."

Whatever Emeric sees in my face makes him reach a hand across the table. It is no small relief to take it.

I told this story when it was just me and him and a fireplace in mid-winter, and when we stood before a court of gods in the wreckage of a wedding. I can tell it to the Ros siblings now.

I tell them how I was born the thirteenth child of a thirteenth child. How my mother believed I was bad luck. I tell Helga how I climbed trellises, snuck in and out of castles, wore gowns of the finest silks. I tell Udo and Jakob how I stole the signet ring off the Golden Wolf himself, how I lie as easy as breathing. I tell them of curses and rubies and a foolish girl drunk on a winter's night, and of the simple lie that grew too fast to stop.

When I am done, the only sound is the furious scuttle of Emeric's charcoal over paper. Then Udo leans forward, dropping something onto the table with an oddly familiar *click*.

A small, perfect ruby casts a fringe of glimmering red over the smooth oak.

"Found it the first night you stayed," Udo says evenly, "stuck in the bottom of the bucket. You must have missed it."

I feel like the stool's been kicked out from beneath me. "You . . . knew? This whole time?"

The unspoken question hangs even heavier in the air: *And you didn't tell anyone?*

Udo leans back. "Jakob said you probably had your reasons."

"And I was right."

"*Were* you, though?" Helga grouches into the rye.

"You're not angry with me?" I ask.

"I wish you'd asked for help the honest way." Udo folds his arms. "We would have got your rubies for a fair price. But that's a lot of faith to put in a strange town. With a story like yours, I can't fault you for acting the cynic."

Emeric coughs politely. "May I ask a few questions?"

"Go ahead." Udo's tone is friendly enough, but his granite eyes narrow.

"Thank you." Emeric slides the Queen of Roses card into the notebook, then flips to a clean page. "At any point in time, did Miss Schmidt solicit you or anyone you know for money, goods, or services on behalf of the Scarlet Maiden?"

My throat goes abruptly dry. I don't know what's worse: how that question feels like a sentencing or how he called me "Miss Schmidt."

"No," Udo says firmly.

Helga tilts her head. "Does getting help with the rubies count?"

Udo waves a hand. "Fine, apart from that."

"And the statues?" Emeric asks. "The chapel?"

"The chapel was Leni's idea," Jakob says, gathering bowls off a shelf. "Statues . . . Who came up with the statues?"

Udo shrugs. "The Red Blessed."

"They came to me with the plans," I add. "I mean, I did tell them the Scarlet Maiden would approve."

Emeric nods but doesn't look up, his charcoal still scratching away. "Did you ever witness Miss Schmidt fabricate signs to suggest the existence of the Scarlet Maiden?"

"Miss Schmidt" again. I feel sick.

Broad knuckles give my shoulder a light rap. "Help me serve the soup," Jakob says, and hands me a stack of bowls.

I get up so fast, I almost knock my stool over, as Udo issues another hard "No."

"Again, the rubies," Helga hums.

"I think the prefect boy can do his own job," Udo says shortly.

Emeric's own stool creaks. "If you're trying to cover for   "

"All we gave Vanja, we gave freely." Udo's voice turns hard. "She took nothing that wasn't offered, and if she lied to folk, it was because they asked her to."

Jakob ladles soup into a bowl. "Everyone who went along with the Red Blessed was an adult of sound mind who ought to have known better."

There's a knock at the door. Udo gets up to open it, still radiating belligerence. It doesn't help that he finds Kirkling on the stoop.

"Pardon me," she says. "I need to speak with Aspirant Conrad." Her eyes catch on the kettle. "It can wait until after your supper, though."

"Join us," Jakob calls over his shoulder.

Kirkling takes a step back. "That isn't necessary."

"We need to discuss this sacrifice business." Jakob tips his head to the table. Udo moves to let the proctor reluctantly enter, shutting the door behind her.

"I will compensate you for the meal," she says, stiff. "As will Aspirant Conrad. His impartiality cannot be in question."

"I don't think anyone can question that," I respond a bit frostily, placing a bowl in front of Emeric with perhaps a bit too much force. Out of the corner of my eye, I see him look up at me, startled, but I ignore it.

"So, you need a drop of blood from each of us." Jakob hooks mugs on his fingers and joins the table as Udo sets down a pitcher of cool milk, then passes around spoons. "The brothers, that is."

Udo takes my previous seat. Good manners would say he's giving Kirkling his chair, which happens to be by Emeric's corner. It also conveniently allows him to glower at Emeric unobstructed.

It does create an awkward moment when the last two seats left are one next to Emeric and one farthest from him, opposite Kirkling. I drop onto the far stool. Jakob settles by Emeric with just a quirk of his eyebrows.

Helga looks like she's trying not to laugh. "Yes, she gave Vanja an awl and a kerchief to collect the blood. Supposedly that will give the Scarlet Maiden enough power to hold back the hellhound."

"You know I don't muck around with the gorge for a reason." Jakob sighs. "*Hellhounds.* Honestly. And blood's the only alternative she gave?"

Udo mutters something into his soup about the other option.

Emeric looks increasingly nervous. "It is."

"Then you've a fair bit of traveling to do." Jakob sets a strange little dice-sized wooden box on the table, then gives it a tap. The sides fold down flat—and continue unfolding with a nigh-endless supply of wooden tiles, spreading across the table. A few squares keep tossing and turning, but the rest settle into a smooth surface that blooms with the lines of a map. It centers on the Haarzlands' corner of Lüdheid Principality, thick with forests and hills that spill out from Boderad's Gorge. Even the rivers in the area all seem to share the same source as the Ilsza.

Helga whistles. "Where'd you get *that?*"

"One of Ozkar's toys." Jakob prods a still-flipping tile. "You know how he is; it wasn't perfect, so he had no use for it. Anyway, the good news is you have to go to only three places for the others. You'll find Dieter to the east, in Dänwik, working at the Golden Bine."

"I thought he had a gig in Glockenberg," Helga says.

Jakob gives her a significant look. "He . . . moved on."

"Oh," she says delicately. "I see."

Jakob's finger moves northwest across the map, from the modestly annotated Dänwik to an area that merits not just a drawing of a city straddling a river but also two separate names: Rammelbeck and Welkenrode. He taps the river's western bank. "Erwin works the docks in Rammelbeck. He may be a bit difficult to track down. Ozkar . . ."

"Ozkar's just going to *be* plain difficult," finishes Helga. "He's still in Rammelbeck too?"

"Welkenrode." Jakob points to the eastern riverbank. "Moved his workshop over around midwinter. And Henrik's in Welkenrode, too, at the Konstanzian Imperial Abbey." He glances at me a moment, then continues, his finger moving to a town in the lowlands north of Hagendorn. "Last you've got Sånnik. He's in Kerzenthal, helping with the family farm. He's getting married at the end of April, actually, so I'd say you could get all seven of us at the wedding, but . . ."

"*Pff.*" Helga snorts. "Only Henrik will probably show. And you two, if you're done with shearing."

Jakob moves his finger in a loose loop over the map. "You'll have to get a coach in Glockenberg, and from there, it's three days and some to Dänwik, then five from Dänwik to Rammelbeck-Welkenrode. With clear roads and fair weather, it's four more days to Kerzenthal, then another four to come straight back here. Shouldn't take more than a month if you hurry, but you've plenty of time until midsummer."

Kirkling speaks up for the first time. "The Library of the Divine in Dänwik could be useful to your investigation, Aspirant Conrad, as its records may date back to the days of the Scarlet Maiden. And the Imperial Abbey at Welkenrode has augurs whose insight could help." Then she seems to recall that her one purpose in life is to be a blight on mine, because she adds, "It would also be . . . inadvisable to let Schmidt out of your sight while you're investigating her."

"What did you want to speak to the boy about?" Udo asks in the tonal equivalent of a *TRESPASSERS WILL BE SHOT* sign.

Kirkling dunks a slice of bread into her soup. "I suppose *this* much isn't confidential: Aspirant Conrad, now that you have begun your Finding, at the close of every day you will provide me with a verbal status report in private. Today's will be brief because of the short notice, but from tomorrow onward, you are expected to show a full prefect's command of the facts of your case. Am I understood?"

"Yes, Proctor Kirkling," Emeric says with a forced sort of tranquility, as if the prospect of a daily quiz isn't the greatest thing that's happened to him since the invention of the T square.

"Our belongings have arrived, so tomorrow I will arrange transportation to Dänwik. Be ready to depart in the afternoon."

"If that works for Vanja." Emeric glances to me, but I find my own gaze skating away.

Udo makes a noise of uncut disapproval. "She shouldn't go on her own. One of us ought to help her track the others down and convince them."

"I believe Schmidt is seventeen," Kirkling returns, "making her an adult and citizen by imperial law. Besides, she will be safe in the custody of the prefects."

"*'Custody'?*" Now a *NO TRESPASSING* sign is posting up in Jakob's voice too. "Vanja hasn't been charged with anything. Udo's right—one of us should go."

In near-perfect unison, he and Udo both look at Helga.

"No," she says immediately. "No teenager melodrama."

Jakob points with his own slice of rye at his brother. "Sheep shearing's this month, we have to stay. And, Helga, you haven't seen the rest of the family in, what, two years?"

"Auntie Gerke's too old to make the walk to town for house calls."

"She can stay with us. Or we'll send Sonja's eldest. They want to apprentice for a hedgewitch."

The siblings go back and forth, but eventually it's clear Helga does want to go and is arguing only to harass Jakob. She stomps off after supper with no real spite; Udo, on the other hand, maintains a frosty front toward Emeric even after Emeric singlehandedly cleans up dinner. Then, peculiarly, Udo offers the house to Kirkling.

"Jakob's got to close down his workshop, and Vanja and I have to put the sheep away for the night," he says. "You two need a private place for your report. This will do."

"Much obliged," Kirkling answers. Udo and I head for the door only to get snagged on her follow-up question. "Oh, is the . . . *sleeping arrangement* still acceptable?"

Every eye turns to me, but I feel Emeric's more than any other.

I . . . I don't know why I'm angry with him, just that I am. But I also got him into this mess in the first place.

"It's fine," I lie again, and follow Udo out.

We get halfway to the barn before he says, "I'll handle the sheep myself. You can go get ready for bed." He pauses. "Going to be a chilly night. May want to warm up your room."

When I connect the dots, I am delighted at Udo's unprecedented craftiness. "Right, chilly," I say. "Good night, then." I turn to go, then find I have a parting question of my own: "Udo? Why are you all helping me?"

When he answers after a moment, all he says is "You had your reasons. We have ours."

Then he continues on toward the barn, whistling into the early twilight. Baffled, I head to my lean-to.

It's dim inside, the dwindling light casting a periwinkle glow, and I take care not to make too much noise. The little iron door in the back of the chimney is piping hot, so I use a rag to ease it open. There's a faint hiss of embers—

Then, more important, voices.

". . . your case thus far."

Udo, that *deviant.*

"Very little I can say for certain." Emeric's voice carries through clear as day. "There is an entity that calls itself the Scarlet Maiden, and it commands some manner of power. It claims to have chosen me for a sacrifice. Hagendorn's new cult worships a god *also* called the Scarlet Maiden. We have not proven they are the same entity."

"'Not . . . proven,'" Kirkling repeats. She must be taking notes again. "And the profane fraud related to that cult?"

"I have nothing certain," Emeric says.

I catch my breath.

There's an uncomfortable delay before Kirkling prompts, flat, "Truly?"

"Truly," he confirms. "If the entity is a true Low God, then there is no fraud. I will—"

"You don't really believe that," Kirkling interrupts.

Emeric pauses. Then he continues with the same ironclad calm he summoned after the Scarlet Maiden speared him through the throat: "I will conduct further questioning of the locals in the morning. At present, the only incident that might qualify as profane fraud is too trivial to meet the standard for trial by the Godly Courts."

Maybe—maybe there's a chance this ends well for us.

"The Ros brothers have stated that, apart from the incident, they have never seen Miss Schmidt use the Scarlet Maiden for her own benefit. It seems more likely to me—"

"Spare me your guesses, Aspirant Conrad." Kirkling sighs. "You've comported yourself reasonably enough for a difficult day, and this will suffice as a report for which you were not prepared. I expect more thorough work going forward. You're dismissed."

I hurriedly light the lantern and sneak the iron door shut before Emeric arrives, but it turns out there's no need to rush. When he knocks at the lean-to door, I've had time to finish washing up, and to even scrub my hair with the nice soap I stole from Castle Reigenbach.

I let Emeric in and spot the cause of the delay: a pack slung over his shoulder. "You got your stuff."

"I did. I . . ." He trails off, a strange look on his face. "Are you wearing perfume?"

"My old soap."

"Oh." He sets his pack down.

I pull a clean linen shift from the plain wooden trunk Udo built for me. "I need to change."

"R-right. I'll just, er." He closes the door, then turns his back to me and faces the corner, rubbing the nape of his neck.

Part of me wants to be charmed by his propriety. Part of me can't stop hearing "Miss Schmidt." I say nothing, just go to work on my dress's ties.

"How much did you overhear?" Emeric asks. "I assume that's why *Meister* Ros gave us the room."

"You wanted me to eavesdrop?"

"I expected no less."

I step out of my dress and chemise and pull the shift over my head. "So you just said what I'd want to hear."

"No, I—" There's a rustle as he starts to turn around and then catches himself. "I want you to know where things stand."

"Your turn to change." I climb into bed and scoot to the far side of the mattress, staring at the wooden slats of the wall.

"Vanja, I—have I upset you?"

"It's nothing," I lie, for a third time. There's a horrid silence punctured only by the *thmp* of buttons slipping through wool and a whisper of fabric I am much, much too aware of. I don't know if my head is burning with frustration or—well, a different kind of frustration. The words pop out before I can reel them back in: "You're just doing your duty."

The sudden quiet tells me Emeric's gone still. After a moment, he says, "I didn't lie to Kirkling. My duty as a prefect is not to trick anyone into incriminating you for something you didn't do. It's to find the truth and to present evidence that verifies it."

"And what if I did do it?" I sit up, my eyes nailed to the wall. "Because I *did* rig miracles, I *did* pretend to have visions, I—"

"As long as it wasn't in exchange for goods, money, or services—"

"Then why did you have to ask if it was?" My voice rises with an embarrassing quaver. I know none of this makes sense, I *know* it's not about me. "*Wh-why are you calling me 'Miss Schmidt'?*"

The mattress shifts. I look up to see Emeric kneeling beside me before my face crumples.

"Vanja—" he starts, horrified, then pulls me to him as I burst into utterly humiliating tears. "Oh no, Vanja, I'm so sorry."

"No, I'm sorry," I sniffle into his shoulder. "I'm being ridiculous."

Chagrin weighs each word. "No, you're not. I thought it would be easier for you if you knew what I was asking, if—if I tried to make it less personal—but I haven't called you 'Miss Schmidt' since . . . Hubert. And that was awful for you." His voice hitches. "*I* was awful to you. And now you're watching me dredge up anything you may have done wrong so you can be put on trial . . . Of course that's distressing. I'm sorry, I didn't think this through at all."

"It's not your fault," I mumble. "I'm the one who started a cult."

"But it's not my duty to—to terrorize you either," he insists. "If

I can't do my job otherwise, then I have no business joining the prefects." He thinks a moment. "Do you still have the amnesty token from Minkja?"

I pull back enough to reach a small bag on the crate that serves as a bedside table. Inside are trinkets I kept from Bóern: a black feather from Ragne, a little leather notebook Emeric gave me for my birthday (which, admittedly, is still completely blank), a luck charm from Winterfast, and, at the very bottom, a pewter coin stamped with the sigil of the prefects.

"Here." I hold up the coin.

Emeric folds his hand over mine and closes his eyes. There's a soft pulse of silvery light between our fingers.

When I realize what he's doing, it's already too late.

"Done," he says, letting go. "It's active again. I'll have the Dänwik outpost formally document your amnesty as a consultant for the Scarlet Maiden case. No prefect can arrest you as long as the case is open."

I'm both overwhelmed and strangely upset that he would take this risk for me. "But you'll have to close it to pass your Finding."

"Then I won't close it without compelling evidence that you shouldn't be charged."

"But what if I *should*—"

"I don't think this is chance," he says in a rush. "It all feels too— orchestrated. You've been here since the end of January, but the Scarlet Maiden first manifests when prefects arrive, just to claim me for a sacrifice? And there just *happen* to be two of seven brothers right here?"

"You don't think she's a real Low God," I say tautly, leaving the rest to hang between us: *And that makes me guilty.*

But Emeric shakes his head. "She very well may be real. But just because she's a god doesn't mean she's *good*. The real question here is what she wants. And in the meantime, you shouldn't have to live in fear."

I'm getting choked up again, but for a completely different reason, so I just lay my cheek over his heart and try to breathe. "Saints and martyrs, this is going to be hard, isn't it."

"Mm-hm. We'll figure out what to do differently in the morning." He presses a kiss to my temple. "But as long as we're in this . . ." He trails off again. I don't mind; I know how it ends.

I can't help a bewildered laugh when he buries his nose in my still-damp hair. "What are you doing?"

"Sorry," he says, with no trace of remorse. "*Gods*, I missed that smell."

CHAPTER SIX

[ONSULTATION

I EXPECT TO WAKE THE NEXT MORNING MUCH AS I DID THE MORNING before: pleasantly tangled with Emeric, but letting it last this time. Instead, I awake to a clear view of the wall, an unintentional success of the separate-blankets gambit, and a slight chill.

When I roll over, Emeric is staring at me with an expression best summarized as haunted. Bizarrely, he seems to have slept under his coat, a towel, and several unbuttoned shirts.

"You," he says blearily, "are an unparalleled devil from hell in your sleep."

"*What?*"

Emeric rubs his eyes. "You stole all the blankets. And then you rolled up in them, like a, a crêpe, so they were stuck on your side. And then, when I tried to take one off the top, you turned over, looked me straight in the eye, and said—and I quote—'I'll kill you.'"

"I *never*."

"You followed it up with 'It'll look like an accident.'"

That unfortunately tracks. Mortified, I wordlessly free one side of the blankets and extend it to him. He sheds the laundry and scoots under with a grumble that subsides when I wrap my arms around his chest. He *is* rather dreadfully chilly. I mumble into his nightshirt, "Well, at least you know I can't come up with a decent murder threat in my sleep."

"Quite the contrary," he says, almost a touch impressed. "I asked several follow-ups. Your plan was shockingly robust."

"Nooo," I groan.

"One of your contingencies involved a pig farm."

"I'm never going to hear the end of this, am I?"

"Not if I can help it." Emeric's voice rumbles through me, huddled together as we are. There's something lovely about this, drowsy and warm and feeling the thin linen shift against my skin with his every breath.

We were both exhausted last night, and barely anything happened before we fell asleep. This morning feels different. That sleepy bone-deep hunger is stirring.

I lever myself up until our faces are even and find the same hazy hunger in him. "Then I'll just have to keep distracting you."

The kiss starts sweet and velvet soft, lingering like the gloaming, fingers sifting through hair and roaming only within charted territory. But perhaps we're both thinking of more, or maybe the wild ride of yesterday made us bolder, greedier. It doesn't take long for me to draw his hands under my nightshirt and let them run deliciously over the bare skin north of my hips. He traces his circles higher and higher, first to ask, then to draw shivers from me, intent like each one is a secret between just us, like he won't rest until he's uncovered them all. Nor am I content to let him be alone in his scrutiny, ridding him of his shirt entirely, the better to reorient myself in the maps of rib and scar, muscle and skin, the lines of the prefect contract mark over his heart. In the mellow early morning glow, it's almost possible to pretend the red handprint isn't there.

It also doesn't take long to have an effect on him that linen does little to hide. I think we both realize this at the same time, when I move a knee and brush something that makes him jolt back with a gasp.

He bolts upright. "Oh gods—excuse me—I'll go to the privy—"

I catch his elbow before he swings his legs over the edge of the bed.

Ordinarily this sort of thing would scramble my brain like an egg, if not send me into an outright panic. It's all fine to think about, but in person? With anyone else, I'd be sprinting for the hills.

But with him, it's always a dance between us, always even ground, even when he has to give something up to level it. That makes it less excruciating to want this. It makes it less terrifying to be wanted.

"Wait," I rasp. "You . . . don't have to go."

Emeric looks back at me, a flush staining his cheeks, dark hair in glorious disarray, eyes locked on mine from behind crooked spectacles. "Vanja, please, tell me *exactly* what you mean."

Maybe it's the rush of testing new waters with him; maybe the way I feel is like a fire that's spread from a single ember, growing beyond what it once was. It's easy to feel, more awkward to say. "I want to . . . to touch you. What do you want?"

He reaches over, traces a small circle between my hip and my belly button. His words stumble out like unsteady foals. "That, but . . . for you first. Is that all right?"

I can't suppress a shiver, and it gets a nervous laugh out of us both. There's a riotous weightlessness in my stomach, and the breathless "Yes" that escapes my lips is not a lie.

"I don't really know what I'm doing," he admits, shifting to a better angle. "Do you, er, know what you like?"

There is a very specific reason that I do. I half garble something under my breath.

"What?"

I feel a whole-body flush coming on. "*Three months*" is all I say.

A *bastardly* smug grin breaks across his face. But it softens as he reaches for one of my hands. "Will you show me?"

I swallow. If it's all like this, maybe—maybe we can manage. This is nerve-racking and wonderful; I have never felt so exposed and yet so safe. I can do this. *We* can do this.

I weave my fingers through his and guide the way.

❦

"Has Helga come by yet?"

I'm aware my voice is high-pitched, nigh strangled; I don't care. Jakob is setting out breakfast, but he pauses to gesture to his workroom. "She's helping herself to my supplies."

"You owe me for this absurd little road trip," Helga snipes from beyond the doorway.

"Thanks!" I chirp through a rictus grin, and march stiffly over to the workroom.

Helga is squinting at an open jar of dried leaves. She shoves it at me. "Here, smell. Do you think they're still good?"

I push the jar out of my face and close the door. "I have a question now," I squeak.

"Don't we all. Why, just yesterday I was wondering what could possibly compel me to seek out my terrible brothers again, and—"

"*Helga,*" I hiss frantically, "I think I'm pregnant."

"Oh." Helga retracts the jar, eyebrows raised. "Then Jakob owes me ten *sjilling*."

"You," I squawk, outraged, "you *bet* on——"

Helga cuts me off. "Wait. Does the prefect boy still have the handprint mark?" I nod. Her mouth twists. "Then I'm pretty sure you're not pregnant. Unless one of you was very determined. And a contortionist. Damn, I could have used the money in Dänwik. They make this witchash out of——"

I interrupt her this time, squeaking a little. "How can you be sure?"

Helga sets the jar down, eyeing me. It might be the first time she's done so without a shadow of suspicion. She clears a few bundles of wool off Jakob's worktable, then pats the wood indicatively before circling to sit on the far side. "Sorry. Sit. Let's do this properly. Why do you think you might be pregnant?"

I sit across from her, heat rushing to my face. "We . . . er . . . were . . . more than kissing, and . . ."

Helga holds up a hand. "You need to be specific for me to help you."

I thought it was hard to tell Emeric what I wanted, but this is *infinitely* worse. I look anywhere but at Helga. "I was touching his . . . him."

She waits.

"You know what I mean!"

"Say it," she says sternly.

I try not to squirm in place. "You're just doing this to embarrass me!"

"I'm doing this," Helga returns, "because if you aren't ready to say it, then you *really* aren't ready to be touching it, and that's a very different conversation."

I bury my face in my hands. A moment later, the vague phantom of a word escapes between my fingers, briefly taking the form of "penis" before evanescing into the ether.

"Sorry," Helga says innocently, "what was that?"

My temper snaps. I slam both hands on the table and bellow, "*PENIS. ALL RIGHT? PENIS.*"

Jakob's kitchen sounds cease momentarily, then resume from behind the closed workshop door with the kind of premeditated clanking that says, *We will never speak of this.*

"Maybe a little to embarrass you," Helga allows. "Anyway. You were using only your hands?" I nod miserably. "That won't get you pregnant."

"But when he——" I halt, more flustered than ever. I can think of a dozen crude ways to say this, but I don't *want* to talk about it like it's a bawdy bar song. I don't want to talk about it at all.

Helga clears her throat. "Was there," she says tactfully, "an emission?"

I duck my head. "And—some got on me. So . . ."

"Did you wash off?"

"Of course," I grumble before my head flies up. "Will that keep me from getting pregnant?"

"No." Helga wrinkles her nose. "Again, you're not pregnant, this is about hygiene. We're *surrounded* with fabric in here, and nobody wants that on their new clothes. The point is, most people get pregnant only when that emission happens"—she gestures vaguely at her hips— "inside them, where it can reach the womb, during certain times in their monthly cycle. There are other ways to get with child, but that kind of intercourse is the only way it happens *accidentally.*"

"Right," I say, feeling very foolish. "Good."

Helga reads me correctly and waves her hand. "Don't feel bad for not knowing. Plenty of parents just decide their teenagers don't need to know anything about sex—"

"Don't *say* it so loud?" I whine, my shoulders bunching instinctively.

She rolls her eyes. "—until they're wed, and that's how you get Johann the Younger, father of five before he was seventeen." At my horrified look, she clarifies, "Five different mothers. He was quite . . . industrious. Anyway, you *can* get warts, boils, and infections from other . . . *activities*, even if your partner hasn't bedded anyone else. So let's talk about protection."

"I would rather get breakfast," I grumble, pushing back from the table.

"Fine." Helga's voice turns stern, almost reproachful. She also leans back, crossing her arms. "Then we can revisit this conversation two days from now, when it burns every time you use a privy."

I scowl at her. "I didn't ask for your help."

Helga matches my scowl. "You *very much* did, and you very clearly still need it. Look, I'm not going to tell you how to feel about sex or that you should even feel comfortable talking about it with me. I *will* tell you that it demands communication, especially about your health and safety. *And* that we're not going to have another chance to speak privately about this until Dänwik, at the earliest, so. Your choice."

Ugh. The only thing that could make this worse is admitting Helga's right, so I just slouch a little deeper on the stool. "Fine. You're the midwife. What do you recommend?"

"You have a lot of options, from daily tinctures to single-use charms, but those are, hmm, fussy." Helga tilts her head as she tucks a stray wisp of auburn hair back into her braided crown. "The simplest method is what we call the root-bind. It's an enchantment anchored to an internal bone of your choice—we typically use your pelvis or lowest vertebra— and it lasts for a year unless you have the enchantment undone early. While it's active, a root-bind prevents things from, well, taking root. You won't conceive or catch any diseases. You'll still have monthly cycles, but they may be lighter and their timing might change. The main drawback is that once the root-bind's set, if you want it undone before the year's up, you need a trained hedgewitch."

"That's the only downside?" I ask, nervous. "No other side effects?"

"It's also usually the most expensive option," Helga drawls. "A root-bind needs high-grade witch-ash. But it'll be free for you because I'm stealing Jakob's witch-ash, because *he* owes me for making me deal with teenagers. If you want, we can do it here and be done before breakfast."

I swallow. It's a strange feeling, actually thinking about whether or not I even *want* to conceive. I was the youngest of thirteen children, a completely unfathomable number. Part of me feels aghast at the idea, and part of me . . .

Well. It's easy to want that family when they're pure imagination, an unconditional fantasy, whatever I want them to be.

Either way, I don't think I want thirteen children, and I certainly don't want even one for the foreseeable future. I spent ten years as a maid, living only to serve others; I spent the next year living a selfish and desperate lie. It feels like my own life, one I control, has barely begun.

"All right," I say. "And—I can pay you. I *do* have a whole bag of rubies."

Helga flaps her hand as she gets up to raid Jakob's witch-ash jars. "Consider it an investment. I want to win that bet, after all."

⁂

"It's going to be very simple," I say later that afternoon, my voice echoing around the stave church, which is empty save for Leni and myself. I can't exactly leave the Red Blessed stranded while we're gone, so for the time being, I'm delegating. "All you have to do is lead the weekly service, starting this Wednesday. You know the rites better than anyone else."

"It's a tremendous honor," Leni answers solemnly, her eyes enormous. "Even if the Scarlet Maiden has not seen fit to grant me with your gift of prophecy, I am humbled to lead the Red Blessèd in worshipping Her in Her glory."

The most uncomfortable thing is that I can *hear* Leni capitalizing that pronoun. "You'll do great. If you have any questions . . . well, pray for guidance. And the Red Blessed—"

Blessèd, Leni mouths.

I wrestle with a patient smile. "Sure. Anyway, they're very, uh, open-minded, if you need to adjust things."

"I was actually thinking of adding a daily morning service," Leni says quickly. "With the Red Blessèd growing by the day, we won't all fit in the chapel much longer. And with the appearance of Her Divinity, it seems only right that we give Her thanks and honor sevenfold."

"That's . . . one way to look at it," I hedge. The Scarlet Maiden is already spearing throats and demanding human sacrifice as is. I'm not sure we should be rewarding that behavior with daily worship. "Maybe start a bit slower? Every other day?"

"We owe Her our full devotion," Leni responds with the kind of supermassive sincerity that draws lesser convictions into orbit around it.

"Er," I say.

I'm saved by a knock at the door. It's Emeric, who distinctly avoids looking at the statue of the Scarlet Maiden. "Vanja, it's time."

I put a hand on Leni's shoulder and say again, through my teeth, "You'll do great."

Then I follow Emeric out, heading to the main road, where our ride awaits. The innkeeper's wagon isn't the most glamorous transportation, but it'll get us to Glockenberg, where we can hire a proper coach. Helga and Kirkling are already inside, having claimed the empty cask and the crate that serve as the only seats.

Jakob is waiting by the wagon, along with Udo, who's clearly repressing his disdain as the Red Blessed start tucking flowers between the wooden slats. We've told the congregants that Emeric and I have been tasked to gather a tribute for the Scarlet Maiden, and—going off the unprecedented number of flower garlands they've crafted for the occasion—they're taking it well. If anything, it's almost a bit unnerving how quickly everyone joined Team Blood Sacrifices Are Great, Actually.

Jakob holds up the bone awl and the cambric square. Since his blood is on the line, it seemed more than fair to let him examine them as he wished. "Nothing amiss that I can see," he says. "Just cloth and bone. Let's get on with it, then."

A hush falls over the growing crowd as he presses a fingertip to the awl's sharp end, then flinches. A bead of red swells from his skin. He quickly presses it to the cloth.

And—that's it. No flashing lights, no horrifying apparitions. There's a single red blot on the pale cambric now. That's all.

Jakob shakes out his hand. A pinpoint of red marks his finger, but it's not even bleeding anymore. He lets out a breath that turns into a half chuckle. "That was anticlimactic. One down, six to go."

He passes the awl to Udo, who adds his own drop of blood with a similar deficit of fanfare. "That's that, then," Udo says as I tuck the cambric and awl into a little leather pouch I'm stowing in my satchel. "Come back safe, Vanja." Jakob elbows him, and Udo amends, "Both of you."

Emeric's eyebrows rise. "Oh. Thank you."

"I meant the innkeeper."

"No he didn't," Jakob says as Emeric stammers an apology. "Safe travels, all of you."

Our departure is unfortunately much more dramatic, involving a lot of singing, showers of petals, and truly wretched flower crowns, which are bestowed upon Emeric and me by the Red Blessed. The only thing that makes up for it is the look on Kirkling's face. To her credit, she waits until Hagendorn is out of sight to sneer, "I hope that wasn't your doing, Schmidt."

I glance at the innkeeper's back. Fortunately, he doesn't seem to have heard Kirkling over the noise of the wagon. I lean forward, my voice lowered. "If it were me, I would have thrown in a burnt offering."

Emeric ignores that as he sets his flower crown aside and begins picking crimson petals out of his hair. "So, we'll charter a coach from Glockenberg to Dänwik. Vanja, do you want to go directly to Dieter Ros when we get there or stop by the outpost first?"

Helga makes a noise, but Kirkling interjects: "She doesn't have any business at a prefect outpost."

The wagon shudders as a wheel hits a rut hard enough to fling us and our luggage briefly into the air. "Sorry," the innkeeper calls over his shoulder.

"It's fine." Helga's gone suddenly terse. Her eyes are on the road behind us.

Emeric and Kirkling don't seem to have noticed. Emeric looks from me to Kirkling and back, then says, "We need to formally register Vanja as a consultant for the case."

"You *cannot* be serious." Kirkling's voice cracks across the road like a whip.

"Calm down," Helga says under her breath.

If I thought the look on Kirkling's face was golden during Hagendorn's flowery send-off, it's diamond-grade comedy now. She opens her mouth only for Helga to shake her head, her lips pressed together, and jerk her chin pointedly at the road.

"Don't all look at once," she grits out of the corner of her mouth. Then she hoists herself up to say something to the innkeeper. The wagon jolts again, the hoofbeats picking up into a trot.

I sneak a glance. Between the unsteady ride and the rustling of the forest, I don't see anything—

And then I do. A vivid green eye opens in the knot of an oak we pass. Another buds on the tip of a hawthorn branch.

In seconds, everywhere I look, the forest around us is looking back.

CHAPTER SEVEN

The Fix

"MOSSFOLK?" EMERIC ASKS QUIETLY. A NARROW BARK-COVERED FACE emerges from a roadside hedge. The hedge uproots itself and starts toddling after the wagon.

"They shouldn't be out in the open like this." Helga sounds perplexed.

There's a creak from the crate Kirkling's perched upon. "Could the Wild Hunt be flushing them out?"

"Not before nightfall. And not here. Brunne the Huntress leads the *Wildejogt* in the Haarzlands, and she's got an agreement with the local Briar Hag. All the Mossfolk under this Hag's care are safe from the Hunt. I think they're watching us."

Another little hedge starts following the wagon's tracks but soon falls out of sight.

"What do we do?" I breathe.

"Keep talking," Helga says with a forced kind of serenity. "Act like everything's normal. But no yelling, no sudden moves. If they talk to us, pay attention. If they ask for something, give it. And hope the Hag herself doesn't show."

"Very well." Now I can barely hear Kirkling over the wagon's rattle. "Aspirant Conrad, you cannot bring Schmidt on as a consultant for a case in which she's implicated."

I flash the amnesty token at her. "Too late. We're just making it paperwork official."

Kirkling's face darkens perilously. "Then this is an immense lapse of judgment, Conrad."

Emeric sweeps a handful of red petals out of the wagon, his brow furrowed. "Vanja's consulted bef—"

"I wasn't finished," Kirkling says tersely, earning a glare from Helga. She softens her tone, but her words stay sharp. "Even in the unlikely event that Schmidt is innocent, you have now exposed your investigation to her influence. Did you give even *one* thought to how you're going to prove she didn't steer you away from incriminating evidence? And, let me remind you, how you will prove that when you make this case *before the Low Gods themselves?*"

A muscle jumps in Emeric's jaw. I know that tick from every time I'm right, and he's annoyed that I'm right. "One would think," he says, in that steely-calm voice he used with the Scarlet Maiden, "that the presence of the Low God Truth might assist with that."

Helga lets out a positively evil snort.

Kirkling narrows her eyes—then shifts her focus to me. "Schmidt, do you know what happens if a prefect aspirant fails their Finding?"

My stomach twists abruptly. Emeric didn't mention a price for failure—but when he was a junior prefect, losing a case meant losing his life. But surely—

Emeric isn't meeting my gaze.

"I don't," I say stiffly. "Is it fatal?"

Kirkling tilts her head. "No, an aspirant like Conrad has received enough of their contract mark to survive the summoning. But if they fail their Finding, they are stripped of their marks—both of them. The process is excruciating and can go on for hours, as every last fleck of pigment must be cut out of them. And then they are permanently expelled from the Order of Prefects."

I think my heart stops.

"It's not going to happen," Emeric says under his breath.

A gangly lichen-gowned figure steps onto the road in our wake, staring with those leaf-green eyes. It begins to trail the wagon, too, like the previous Mossfolk.

Unlike the others, it's keeping pace with the trotting horses somehow, even though it's moving at only a walk.

"Woodwife," Helga mutters. "They come by Auntie Gerke's sometimes. Just don't upset her."

"What happens—" Emeric starts.

Helga cuts him off. "Just don't."

Branches sway, roots creaking. The trunk of an oak twists with a groaning *crack*. More and more eyes bloom all through the woods, staring, measuring, judging. Every single one seems trained on us.

Not us—me.

It feels as if I'm already on trial.

"I don't have to be a consultant," I tell Emeric quickly. "We can—we can revoke the amnesty—"

He shakes his head, resting his hand on mine. "Even if I could, I wouldn't. I stand by the decision." Emeric meets Kirkling's eyes. "Vanja was in acute distress—"

"Of her own making," Kirkling interjects.

"—and no matter the outcome, I will have to answer in court for causing that distress and for prolonging it for the time it takes to conduct a proper investigation. My job isn't extrajudicial punishment; it's to find the truth." He purses his lips, and I hear the faintest prick of claws emerging. "At least, that's how Hubert trained me."

Kirkling's scowl deepens; I know that had to have drawn blood. After a furious silence, she says, "Then out of respect for the memory of Hubert Klemens, allow me to advise you, Aspirant Conrad: If Schmidt is found to have tainted your case, you *will* fail your Finding. Your best hope is to exercise extreme prejudice in what Schmidt consults on going forward. In fact, I would keep everything—your leads, theories, notes, and collected evidence—between you and me alone, until the trial."

So I'll be completely in the dark. Completely on my own.

Well, not completely. I just . . . have to trust Emeric.

I think of Minkja, of calling the Godly Court, how he put his faith fully in me to pull off a miracle.

"Fine," I say swiftly, before he can argue and before I can change my mind. "If that's what it takes, fine. Leave me out of it."

Both Kirkling and Emeric seem taken aback by that. "Are you sure?" Emeric asks. I nod.

"Then tonight, when you make your report . . ." Kirkling starts rattling off what she expects from Emeric, and he scrambles for his notes and charcoal. Some of the tension seems to wane.

Even the eyes and the faces of the Mossfolk are fewer, farther between. The woodwife seems to have lost interest, and none of the other vegetation looks to be on our tail. Helga taps the innkeeper's shoulder. The horses slow to a walk again.

Then, as we round a long curve, I see her lumber out into the road behind us: an ancient hillock of a woman, wrought of earth and root, draped in a thick shawl of moss, face streaked with rusty-iron veins. Her eyes are the same vivid emerald as the other Mossfolks'; a tangled nest of snow-white hair crowns her stern face. One hand is wrapped around a gnarled wooden staff laced with living vine. The other clutches a fistful of the red petals the wagon's been shedding.

It's the Briar Hag, queen of the Mossfolk.

She points her gnarled wooden staff straight at me. In my head, I hear a snarl like splitting branches.

"FIX IT."

The wagon hits another rut with a gut-wrenching lurch. By the time I look back again, she's gone.

"Did anyone else . . . ?" I start, only to realize the conversation's carrying on without me. Not even Helga, fussing in her satchel, seems to have noticed the Hag.

Her message was for me alone.

I'm not sure if I'm being asked for something so much as commanded. Either way, I'd wager Emeric isn't the only one with hell to pay for failure.

❧❧❧

Four days later, our carriage rolls into Dänwik, a town beautiful in a way reserved explicitly for things built on spite.

See, a few generations back, Lüdheid Principality was governed by the united House Eisz-Wälft. Unfortunately, the *prinzessin-wahl* was rumored to have discovered her husband, Prince Nibelungus von Wälft, in the most flagrante of delicto with her cousin, and thus was launched the messiest divorce in the history of the Blessed Empire. Princess von Eisz kept the palace turned Imperial Abbey in Welkenrode, along with administrative control of Lüdheid as the first imperial abbess. The *prinz* . . . Well, he got the hunting lodge in Dänwik.

Supposedly he threw himself into making Dänwik a jewel of a retreat, to bribe his ex back to matrimony. And I can buy that: The little city is picturesque as hell, all immaculate plaster and intricate timber. Beyond the neat lanes lie the sparkling sapphire waters of Wälftsee, the adjacent lake (you can guess where the name comes from.) Somehow it even smells consistently of fresh-baked bread, *everywhere*.

But eventually, the *prinz-wahl* realized that no amount of artful landscaping would win his ex-wife back. And that's when he got *petty*.

The architectural dissonance says it all: A rosy marble chapel capped with a demure dome, only to sour under a crown of bristling spires and snarling gargoyles. Dainty flowering hedge walls impaled on combs of iron spikes. The bones of an old hunting lodge are still there under lavish, impractical gilt, but now they're guarded behind ranks of scantily clad marble statues in varying sultry poses. Legend has it the statues are carved mostly in the image of the *prinz*'s subsequent mistress. I can't say if it's true or not; all the white stone faces look alike through the carriage window.

The atmosphere inside the carriage is a similarly uncomfortable blend of anticipation and resentment, a calcified silence having kept a chokehold on us for most of the day. We're so accustomed to it that everyone but Emeric jumps when he clears his throat.

"When we get to the inn," he starts with the subtle precision of an optical surgeon, "it seems practical to drop off Miss Ros and Proctor Kirkling to get settled, and Vanja and I will continue to the outpost to register her consultancy."

"Fine," Helga bites out, as Kirkling emits a surly "Hmph."

Helga rolls her eyes at the proctor. "Do you really want to be around"—she waves at Emeric's and my joined hands—"*this* situation even longer?"

(Truth be told, part of how I've kept myself entertained the past four days is seeing how saccharine I can get with Emeric before Kirkling's lip curls so far that it looks like it's escaping up her nose. It's a very low bar.)

All she says is "Schmidt will make her own arrangements with the innkeeper."

That, you see, is how Kirkling has kept herself entertained: insisting I pay my own way for every step of this fun little countryside jaunt, while also brainstorming any possible thing she can tack onto my bill. Everything from a quarter of the carriage fees to the cost of the overpriced smelly corner cots I slept in when we crammed into a communal bunk room each night. Shockingly, roadhouse options are not great in the backwaters of Almandy.

I can handle the expense—I changed plenty of rubies to coin in Glockenberg, and the rest still constitute a solid twenty-inch layer in the bottom of my very large rucksack—but it's more the principle. And the indignity: I'm not even sure I needed a root-bind, because Emeric and I have not had a single moment of privacy since we left Hagendorn.

Apparently that's on his mind, too, because he says, "Vanja can share my room." Then he hastily adds, to me, "If that's what you want."

Kirkling looks like she's bitten into a lemon, if that lemon were made of bees. (So a fig, I suppose.) My mood absolutely soars.

"That sounds perfect." I beam up at him, then turn that sunny smile on the rest of the carriage as I twist the knife further and lay my head on his shoulder.

"Gross," Helga mutters.

Kirkling, in turn, dictates: "Then Schmidt will pay for half your room."

"Done," I say before Emeric can object. If it means we'll have some alone time, it's worth it.

The carriage finally slows to a halt at our inn, the Book and Bell. It's hard to hide the impatient bouncing of Emeric's knee without the bumpy ride; it grows worse as we wait for Helga and Kirkling to get out, then as they painstakingly unload the luggage. By the time the carriage jolts into motion again, I'm pretty sure he's going to wear a hole in the floor.

"How far is it to the outpost?" I ask, squinting through the window, only for an arm to reach past me and yank the curtains shut before looping around my waist.

"I don't care," he mumbles into the side of my neck, and a moment later, neither do I.

There's a nagging worry at the back of my skull—I've had to make do with rustic washstands for four days, and I *know* I smell and my hair's dirty and you could scrape enough oil off my face to fry a *schnitzel*—but that certainly doesn't seem to slow him down at all. I wind up awkwardly straddling his hips as he keeps a steadying hand near the base of my spine, and *damn* if it doesn't feel amazing every time the carriage lurches and his grip tightens, and every time we break apart, laughter spilling into the gap before we close it up again.

Eventually the coachman has to knock on the door to let us know we've arrived. He's unsuccessfully hiding a smirk as we stumble out in a flurry of straightening hems and fixing buttons. "Will you be needing a return ride to the Book and Bell, sir?"

Emeric looks to me, half sheepish, half hopeful. "I think we could use the walk?"

"We could," I confirm, adjusting the strap of my satchel to better sit over my coat. I suffer no delusions that, once we get back, Kirkling won't resume her one-woman crusade against youthful canoodling, and I'm determined to manage at least one more respectable indiscretion beforehand.

Dänwik's outpost of the Order of Prefects of the Godly Courts isn't too different from the one in Minkja: a neat little stacked-stone affair among a handful of chapels that make up in grandeur what they lack in numbers. There's a faint chime as Emeric pushes the outpost door open, revealing a simple, well-furnished reception area almost uncannily alike to the one in Minkja, down to the winding hallway opposite us. There's no one at the polished walnut reception desk, but a voice calls from beyond the hall, "A moment, please!"

Emeric pauses beside me, tilting his head, and mutters, "*Vikram?*"

Then a smile breaks across his face as a man bustles into the room. The man looks about Helga's age, with warm brown skin, hazel eyes, and loose dark curls pulled into a haphazard knot at the top of his skull, in the fashion some Surajans favor. He's cleaning what appears to be soot from his hands with a rag, utterly oblivious to both the streak of soot emblazoned across his uniform's waistcoat and the holes scorched into his rolled-up sleeves. A dark jacket is draped over his shoulders. What looks like a blackened jeweler's loupe on a chain is bouncing against his chest, and there's a distinct clean circle around one eye, where it seems he took the brunt of the soot.

He barely glances our way, digging under his nails with the rag. "Apologies, there was a slight issue with a small fire the size of, well, a large fire, and—"

"Vikram," Emeric repeats.

At that, the man—Vikram, clearly—blinks at us for the first time, his thick eyebrows cresting like a wave at the top of his forehead. Then he promptly throws his rag at Emeric.

"Conrad, you convenient little weasel," he says, with a delighted kind of outrage. There's an unnerving current of relief below, though, when he follows with "Thank all the gods you're here."

"Thank you for that." Emeric plucks the rag off his chest, his nose wrinkling as he brushes away a faint trace of soot. For most people, hitting Emeric with a dirty rag would be the beginning of a very bad time for them, so the fact that this Vikram is still intact says quite a bit. "I thought you were finishing your mastery certification at Aederfeld."

"Mathilde and I have a temporary assignment here. The Northern Artificers' Guild is negotiating their ten-year contracts with the Merchant League, and Prince Ludwig specially requested impartial arbiters." Vikram gestures at the clerk's empty desk, like I'm supposed to understand any of the words he just said. "Mathilde's from Rammelbeck, so they sent us. She's at the convention now with our clerk, Linn, but with the Library of the Divine closed, they've had to send out for—"

"The Library of the Divine is closed?" Emeric interrupts.

"Yes, for the past week. It's too dangerous to let anyone in."

Emeric and I trade looks. "On a scale of one to immediate disembowelment," I start, "how dangerous are we talking? Because that library's at least half the reason we're here."

Vikram purses his lips. "Closer to immediate disembowelment than not," he admits, "but I'm rather hoping you can fix it."

CHAPTER EIGHT

CRYSTAL AND GLASS

EMERIC OPENS HIS MOUTH, AND I CAN SEE THE GEARS IN HIS HEAD creaking into motion. I know what happens when you give him a puzzle: He'll drop everything until it's solved.

I cough. "We're actually here to register me as a consultant, so maybe that first?"

Vikram starts, as if he forgot I was here. "Oh! Sure. Er, I think I know where Linn keeps the forms . . ." He produces a sheet of parchment from a cabinet and slides it over the counter to me, along with a quill. "Fill out everything except for this bottom section, and sign on this line, not that one—that one's for the authorizing prefect. Conrad, I'll catch you up on the library situation in a moment. What the devil are you doing here, though? Last I heard, you were still in Helligbrücke, pining over some floozy."

I look up from the form, startled enough to keep from laughing. "Oh, was he?"

Vikram doesn't bother hiding his own smirk. "Apparently he met her on a big case over midwinter and spent all of January—"

"Vikram," Emeric starts tightly.

"—and most of February looking out the nearest window and sighing."

"*Vikram.*"

"I heard it got so bad, he wrote *poems.*"

I pause in the middle of drawing a pair of gleaming buttocks under *Please list any specialized or relevant skills* and glance sidelong at Emeric. "Poems, *plural?*"

He's beet red. "*Will you just fill out the form.*"

"Was this the Minkja case?" I ask innocently, adding stink lines to the butt. "I've heard about that one."

Vikram's face lights up. "It was. Wildest file I've read in years. The whole order was in an uproar that a wee junior prefect brought down the margrave of Bóern by himself."

"I had significant help," Emeric protests.

"Entirely on his own," Vikram continues blithely, ignoring Emeric's muttered "*Again, incorrect.*" "Completely unaided, particularly not by some mysterious absent floozy."

I scoot the form over to Emeric along with the quill, resting my hand on the parchment for strategic buttock concealment. "Sign, please." He obliges me, scowling at Vikram the whole time. I push the completed form over to Vikram.

"Thank you, Miss . . ." His eyes land on my name and widen.

"It's me," I say serenely. "I'm the floozy."

His mouth purses for a beat. Then Vikram says, with a remarkably straight face, "Conrad, you didn't tell me she was an artist."

Our eyes meet. In that moment, an unspoken ironclad alliance is forged, and I know we are a united front with the sole objective of haranguing Emeric.

"What do you mean—" Emeric cranes to look at the form and sees my creative contribution. "*Vanja*."

A heavy and official stamp thuds onto the bottom of the page before he can swipe it.

"Entered into record April third, 761 Blessed Era," Vikram says briskly, whisking the parchment away. "Now let me grab a decent coat and you can see this library problem for yourself before it gets dark." He vanishes down the hall again, only to thrust his head back out. "Oh. Miss Schmidt, I'm Vikram Mistry, journeyman research officer for the Order of Prefects of the Godly Courts. You've probably figured out the 'Vikram' part on account of Conrad saying it so much. Lovely to meet you." He disappears again.

"I'm shocked," I say to Emeric. "I thought the first rule of your prefect charter was *I solemnly swear to keep a stick up my ass, permanently, no takebacks*."

"Article One is '*A prefect is bound to investigate and resolve any case they are assigned by their superiors, to the full extent of their ability*,' and you know that," he grouses. "Vikram and I were in the training academy together. I wound up taking the track for field investigators, and he went into the research and engineering division. He was one of the few people who would actually spend time with a ten-year-old know-it-all."

"We were both little outcasts." Vikram returns, pulling on a heavier uniform coat, much like Emeric's but embroidered in striped black-and-white trim instead of silver. "Him for being a literal infant, me . . . Well, some of the Almanic cadets had strong opinions on a Surajan joining their ranks. Any path to authority is going to attract bullies, and the prefects are hardly an exception. Lot of spares-to-the-heirs who saw a little smartass and a son of silk merchants as safe targets." He holds the door open for us with a wink. "Hence why I was also the first person to teach this lout how to throw a proper punch."

"Which was great," Emeric says darkly, "until I got stabbed."

Vikram rolls his eyes. "What eleven-year-old *hasn't* been stabbed, honestly."

Emeric turns to me for backup, and I hold up my hands. "Don't look at me, Junior. I did very much try to drown you."

"Ah, *romance*," Vikram hums. "But wait—'Junior'? I thought you'd be fully ordained by now."

I pull a face. "It's a nickname. If I call him 'Aspirant,' I sound like Kirkling, and I think that'd traumatize us both."

"*Kirkling* is your proctor?" Vikram whistles. "High Gods and Low ease your way, friend. What's your Finding, then?"

Emeric provides a recap as best he can, including Kirkling's embargo on what I'm allowed to know, as we wind through the lanes of Dänwik. Our path slopes gradually upward as we pass manicured hedges and tidy little street markets. They're mainly for tourists, given how many stalls hawk souvenirs, from novelty stoneware mugs to wooden toy ducks and somewhat incongruously elegant glass goblets. As we walk, a set of sharp steeples starts poking over the rooftops, marking a building at least as large as the *prinz-wahl*'s hunting lodge. The closer we get, the more popular the goblets become, with vendors shouting something about replicas.

"What's the deal with the glassware?" I ask, only to realize I've fallen a few steps behind Emeric and Vikram.

". . . weren't many signa available when I did it, but I picked the Alembic," Vikram's saying as I catch up. "Seemed fitting. Did you take up the Oak from Klemens?"

Emeric shakes his head. "Hubert was always adamant I follow my own path, so I chose my own signum."

"Your what?" I pipe up behind him.

Both boys look back at me, chagrined. "Stop neglecting your lady," Vikram scolds.

I make a noise of indifference but am secretly delighted when Emeric hurries to loop an arm around my shoulders. "What's a signum?"

"It's part of the second contract mark." He ducks his head. "I can show you when we get to the Book and Bell."

Considering he has to be shirtless to do that, I find the idea extremely motivational. "Right. So. This library problem isn't going to take long, is it?"

Vikram sucks in a breath through his teeth. "Ah, we'll see soon enough. Some particularly nasty *grimling* got into the Library of the Divine last week, and it's been attacking anyone who sets foot inside ever since. The Merchant League and the Artificers' Guild are blaming each other since they can't access the spell registry for negotiations, and neither Mathilde nor I have the field prefect training for wrangling *grimlingen*."

The Library of the Divine begins to fill in under its steeples as we draw nearer, looming even larger than I'd originally thought—and too large to be unprotected. "Shouldn't there be a *kobold* to keep them out?"

"The library has its own guardian entity called the Armarius. Some kind of spirit or the like, I don't know." Vikram shrugs. "I do gadgets, not ghouls. But no one's seen the Armarius since this all started. A few local hedgewitches and warlocks have tried to put the *grimling* down with no luck either. It's not enough of an emergency to call in backup, but since a field prefect happens to be in the neighborhood . . ."

"Prefect aspirant," Emeric and I correct at the same time.

Then he pulls a face at me. "Oh no, that's horrible. It really does make you sound like Kirkling."

"But if I use 'Junior,' it's going to bother you, since it's outdated."

Vikram grins. "She *does* know you."

We turn a corner, and the full bulk of the Library of the Divine breaches our view for the first time, crouching, ancient, at the crest of a hill. Unlike most of Dänwik's prim and posh façades, it's a monolithic granite gargoyle of a building that predates the others by at least two centuries. Baring fangs of turret and spire and collared in blocky trim, its darkened windows leer like dozens of vacant, hollowed eyes. The double doors are shaded by a massive ribbed archway, and the lane ends at the front steps, imparting the impression of a lolling stone tongue.

"As you can see, huge tourist attraction," Vikram drawls.

I spy a padlock on the door as we approach, one unlike any I've seen—for starters, there are two keyholes instead of one. "I'm not sure I can pick that. At least, not fast."

"No need." Vikram flashes a key ring. "I made it. But"—he correctly interprets the excitement that sparked in my face—"I would love for you to take a crack at it later. Always room for improvement."

Vikram makes me turn around while he removes the padlock, "just to preserve the mystique," but Emeric stops him before he can push the doors open.

He eyes the dark windows warily. "There's no need for you two to put yourself in harm's way. I'll—"

"Handle the *grimling* while I search for your records," I finish.

Emeric sees the stubborn jut of my chin and sighs, then turns to Vikram, who's donned a similarly obstinate frown. "I suppose there's no convincing you either. But . . ." He winces apologetically. "Vikram and I should find the records, to avoid any issues. Vanja, you can be our lookout. You'll notice if our luck's turning."

I squint at him. It sounds like a flimsy excuse, but it beats waiting outside. "Sure."

Emeric squares himself to the arch, lays a hand on the oak, thinks better of it, takes a step back, and prods one door with the inexplicably spotless toe of his boot. It swings inward with an arthritic creak, and all three of us freeze, bracing for a monstrous onslaught.

Nothing happens.

Emeric runs a hand through his hair. "Vikram, tell me this isn't a very elaborate joke—"

The door slams shut so hard, it rattles on its hinges.

"It is not," Vikram deadpans.

A line appears in Emeric's brow. (It's actually a little cute, but I don't feel like that would be a helpful observation right now.) He reaches for his belt and draws a dagger, plain but for the copper coating on the blade. It's one of a prefect's set of five, the others being gold, silver, steel, and iron; they're each wrought to be effective against different sinister things, but I always forget which. That is, save for copper. Copper I saw enough of in Minkja to remember: best against *grimlingen*.

Emeric's lips move in some sort of incantation, and a gust of silvery light wrenches the doors open, straining against an unseen force. "Hurry."

The doors bang closed again moments after we three scuttle inside, snipping off the last umbilical of light until Emeric digs out his prefect coin and ignites it.

Vikram is also scrounging in his satchel. "Hold on, I've been working on something . . . Here." He emerges with what looks like a fistful of marbles, only to toss them into the air. They kindle with the same colorless light as Emeric's pewter coin and hover around us like a cloud of sedate but extremely potent fireflies, casting an easier, wider glow than the coin's.

Emeric whistles in appreciation. "How is *that* not standard-issue already?"

"Single use, and lasts only five minutes for now," Vikram says. "Save your dirty jokes, Mathilde's already made them all. Let's go get your records."

Emeric holds up a hand, peering beyond the light. "Do you see anything, Vanja?"

I look around, a smidge baffled. We're in a foyer of sorts; pale light glazes over stone columns and a vaulted ceiling embellished with an iron chandelier long gone cold. There are signs of a hasty exit everywhere, from scattered papers and abandoned cloaks to a forlorn porcelain doll swooning at the foot of a statue. The statue itself bears only the inscription *THE FOVNDER* on the base, but judging from its old-fashioned robes, I'd say it's meant to be a friar, the kind who goes by something like Sextus and entirely deserves it.

I don't know what Emeric expects me to find, but nothing's leaping out. "No."

We pause for him to quickly consult the floor plan and directory posted on a nearby wall, then head into the library itself. Given the size of the building, I expected it to be separated into different chambers. Instead, the only partition is a ring of waist-high walls that section off something like an open-air rotunda at the main floor's center. That area's crowded with chairs and sturdy tables, some still bearing open books, parched inkpots, and half-written notes.

Radiating out from the rotunda's rim is a towering forest of cylindrical columns—no, not columns, *bookshelves*, like massive tree trunks with scrolls and manuscripts for bark, rising all the way to the chandelier-dotted ceiling three stories above. Each one is spiral-bound with spindly staircases, and ruffs of narrow balustraded walkways offer brief respite before the next steps climb higher. Most of the shelves are bare above the second story, a few patches of books and scrolls clinging like lonely barnacles, but there's clearly room for the various collections to grow.

"This way." Emeric cuts an unyielding line across the rotunda, allowing only a wobble or two for avoiding furniture. "Vanja, you'll have the clearest vantage in the middle. We'll be just over at that section." He points to one of the nearest columns. It's still far enough away that I won't be able to see what he's searching for.

It can't be easy for him to balance between Kirkling's insistence on my exclusion and keeping me from feeling utterly useless, and for that reason alone I repress an eye roll. "Right then, lookout it is."

Emeric passes me his coin. "Here. The *grimling* should show up before Vikram's lights run out. Just shout if you see our luck change."

I suppose that's one way to say, *Holler if we're in mortal peril.* The boys continue on without me as I scan the area and conclude only that there are probably about a thousand pounds of cobwebs in the unlit chandeliers.

Emeric's voice floats over to me: ". . . looking for . . . before 398 BE . . . Hagendorn or Boderad's Gorge." There's a formless query from Vikram, and I catch in reply: ". . . prefect accords."

I shouldn't eavesdrop, not if it could put his case in jeopardy.

But I really, *really* want to, is the thing.

I look around for a distraction. There's a sort of dais in the chamber's dead center, with a stone pedestal right at the bull's-eye, and bolted to that pedestal is a very robust-looking display case that stands no higher than my sternum. Something is glittering inside.

Something presumably *quite* valuable.

I am officially distracted.

I mince over, keeping one eye on Emeric and Vikram to make sure some hellion isn't descending upon them, at least not unnoticed. When

I reach the display case, I'm surprised to recognize its contents: a clear, intricately cut crystalline goblet identical to those the souvenir peddlers are hawking outside. There's a polished bronze plaque affixed to the pedestal. It reads:

THE MOSTE HOLYCH CRYSTALL GOBELET BORNE IT OF SANKTVS VVILLEHALM THE SCRYBE

This isn't a display case, I realize with a start, but a reliquary.

There's a shuffling rasp from behind me. I whirl around. Some deserted parchment sheets flutter into the air as a faint breeze rings the rotunda. It almost—almost sounds like a whisper.

Then it's gone.

"We've been noticed," I call to the boys. There's only a brief grunt of acknowledgment. A little annoyed, I turn back to the reliquary.

Something catches my eye as I move the coin light. I catch my breath and wave the coin from side to side, watching rainbows dart through the goblet.

I check on the area Emeric and Vikram are picking over. No sign of a *grimling*, though, as I watch, one of Vikram's glowing marbles winks out and disintegrates. All that hits the floor is a thimbleful of dust.

That's enough of an all clear for me. I circle the pedestal, scouring the reliquary's base until I see a narrow keyhole in the dull brass. I crouch for a better look. Sure enough, the coin light sparks on a few bright scratches around the keyhole—too new to have faded, too few to have come from anything but a seldom-used key.

Someone's unlocked this. *Recently.*

I send one final glance over my shoulder, this time to be sure Emeric and Vikram are wholly occupied, because Emeric won't like this and Vikram may not find it as amusing as a butt on formal paperwork.

Fortunately, they're both immersed in the bookshelves. Less fortunately, the remaining light-balls are flickering. Another two go dark. I'll have to work fast.

I set the shining coin on the pedestal so I can see, then reach into my satchel and slip out my lockpicks.

It's not a very difficult lock, especially because I'm not worried about leaving a trail. If I'm right, it won't matter anyway. All it takes are a few prods of the pins and a flick of the tension wrench, and the base of the reliquary releases from its frame with a soft rattle.

"About a minute of light left," I hear Vikram warn.

That's enough time for Emeric to stop me, so I try to keep it down as I rock the case, easing it off its base. The light-cloud in my peripheral vision is shrinking, shrinking—the case comes free with a jolt—I hold my breath as I lay it on its side on the nearest table, nearly folding myself in half to do so quietly—

When I straighten, I see my face reflected in the dark glass—

And a twisted, gray, half-rotted face gaping over my shoulder.

I scream.

"*LIAR*," a wretched voice shrieks in my ear as I dive under the table, my heart thrashing, every nerve ablaze with adrenaline. "*LIAR!*"

The table goes flying, crashing somewhere in the rotunda with an ugly splintering sound. The reliquary case falls to the stone floor nearby, cracks spiderwebbing the glass panes.

The *grimling* hovers above me, unlike anything I've seen (and a *kobold* eating a man-horse monster doesn't make it into even the top ten weirdest things I've seen, so that's saying something). Its ghoulish face looms in a swirling incorporeal pool of coarse-woven black rags, the ruined features contorted with fury. Threads of darkness twist into two gaunt arms, with long fingers ending in mortally sharp points. "*Thief,*" it half sobs as I try to crawl away, "*liar, get out, bring it home, GET OUT!*"

It lunges for me—only to be dragged back, shrieking, as silvery light spears it through. I push myself up and see Emeric halfway across the rotunda, feet planted wide, one fist holding the other end of the spectral light. If I thought the *grimling* looked furious, it's nothing compared to the look on his face as he makes a swift, savage gesture. The light frays at both ends, splitting into a dozen ties that anchor to rafters, columns, even the base of the pedestal.

The lenses of Emeric's spectacles flash as he looks frantically around the room. "*Vanja!*"

I roll to my knees, keeping a table between myself and the *grimling.* "Here!"

Relief washes over him. "Are you hurt?"

"No, I—"

"Get clear," he grits out, then adds a conciliatory "please."

The creature writhes on the shining hook. "*Lies, lies, LIAR, mine, mine, it's mine—*"

I want to get away, but . . .

The goblet's still glittering patiently on the pedestal. And if I'm right, it'll give us just as many answers as the records Emeric was digging up.

Vikram's voice echoes from behind me: "This way, Miss Schmidt!"

"I need that goblet," I call, bracing myself to stand.

Emeric twists to look at me, almost offended. "Is now *really* the time?"

I feel a small little crumple of dismay. He thinks I just want to steal it. It's not the wildest assumption to make, all things considered.

I just hate that it's his first.

But we don't have time to interrogate that. With an unearthly wail, the *grimling* tears loose. "*GIVE IT BACK!*"

It strikes like an adder, those needle-sharp fingers darting toward me—

They shatter against a sudden arc of silver light. It yanks its hand away, screaming. Emeric's saved me again.

It can't be for nothing.

Emeric ducks another hurled table, squinting up at the howling ghoul with the expression he gets when he's found the first loose end in a complicated knot. He draws a dagger. To my surprise, it's not copper but silver—the one meant for the undead. "*Poltergeist*," he calls up to it, "tell me what you need to be at peace."

A *poltergeist*? Why is a hostile spirit in a library, of all places?

"*LIAR*," it accuses, sending a chair his way.

"I can banish you," Emeric says sternly, "or we can put you to rest, your choice. Why are you here? What do you want?"

In response, the ghost chooses violence. A chandelier rips from its moorings and flies at him as the *poltergeist* screams, "*I want what's MINE!*"

A burst of light knocks the chandelier aside. Emeric scowls and makes a complicated-looking gesture, his mouth moving in an incantation. Wheels of silver light wreath the *poltergeist*, trapping it in place. It lets out a half growl, half whine.

Now's my chance. I roll out from under the tables and bolt for the pedestal.

My hand has just closed around the stem of the goblet when I hear Emeric's incantation stop. I look up. The rings of light are constricting, tightening until they've just about sliced through the squirming, screeching *poltergeist*. Emeric draws his arm back, then flings the silver knife up and into the heart of the dark shrouds.

There's an explosion of shadow and screams—

—and the *poltergeist* breaks free.

Emeric staggers, briefly stunned as if by recoil, the silver knife ringing against stone at his feet. A terrible shudder rocks the rotunda. Tables, chairs—anything not bolted down—are pitched into the air. I see Vikram running toward us, see the ghost's horrible face fix on me; I know what's coming—

I toss the goblet to Vikram just before a table rams into me like a runaway wagon.

Here's the thing about a bad fall: The worst part isn't the impact, not really. It's the moment you're airborne a little too long, when you know that once you hit the ground, you aren't getting back up.

I crash down onto something that crunches awfully beneath me, my arm snaring with another horrid snap. A different, sharper pain blooms all along my left side. Everything fogs red. A tinny scraping sound fills in the gaps: I've landed on the shattered glass of the reliquary.

I hear Emeric calling my name. Everything hurts too much to answer in more than a whimper. I'm dimly aware of being picked up, the stagger of an unsteady run, urgent shouting. Rumbling and roars of "*GET OUT, LIARS, THIEVES, GET OUT!*" echo dully in my ears.

I glimpse the hideous specter behind Emeric, its face twisting even more horribly as it reaches for us—

And then, for a moment, I think I see a shrouded figure drag it back.

The fog lightens. There's a rush of fresh air and a *crack* from the doors thundering shut behind us. We're outside again. I am carefully lowered to the ground. Numbness spreads down my side a moment later, loosening the hurt's stranglehold on my head.

". . . my fault." Emeric's voice fades in. "I should have gone in alone. Vanja, I've stopped the bleeding, and you shouldn't be in pain. You just have to hold on until we get to the inn."

My head lolls as I try to look at the damage. I catch a glimpse of a pink splinter jutting from my wrist before Emeric turns my chin. Guilt burns like acid in his dark eyes. "You don't want to see, trust me. I'll—I promise I'll fix it, you'll be fine, all right?"

"Not your fault," I croak. "I went after the goblet."

"I should have known better than to leave you unsupervised around a priceless artifact, then." He's trying to force it into a joke, but there's too much frustration seeping through for plausible deniability.

He still thinks I was just after it for larceny's sake. I try to gulp down the sudden knot in my throat, my heart still racing a million miles a minute.

"You owe the lady more credit than that." Vikram's peering at the goblet through his loupe, turning it in his hands. "I'll be damned, Miss Schmidt. Spotted it even inside Saint Willehalm's reliquary. Well done."

Emeric looks between us. "Spotted what, exactly?"

"What our ghastly nuisance is after, I wager." Vikram licks the tip of his index finger and runs it around the rim experimentally; there's only a muted yet audible squawk.

Crystal sings. The prisms cut into it should throw rainbows like the sun after a storm. I handled too much crystal at Castle Falbirg not to know it on sight.

And all I saw in the reliquary was glass.

"That goblet's a fake," I push through my teeth. "The real one's been stolen."

CHAPTER NINE

HANDS AT WORK

THE TRIP BACK TO THE BOOK AND BELL IS A BLUR. JUST BECAUSE I CAN'T feel my injuries doesn't mean I'm not going into shock, sinking into a gray haze in Emeric's arms. It's only occasionally broken when his voice throbs through in rumbles and murmurs and, once, a curious spur of anger.

When lucidity waxes back in, I'm facedown on a mattress. Late-afternoon light streaks around the morning-glory tendrils framing a window on the far side of the room, and I see my luggage and Emeric's in an oddly haphazard heap near a door. Emeric is sitting at the bedside to my left, his coat tossed over the bed's footboard. A prefect coin is set on a bedpost, casting clearer, steadier light than the nearby oil lamp's. Emeric pauses rolling up a sleeve when he notices me stirring.

"Welcome back," he says softly, brushing a loose strand of hair behind my ear. "The worst of your injuries are gone, and I would rather you slept through this last part, but it wouldn't be . . . I need to . . ." He grimaces. The words come out in a rush: "I need to remove the glass from your wounds but since it went through your clothes it's caught on fabric, too, so I need to cut through the sleeve of your shift and the side of your bodice and I think some of your skirt. And. That is. I don't know if you're comfortable with that."

"Well," I slur dizzily, "it sounds sexy when you put it that way."

He lets out a strained laugh, but it doesn't dispel his nerves. "To be clear, you have glass in your arm, your upper shoulder, your hip, and along your left side. I . . . might see more than you want me to."

That's when it sinks in. It's one thing to let his hands wander under the safety of a hitched-up linen shift, or in the forgiving dark, or when his spectacles are on the nightstand. But there's no lenience in this light; he will see me as I am. The blemishes, the hair, the—the scars. Even though he knows the von Falbirgs whipped me for someone else's lie, he's never seen the full ruin of my back.

And as with so many ugly parts of me, I am terrified that once he sees it, he will know he deserves better.

I try to catch my breath. "How much will you—I mean— where—Oh, you already said—"

"I can put a sheet over most of you," he offers swiftly, "so the only area that'll be uncovered is just around the injury, even if—if anything else slips?"

"Even sexier," I mumble. "Go for it."

Linen settles over me, and it does help, a little. "Do you want to sleep through this?"

"No." I want to know what he's seen, so I can brace myself for the worst.

"Right. Then . . ." I hear him uncork a vial. "You're under the strongest pain-suppressant spell I can balance against other physiological—er. This mostly won't hurt, and feeling should return once . . . Why are you smiling?"

I point with my chin at the vial. "You got juniper."

"Oh. Yes, the *poltergeist* was more tiring than it had any right to be, so Vikram brought over witch-ash oil from the outpost. I'm going to start now, if you're ready?"

At my nod, his fingertips rest on my left wrist. After a moment, I understand what he meant by "mostly won't hurt": There's a strange little jolt when I feel him brush against a glass shard buried in my forearm, like the wiggle of a milk tooth ready to slip the gum. I suck in a breath. He pauses, and I bite out, "It's fine, just . . . odd."

"Tell me if you need a break."

"I will." I'm not sure I mean it. Especially as he moves up my arm and, with a preoccupied apology under his breath, begins cutting the sleeve of my shift with a pair of what looks like sewing shears. I can't help stiffening, then squeezing my eyes shut as I feel bits of glass dig into muscle in response.

He pauses again, and I steel myself for a rebuke. Instead, he says, "I'm sorry for earlier."

"What?" I know when I'm being distracted, but I'll allow it.

"What I said about leaving you unsupervised. And assuming you wanted the goblet for . . . mundane reasons. I acted like you can't be trusted, and you don't deserve that. Especially not when *I* brought you into a dangerous situation unprepared and *you* secured our only lead." There's a soft *plink*.

I open my eyes and see a red-stained shard sitting in a nearby clay dish. Bits of bloody fabric are still caught on its edges. "Ew."

"There's unfortunately more where that came from." Emeric is carefully cleaning the tips of a pair of forceps, a furrow in his brow. "I've never encountered a *poltergeist* like that . . . A simple banishment should have handled it."

"Historically," I note, trying to focus on the bright white petals of the morning glories outside, rather than the forceps, "banishments have not been your strongest suit."

He makes a noise of indignation. "My banishments are *fine*. The *nacht-mahr* in Minkja was an anomaly because it was tethered to a material—I won't bore you with the theory. But . . . I left you in the rotunda so Fortune could give us warning. Didn't she tell you danger was coming?"

There it is again: some sort of foresight I'm supposed to have. "What do you mean?"

"Well, you haven't told me of the precise mechanics"—he drops another piece of glass into the dish—"but didn't you see Death or Fortune before the *poltergeist* attacked?"

My mind goes blank as he folds the sheet over my back, the crease parallel to my spine. The sewing shears creep along my arm, up to my shoulder, and my throat tightens as they get closer and closer to where I know my scars begin—then, mercifully, they stop. He peels the bloody fabric away from the wounds, but the old scars stay hidden. I'm so relieved, I barely mind the unsettling dig of the forceps.

Then my mind catches up to what he said about seeing Death. "Sorry, what?"

"Death or Fortune." Emeric lifts one more shard free. At my puzzled stare, he sets down the forceps. "Because . . . you can see their hands at work."

"I have no idea what you're talking about," I say.

Emeric studies me a long moment. "Vanja, when was the last time you saw your godmothers?"

"What?" It's a perfectly normal question, I know it is, but—but there's no *traction* when I try to think of an answer, the question whirling aimlessly like a spindle with no thread.

"Your godmothers." Emeric leans closer. "Death and Fortune. When did you last see them?"

I shake my head slightly. "I . . . don't have godmothers."

He doesn't say anything, only searches my face, and it feels like I'm coming up short somehow. Finally he repeats, "You don't have god-mothers?" At my nod, he steeples his fingers, blinking at the mattress. "Forgive me, I have to . . . clarify something. How did you end up in the service of the von Falbirgs?"

The memory catches in my throat more than usual. It's a blur of frost and night and murmur, the only fixed star the iron lantern in my mother's hand as she leaves. "I told you in Minkja. My mother aban-doned me on their doorstep when I was four. What does this have to do with—with Fortune? Or *Death*?"

"I can't be certain," he says slowly. There's a muffled, furious sort of spark in his face, and I'd swear it looks almost like hope. "But . . . it's going to be all right, Vanja. That I can promise you."

It's distinctly unsettling being the puzzle he's trying to solve when I can't watch him move the pieces. "If you say so."

Emeric doesn't respond other than to take up the forceps once more, but he's clearly mulling over something. "I . . . know it bothers you, not knowing about this case. I may not be able to tell you every-thing, but there's no reason you can't ask me questions. I'll just be care-ful how I answer."

So there's something he wants me to figure out. Or he just wants to even the ground between us again. No matter what, I'll take it. I just have to think of safe-ish questions.

Well, there's a very easy one that should suffice. I don't even know what, exactly, I'm being charged with. "What is profane fraud?"

Emeric hums a little, and I take that as a sign I've picked a good one. "I'm assuming your g—er . . . *somebody* explained to you how Low Gods are sustained by their believers?"

"Yes." Someone told me once that they are like rivers and valleys, each shaping the other over time. The whole of Almandy believes in the Wild Hunt, for example, but in the Haarzlands its leader is Brunne the Huntress, who favors a merry chase over a bloody kill. Other parts of the empire believe the Spindle-dam leads the Hunt and steals away disobedient children. Or it's called the Furious Host instead, and its riders are restless ghosts of warriors who died without honor, led by the Knight Unseen to endlessly seek their redemption. In each region, the Wild Hunt becomes what the people believe it to be.

Another piece of glass falls into the clay dish. "It is hypothetically possible to fabricate a Low God by deceiving a massive number of people into believing it exists. So if you had—" He stops. "I shouldn't give specifics about your situation. But essentially, profane fraud is the crime of intentionally misleading people into believing in a falsified Low God with the intent to manifest the Low God and use their powers for personal gain."

No wonder this case is complicated. I certainly misled Hagendorn into worshipping the Scarlet Maiden, but I had no intention of manufacturing a god, let alone waking one. I suppose that's my next question, then. "How do you prove someone committed profane fraud?"

When Emeric's answer comes, it's heavy with resignation. ". . . I can't answer that."

"Right." I need a new diversion while the shears snip along my side, down to my hip, as he promised. I can't help shivering from the chilly metal.

"Sorry," he mumbles.

I don't know if he's apologizing for the nonanswer or for the cold. "You know I'm making you buy me a new dress."

"When we're done with this," he says absently, "I will buy you fifteen dresses, if it means you stay out of trouble."

"Hmph. I can retire from arson for twenty."

"Arson *and* theft for twenty-five."

"Horse theft for thirty dresses. I feel like that's a win for us both." I have to duck my head when he huffs out a laugh, because it buffets my bare side in a way I was significantly underprepared for. Then another question coalesces—but I'm not sure he'll be able to answer it either. "Emeric . . . do you think the Scarlet Maiden is a real god?"

"I . . . I can't . . . Hold on." There's a faint dart of pain, now at my hip, as a shard is extracted. He sighs. "This falls under things I can't say outright, so bear with me. There's a saying here in the north: 'A child's eye fears the painted devil, but an elder wields the brush.' We fear what we're taught to fear, not necessarily because it's worth fearing. I see a devil on the wall. Real or not, the question that matters is who put it there."

"Well," I say slowly, "I have no idea what any of that means, so I think we're safe."

There's one last *plink* and a waft of juniper, and then a soft *whoosh*. The numbness ebbs from my side, leaving a slight ache in its wake. I stretch my arm out from under the sheet to watch as hair-thin scabs slough off of fine raw pink lines, which shrink away to nothing.

Emeric catches my outstretched hand with one of his. Morbidly, there are still a few flecks of my blood stuck under his nails. "I know today's been—strange. Difficult. Are *we* all right?"

I tug him closer, and he obliges, crooking his free arm on the bedside by my face and resting his chin on his wrist. He looks *tired*, in a way I rarely see. "We're all right," I confirm. "And tonight we're both going to have decent baths and a good night's sleep, and in the morning I'm going to wake up and see you instead of some moldy bunk room, and then we're going to be *great*."

"Well," he says with a lopsided smile, "it sounds sexy when you put it that way."

Once again, I find myself ruing the day I gave this smartass tentpole the power to be-twitterpate me. Before I can summon a response, my stomach does so for me, grumbling like it's trying to wake the dead.

Emeric stands with an even wider grin, depositing the forceps in a washstand. "Vikram and Mathilde wanted to work on this *poltergeist* problem over dinner. If that's fine by you, I'll just, er, look at this very interesting corner of the room until you're dressed, and we can meet them downstairs."

It doesn't take long for me to dig up a change of clothes and my coin purse, and then we head down. The Book and Bell is a nice inn by Minkja standards, middling by Dänwik standards, and pure decadence by Four Solid Days of Roadhouses standards: clean floor timbers, fresh white-wash on the walls, and practical brass chandeliers. The dining room is a reasonable pandemonium by anyone's standards, permeated in the dull roar of many, many conversations competing for volume dominance. Even among the chaos of servers weaving between rowdy tables, it's easy to spot Vikram and a woman I'm guessing to be Mathilde. Their stark black uniforms stick out almost as much as the seats they've saved for us.

Before we can make it even halfway across the dining room, though, we're intercepted by a man in pristine livery that boasts the badge of a *prinz-wahl*'s personal messenger. "Prefect Conrad?"

"Close enough," Emeric mutters. "Yes?"

The messenger hands him an envelope sagging with a wax seal so elaborate, you could wear it as a brooch. "From His Highness Prince Ludwig von Wälft."

Frowning, Emeric shucks a gilded missive from the envelope. I glimpse a few snippets: "*the great prefect Emeric Conrad,*" "*honor of your presence,*" and, most crucially, "*tomorrow evening.*"

"I see," he says. "Thank you." He tucks the invitation into his uniform coat and continues on.

We've nearly reached Vikram and Mathilde when the messenger's voice bugles across the dining room: "Sir! Prefect Conrad! *Sir!*"

Emeric spins on a heel as a curious pause ruffles through the diners. Having spent quite a lot of time gleefully trampling his last nerve myself, I can tell that we're on it. "*Yes?*"

"Your reply, sir?"

"I accept," Emeric says shortly.

"Very good, sir." The messenger's gaze flicks to me. "I believe the invitation is just for you, sir."

"Thank the gods," I say under my breath. Emeric just nods and keeps heading for our table. The conversations begin to pick back up, and this time they're scattering breadcrumbs like "Conrad" and "Minkja" and "von Reigenbach." I suppose I shouldn't be surprised—Bóern is the largest territory in the southern empire, and when its margrave binds himself to literal nightmares to attempt overthrowing the Blessed Empress, word's bound to get out. I suppose I just never thought it would make Emeric Conrad a household name.

I don't know how I feel, that no one's saying mine.

We make it to the table, where Mathilde has covered her mouth with a hand and Vikram is trying not to laugh as he pours a *sjoppen* of cider for each of us. Emeric's just pulled out my chair for me when the courier's call splits through the room yet again: "Sir!"

Emeric sends a look over his shoulder, barely smothering his annoyance.

"A carriage will be sent for you at six in the evening, sir."

"Wonderful," Emeric says as enthusiastically as if he'd been invited to have a tooth pulled. "Please excuse me."

"You ought to tip the man," Vikram says as Emeric sinks into his own seat. "That was the most entertainment I've had all week. So Prince Ludwig wants you to come to dinner tomorrow?"

Emeric nods, glum.

"That's going to be awkward," pitches in the woman I'm still presuming to be Mathilde, "considering he's almost certainly the one who has the real goblet."

I choke on the cider I've just swigged. "How do you know that?"

"She's Mathilde," Vikram says with a twist of rue. "She just does. You get used to it."

Mathilde sniffs. She seems to be in her midtwenties, like Vikram, with curly smoke-brown hair cut nearly as short as Emeric's, wide gray eyes, and pale skin dusted in a more moderate amount of freckles than mine. Her uniform has the same striped black-and-white trim as Vikram's as well.

"It's very simple," she says at a rapid-fire clip. "The problems with the—You're certain it was a *poltergeist*? Usually *poltergeists* die angry. Who dies angry in a library?"

Emeric helps himself to a rye roll from the basket on the table. "It displayed all the classic indicators: ghoulish appearance, violent rage, and the ability to move physical objects with great force. Yes, I believe it was a *poltergeist*."

"In a *library*, though?" Her mouth pinches.

Vikram shrugs. "More likely than we thought."

"Sorry," I say slowly, "can we go back to the *prinz-wahl* having the real goblet?"

"Oh, right, well, *so*." Mathilde holds up five fingers and starts ticking them off. "First: There's a legend that says so long as Saint Willehalm's goblet is in *its home*, Dänwik will be protected. Second: House Wälft claims it as a family heirloom, but it's been displayed in the Library of the Divine for . . . forever, basically. Third: Prince Ludwig has been pushing the head librarian to let the goblet move to his residence. Fourth: It's rumored that the Armarius, the library's guardian spirit and master recordkeeper, is tied to the goblet somehow. That explains how the *poltergeist* got in if the real one was stolen. And fifth . . ." She starts to curl in her final finger but stops halfway. "I'm not going to tell you until Vikram puts in our order for dinner."

Vikram makes a noise of outrage. "You see this, Conrad? She won't even tell me how she does it."

"I'll have the white asparagus soup, thank you. And, Miss Schmidt— you *are* Vanja Schmidt, I presume—will have . . . ?"

I'm too startled not to answer. "Soup for me too."

"Traitor," Vikram grumbles. "Conrad, I'm getting us both trout."

Once he's set off toward the bar, Mathilde leans in. "It's just the women's privy," she says bluntly. "That's the secret. You hear *everything* in there." Then she extends her hand to me. "Mathilde Richter. Vikram's my partner."

I shake it. "Vanja. Emeric's poetry muse, apparently."

"I wish you'd forgotten that," he grumbles into his cider.

"Not even if it'd save a burning orphanage," I say breezily, "and I've been in one of those, so you know I mean it."

"So is there a reason Proctor Kirkling hates you?" Mathilde asks me, in the cheerful, direct tone typically reserved for questions like *Read anything good lately?*

I give her a startled look. "Don't tell me you heard *that* in the privy."

She shakes her head. "No, I was here when Conrad brought you in. I heard the whole bed argument unfold."

"Bed argument?"

Mathilde gestures to Emeric. He looks both annoyed and embarrassed. "The room Proctor Kirkling originally got for us was meant for one person. Including the bed. I was somewhat . . . irate."

"It was definitely a bold move, yelling at the proctor of your Finding," Vikram says merrily as he drops back into his empty seat. "Mathilde told me all about it."

"I didn't yell," Emeric protests.

"Raised your voice. Spoke strongly. Whatever you want to call it. Kirkling definitely hates you, Vanja."

"I'm aware," I say. "You *yelled?*"

Emeric buries his face in his hands. "I asked for a different room. Firmly."

"He yelled." Vikram turns to his partner. "Order's in. *And* I got the pudding for dessert."

To my surprise, Mathilde leans over and plants a kiss on his cheek. "Yes you did. My fifth point: The goblet of Saint Willehalm is cleaned and inspected once a year by a professional that House Wälft appoints. That happened just over a week ago, and instead of the local jeweler who traditionally does it, the *prinz-wahl* hired someone new."

"Suspicious timing," Emeric says, "and our only lead at the moment. I'll try to confirm it tomorrow night."

Mathilde scrunches up her nose. "I hope I'm wrong. If Prince Ludwig doesn't return the goblet willingly, we're all going to be stuck here for another two months at *least* while the paperwork goes to Alt-Aschel and back."

Emeric and I both blanch. Alt-Aschel is the High Imperial City, the capital of the empire itself, home to the Blessed Empress. It's also on the opposite end of the empire. "We don't have two months," I say slowly. "Can't it happen faster?"

Emeric pinches his nose. "I forgot how messy it gets when it's a relic and not just property. No, we'll have to petition the archcardinal for authority to seize the relic, so the paperwork has to go through the Kathedra."

The Kathedra is the administrative body responsible for the temples and clergy of the myriad Low Gods of the Blessed Empire, located in Alt-Aschel. "I don't suppose anyone knows what the archcardinal's signature looks like?" I ask. "I'm already being investigated for profane fraud, I might as well throw in some actual fraud for free."

"Aspirant Conrad."

The incredible thing about this moment *isn't* that I'm there to witness the perfect and instantaneous exodus of Emeric's soul from his body. Rather, it's that he still manages to turn in his seat and rattle out a disembodied "Yes?" to Kirkling, who's looming behind us. Judging from the look blistering down her nose, she absolutely heard me.

"You are to make your report to me by no later than eight o'clock tonight. You know where my room is. That is all." She stalks off without another word.

Emeric hides his face in his hands once more. I'm not optimistic about luring him back out with anything short of a subscription to an Abacus-of-the-Month Club.

"So that's a no for forging the archcardinal's signature?" I venture. "Just to confirm?"

"It's a no," Emeric mutters into his palms.

"How badly do you need to get into the library?" Mathilde asks. "Didn't you get some records earlier?"

"We found the section, but not . . ." Emeric hesitates, glancing sidelong at me. "What I'm looking for may not even be there. I need to review a significant number of documents either way." He sighs. "I'm . . . sure I can make Prince Ludwig see reason."

Vikram and Mathilde trade unencouraging looks. Vikram shrugs again. "If anyone can, it's Conrad," he says, more to Mathilde than us.

Mathilde does not look convinced. For that matter, neither am I. I don't know Prince Ludwig, but I do know thieves. Little thieves tell themselves they take what they need to survive, and sometimes that's true, and sometimes it's a lie. Great thieves don't fool themselves about their motives; they take things because they want them, end of story. The only lie they tell themselves is that there's no difference between wanting something and deserving it.

Dinner passes easily enough, all things considered. Vikram produces a copy of his padlock to test against my picks (it lasts five minutes the first try, less than one minute after), and Mathilde presses for details about the Scarlet Maiden (we skimp on details about her "unclaimed" criterion and skip straight to the blood sacrifice). Surprisingly, they've heard of the Ros brothers—or at least one of them.

"You may not want to mention Ozkar Ros around the artificers," Vikram says out of the side of his mouth. "There was a whole debacle where they tried to recruit him into the Northern guild, and the only way he'd agree was if he paid no dues and didn't have to heed the bylaws."

"Why would they even want him, then?" I ask.

"Because he could have retired three inventions ago. No merchant would cross the guild if it meant losing access to Ozkar Ros . . . but Ros didn't want to limit his clients either. Half the guild wanted to bring him on anyway. The other half just thought he was stringing them along, and they were right."

I'm starting to see why Ozkar's siblings call him difficult.

Emeric has to go make his report after dinner. Vikram insists on paying for the meal, leaving me alone with Mathilde for a moment.

It's a moment I need, because there's been something stewing in my head since I saw her kiss Vikram on the cheek. "Can I ask you a personal question?"

Mathilde leans back, squinting at the window; the daylight is starting to fade. "Yes, if you hurry. I have to leave for sabbath prayers before the sun's completely gone."

"Saints and martyrs, it's Friday. I keep forgetting." I rub my eyes. Followers of the House of the High worship the Low Gods as facets of a single High God, and most observe a daylong sabbath at the end of each week. I see some of the other diners excusing themselves too, a few slinging prayer cords around their shoulders on their way out. I have to make this fast. "You and Vikram are . . . more than professional partners?" At her nod, I try to sort out my question and find it's so simple, it can't be put delicately: "How do you do it?"

"What do you mean?"

"You're prefects. You don't get to—to be wrong," I babble. "So do you just agree on everything? What if one of you makes a mistake? Or if you have a fight? How do you keep your job out of your . . . life?"

"'How do you have a relationship with a prefect' seems to be your question," Mathilde says shrewdly. "I'll be honest, I have no idea how it works when only one of you is part of the Order. We both love what we do, and we both know when we need a break from it. When we disagree, we talk through it, and if we don't have time to talk, we just trust each other until we can make time. The hardest part was waiting out the first journeyman year after we were fully ordained. We already knew how we felt by then, but . . ."

I give her a blank look.

Mathilde's eyebrows rise and quickly flatten. "Oh. Er. Journeyman prefects are expected to remain single and childless for the first year following their ordination, at minimum. It's so we can get a full sense of the work and can judge for ourselves whether we are willing to pursue relationships and families outside the demands of the Order."

A *year?*

I feel—I feel like I'm lying under the sheet again, and those cold shears are creeping much, much too close to the scars.

I've shared parts of myself with Emeric that I wasn't even sure I could share with another person. I got a root-bind to share even *more* of myself. And when this case is closed, and he's fully ordained . . . none of that will matter. He will move on alone.

Tentative, Mathilde asks, "Conrad hasn't mentioned it?"

"No," I answer distantly. "He didn't say a thing."

Mathilde shakes her head, pushing back from the table. Sunset-gold light is sceping through the window; her time's up. "Then this is your chance to practice the talking part. That's how you build trust for when you can't talk. And if you want to make it through that year, you're going to need it."

CHAPTER TEN

ℜISE AND SHINE

MAKE A QUICK VISIT TO THE BOOK AND BELL'S UTILITARIAN BATHHOUSE, scrubbing off the accumulated grime like it'll clear out my doubts and pores alike. Helga catches me on the way out to tell me to be ready first thing in the morning. She's tracked down the Golden Bine, and we'll be going there to badger Dieter Ros into contributing his drop of blood.

Emeric's not in our room when I return. I light a candle, change into my nightshirt, and climb into bed, resolved to wait up for him. Mathilde's right. If we want to make it through this, we need to talk.

Unfortunately, the moment I lean back against the pillows, I pass out.

I'm the kind of tired that doesn't allow for the delineation of dreams, only soft dark shadows that swallow me whole. I don't know when Emeric gets back, just that the stillness shudders, and then there's a weight beside me, somehow comforting, somehow unsettling. I slip under again.

Then—

I'm standing in the Library of the Divine.

The chandeliers are lit, the tables and the chairs of the rotunda restored to their neat array. There are no scattered papers, no abandoned dolls.

There are, however, ghosts.

Or shades, rather: indistinct blurs of people poring through tomes, scouring shelves, depositing a heap of books at a desk. My sight goes briefly gray, and then a broad back materializes before me, shrinking as the shade strides away. It walked right through me.

"*You.*"

I whirl around. Behind me is the foyer of the library. The friar statue is, bizarrely enough, staring at me. No, not a statue—he seems to be flesh and blood, and there's no pedestal in sight.

I've heard that voice before. And as I take in the coarse weave of his robes, I abruptly know where.

"You," I stumble, "you're the *poltergeist.*"

A terrible look crosses his face: not anger but . . . sorrow. "Please," he says. "I know what you are. And only you can help me."

"Pass," I say darkly. "You threw a table at me."

The friar bobs his head, sheepish. "I am not myself without the goblet."

I look around for a door. Unfortunately, in the dream-foyer, there's solid stone where the entrance should be. That only vexes me more. "Correction, Sextus: You threw a table at me *so hard* it broke my entire body, like a little twig, on the spot."

"That seems improbable," he says meekly, "and my name is not

Sextus. We don't have much time; it is a great strain to speak to you this way, while I am sundered thus. You must understand, my very ashes were melted into the crystal of the goblet and mixed with the mortar of the pedestal. I chose to remain bound to my library to guide and protect it, but the goblet and the pedestal *are* the binding, and without the goblet, I am . . . undone."

I catch myself pinching my nose like Emeric does and have to brush off the pang in my chest. "Wait. Hold on." I think of the statue pedestal's plaque that read THE FOVNDER, and of the one on the reliquary, too, and of the other unanswered question: why the library's guardian spirit let the *poltergeist* in to begin with.

It didn't. *Of course.* He had been there all along.

"You're the Armarius," I say slowly. "That's why Emeric couldn't banish you. You're already where you belong."

"Correct."

"But that's Saint Willehalm's goblet. So . . ." I swallow. "You're Saint Willehalm the Scribe. And this is your library."

The friar pushes his hood back, revealing a lined pale face and a scraggly white beard. He offers a weary smile. "I must confess, I've not heard that name for a long, long time."

I'm still less than awed. "Sadly, Sextus—"

"Not even close," he says gently.

"—this all sounds like a personal problem," I finish. "And I count at least three prefects in this town who are a lot more qualified to handle it."

The smile fades from Willehalm's face. "They cannot help me, God Daughter. I came to you for a reason."

All this is weird enough that I don't think too hard about why a saint is calling me his goddaughter. Instead, I'm stymied by a peculiar feeling blooming in my chest.

For most of my life, I've held to a theory I call the trinity of want. It states that people are desired for three reasons: power, pleasure, or profit. If you provide three of those, others serve you. Provide two, they see you. One, they use you.

This came from my life as a servant, where people didn't want me, they wanted steady hands, a sturdy back, and a closed mouth. The von Falbirgs were sound of body and mind; they could have laid their own rushes or emptied their own chamber pots. They just made me do the things they didn't want to.

But I am a stranger to being . . . sought.

Saint Willehalm continues, encouraged by my pause: "The prefects are an axe. Their justice falls absolute and irrevocable, and so they must take the time to be sure of every strike. But there is more to justice than an axe; sometimes it calls for leaving no trace but a mending. Sometimes justice must be a needle."

I drag a long breath through my teeth. "Great metaphor, perfect, comprehensible, ten out of ten. Just for fun, let's pretend I didn't understand any of it. What do you want from me?"

The old saint lets out a bemused chuckle. I realize his outline is growing dimmer, blurring along with the rest of the dream-library. Our time is coming to an end.

"I'm glad this is funny to you," I grumble.

He shakes his head. "I just think I've been very clear. The years will do that, I suppose. Again, God Daughter, I know what you are. What do I want?"

The world melts into shadow, Saint Willehalm last of all. His final words ring my skull like a belfry.

"I want my damned goblet back."

I sit up with a gasp.

At first I don't know where I am. Then I hear an indistinct mumble at my side. Emeric's asleep on my left, the wall is on my right, the room itself is still heavy with dark. I seem to be cocooned in an unnecessary number of blankets—and then I realize I've hoarded them in my sleep again, as Emeric is shivering under a thin sheet.

I carefully extract myself and redistribute the bedding more equitably, then lie back down, staring at the ceiling. Unless I'm horribly mistaken, a saint just quested me to retrieve his relic.

No, not just retrieve. He said he knew what I am; he said this called for not an axe but a needle. Slight enough to leave no trace, sharp enough to pierce deep.

He wants me to steal it.

He wants *me* to steal it.

He wants me to *steal* it.

And I can say, with an equally horrible degree of confidence, that the prefect aspirant in my bed right now does not.

✺

When my eyes open again, it's to the pale glow of a plaster wall in morning light. And for a heartbeat, everything is perfect: the warmth where my back is pressed to Emeric's chest, the snugness of his arm tightening around my waist, even the scratch in his voice as he sleepily mumbles into my shoulder, "Morning."

I can't remember why I was mad at him. Then, with a sting, I do.

Emeric goes still as he feels me tense. "What's wrong?"

It would be so, so easy to lie to him, to say it's nothing and try to stretch the cozy peace as long as I can. But it wouldn't be real. I would still know.

So I make myself roll over, try to quell the fear that only feeds my anger, and face him. "Why—" My voice cracks. Emeric turns, reaching for a cup on the nightstand. His hand closes around it just as I say, "Why didn't you tell me about the first year?"

BANG-BANG-BANG-BANG-BANG. Furious pounding rattles our room's door on its hinges. Emeric knocks over the cup, swearing.

"Get up!" Helga barks from the other side. "I'll be back in five minutes!"

"*Why,*" Emeric wheezes blearily.

"*Scheit,* I forgot." I climb over Emeric's legs and lever myself off the bed as Helga's footsteps fade down the hall. "We're going to meet with Dieter Ros. Forget it, we can talk about this later."

He pauses mopping up water with what appears to be his own nightshirt. "No, I don't want you to think—I wasn't trying to hide any-thing from you—"

"Right." I yank open my traveling pack a little too hard.

"It just doesn't matter."

I stop in the middle of pulling out a kirtle, trying to wrestle my squirming anxiety into words, and surface only with "It matters to me."

"That's not . . ." Emeric removes his spectacles and rubs his eyes. "That didn't come out right."

"No, I get it," I say, turning away as I pull the kirtle over my head. A bitter note seeps in. "But it would have been nice to know you were planning on ditching me after you're ordained."

There's a startled silence. The hurt in his voice makes me want to shrivel when he asks, "Is that really what you think of me?"

That's when I feel it: the vertigo of losing the high ground. I can't make myself face him this time, so I just try to focus on the kirtle ties. "What am I supposed to think?"

Another beat passes. Then the bed frame creaks, and Emeric says exhaustedly, "I don't know what more it's going to take for you to trust me, Vanja."

I haul on a stocking, trying to work through the tears I feel burning behind my eyes. Every answer I scramble for slips into a sinkhole I can't patch over: I don't know either.

The cold truth is, some part of me is always waiting for the other shoe to drop.

And it's for no good reason other than the truth beneath, colder still: Even after everything we've been through, I still know myself. And deep down, I cannot believe someone would want me, without agenda, as I am.

Before I can scrape together an answer, Helga's thunderous knocking erupts once more. "Time's up, let's go!"

"In a *minute*," I snap as I shove my feet into my boots, absolutely certain that five minutes have not passed. The irritation pushes my anger with Emeric from simmer to boil. "You know what would help me trust you? If, at any point in the past week, you had actually told me——"

"When?" His voice rises. I look up from my bootlaces and find a flush staining his face, his hands fisting in the sheets. "When was a good time, Vanja? When we were stuck in a carriage for four days? When we were in a cave, parsing out how your cult is going to feed me to a hellhound? Was that a good time?"

He's not really asking, so I just grab my satchel and cloak. My jaw is clamped so tight, it aches.

Emeric keeps going. "Or how about earlier? How about January, when you said you'd meet me in Helligbrücke? Would *that* have worked for you? Because for someone who's so afraid of being left behind, you had *no* problem leaving me."

I——I have no answer, because he's right, damn him, but it still cuts, hearing it out loud——

"Thanks," I hiss, "but I didn't need *another* reminder that I'm not good enough for you."

Emeric looks as stunned as if I'd slapped him.

I should feel relieved to air the words, triumphant to have shocked him into silence. Instead, I only feel worse.

Helga's knocking starts up again just as I wrench the door open. It's humiliating, but I know she can see the tears in my eyes, so I don't even bother trying to hide them. "We're in the middle of something."

Helga, for her part, is clearly totally unprepared for what she's walked into. She looks from me to Emeric, back to me, drags a hand down her face, then seizes me by the elbow and steers me out. "Not anymore, you aren't. There's a cute little garden park by the Golden Bine. You two can sort this out over lunch."

"Wait—" I hear Emeric get to his feet.

"Be there at noon," Helga flings over her shoulder as she hustles me down the hall.

She doesn't say anything else until we leave the Book and Bell, the cool morning air stinging against my hot cheeks, and start down the street. Then she offers me a hankie, uncomfortable. "Sorry for the rush. But whatever that was . . . you weren't talking, you were just hurting each other."

"He's the one who—"

"*Ah-ah-ah.*" Helga holds up a hand. "Not getting involved. I don't do relationship drama, I don't do teenage drama, and I *especially* don't do teenage-relationship drama. Work it out among yourselves. I got you out because our best chance of catching Dieter sober is before breakfast. Come on, hurry it up."

The brisk walk does help clear my head, or at least dulls the hurt. And it's a decent walk: The Golden Bine is past the prefect outpost, planted right on the shore of Wälftsee, adjacent to the grounds of the royal hunting lodge itself. There's even a rather gaudy painted wooden statue posted in front of the beer hall: a towering nobleman in old-fashioned robes whom I suspect to be Prince Nibelungus von Wälft.

The Golden Bine has the same florid embellishments as the architecture that the prince commissioned to win back his ex-wife, though mercifully it seems to have been completed before his vengeful gothic rampage. Ornate lattices of dark timbers crisscross the plaster, vivid murals are painted on the whitewash, and a man is perched on a ladder by the double doors, applying a fresh coat of golden paint to the trim.

"Morning," Helga calls up to him as we approach. "Dieter Ros in?"

"In a devil of a mood, more like." The man spits off to the side, then jerks his thumb at the doors.

Helga curses under her breath and pushes inside. The interior is even more of a visual assault than the façade, every wall painted with gilded portraits of House Wälft and scenes of nobles hunting and fishing, apples being gathered by buxom and impractically dressed maidens, and so on. By contrast, the long pine tables are mostly empty. A handful of people are trying to enjoy what looks like a decent breakfast; this requires them to steadfastly ignore the slurred ramblings of a young man huddled at the end of a table beside a lute, his head cushioned on an outstretched arm, fairly surrounded by empty *sjoppen*. Some are lying sideways on the table, dribbling out the last dregs of beer.

Helga's long sigh comes out like a wordless grievance. She stalks over and seizes the man's ear as he emits a bawl of protest. "What is this, Dieter? Are you *trying* to lose another job?"

Dieter Ros swats her away. "Nothing matters," he hiccups. "I had one chance, one single chance to make it big, and I just—it just slipped—" He bangs his fist down on the table so hard, all the *sjoppen* jump. "And now I'll *never* play for the prince and *never* make it out of this backwater town and *never* win back Betze and—" He dissolves into furious groans, his head in his hands. An older Sahalian merchant sitting nearby picks up his breakfast and moves a few seats farther away.

I have the strangest feeling, like I've seen Dieter Ros before. I can't quite place it, though I see the resemblance between him and Helga. His hair is redder than hers, and right now, so is his face, but they have the same sharp eyes, and the only difference in their narrow jaws is the goatee carving out a bleak existence on Dieter's.

Helga passes me an empty *sjoppen*. "Can you go get some water?"

"*Nooo*," Dieter groans.

She presses her lips together and hands me another. "Two waters."

The barkeep obliges me with an irate sneer on his face, though it's directed primarily at Dieter. When I return, Helga empties a little packet of herbs into one *sjoppen*, mumbling a charm under her breath; I see traces of witch-ash on her fingertips.

Then she empties the other *sjoppen* over Dieter's head. He splutters, shocked. She shoves the herbed drink into his hands. "Here, it's your favorite."

"Leave me *alone*," he snarls.

"You promised you'd do this for me. *Drink.*"

He reluctantly downs the concoction. His face turns even redder, then the flush subsides. There's less of a drunken slur when he speaks. "Saints and martyrs, Helga, did you have to throw water on me?"

"You wouldn't ask if you could smell yourself." Helga sits next to him. "What happened, little brother?"

Dieter rubs his face. "Supposed to play for the prince tonight. Some fancy dinner. If it went well, it'd be a steady gig performing at parties for at least another two months. It could have been my big break, but some hotshot bard is in town from down south and"—he flaps a hand—"tossed me aside. Just like Betze did, and now she'll never . . ." He reaches for a *sjoppen* only to curse it when he sees it's empty.

Then he finally looks up at me, standing awkwardly a few feet away.

"*YOU*," he thunders.

"I'm getting that a lot today," I say. "Where do I know you from?"

"You cost me my gig in Glockenberg," Dieter accuses, pointing a shaking finger. "I never forget a redhead. You kept heckling me in the middle of a song."

"I don't remember that," I lie, recalling it, in fact, with perfect clarity.

"You tried to take my lute. You said you were confiscating it on behalf of Glockenberg."

"Are you sure it was me? There are a lot——"

"You said my singing was a public health hazard."

I wince. "I was extremely incapacitated."

"You said the Red Maid of the River would drown me herself if there was a repeat performance."

"Does it help that that spectacularly backfired?" I offer, and start digging in my satchel for the cambric and the awl. "Speaking of . . ."

"No," Dieter says, stone-cold.

I glance up at him. "No, it doesn't help?"

"No, I'm not doing this . . . blood thing anymore." He scowls. "Not for *you*."

"Dieter!" Helga gets to her feet. "You promised!"

"She threw up on my stage! The innkeeper made me clean it!"

"I'll——I'll tell Aunt Katrin you were drunk before noon——"

"I was fired the next day!"

Helga puts a hand on the table in front of Dieter and leans in. For someone who looks to be a handspan shorter than him, she summons a remarkable amount of menace. "*Do it*, little brother," she says slowly, "because I asked, *for family*."

Dieter shrinks a little. His eyes flick over to me and narrow.

"If she pays my tab," he says grudgingly.

"Agreed. You handle this part." I try to hand the cambric and awl to Helga.

She shakes her head. "Call it a hunch, but I think you have to do it. Come back once you've settled up."

I handle the tab, then return to collect. Dieter complains bitterly the whole time, claiming he won't be able to play for a week despite the wound healing almost as soon as his fingertip presses to the cloth. Helga makes him down another flagon of water before we go, sternly ordering him to attend their brother's wedding at the end of the month or face her wrath.

I listen with half an ear. Something's sticking in my skull about all this, something I don't have a clear picture of yet.

Helga found Dieter on her own yesterday and apparently got him to promise a drop of blood before he even met me. I'm certain that, without her bullying him just now, he'd have told me to piss off.

But Helga didn't even want to go on this trip in the first place. And in my experience, help never—well, *almost* never—comes without an agenda.

So why is she helping me?

Familiar, spiteful notes rise behind us as we leave the Golden Bine. They, too, take a moment to place until I catch the lyrics trailing us out.

"Red maid, red maid, red maid o' the river . . ."

Helga rolls her eyes so hard, it seems they ought to clank. "Asshole," she says under her breath. "Come on, I'll show you where the park is."

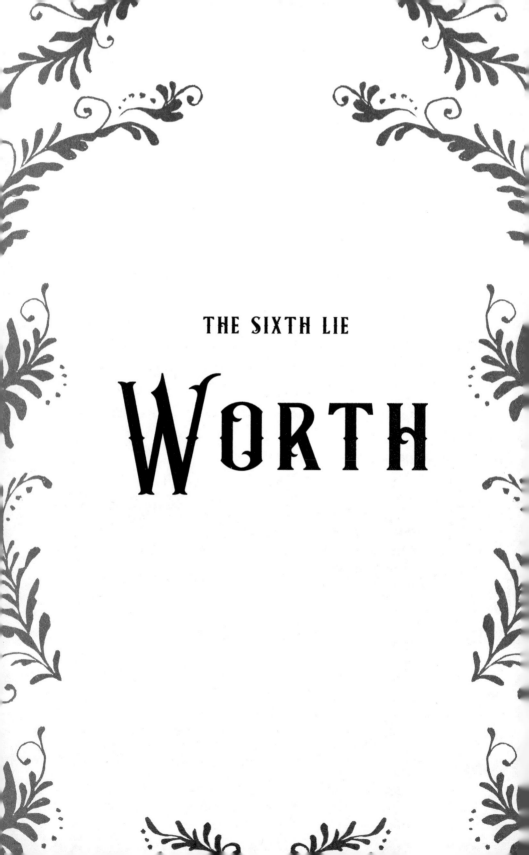

THE SIXTH LIE

WORTH

ONCE UPON A TIME, A GIRL SET OFF INTO THE GREAT WIDE WORLD, leaving behind everything she knew, bound for a new life . . .

For the fourth time.

The first had not been her choice, led into the midwinter woods by her mother and handed to Death and Fortune to do with her what they willed.

The second time, too, was not her choice, led by her godmothers to a castle and left to the whims of those who ruled it.

The third time, she did not so much leave her life as steal another. It was, and was not, her choice. There were other ways to survive, but she took the path that was open to her.

This fourth time would perhaps be different, perhaps be the last. It was wholly of her own choosing: She would leave Minkja and her friends there behind for now and follow her sweetheart to Helligbrücke. Once she arrived, they would seek out the family she'd lost, somehow, together.

The problem was, the girl did not quite know what to tell that family. How to face the mother who turned her out into the cold. How to ask if her mother regretted it, even once. How to say who she'd been, who she was now; she did not even know yet who she wanted to be. Years of pain had smelted her down to a knife, and only now was she relearning to touch others without drawing blood.

It was for the best, she supposed, that it would be a long ride to Helligbrücke.

She left with three strangers in a coach. Two departed in Okzberg. A mother and her damp-faced daughter took their place.

"Stop sniveling," the mother ordered as they climbed into the coach. "You should feel lucky the convent will even take in a little sneak thief."

Her daughter, wobble-mouthed and red-eyed, looked to be no more than thirteen. "But I don't know anyone in Quedling."

"Then you can't make trouble there too." The mother's voice was hard. "You're not to leave the cloisters anyway."

The daughter said nothing.

"I warned you, but would you listen? Your sister helps with the store, your brother sends us flour from his mill, and what do you do? Steal and lie and bring grief to our door. I've had enough."

No one in the coach said a word.

At the roadhouse that evening, the Minkja girl found herself drinking with the other passenger, an old soldier.

"Sad it is," he said into his watery ale, "but it's the way of the world. You want to live with others? You have to do more than take, you've got to bring something to the table. Sending her to a convent is kinder than turning her out into the street."

The girl thought of a lantern at a crossroads on a midwinter night, and of all the things she'd taken. Of who she'd been at thirteen, with fresh scars on her back and a pitiless sinkhole growing in her heart.

She wondered again what she would tell her family when she met them.

What she would tell her sweetheart's family, his friends, if she met them.

Whether they, too, would ask themselves if she did anything more than take.

When the coach reached Lüdz, the soldier got out and the mother and daughter remained. When they paid for the next leg of the trip, the girl from Minkja was careless in opening her own purse; she saw the Okzberg daughter's eye catch on the rubies glistening inside.

It came as no surprise when, in the dead of night, she caught the daughter trying to ease that purse out from under her pillow.

"You're not a very good thief," the Minkja girl said dryly. But there was fear in the daughter's eyes—fear and a pain the girl knew all too well.

They were, after all, what had worn her down into a knife.

She took five rubies and handed them to the daughter. "It's not safe for you to carry more than this. Go to the temple of Fortune and tell them Vanja sent you. They'll take you in, and you can start over, understand?"

I did not know what she had done to be exiled to a cloister; I could not say whether this was any better. I just knew that if someone had offered me a way out at thirteen, I would have taken it, instead of trying to cut my way free.

In the morning, when the mother found her daughter gone, she cursed and raged but shed tears only for the coin wasted on the trip. She didn't even lift a finger to look. She just set about arranging for her ride back to Okzberg, muttering, "Good-for-nothing . . . ingrate . . . Little wretch was never worth the trouble."

As our coach set off again, only a few days from Quedling, a relentless whisper of memory echoed louder and louder with each heartbeat—my own mother telling Death and Fortune, *Whatever she touches falls to ruin.*

And not for the first time, I wondered: What would I have to be, to be worth what followed?

CHAPTER ELEVEN

THE NEEDLE

HELGA SHOWS ME THE PARK. THEN SHE SHOWS ME THE NEARBY MAR-
kets and the best bakeries, and effectively keeps me occupied until it's
almost noon. I suppose I've figured out this much about Helga: She'll
roundly deny doing anything for any purpose beyond self-interest, but
that doesn't mean I should believe her.

She leaves me on a bench by the park's entrance with plenty of time
to mull over what I want to say to Emeric. I'm angry he didn't tell me
about the end date on our relationship. Especially since, well, I'm not
sure how I feel about losing my virginity to someone if we're just breaking things off soon after. It feels like . . . being used.

And I don't like that we started off talking about why I was upset,
but then it turned into me defending myself. Even though he's right: I did

leave him first. And I've assumed the worst of him—something that hurt when he did it to me just yesterday. But what else am I supposed to think?

It all feels like too many pans crowded on a stove, some smoking, some boiling over, all too hot to touch. Still, I can at least look at it from above now, instead of trying to talk with one hand in the fire.

The noon bells toll as my stomach growls. Helga and I did stop for some sweet buns, but I didn't have a proper breakfast, and the smell of sizzling *wurst* is wafting from a nearby food stall.

By the time bells chime for the quarter-hour, I'm very aware of how hungry I am, my legs swinging impatiently on the bench to keep the early April cold from locking them stiff. There's still no sign of Emeric. It's not like him to be this late.

That not-assuming-the-worst thing is getting more and more difficult.

I make myself think about the goblet instead. Or rather, how I'm going to sell Emeric on the idea that I have to steal it because a saint asked me to. Emeric did say he'd try to persuade the prince to return it, but . . . Saint Willehalm appeared to *me*.

It's just odd that Prince Ludwig *invited* Emeric in despite having stolen property on the grounds. Apparently Ludwig's even hiring per-formers for the dinner—

Wait. No. Not just tonight, but at least the next two months, Dieter said.

The two months it would take to get the goblet back through the authority of the Kathedra. The prince knows he'll have the goblet that long no matter what.

It's a trial run, I realize. He's testing whether a prefect can sniff out the genuine article, but he won't surrender it no matter what. If he gets caught, he can claim it was a mix-up with the cleaning and use the paper-work to keep it in his custody for months. If he doesn't get caught . . . Saint Willehalm will be waiting a long, long time.

And either way, I'd bet every last ruby that Ludwig will throw nonstop parties to show off his *acquisition* until Alt-Aschel twists his arm.

If we want to get into the library before midsummer, we'll need more than Emeric asking nicely.

My mind starts lining up the picks for this lock all too easily as I gnaw on the tip of a thumb. I've robbed backwater manors that posed more of a challenge, really, when the *Pfennigeist* was haunting Bóern. It's the sabbath, so any servants from the House of the High won't be working, and that means the hunting lodge is likely scrambling to cover staff shortages for tonight's big dinner. (Not to mention hiring for the next two months.) If I can get in, Emeric can keep the prince distracted for me, and the goblet will be gone before Ludwig is any the wiser. I just need Emeric to play along.

The bells ring out for the half-hour.

Where *is* he? This isn't like Emeric. He'd feed his own notebooks to swine before being even a minute late.

The worst-assumption road starts veering in a completely different direction.

Adalbrecht was the last aristocrat to invite prefects to his lands midfelony, but it was to kill Hubert Klemens for the contract mark inked into his skin. Maybe the prince has sinister intent for Emeric.

Suddenly I can't shake the memory of the dead man's tattoo sewn into Adalbrecht's back, the Scarlet Maiden spearing Emeric through the throat—

I'm on my feet before I can help it. I barely know where I am, but I do remember passing the prefect outpost on our way here, and I can make it back there easily enough. It's embarrassing; it feels almost like groveling to come to him instead of meeting on neutral ground, but it's better than letting my own mind terrorize me until he arrives.

I'm nearly at the outpost when an awfully familiar voice carries around a corner: ". . . supposed to do about it."

I whirl around, yanking up my cloak's hood, and shift to the hunched shuffle of an old woman picking her way down the street. The reflection in a nearby windowpane shows me what's going on over my shoulder.

I see Emeric and Vikram emerging from an alley and heading for the prefect outpost. They both carry half-eaten food-stall *wurst* rolls. It's harder to eavesdrop as they walk farther away, but I catch one last scrap: ". . . Vanja's problem."

His words from this morning burn like bile: *You had* no *problem leaving me.*

First my heart sinks. Then blood rushes to my head.

There's no getting around it. I can't even pretend that he forgot or lost track of time. He just chose to leave me on my own.

I feel almost unmoored. Even though I keep worrying about the other shoe dropping with Emeric, I wasn't really prepared for him to choose cruelty. But making me wait on him like a pathetic little fool— letting me *hope*—

Inchoate, explosive fury overthrows me. I want him to *hurt* so he learns to never hurt me again.

I don't even think, just spin on a heel, swipe an apple of horse dung out of a gutter, and throw it as hard as I can. It hits him on the shoulder in a tiny, foul explosion of brown.

That's about when my brain kicks in again and I realize throwing feces at a prefect (aspirant) was probably not the brightest move.

A confused shout follows me as I bolt around the corner he and Vikram just came from. It leads to a tidy but cramped little alley—more of a polite distance between two buildings. I don't know if they saw me; I'm not going to risk a foot chase either way. There are decent handholds in the lane's timber- and stonework, and I definitely scaled worse in my *Pfennigeist* days. I scramble up the wall until I reach a balcony, then climb it and a window gable until I reach the roof. It's lamentably steep, built to shed snow, so I scuttle along until I reach a roof with an easier slope. Then, satisfied I'm not being followed, I plop down on the shingles and try to collect myself.

Emphasis on *try*.

My sight streaks with tears once more. I still have Helga's hankie, which is even more valuable because, as it turns out, you can't throw dung at someone without getting shit on your own hand. I mop my face with my clean palm and wipe my other on the wooden shingles as best I can, only to curse when I pick up a splinter. Then I tip my head back and stare into the cloud-patched sky, wishing I could fall into it, if only to feel something uncomplicated.

I don't know how to fix this. I hate that I don't. I hate that I want to hurt him. I hate that he keeps hurting *me*. I want to go back to that final night in Minkja, when I cared for him and he cared for me and it was as simple as that.

All I had to do was follow him to Helligbrücke. All I had to do was trust he'd still want me.

But I ruined it, and now, here we are.

I scrub my face again with the hankie, angry with the both of us, as bells let out one lonely toll for the hour. Whether I like it or not, I still have to get Saint Willehalm's goblet, and tonight's going to be my best chance. I just have to do it without Emeric seeing.

Which means I can't do this as a needle, moved by a saint's hand.

I'm going to have to do this as a ghost.

"Marthe," I tell the guardsman at the rear gate of the royal hunting lodge, hefting a basket of produce. "From the greengrocer? I have a delivery for Cook Grett."

The guardsman eyes me suspiciously in the early evening light. Emeric should arrive in an hour, so I anticipated some wariness. "Bit late for that. You got an order?"

I give him a handwritten list on a scrap of parchment. "She said His Highness set the menu only this morning."

He scans it, still frowning. I know the list will pass muster, because I pickpocketed it off a scullery maid I tailed around the produce market a few hours ago. The maid was full of all sorts of interesting stories for her friends at the stalls: A renowned prefect is coming to dinner tonight, poor Grett the cook is in over her head, the steward is in a hiring frenzy to keep up with the months of parties the *prinz-wahl* has in store, and so much more gossip. Each insight is as good as a lockpick when it comes to breaking in.

The guard hands back the list and waves me on. "Be quick about your business."

"Yes, sir," I lie, and trot over the shallow stone bridge, heading for the kitchens. One thing I learned from burgling the rich is that architectural innovation tends to be reserved for upper stories. Kitchens, larders, laundry—they're always low to the ground and in the rear, so important people don't have to see how the sausage gets made.

Sure enough, I can hear a chaotic clatter of pans and frantic voices as I approach an open door near the cellars, where light and steam are spilling out. I make sure my hair's completely covered by my cap and kerchief, then quickly empty my basket into the slop trough and discard it in a discreet corner.

Then I hover by the door, taking in the kitchens' pandemonium.

It's a hurricane of servers with a harried-looking woman at the center: Grett, the main cook for the Golden Binc. The prince's personal chef, Dorlein, belongs to the House of the High, so Grett covers for her every sabbath. It's difficult enough to feed a prince from someone else's kitchen once a week, but Grett's also been saddled with preparing a dinner much finer than the Golden Bine's standard fare, and, according to the gossiping maid I trailed, she found out only this morning.

She spies me fluttering on the doorstep and scowls. "What's your business, girl? Who are you?"

"M-Marthe Schmidt," I stammer, falling back on my old standby alias from Minkja. "My mother's a friend of Dorlein? My brother just started as a groomsman today? And Dorlein said you need more maids tonight? I can come back later?" I take a timid half step back.

"No! No." Grett waves me in. "We need all the hands we can get. Do well tonight, and maybe we'll keep you on. Pay's four *sjilling* a d—*Watch it!*"

"O-oh," I say feebly as I step right into a manservant carrying a gravy boat. He leaps back quickly enough to save most of the gravy, but not without splashing us both.

"Damn you, Karl, you can't serve the prince looking a mess." Grett lunges for a pot that's begun to smoke. "Go change, and show her where the uniforms are while you're at it."

We pass a stack of wood for the stoves on our way out, and I sneak a dusting of Joniza's flash powders over the logs. Not enough to hurt anyone—just enough so that, in about five minutes, everyone will forget about Marthe Schmidt.

Karl dourly leads me down a hall to a storeroom with shelves of uniforms in obnoxiously bright red, blue, and yellow, everything from serving maid's livery to coachman's waistcoats. I pull the largest dress from a stack as Karl ducks into a nearby changing room with a fresh pair of breeches. I change in another little closet, tucking my own dress and cap into my satchel and securing the satchel itself under the oversized skirt. Once the apron's tied on, it masks the bump. I keep the kerchief on over my ginger hair; considering I don't know when we'll leave Dänwik, I don't want to risk being recognized.

Then I wait. I hear Karl leave, then a few powder-borne bangs and surprised yelling from the kitchens. I huff a silent laugh and slip out to wait elsewhere, since this has all but guaranteed a run on clean uniforms.

I hole up in a dusty storeroom among barrels of pickled herring to give Emeric plenty of time to arrive. Most of my heists in the past involved playing both a princess and her maid, so, comparatively, this feels downright restful.

I wait until the bells chime a quarter past six, to be sure Emeric's here and everyone is fully occupied with entertaining him and the prince. Then I leave the storeroom and hurry down the hall. Most of the staff ought to be shuttling between the dining hall and the kitchens, but the laundry should have its own route to the living quarters upstairs. I grab some mostly dry towels off a clothesline as I pass, quickly folding them into a neat stack, then climb the first set of stairs I see.

After only two short flights, I'm let out into a hallway whose arching ceilings and polished marble floors seem to contradict my vision of a residential wing. I pause, looking around. This was always going to be the hardest part: tracking down the goblet in a strange mansion.

"You, girl." A voice cracks behind me like a whip. "What are you doing?"

I don my best startled-yokel face and turn to find a guardsman with an outrageous mustache bristling by a nearby corridor. "Oh, excuse me, sir, I'm new. I was just bringing towels up—"

"Where's your badge?" he demands.

I falter. None of the servants I've seen has worn a badge. "I don't think I've been issued one yet?"

"You can't be in this wing without the badge," the guardsman growls, rubbing the waxy ends of his mustache. "The housekeeper would have told you."

For the second time today, I catch a familiar voice—a different one this time. "Oh good, you got my towels."

It takes every ounce of control to keep my jaw from dropping as Joniza Ardîm, bard of Castle Reigenbach and my oldest friend, strolls into the hall.

The past few months have been *great* for her, by all appearances. She's traded out her neat dark braids for a cascade of narrow, tightly wrapped tresses in soft corkscrews, pinned up tonight with delicate lacquered lilies. Her long brocade tunic and silk shirt are a significant upgrade from Minkja, too, but her Sahalian *koli* is slung over a shoulder in her usual fashion. Her lips and fingertips are painted in gold, her standard glamorous touch for a performance.

It clicks. *She's* the bard Dieter was bawling over.

"I'm sorry, this maid's attending me this evening, but I don't think the staff have had time to do much more than point the poor girl to the laundry," Joniza says smoothly. "I need these towels run up to my room, and I don't want anyone hassling her. Where can she get the"— she waves an elegant hand, golden rings flashing against her deep-umber skin—"key? Password?"

"Badge," the guard relents. "One moment."

He disappears down the corridor. We wait until his footsteps are gone, then Joniza turns on me, half amused, half livid. "What," she says, "did I *tell* you about vanishing on us for months on end? What in the name of all your nonsense gods are you *doing* here?" She holds up a hand before I can answer. "No, I can guess. Does Conrad know?"

"It's complicated," I grit out. Her scowl says that's not enough. "We're staying at the Book and Bell together. He's distracting the prince for me tonight. He just doesn't know it."

"Healthy," Joniza says sardonically.

"I'm not talking to him right now anyway," I mutter. "I'm here for a crystal goblet the prince stole. Has he——"

She elbows me as the guard's footsteps return. He reappears, handing me a little brass pin. "Fix it by your collar so we can see it."

"Thank you, sir, I won't forget again." I bob a curtsy.

"Come along, girl." Joniza steers me away. Once we're out of earshot, she whispers, "I overheard something about a gallery upstairs. That's the best I've got. If you get caught, say I sent you to get my powders and you got lost. And if you don't meet me at the Book and Bell for breakfast first thing tomorrow and explain yourself, I *will* come back and tell the prince exactly who has his vase."

"Goblet."

She gives me an absolutely scorching look.

"Right, going now, thanks and see you soon," I babble, and run off.

Once I'm clearly in the guest wing, it's not hard to spot Joniza's room; it's the only one with a faint red firelit glow flickering under the door. I let myself in, ditch the towels, switch the clownishly bright servant uniform for my own plain gray dress, and then crouch-walk out onto the balcony to study the hunting lodge's façade. Most of the building is thick walls and small windows, meant to keep heat in the winters. But a gallery calls for as much natural light as possible, the better to show off the collection within.

There. A long stretch of tall windows at the southwest corner, one floor up. When I look down, I see another story between the ground and me. Three floors is high enough to feel secure but not too far away from the entertainment of the main floor. That's my best bet.

I turn my attention to the handful of guards patrolling below in the thickening twilight, counting the halos of torchlight and the seconds that pass before they move. They're looking for intruders outside, mainly, but I still can't risk even being caught in the corner of an eye.

By the time I've tracked their patterns enough to be certain, full dark has fallen. There's a brief window every minute or so, no more than a count of ten, when the guard most likely to spot me passes down a long hedge tunnel that blocks his view. I make sure my satchel's buttoned tight, untie my apron, twist it into a rope, and wait.

When the torch passes behind the leaves, I leap into motion. *One.* I hop onto the railing, one hand braced on the wall. *Two, three.* I work my apron around a sturdy baluster of the balcony above. *Four, five, six, seven, eight*—I drag myself up, halfway over the balustrade—*nine*—I flop over and onto the balcony—*ten.*

The guard passes the hedge.

He's three stories down and looking another direction, but I don't dare move an inch until he loops through the tunnel again.

It takes me another four loops to cross all the way over to the gallery corner. Its windows are surprisingly latched, albeit with a simple hook-and-eye fixture, just to keep them from blowing open in the wind. Most people don't bother locking third-floor windows, especially not in a place like the royal hunting lodge, with guards posted at each entrance.

That's the funny thing about people who have never truly felt unsafe, though: They expect danger to ride right through the front gate. (And usually wearing a sign that reads, *I am danger*. I *cannot* emphasize enough how easy it was to rob people when they believed I was rich.)

When I reach the first of the gallery's balconette windows, I linger behind the heavy velvet drapery on the other side of the glass, moving slowly to peer inside. It's completely dark. That doesn't guarantee it's safe; sure enough, when I move farther down the line of windows, I see a faint glow at a doorjamb. It could be candlelight, but it could also be guards. I'll have to keep quiet.

I slip a thin file between the window casements and flip the hook latch from its eye. When I give the pane on the left an experimental tweak, it sticks on stiff hinges, so I leave it be lest it squeal a protest. The pane on the right doesn't exactly glide like butter, but it eases open quietly enough for me.

I hop over the sill and close the window behind me, then look around. The shadowy gallery is packed with paintings, ornate statues and statuettes, marble busts—typical fare for show-offs. There isn't a dust sheet in sight, nor a speck of dust; that makes me suspect I'm in the right place. This room is ready for Prince Ludwig's parties, once he's sure the goblet will stay awhile.

Speaking of the main attraction . . . I scour the room, but it takes me a moment to spot Saint Willehalm's goblet in the west end, because the crystal blends right into the drapery drawn behind it. It's perched on a lavish pedestal beneath a pristine glass cloche. I have the oddest feeling as I study the pedestal for any sign of a magic ward, like—like I'm forgetting a trick to this, but I don't know what.

Magic security wards are rare anyway; they're dreadfully finicky, and infamous for going off for something as slight as a spider touching a glass case. Prince Ludwig does not strike me as someone who'd risk dampening a party with shrieking alarms. Sure enough, when I use my apron to pick up the cloche, nothing happens.

I carefully lift the goblet off its hideous velvet cushion, which is embroidered with the garish arms of House Wälft. Then I remove a souvenir replica goblet from my satchel. I got the best one I could find, so it's close enough to hold up under casual inspection, but it won't take an expert to spot it for a fake by daylight. It just has to pass muster until I bring the real goblet to the library tonight.

There's one final touch, though. I want Ludwig to know (eventually) that this wasn't just some grift from the "cleaner" he hired to make the switch, or a miracle from an angry saint. I want him to know he had the goblet and lost it.

So I lay a red penny in the middle of the velvet cushion and set the fake goblet on top of it. Cut glass refracts copper into the loud patterns of the coat of arms; it won't be easy to spot until someone picks up the fake.

I use my apron to replace the cloche once more. Then I start bundling up the real goblet, trying not to think too hard about Willehalm's ashes being infused into the crystal and whether that makes it a corpse goblet—

—when I hear a shouted salute from the guards at the door.

My heart just about leaps from my chest.

He *wouldn't*. Brazen the prince may be, but no one in their senses would wave a stolen holy relic in front of a prefect's nose.

There's a jolly shout in answer. *Someone* is coming in, and judging by the volume, I have a matter of seconds to get out of sight.

I dart to the windows behind the pedestal. As I lean over the sill, I see the western side of the gallery offers no balconettes—only a sheer three-story drop. If I had time, I could use the drapery to lower myself, but I hear voices at the door, a knob turning—

I climb up onto the broad windowsill, clutching the goblet and the apron in one hand, and yank the drapes closed in front of me with the other.

". . . tour wouldn't be complete without my pride and joy." The *prinz-wahl*'s voice echoes off the walls. It's not unpleasant exactly; it makes me think of schnapps, sweet enough to mostly cover the bitter burn below. "I've dedicated my life to curating this particular gallery."

"So I see," Emeric says politely.

He's really doing it, the absolute madman. Prince Ludwig is showing Emeric the goblet.

CHAPTER TWELVE

ᛈATRONS

"EVERYTHING IN MY GALLERIES HAS BEEN HAND-SELECTED BY HOUSE Wälft, but I've doubled our collection in the past two decades, to be truly peerless." There's a lilt in Prince Ludwig's voice. I know it immediately.

Whenever I need to make a quick *sjilling* or fifty, I find a busy street corner and start a game of Find the Lady. Without fail, men like Ludwig show up with that kicky little lilt to lay down their coins. They're convinced they know the trick of the game, absolutely certain they'll win. They speak to me like it's all a private joke, like I don't know I'm their intended punch line.

How could Emeric think, even for a moment, that he might shame a man like this into giving back what he stole?

Ludwig delays the inevitable, detailing the histories of portraits, *this* sculpture, *that* urn, but he can't hold out long. Candlelight brightens the walls as he steers Emeric to the pedestal, then sets a candelabra in a sconce. Through a tiny gap in the drapery, I spy the prince a few feet away. He's hard to miss, sporting a canary-yellow silk coat that clashes with his hot-curled blond ringlets. They give a disconcertingly boyish cast to his weathered pink face, which suggests a man in his late forties. "And my greatest treasure . . . the goblet of Saint Willehalm."

"My word." Emeric does a credible imitation of surprise.

"Or rather . . . the finest replica I could commission. Just like the real thing." A smirk teases the edge of Prince Ludwig's smile. "Though House Wälft has both the replica and the real one cleaned each spring. I suppose some year the jeweler might make an error."

"I should hope not, for your sake," Emeric says with a short laugh. "I was asked to review the situation with the library, and, having seen the custody agreement for the goblet just this morning . . . It would be costly to say the least."

Ludwig lets out a parrying chuckle. "My dear boy! The prefects *must* increase your commission if you think that's real money. The fine's a mere fifty *gilden*. May as well be a rental fee."

Fifty *gilden* is half a year's income for a common laborer. It's real money to people who don't live in royal splendor.

"May I?" There's a scrape of glass. I see the cloche handed off to Ludwig before he can object. Emeric's voice stays light, but there's an edge to it now. "Remarkable. What an extraordinary likeness. I take it Your Highness hasn't received February's legislative adjustment dispatch?"

"*Pff.* Boring stuff. I pay my steward to read that."

"The new margravine of Bóern swung a vote to pass an amendment to the articles covering financial penalties for noble houses. Fines are now structured as a percentage of the previous year's income, rather than a flat fee." Emeric shifts into view, peering pointedly at the goblet. "Unlawful possession of public property is now punishable by a fine of five percent of your house's yearly income, but it increases to ten percent when the property bears religious significance, like Saint Willehalm's goblet. For you, that would be, oh, three thousand *gilden*, I believe?"

He's underestimating; I'd put it at five thousand. I suspect it's to rattle a showboat like Ludwig even further, to make him do the math himself.

It seems to be working.

"R-roughly." Prince Ludwig sets the cloche on the floor and strides over to another painting. "Come, look at this! Finest portrait artist in the north."

"Just a moment, I'm admiring the craftsmanship. Who did you say does the cleaning?"

"A . . . a passing specialist. She left for Quedling last week. My boy, you must see this statue—"

Emeric leans even closer, candlelight flashing on his spectacles. "Did you know, according to records at the outpost, Saint Willehalm's very ashes are integrated into the crystal? I've a particular enchantment for my lenses—allows me to see various associated magics with anything on contact. I wonder if . . ."

He reaches for the goblet.

"I just had it cleaned," Prince Ludwig almost yips.

Through the gap in the drapes, I see a hint of curl to Emeric's lips.

I'd be lying if I said this wasn't doing . . . *distressing* things to me, especially given the day we've had.

And especially when Emeric's gaze flicks up and locks with mine.

His eyes nearly bug out of their sockets.

It takes a heartbeat or two for him to progress from shock to outrage. Then he silently mouths, *WHAT. ARE. YOU. DOING.*

I could play this sheepish, choose the conciliatory approach. After all, at some point tonight, we have to go back to the same room and share the same bed, and I don't think either of us is ready to introduce manacles into that equation.

But I think I'm done with trying to control the damage.

(Arguably, I've been done since I hit him with horse shit.)

So instead I toast Emeric with the real goblet and blow him a kiss.

His brow furrows as he lifts my fake goblet off the cushion. His eyes land on the red penny that was hidden under its foot, lying brazenly in the open now. Then he looks back at me and cocks an eyebrow.

"Fascinating," he says loudly, holding the fake up to the candlelight.

"Please, my boy, put that down," Prince Ludwig pleads from across the gallery. I hear his steps hasten across the marble floor.

Emeric doesn't move, only shoots me a thinly smug smile. And that's when I realize he's drawing Ludwig over here to discover the penny. He'll figure out he's been robbed approximately twelve hours earlier than I want him to know.

That—that little *bastard*—

I set the real goblet on the sill and shift forward, snaking a hand past the drapes to snatch the penny from the cushion.

Just as my hand closes over the coin, Emeric's hand closes over mine and doesn't let go. He pivots to stand behind the pedestal, folding his arm behind him and blocking my view through the drapery gap entirely. From the prince's perspective, Emeric is just standing genteelly, one arm resting at his back.

From mine, this overgrown love child of a beanpole and a dictionary still has my hand in an iron grip, and if I move even a *little* in this awkward crouch, I'm going to tip over and yank the drapes down while I'm at it.

I can't decide if I want to throw him out the window again for old times' sake or drag him into a linen closet for an entirely different old times' sake. Probably both. At the very least, I'm revisiting my stance on the manacles.

"Truly an impressive level of detail"—Emeric tips the goblet at the *prinz-wahl*—"for a replica."

Prince Ludwig's steps slow as he gets closer. I can hear guarded confusion in his voice. ". . . Isn't it?"

"Particularly for glass." Emeric lets go of my hand. Then he slips the briefest glance back at me, licks a fingertip, and runs it around the rim of the fake goblet as he sets it down. It barely makes a noise.

My useless brain, on the other hand, is very loudly and insistently sprinting to a number of different places. Every one of them makes my face burn. And the worst part is I'm still mad at him, but that isn't slowing down my terrible, useless, *treasonous* brain in the slightest. It might even be greasing the wheels.

Thankfully, Prince Ludwig has urgent business to attend: figuring out if he ever even had the genuine article at all. "Glass," he repeats slowly. "Yes. Yes, quite skillful. I . . . shall pass your compliments on to the glassblower. Well, this has been a lovely evening, my boy, and you're welcome to a drink before we call your carriage . . ."

Party's over. Emeric only casts one more look over his shoulder as the prince all but drags him out of the gallery. I poke my head around the drapery and wink, dramatically holding a finger to my lips, on his way out. He wrinkles his nose.

I catch the prince's muttered orders to the guards as they leave: "Lock the gallery doors and gather all the servants in the dining hall. And send word that, apart from the carriage service, no one's to leave the grounds until they've been searched."

The gallery goes dark as the doors shut with a terminal click of a bolt.

Security is about to get a lot tighter. I have to get out, *fast*.

I swiftly wrap up the real goblet in my apron and stow it in the satchel, mind racing. I can't get down and off the grounds before the order reaches the guards . . . but maybe I don't have to. I just have to get to the bottom floor.

I look around and spot what I suspected was there: a serving lift in a discreet corner of the gallery. (Making servants climb one flight of stairs to a dining hall is low-risk, but anything more and you're risking an appetizer catastrophe.) I pop it open and haul at the ropes until an unusually generous wooden shelf rises up. Ludwig's zeal for hospitality may just come in handy after all.

Before I get inside, I dash back over to the pedestal and slide my red penny, crown-side up, under the cushion. I don't want Ludwig to know immediately, but I still want him to *know*. Partially so the jeweler he hired doesn't take the blame.

Then I climb into the lift, hanging on to the ropes, and close the cabinet door behind me. I carefully winch the ropes, letting my weight sink the lift down all three stories until I hear the roar of the kitchens. It gets quieter, paradoxically, the closer I get, but I expected that. All the servants are being mustered to the dining hall. There's no noise but the creak of ropes and pulleys by the time the lift stops, and no light but the dim outline of the cupboard door.

I wait a moment to be sure, then push it open and creep out, setting foot on the stone floor of the now-empty kitchens. The back door is still wide-open, and through it I see the carriage house. But I'm not bound there yet.

Instead I run for the uniform room. Once there, I hurriedly yank on a footman's livery, tucking my dress into breeches and buttoning a large waistcoat over the top to hide the strange lumps. When I pull on the outer coat and stuff my braids under the standard brimmed hat, I pass for an awkward stripling of a boy. On my way out, I dump the servant dress I'd borrowed earlier into the soiled laundry.

Then I hurry out to the carriage house behind the kitchens, praying I'm not too late. Guards are stalking around, arguing with grooms and shouting orders. Near the open carriage-house doors, I spot a footboy harnessing a team of harassed-looking geldings to a coach, alone. On his face is the bewildered, intent look of a lad who's been summarily tossed into a lake to learn how to swim—one of the many new hires. Perfect.

I skulk out of sight until he steps back from the yoke and breathes a sigh of relief. Then I bluster in, my voice pitched as low as I can. "What are you doing? Didn't you hear the orders?"

The footboy jumps like a cat confronted with a cucumber. "What? I—I was told to ready the carriage for—"

"We're all supposed to be searching the grounds," I bellow. "You're to check the lakefront walk! Go before they see you slacking!"

I duck out the door and start jogging away. Almost immediately the footboy stumbles out, too, running from the stables. Once he's passed me, I double back and take his place, tugging on leather straps and nodding like I have any idea what they do.

The coachman arrives a minute later. He's much too busy inspecting the yoke and the harnesses to spare more than a glance for me. "All set?"

"Ready, sir," I grunt. The coachman and I lead the horses out of the carriage house and into the yard, then he climbs onto his perch at the front and slaps the reins. As the coach jolts into motion, I grab a handle and swing up to stand on the rear footboard. We roll up to the grand main entrance of the hunting lodge, where Joniza and Emeric are both waiting with politely rigid smiles as the prince prattles on.

I get down to open the carriage door for them while Prince Ludwig offers an emotional farewell with all the substance of a soap bubble. As

Emeric and Joniza get into the coach, I keep my head lowered, hiding as much of my face as I can behind the brim of the hat. When the coachman asks for destinations, Joniza names the Golden Bine.

Emeric, the relentless bastard, asks for the Library of the Divine. He knows that's where I'm headed with the goblet; I'd bet my last penny he's planning on lying in wait until I stroll up.

I shut the carriage door. The coachman cracks the reins, and as the horses break into a trot, I jump onto the footboard once more.

And that's how I leave the hunting lodge: with the prince's prized goblet in my satchel, on the prince's own carriage, right out his front gate. It's not how danger usually arrives, but this time, it's how it leaves.

That's the thing about men like Ludwig, who are so convinced they can win because they already know it's a scam. I win more money off them than anyone else, while they're distracted looking only for the trick they know.

When we stop at the Library of the Divine, Emeric barely notices me as I open the carriage door for him; he's too busy scouring the shadows and the corners and the hedges. Joniza, on the other hand, looks right at my face. She has a sudden coughing fit as Emeric climbs out, and I give her a chipper salute.

I hear the snap of the coachman's reins. This time I let the carriage continue into the night and turn my attention to the library.

Emeric is at the front door, his coin light in one hand, a key for Vikram's padlock in the other. I sneak up behind him while he fusses with the lock. Once the padlock falls open, I tap him on the left shoulder.

He immediately whirls to his left. I sidestep around his right side, staying hidden behind his back as I push open the unlocked library doors. Then I step backward into the foyer.

The hinges betray me with a massive groan, and it's too dark to find a lock or a bar that I can use to keep Emeric out like I was hoping. He follows a moment later. I don't know if it's the harsh coin light or if he really is angrier than I expected.

"What the hell was that, Vanja?" he demands.

"We both showed up to the party wearing the same take-the-goblet plan," I say acidly, digging in my satchel. "Etiquette says one of us has to change, and I was there first."

"*My* plan didn't jump straight to *committing multiple crimes* as the solution," he retorts, and I know he's mad from the way the coin light swings in his hand as he talks. "Ludwig would have returned the goblet on his own if you'd just let me handle this!"

"You want to bet on that?"

"You *used* me to—to distract from *robbing a prince-elector*—you didn't even talk to me first—"

I pull out the apron and start picking open the bundle, sniffing, "I'll have you know, I was asked to."

"Oh, by whom, the gargoyles?" he says sourly.

"Saint Willehalm, actually," I fire back. "He showed up in my dream last night. He's the *poltergeist* and the Armarius, and this"—I heft the goblet—"is part of the binding spell that keeps him here. Which I would have told you if *you* hadn't stood me up for lunch."

I catch a glimpse of the gears turning for Emeric but don't stick around to watch them click into place. Instead I turn on a heel, narrowly avoiding the abandoned doll by the friar statue, and head for the wreckage in the rotunda. "Sextus!" I shout. "I've got your fancy cup!"

The chandeliers ignite a path to the pedestal, flames leaning in the sudden draft. "*Pleeeeease,*" howls the wretched voice that last called me a liar, "*please, give it back!*"

"Yeah, yeah," I mutter as I step over a broken chair, "keep your cowl on."

"Hang on—" A *thunk* reverberates through the rotunda; judging from the startled curse, I'm pretty sure Emeric just walked into a capsized desk. "I did show up for lunch, I waited—"

I stop and turn to face him again, furious that he'd try to sell me (*Me!* A renowned expert in the field of bullshit!) such a blatant lie. "I waited at that park like a little fool for over half an hour, so *don't* tell me you were there."

Emeric looks up from the debris he's wading through. "The park? Proctor Kirkling said she saw you and Helga return to the Book and Bell, so I . . ." He trails off, connecting the dots.

"*Can this waaaait?*" wails the eldritch voice of Saint Willehalm.

"Coming," I snap, and resume picking my way over to the reliquary base. "Right. I see the problem: the words *Kirkling* and *said*."

Emeric's voice frays a little. "Vanja . . . I don't think that's our only problem."

He's right. Kirkling keeps throwing lamp oil on the fire, but we're the coals it's feeding.

I just . . . don't want to talk about this anymore. I'm tired of fighting, of feeling like this. I want to black out for five minutes and wake up and have everything fixed.

But maybe the biggest problem is that I don't even know what *fixed* looks like.

"One thing at a time," I say wearily. I reach the middle of the room, where the remains of the reliquary base are still bolted to the pedestal, and unceremoniously plunk the goblet into place.

A shiver runs through the floor. Hundreds of tiny flames sweep out from the pedestal as every candle, lamp, and torch in the library ignites. A symphony of groaning wood tears through the rotunda, the shattered tables and chairs lurching upright, their splinters knitting into smooth timber. It's hard not to gawk; the empire is full of beasts wretched and divine, but for some reason I never expected a ghost to command this scale of power.

There's a sound like a cascade of parchment, and then the specter of Saint Willehalm towers before me, a little too tall to be human. "*My thanks, God Daughter, for your assistance. Please let me know if there is anything I can do to aid you in the future.*"

"Actually, we first came here to look for records," Emeric says over my shoulder.

Saint Willehalm blinks at him. Then he says stonily, "*I recall you. I believe you threw a knife at my face.*"

There's a thoracic little death rattle behind me. I'm pretty sure it's the sound of Emeric's world crumbling at the fact that he's pissed off the saint of libraries.

Saint Willehalm tips his hood to me. "*Again, please let me know if you require my help in the future, God Daughter. Farewe—*"

"No, no, hold up," I sigh. "Again, you broke every bone in my body"—("*gross hyperbole*")—"so let's let bygones be bygones, all right? I would really appreciate it if you helped Emeric find what he's looking for. Besides, isn't that your whole job?"

"*Fine,*" the ghost grumbles. "*What do you seek to know?*"

I have to motion Emeric forward before he speaks, fussing with his *krebatte* until I pull his hand to his side. "A—" His voice squeaks, and he clears his throat hastily. "Any records you have pertaining to a Low God known as the Scarlet Maiden."

The saint closes his eyes. When he opens them again, he is the Armarius, master of records of the Library of the Divine. The sockets look like vellum held up to the sun, glowing a cloudy, muted gold as symbols and letters scrawl over them.

Then he blinks again and shakes his head. *"I apologize, but I have nothing that mentions a Scarlet Maiden."*

I go abruptly cold.

I did this, then. I conjured her into being myself.

And that means I'm guilty of everything Kirkling said.

Emeric frowns. "Not even prior to the Accord of Prefectorial and Godly Alliance?"

"No."

That's the nail in the coffin. She's lying about predating the accords. And she's doing it to try to claim—no, to kill—Emeric.

Then—I remember Dieter's song trailing out of the Golden Bine. "What about the Red Maid of the River?"

"The Red Maid of the River?" The Armarius's eyes flash that bright vellum again. This time, as letters race across them, I see some ignite, sparking an even brighter gold.

Thuds and rustling echo all around the shelved columns. A veritable swarm of parchments, books, and scrolls bursts from the shelves, weaving around stair and railing, and convenes on the rotunda like a literal cyclone, then settles into an enormous stack that takes up at least three tables. I'm not even sure if we could fit it all into a coach.

The Armarius asks, *"Where do I begin?"*

CHAPTER THIRTEEN

ℝIBBON

"S HE . . . SHE'S REAL, THEN." EMERIC LOOKS A BIT PALE. HE REACHES
for his *krebatte* again but stops short, his fingertips resting over the
red handprint below his shirt.

"Very much so."

I don't feel any better for it. Even if it means I'm off the hook . . .
the seven blood drops will be the only way to save Emeric from the
Scarlet Maiden.

"Do any of *those* records predate the prefect accords?" I ask swiftly.
She could still be lying about evading them.

Some part of me sinks when the Armarius says, *"Nearly all."* He
waves to the stack on the table, returning to Saint Willehalm again as
the vellum fades from his eyes. *"That does mean there are many versions of*

her story, and few can say which are true—certainly not I. But hers is an old, sad tale at its heart. She was a princess before the days of the empire, back when a castle stood in the shadow of the Broken Peak, and was betrothed to the love of her life. Then she lost him to the hellhound, and it's said his blood dyed her red from head to toe. Her tears swept her own castle away and made the river that runs through the gorge now."

"That . . . would explain some things." Emeric thinks a moment. "I'm also going to need any records you have on Low Gods going dormant, especially if they revived at a later date. And ritual sacrifices common to the era. And ritual bindings, siphoning magic, paras—"

"*And how,*" Saint Willehalm asks, mild, "*will you be carrying that out? And returning it?*"

"It's a lot, isn't it?" I sigh.

"*Some two hundred records and counting.*" Saint Willehalm pauses, looking off to the side a moment, as if listening to an unseen speaker. "*I suppose . . . yes, that would be a novel approach. I have an alternative. Wait here, please, I'll return shortly.*"

He winks out, a few papers fluttering in his wake, leaving Emeric and me alone in the enormity of the rotunda.

A stiff beat passes, then I say, "What do you think 'shortly' means to a centuries-old ghost?" at the same time Emeric blurts out, "I should have told you about the first year earlier."

I turn to face him properly, a little surprised. "Uh. You really want to do this now?"

"At this rate there's decent odds we'll be interrupted by—I don't know what next, a haunted doll with a quest? So yes. I need to say this while we have the chance." He steps closer, and his hands are back to fidgeting, tangling with each other. "I *am* sorry I didn't tell you. We didn't really have time before, but I should have made it. I didn't think it would come up this soon and—and I didn't want to scare you."

"Because *this*"—I gesture between us—"has an end date."

But Emeric shakes his head. "Because it doesn't. I mean, not for me."

I blink at him, uncomprehending.

His mouth twists. "I understand the reasoning behind the first-year tradition, but it's an expectation, not a rule. Vikram and Mathilde both say it was awful and didn't teach them anything they didn't already know. And I think it does more harm than good, keeping people from joining the prefects if they already have a partner or children. So I have no intention of following it."

I want it to be true, and yet—"Is that really something you can just *do?*" I push, trying to stifle the tremor in my voice.

"It's not in any prefect code, any charter, anything formal." Emeric's chin stiffens, stubborn as ever. "I looked through them all in January to be certain. This, *us*, is too important to me to throw away for a bad tradition. I'd rather force them to change it than . . . lose you. Again." He swallows. "But I was afraid that might be too much to put on you, too fast." When I don't respond after a moment, he starts knotting his hands together once more. "Please say something."

With tremendous effort, I squeak out, "*January?*"

All this time, he's been ready to fight. To stay with me. And all I did was run.

His ears turn pink. "I—I thought you would be there soon, and the Finding wasn't supposed to take this long, and—oh." He stops short as I collide with his chest, my hands balling up in his lapels.

"I'm sorry I said that stupid thing about ditching me," I say into his *krebatte* in a rush. "I'm—I'm sorry I left you in Helligbrücke—"

"No, you told me what happened and I threw it in your face." Emeric's arms wind around me as he huffs a short tense laugh. "Much like the dung *you* threw at *me* this afternoon."

"Oh. Sorry for that too."

"You absolutely are not."

"I'm really not," I confess. "It was hilarious."

"Agree to disagree," he says dourly. Then he pulls back to look me in the face, concern stealing over his. "There's something else. You said you're not good enough for me, and, Vanja, I have *never* thought that."

"The first week we met, you recited the specific prefect chapter and verse that says you're better than me," I fire back. "'*Something something association with miscreants, something something taints your character*' ring any tainted bells?"

Emeric mutters, "*Charter of the Prefect, Article Seven,*" under his breath. "Fair point, and I almost *immediately* learned how wrong I was. But for as long as we have been together, I have never thought you're not good enough for me. And I think you know that." His voice turns tentative, careful. "I think the real issue might be . . . you don't believe you're good enough."

It's the kind of truth too painful to deny, even worse to own, and all the more terrible to hear someone else say aloud. I squeeze my eyes shut and lean my forehead against his sternum, trying to keep my face from crumpling. It's enough of a confirmation, even without words. The weight of his chin settles between my braids a moment later.

"I don't know how to help that," he whispers, "but, High Gods and Low, I'm going to try. Starting here." There's an odd crinkle, then paper is pressed into my hands. I open my eyes.

It's a folded page, a muted stain along one edge, that lets off a whiff of coffee when I peel it open. Words scrawl before me, familiar even though I read them only once, months ago. *I know bravery is real because I see you choose it every day.*

Emeric wrote this to me in Minkja, when everything seemed lost and all we had was hope traced onto mirrors.

If you want me to chase you, I will chase you. If you want me to find you, I will find you.

"I want you to keep this, so anytime you feel that way, you will know I couldn't disagree more," he says fiercely. "I want you to remember that, as long as you'll have me, I will choose you every time."

I can't—I can't find the words, because for so long I have lived afraid of feeling like this, like roots might grow through my skin instead of thorns, and I wonder if roses, too, fear the moment the petals break through the bud. But bloom they must, and answer I must, so I lift my face to the sun, feeling the tempo of his heart quicken as my lips brush his.

I don't know if he'll be able to just ignore tradition, written or not; I don't know if I can find it in me to believe I'm worth the trouble I bring to the door. But when he returns my kiss, it feels like a promise, and for now, that is enough.

I let myself be still a moment, let myself be held the way he does it, like letting go means losing something. Finally I mumble, "You're not going to let me say I don't deserve this, are you?"

"I am not," he says archly, his arms tightening. "I might not let go until you say you do, in fact."

"Hm. Terrible disincentive." Then I hold up a fistful of ribbon I found while rummaging through his pockets. (Old habits, you know the saying.) "Now what is *this* for?"

Emeric's eyes widen, and one arm peels free to make a frantic swipe for the ribbon. "That's not—you weren't supposed to—"

I flick my hand out of reach, grinning, and take a better look. It's not one ribbon but two, tablet-woven, fern green, laced with a pattern of leaves in cream thread, dotted periodically with red roses. Then I connect the dots. "Is this for *me*?"

"I, er." Emeric appears to be going into rigor mortis, apart from his ears turning a distinctly vibrant crimson once again. "You always pick the Queen of Roses for your card, and I saw it in a store this morning, and I—I thought it might—look nice with your hair—and then I went into a sort of fugue state, and when I came out I had two lengths of ribbon and one less *sjilling.* So yes. It's for you."

"But you were mad at me this morning," I say, confused.

He shifts in place, the flush spreading to his cheeks. "I can be upset and still think you deserve nice things."

I look from him to the ribbons and then back. I can't quite wrap my mind around it, him buying something just because I might like it.

"Please don't look at me like that," Emeric says wretchedly. "I already want to die. This was a terrible idea. Forget I—"

I hand him the ribbons. "Will you tie them on?"

It's his turn to be rendered speechless; he only blushes a bit harder and nods. He draws my right braid over my shoulder, slides the simple string tie off the end, and deftly winds one ribbon into a neat bow in its place. He takes a bit more time with the left one, letting the braid run through his fingers before undoing the tie, and as I watch his hands work, I suddenly wish we were at the inn so he wouldn't stop with the string.

Emeric pulls the second bow taut just as the ghastly creak of Saint Willehalm's voice rasps from off to one side, "*I can come back later?*"

Both of us jump nearly out of our skins. "*Saints* and martyrs," I gasp.

"*Present,*" Willehalm says with the air of someone who has been saving the joke for a special occasion. "*I have a way for you to access any record in my library from anywhere in the Blessed Empire. I would like you to meet Lady Ambroszia.*"

He drifts over and, to my utter dismay, gently places the ceramic doll from the foyer into Emeric's hands.

"Oh," Emeric says, all but vibrating with discomfort. ". . . Thank . . . you."

Up close, the doll is even more unsettling. Tailors use dolls like this to mock up and advertise clothing without committing to the full garment, and it's not uncommon to give them to local children once they're damaged or out of date. Lady Ambroszia is a particularly enthralling combination of both. She's wearing a black gown that would have been the height of fashion fifteen years ago, and her yellow horsehair curls have faded to a dingy oatmeal hue that still clashes with the rosy red blotches painted onto the apples of her bone-white cheeks. One blue eye is weighted and painted, so it should slide shut when she's laid down, but it rolls and darts like a real eyeball. I'd say the other eye is less upsetting, as it's just an empty black hole in the porcelain, if not for the single pinprick of steady white gazing out.

Her faded pink painted lips do not move, but a woman's reedy voice says clear as day, "I apologize for this unworthy vessel. In life, my pulchritude was the subject of *great* renown."

Emeric almost drops the doll.

"*Lady Ambroszia is an old friend of mine who knows these records nearly as well as I do,*" Saint Willehalm chuckles. "*She has always wanted to see more of the world, and while she is in this vessel, I have granted her the power to show you any document within the library at your request. She will be your link here while you travel.*"

Emeric's brow furrows. "I didn't know this was possible."

"Unique circumstances," Lady Ambroszia chirps. "Most of us are inherently connected to the place where we . . . became unalive. With sweet Willi's help, I can use that connection to summon a projection of anything in the library, like thus."

A blinding beam of light bursts from her empty eyehole, shining directly into Emeric's face. He does drop the doll this time, swearing.

I swoop to catch Lady Ambroszia before her porcelain can shatter on the floor. She blinks the light off. "Apologies, again. I will have full control of this vessel's movement eventually, but at present, certain . . . regulations are beyond me."

"Not a problem. One key question." It's decidedly weird to address a doll in my hands, so I sit her up on a stack of books. "You *died* here?"

There's an uncomfortable pause. Saint Willehalm coughs, sheepish. "*We . . . didn't always have railings for the shelves.*"

"You're not planning on venturing to great heights anytime soon, yes?" Ambroszia asks. "It's rather a *thing* for me."

Emeric's still rubbing his eyes. "We'll figure something out. Thank you very much, Your Hallowedness. This will be immeasurably helpful."

"*Thank the God Daughter,*" Saint Willehalm says. "*She aided me when none else could. Now, if you'll excuse me, the reshelving's backed up atrociously while I've been gone. You know where to find me—unless someone steals the goblet again. Then it might be something of a treasure hunt.*"

He waves a hand. Ambroszia floats over to us as the bookstack takes to the air and trails Saint Willehalm out of the rotunda.

"You may carry me in your satchel," Lady Ambroszia announces imperiously. "Keep me away from your silver knife, though. And make certain my head clears the top so I can see."

"As her ladyship wishes," Emeric says, a little strangled, only to have to pass her off to me when it turns out his cloak blocks her view. Once I'm done arranging the doll in my satchel, Emeric holds out his hand. "We never did get that walk."

"Better late than never." I take it and let him lead us out.

There's a strange current between us as we step into the night under the watchful eye of a full moon. It's not as if we haven't held hands before, but I'm unnervingly aware of his thumb running along my knuckles, of the simmer in my belly, of the moments I glance up and see his eyes lingering on me too.

I don't know what I want when we get back to our room at the inn.

I think—I think I want more of him than before. I might want all of him. I still know wanting and getting are not the same.

But if there were any time I believed we could be wholly, dangerously vulnerable with each other, it might be tonight.

We detour by a night market so I can grab something to eat, but don't speak much beyond humming vague acknowledgments as Ambroszia exclaims over the changes to Dänwik since her time. The butterflies in my stomach only swell in number, and by the time we see the morning glory–spangled face of the Book and Bell, I'm afraid to open my mouth lest they come bursting out.

The evening's still young enough to have a respectable number of people in the dining room, though it's nowhere near last night's crowd. Before we make it to the stairs to our room, I hear raised voices from another table. When I look, I find Helga arguing with a woman I don't know. All I catch is Helga's snarl of "... *you to wait!*" before her gaze lands on me.

The other woman twists in her chair. She looks to be a couple of years older than Helga, pale-faced and stoutly built, with deep brown hair and sharp eyes black as coal. Those sharp eyes widen when they find me, her expression awash with apprehension as she gets to her feet. Helga seizes the woman's arm and says something inaudible. She doesn't let go until the strange woman nods.

Only a fool would still believe that Helga Ros is helping me solely out of the goodness of her heart.

Then the stranger walks toward me, Helga on her heels. "Vanja?" she asks.

Strange motives or not, I automatically distrust anyone Helga's suspicious of, considering she knew to distrust me from the moment we met. "Who's asking?"

The woman stops short, drawing her clenched fists up to her throat.

There's something . . . odd, I decide, about her face. Not familiar in the comfortable way, or even in the same way as Dieter Ros. It feels like I've seen disparate parts of it before, just never assembled like this.

"My name is Eida," she says, with the slow deliberation of someone waiting for a reaction. "I—I—" She looks over her shoulder to Helga, almost guiltily.

"*Don't*—" Helga starts, reaching for her elbow.

Eida knocks Helga away and steps forward, then grabs my free hand in hers. "Vanja, it's *me*. Your sister."

PART TWO:

SCARLET THORNS

THE FIFTH LIE

DESIRE

ONCE UPON A TIME, THERE WAS A PRINCESS, A COUNTESS, AND A MAID-servant who grew thorns from her back.

At least, that's what the maid thought they looked like: briars of welt and scab that branched all over her shoulders and lower, climbing her spine like a trellis. They had been planted in her flesh a week earlier with a whip and a clumsy hand, because the cruel little countess told a lie about the maid, the princess kept the truth to herself, and nothing the maid said made a difference.

The hedgewitch who had treated the maid afterward said there would be scars from the whipping, but that her salves would help. The maid had to take her word for it; the castle's mirrors were scarce and the time to gaze upon her back even scarcer. Her one friend in the castle, a magician, told the maid what she saw when she helped dress the wounds each night, and most days that had to be enough. The maid told herself no good could come of seeing the ugly marks with her own eyes.

One morning, the maidservant felt the hot itchy pull of a too-tight scab tearing as she scrubbed the floors, felt the sticky damp patch spread between her shoulders, and in the afternoon, she finally had a chance to survey the damage. She had just finished laying down clean rugs in the princess's bedchambers—rugs were for company, after all; no one of import was to know they used straw for rushes in Sovabin most of the time—when she spied the princess's small hand mirror on the vanity.

The vanity, too, had a mirror, and the princess was off keeping the countess entertained, and all was quiet in the living chambers, and so the maid decided to take the risk.

She undid her kirtle ties and loosened her shift collar and gingerly freed the linen where it had stuck to skin until finally her back was bare. Then she picked up the hand mirror and faced away from the vanity, and saw what had been done to her.

The whipping gashes were a dull red, still feverish and tender around cracking scabs. The longest of them had split earlier, and the maid was trying to see if the blood had dried when a voice carried across the room: "Hideous."

The maid froze.

The cruel little countess stood in the doorway, a sad little smile curling her lips. "Don't move," she whispered, "don't speak, or I'll say I caught you stealing again."

The maid did not move.

The little countess gamboled over, arranging herself behind the maid, head tilted and lips puckered as she inspected what she had wrought. "Disgusting," she mused, "like great bloody worms. How are they healing so fast? Tell me."

The maidservant did not want her salve to be taken away, so she said, in a shaking voice, "I clean them every day, my lady."

The little countess met her gaze in the hand mirror. Then, to the maid's surprise, the countess slapped herself, hard. A vivid red mark began to bloom on her pale cheek.

There was something like a fever in her eyes when the little countess said, "I'll say you struck me, and they'll hang you like a dog for laying a hand on a noble. Tell me *now*."

The maid knew that, or worse, would befall her. She swallowed. "A-a hedgewitch gave me a salve, my lady."

"I see." The countess twirled a soft nutmeg ringlet around a finger, one the maid had curled into the countess's hair with a hot iron this morning. "You know, Father says servants are like hounds. The best ones are loyal, obedient, don't think themselves clever." The countess let the ringlet fall away and touched the edge of a scab. "The worst ones—not a sound or I'll scream"—the hard crescent of a fingernail dug into the maid's sore back—"the *worst* ones won't learn a lesson without *pain*."

The countess ripped the whole strip of scab off the maid's back.

The maid jerked, trying to strangle a cry as best she could as searing-bright agony flashed between her shoulders. A warm trickle seeped down her spine.

"You need to suffer so you'll learn your place," the countess hummed with bliss. "You think you're clever, don't you? And maybe you're clever enough for that cow Gisele, but I know what you are. Now your back is as ugly as your front. No wonder you were abandoned here, you're horrible to look at from every side. It's what you deserve. No one will ever want a lover who's covered in worms."

Quick as a flash, the countess peeled away another long scab. The maid bit her tongue to keep silent, squeezing her eyes shut.

"Look at me," ordered the countess.

The maid forced herself to obey, meeting the countess's icy-blue eyes in the mirror once more. The red mark of her own hand had not faded. All it would take was one scream and one more lie, and the countess could end the maid's life.

The countess cooed, "I want you to say it. Show me you've learned. Say you're ugly."

"I'm ugly," the maidservant said, for she knew what she was.

"Say no one will ever want you."

"No one will ever want me," the maidservant repeated, in a voice that cracked like her scabs, for in her thirteen years of life, no one had. Her mother had left her to her godmothers, and her godmothers had left her to the von Falbirgs, and the von Falbirgs had left her to the whipping post.

"Say you don't *deserve* to be loved."

The maid told herself this much was a lie. Even so, the words didn't taste like one; there was only blood on her tongue when she said, "I do not deserve to be loved."

With a vicious twist, the countess tore one last ribbon of scab free.

"Remember your lesson," she hissed in the maid's ear, and by the time the pain had faded enough for the maid to see again, the countess was gone.

❧

That night, I was startled to find the precious jar of salve still hidden beneath my bedroll by the hearth; I'd thought for certain Irmgard would take it. The hedgewitch and her salve had cost Joniza all the month's wages she hadn't already sent to her family in Sahali. Nevertheless, when I had tried to work through the sums and figures for how much I could repay her each month, she only waved her hand. "My father would say your name is not in my ledger. Pay me when you have the money." On our meager earnings, we both knew that would take a very, very long time.

But after Joniza had sucked her teeth in anger and sympathy at my rebloodied back and began carefully salving the marks once more . . . that was when we learned Irmgard's game. Joniza was nearly done daubing the dark paste over the gashes when the salve began to burn everywhere it touched. Even Joniza began to curse, shaking her hand to no avail. She rushed to wipe the salve off us both with a wet rag, but still it burned and burned and burned.

The hedgewitch would later tell us someone had mixed in soot and the juice of starch-root berries. The juice was for pain; it raised blisters on the broken skin. The soot was to leave a permanent stain in my wounds. A reminder of what I was.

At the time, I knew Joniza could not afford to replace the salve. Neither would I ask more of her. After all, Irmgard was right: I was already abandoned, already too ugly to be desired. Nothing a hedgewitch brewed could salvage that.

You would think Irmgard wouldn't let me bring a hot iron anywhere near her the next morning, but once again, she insisted I curl her hair. And I did it, meticulously winding the locks around scalding metal just inches from her bare neck. She smiled at me the entire time.

She never once believed she was in danger. She had no fear that I might "slip" and burn her, might swing the iron into her jaw, might inflict on her even a moment of the torment she bestowed on me.

We both knew I wouldn't do any of that.

We both knew I would remember my lesson.

We both knew what I was.

CHAPTER FOURTEEN

FLAME TO FUSE

*S*ISTER.

The impossible word is a fist around my throat. No, no, it's wrong. It can't be.

I tear my hand free from this stranger's. "I don't know you," I gasp.

"You were so little when we lost you," the stranger—*Eida?*—says in an urgent, ecstatic rush, "I used to braid your hair every night, Katrin Little made you a rag doll you called Strietzelina, like the bread—"

Maybe if I'd known, maybe if I had time to think, I could have steeled myself, but I can't—she's so happy, and I don't know what to say, how to tell her what I am—"I don't *know you*," I repeat helplessly, trying to step back and colliding with Emeric as I do.

Eida babbles on: "You carried her everywhere, you cried for a whole day when one of the horses bit her and—"

I don't know what to do, I don't know if this stranger is really my sister, I am terrified she is and terrified she isn't, I should be weeping with joy, I've already ruined it—

"Enough," I hear Helga bark.

"Luisa had to pretend to be a hedgewitch who healed her—"

"*Enough, Eida!*"

I think I hear Emeric say my name; I am shrinking inside myself, haunting my own skull. The world is a blur, one I am moving through like a ghost, untouched and untouchable.

It was a routine, comfortable ache, the hole where my idea of a family had been. I knew I wanted answers. I just wasn't ready to ask the questions, not yet.

When my head clears, the first thing I'm aware of is the anchor of Emeric's hands wrapped around mine, resting on a tabletop. We're in a quiet corner of the dining room.

Eida is gone. Helga is maneuvering around tables and chairs, heading for us.

"What," Emeric asks tautly when she comes into earshot, "was that?"

Helga runs a hand over her face, then fixes her squint on me. "Vanja? Are you back with us?"

"Sorry," I mumble. "Yeah."

"No, it's not your fault. That wasn't supposed to . . ." Helga drops into the seat across from me, chewing on her bottom lip. "Eida is an old acquaintance of mine. Her youngest sister, who happened to be named Vanja, went missing when they were very young. I knew the chances were slim, but she lives a little north of Welkenrode, so I wrote her to suggest setting up a meeting between you two when we get there.

Instead she arrived here an hour ago and wouldn't leave. I *told* her this was too sudden, but . . ."

I don't know what to say. It still doesn't seem real. It can't be this easy.

"Either way," Helga continues, ire rising in her tone, "she's not coming back unless you tell me you want to speak to her, all right? She won't ambush you again."

"Do you know how many siblings she has?" Emeric asks. "Where the family's from?"

Helga's mouth purses. "She has three sisters, apart from the lost one," she says after a pause. "The family's from Kerzenthal."

My stomach wrenches. I spit out a sick little laugh, angry with myself for my dismay as much as for my infant hope. "Then she's not my sister. I had twelve siblings. And I was abandoned in Sovabin. I doubt my mother walked all the way across the empire to do that." I stand abruptly, feeling like a fool, like this corner is a prison cell. "I'm going to bed."

"Vanja—" Helga starts.

"I appreciate the intent," I bite out, "but I'll decide when I'm ready to find my family."

I hear Emeric say something to her as I head for the stairs to our room. He falls in step behind me and doesn't speak again until we're inside, the door shutting behind us. There's a rustle of a gesture, and the candle on the nightstand lights, shedding just enough light to see by. "Do you want to talk about it?"

I've wandered into the middle of the room, my cloak hanging loose in my hands, and I can't think of why, can't think of anything but how I'm almost certain I've seen Eida's face before. How I'm just as certain I'm deluding myself so I can believe someone would drop everything and ride for days to see me.

How I want more than anything to hear my mother made a mistake that midwinter night, and how I thought, for a moment, Eida could tell me.

"No," I say, hoarse.

Everything I've felt today is swelling again, shame like a baritone, brassy anger, piped riffs of euphoria, and forlorn strings, straining at the drumbeat seam of fear, a cacophony I can't shut out.

My back warms as Emeric draws close, runs his knuckles down my arm. It's meant to be comforting, but it's touching flame to a fuse.

The hairs on my neck stand as he says softly, "Whatever you need."

I need to *not* talk, to not think. I need the anchor of him, to feel like I belong somewhere, to someone.

I turn and pull him to me, into a kiss that draws a faint startled sound from him. It's followed by another when I rake my teeth along his bottom lip. He matches me after a moment, his fingers flexing against my back with each shudder when my nails press into the sides of his throat, but he breaks away long enough to gasp, "Vanja, are you *sure* this is—"

"*Yes.*" I shrug off my satchel and let it fall to the floor with a *thunk*, then pull his over his head and let it follow suit before grabbing his *krebatte* to bring our bodies flush. This, this is simple, this is easy, this is good, and I need that right now.

I half push him onto the bed, half let him drag me there, too, both of us awkwardly kicking off boots. He keeps his mouth on mine as he goes to work on my stolen waistcoat. It feels like its own kind of magic—at least until I shrug it off and he makes a face at me. "How do you have a whole dress on under there?" he grumbles. "That's not fair."

"Thought you'd mind the breeches more," I admit.

Emeric shakes his head, a faint hazy gleam in his eyes as a flush stains his cheeks. "The breeches are . . . they look . . . I like them." The last words come out in a stilted hurry. His hands run down my sides, lingering at my hips. "But can they, er . . . go?"

"Trade you," I return. "My breeches, your shirt."

His grin is positively unholy in the dim candlelight. Then I feel fingers on my waistband and forfeit the ability to think a coherent thought. "Dress?" he murmurs, and I nod, a little too addicted to the feeling of being undone. I'm left only in my linen shift when he sits up, and as I pull his shirt over his head, he sucks in a breath. A hand grazes my bare knee. As it slides higher, it's my turn for a startled noise and my turn, too, to double it when he bows his head to trail kisses down my collarbone, each one longer, more insistent, than the last.

Then we're shifting again, Emeric's weight bearing me into the mattress this time, our legs tangling in a way that somehow feels lush. His lips return to mine, and we slide into something almost like a rhythm—

I think we both realize what's happening at nearly the same time. He pushes himself up on an elbow to look down at me, a soft desperation in his eyes, somewhere between hope and apprehension. I know it because it's thrumming through my bones. Neither of us seems to have the words, a long, volatile pause expanding between us.

Then Emeric lifts my hand in his, eyes never leaving mine. Slowly and deliberately, he traces a circle into my palm with his thumb.

I know exactly what he is asking.

This is faster, sooner than I thought it'd be, but I might be ready. I know I want more—I want to know what happens with nothing between us—

But I will have nowhere to hide.

The thought knifes through the haze, straight into the part of me that may never leave Sovabin. The candlelight is meager, but it is not enough to cover my back, my scars. I know Emeric cares for me; I know he has said again and again that he wants me as I am. But this is not a fear that listens to reason. It's a fear borne of saying *No one will ever want me* and having only silence answer.

Then a whispery rattle of a voice trickles up from the floor: "If you are going to commence conjugal relations, you may wish to turn me to face a wall."

The heady bubble of intimacy between us unceremoniously pops.

It turns out there are few things that kill the mood faster than realizing you have a haunted doll for a voyeur.

"I regret to be so forthright," Lady Ambroszia adds as Emeric and I stare at each other, teetering on the precipice of unbridled hysteria. "There just seemed to be quite a lot of personal matters being addressed, and then you took up with each other so quickly, I scarcely had time to remind you of my presence."

My gaze slides off the bed, over to the floor. Sure enough, Lady Ambroszia is lying half out of my satchel, both her painted eye and the glowing white light in the missing one fixed on us.

"Thank you," I croak, "for bringing this to our attention."

Emeric presses a brief kiss to my fingertips, then lets go, pushing off the bed. "Privy," he tells me under his breath. "Be right back."

"You needn't worry about offending my sensibilities, young man," the doll calls after him. "I merely wished to advise you that I am at an unfortunate angle to observe your activities. Low Gods know I engaged in salacious intrigues aplenty in my youth."

I take a moment to collect myself, both disgruntled and . . . relieved. Relieved? That can't be right.

It's tossed onto the growing list of things I'll dissect later, once my head's less of a muddle. I roll out of bed, brushing off my shift, and pick up Lady Ambroszia. "I think that's the end of that for the night, but I'm guessing you'd rather be looking elsewhere anyway."

The light in her eye socket blinks. "Indeed. We shall discuss privacy arrangements in the morning, but for now, you may place me to gaze out the window."

I get her set up in a window overlooking the street outside. "Tell me if you see anything juicy."

"Most assuredly." After a beat, she adds, "Earlier it seemed that you had your concerns, but that boy is really quite smitten, you know."

I can *feel* my entirely undignified, revoltingly sappy smile. It feels good to be honest for once when I say, "I know."

ᴄᴜᴊᴜᴖ

The next morning starts off infinitely better than the day before: I wake up curled against Emeric again, but this time I stay that way, content just to feel the rise and fall of his chest under my cheek.

Part of me can't help but wonder how this would be different if we hadn't stopped where we did, if Ambroszia hadn't been here. Would I still feel this safe, this wanted? Or would I be replaying every moment, trying to pinpoint when I lost him?

Maybe . . . maybe that's where the relief came from.

I thought I was ready. No, I thought I *might* be. But *so much* happened yesterday. I know I wanted to shut everything out, I know I wanted to disappear into something, anything.

Emeric deserves so much more than to be used as my escape. And I don't want to *think* I'm ready; I want to know.

But the red fingers of the handprint on his chest shiver with every heartbeat below my cheek, a cold reminder: We have just over two months to track down the four remaining Ros brothers, or I'll have to stake my own claim on Emeric, ready or not.

Emeric goes still a moment, then draws in a long breath through his nose. He opens an eye to peer at me. "Good. You're here. I have an idea."

"Good morning to you too," I huff, flustered. Apparently abandonment issues are still on the agenda. "What do you mean, 'you're here'?"

The worry dissipates as he rolls over, flops bonelessly onto me, and plants an onslaught of kisses on the side of my face. "Rude," he mumbles between deliberately obnoxious smooching, "now I'm not telling you my idea."

I make an entirely insincere effort to stop giggling and push him off, more for dignity's sake than anything. "You like it when I'm rude."

"I do. It's very inconvenient." He relents and reaches over me to get his spectacles from where they sit next to my ribbons on the nightstand. "And what I *meant* by 'you're here' was, last night Miss Ardîm told me she'd be meeting you here for breakfast at seven o'clock sharp. Unless I'm mistaken, that should be . . ." He pauses, holding up a finger.

A moment later, the seven o'clock bells begin to chime.

I gawk up at him. "No. You can't just *decide* you'll wake up at seven."

He shrugs, smug and unrepentant as he settles the spectacles on his face. "It's a gift."

"You're a monster."

"Only when called for." He whips the blankets off me as I yelp. "And *you're* late."

I put a pillow over his face and scuttle out of bed, grumbling. Only then do I realize Lady Ambroszia isn't on the sill anymore; she's seated on the floor, near our discarded clothing, flipping awkwardly through Emeric's notebook with her stiff porcelain hands. It seems her mobility's increased since yesterday. "Oh, good morning, your ladyship."

"Ambroszia will do," she says distractedly. "One tends to surrender the need for formality after observing one's companions in the throes of passion, however truncated. Young man, is this all of your documentation concerning the situation with the Red Maid of the River?"

Emeric's eyebrows rise. "Not precisely. My supervisor, Proctor

Kirkling . . . *suggested* I leave some of my notes in her custody overnight. I'm going to report to her shortly if you'd like to join me."

"Thank you, I would indeed." She turns a page. "I should like to assist you as best I can. My Nibelungus may not have taken me traveling as much as I wished, but I still found ways to be useful in life and will continue to do so now."

I frown, wondering where I've heard that name before. Emeric provides the answer a moment later as he teeters to his feet. "You mean . . . Nibelungus von Wälft?"

"*Prinz* von Wälft, if we were nasty." She chuckles upsettingly. "I mostly called him 'Nibsi.' You may have seen some of my statues around the hunting lodge."

I stop in the middle of tying on the first kirtle I could find. "You were his mistress?"

"Not the first," she says haughtily, "but certainly the last."

Emeric tugs on one of my braids. "I hate to interrupt, but Miss Ardîm *is* waiting."

"Then you'd better get my ribbons," I return, reaching for my boots.

"Oh. Right." He puts on his best calm-and-collected front as he fetches them from the bedside table, but I can't help noticing him stand a bit straighter, a pleased quirk in the corner of his mouth, while he ties the bows.

I stand on tiptoe to kiss his cheek. "Meet us downstairs after your report. And maybe kick Kirkling in the shin for me."

"Done." He cocks his head. "Minus the kicking. I suspect that would result in considerable setbacks all around."

"Ugh." I duck out the door, calling back, "It'd be worth it!"

Joniza is, in fact, waiting for me downstairs. Thankfully, she doesn't have the crease in her brow that comes with waiting long. She's also dressed more plainly than usual, in a long tunic of Sahalian make, practical woolen leggings, and sturdy boots, her twisting locks arranged in a simple knot atop her head and secured with a cloth headband. The stage cosmetics are gone; only hints of golden paint are under her fingernails.

Before I can speak, she holds up a hand. "Here's what's going to happen. We're going to order breakfast. Then we're going to sit down. And then you're going to tell me exactly what I was an accomplice to last night, and why, and both of those answers better be *damn good*, understand? Then, and *only* then, will we discuss why we both are here. Any questions?"

"Um." I twist a braid around a finger. "Should I start with the corpse goblet or the cult?"

Joniza closes her eyes. "I know better," she mutters to herself. "I *know* better, so *why* do I keep getting into these situations?"

I adjust my approach. "*Orrrr* I could start by buying you breakfast."

It doesn't take as long as I expected to catch her up over egg pancakes doused with applesauce. (This is almost certainly due to her familiarity with my particular brand of idiocy.) The only thing she seems to find more entertaining than the goblet's misadventures is the desolation of Dieter Ros.

"If he wants the gig as Prince Ludwig's bard, he can have it," she scoffs around a mouthful of pancake. "The only thing that man loves more than himself is the sound of his own voice. Besides, I'm leaving the day after tomorrow, so there's a job opening."

"Right, not to be rude, but . . ." I gesture with my fork. "What are you even doing *here*?"

Joniza heaves a sigh. "You remember my baba?"

"*Meister* Bajeri!" In an instant I'm eight again, running around bright painted wagons with a bright paper bird on a wire flapping its wings behind me. Every three years, the Ardîms' trade caravan would pass through Sovabin on its route, with Joniza's father and sister at the head. "Is Fatatuma with him?"

"No, and *that's* why I'm here." Joniza sighs. "This was supposed to be her first circuit as caravan leader, but she's pregnant, and even if her wife wouldn't worry herself sick, Baba doesn't want to risk his first grandchild being born up here. He's too old to do the circuit on his own—don't tell him I said that—so I told him I had an ugly breakup and wanted to get out of Bóern for a while."

"Aw. I thought you and Bastiano were cute. You know, for archnemeses."

"Oh, we are, he's still waiting for me in Minkja." Joniza tries to toss her hair over a shoulder, then remembers it's all bound atop her head and smoothly turns the toss into a shrug. "Don't tell Baba that either. We're headed to Rammelbeck on Tuesday, and with any luck, we'll sell enough there that he can start the return trip and get back before Fatatuma has her baby."

"We're going to Rammelbeck next, too, but probably not that soon." I look up as the chair beside me scrapes back. "All done with your report?"

Emeric drops into the seat with his own plate of pancakes. He's all but cloaked in a suspiciously self-satisfied air. "Good morning, Miss Ardîm. And yes, I'm done. You'd be amazed at how well Proctor Kirkling gets along with Lady Ambroszia." He slices into the stack. "Which is good, because she'll be spending her nights with the proctor from now on."

"How did you manage that?" I demand. "If anything, I thought Kirkling would find *more* haunted dolls for our room just to spite us."

"Exactly." Emeric spears a bite on his fork with a smirk. "So I told her you and Ambroszia were nearly inseparable already. She insisted on *confiscating* Ambroszia at the end of each workday so you can't"—he makes a vague gesture—"something something 'taint the case,' you know. It was just an excuse. And credit where credit's due, Ambroszia's performance was a triumph. I'm actually starting to get quite attached. But this should buy us at least a few days of privacy before we leave for Rammelbeck."

Joniza looks from him to me. "Have you reserved a coach already?"

"No," Emeric says, "I thought if we left on Thursday, we'd make it to the city by . . . oh no. The Week of Barley starts Saturday, doesn't it?"

Joniza nods grimly.

"*Scheit.*" I gnaw on a thumb tip. The Week of Barley is a weeklong holiday for the House of the High, one typically celebrated as a family. "We can double-check with Mathilde, but that sounds right. And it's going to be even harder to leave with the guild negotiations."

"At least a fifth of the attendees will leave town no later than Wednesday to make it home in time," Joniza confirms, "which means the contract negotiations have to wrap up in the next few days, so *everyone* will clear out anyway, not just the House of the High. On the walk here, I heard a coach service tell a man they're booked solid until next Saturday."

"Unfortunate. I wonder if . . ." Emeric keeps talking, but I miss it. My attention has been poached.

There's a woman standing near the dining room's entrance, pretending to read a menu. I know her face; I remember the hunger in her black eyes when she called me "sister."

Eida sneaks another look my way, only to blanch when our eyes meet. I jump to my feet to try to catch her. I don't know why—she's not family, I don't know what I'd say, only that I'd be a disappointment—

Then, without warning, my vision floods with red.

It's as if I'm floating in a sea of crimson mist, awareness without form. Something like a distant current roars in my ears, weaving into words.

"*My prophet*," the Scarlet Maiden coos. Burning roses bloom all around me in the haze. "*I have grave news. The hellhound's hunger grows more terrible by the hour. If we wait until midsummer for the sacred feast, it will be too late.*"

The scarlet handprint pulses in my sight, emitting a spray of embers.

"*Bring me my servant, or my sacrifice, before the moon wanes, waxes, and wanes again. Fail and Hagendorn will be damned.*"

The full moon was last night; that's six weeks. And it's going to take at least three weeks to track down the rest of the Ros brothers and make it back to Hagendorn.

No—four, now that every ride out of Dänwik has been claimed.

I have no mouth to tell this to the Scarlet Maiden, though, and she doesn't seem to want to listen; the mist yields to dark as abruptly as it took me. New voices pierce through.

"—*nja*," Emeric is saying urgently. "Vanja, please—"

"Her eyes." I hear Helga too. How long have I been out?

Not that long, it seems—the ceiling of the Book and Bell's dining room is slowly fading back into sight, blurry shadows sharpening into Emeric, Helga, and Joniza as they hover over me. An ache radiates from one side. I don't see Eida anywhere.

"There you are." Emeric presses fingers to the pulse in my chin, relief all but bleeding from him. "Are you hurt? What happened?"

I let him help me sit up as I croak out, "We have a problem."

CHAPTER FIFTEEN

THE LANTERN

THE FIRST TIME I MET BAJERI ARDÎM WAS IN COLD SOVABIN.

I was four months away from turning nine, and he was passing through as part of his trade route. Or at least, that's what he said at the time; looking back on it now, I know it hardly made business sense to pass through a minute, half-beggared principality in the southeast corner of the Blessed Empire every three years, coming or going. But in those days, Joniza was only a little older than I am now, and it did not take long for me to understand that Bajeri would have crossed every ocean in the world twice over if she needed him.

That, however, does not make him any less shrewd of a business-man. It's probably why we got along so well whenever he arrived in

Sovabin. And now, as he sits rubbing his chin in the parlor of Dänwik's prefect outpost, I can tell he's weighing his options.

Bajeri knows as well as I do that the Order of Prefects of the Godly Courts is hardly suffering from a budget shortfall. He's seen the impatience in Kirkling's stare, the jitter of Mathilde's fingers drumming on her armrest, how Emeric keeps adjusting how he's sitting. Joniza and I know precisely how this will play out, and we're both content to watch Bajeri do what he does best.

He takes his time, adjusting how the drape of his vivid blue agbada falls over his broad chest, thoughtfully tugging at the matching brimless damask hat that covers his bald head.

"So," he says, "you wish for me to take four of you prefects, and two additional passengers, to Rammelbeck with my caravan."

Mathilde's brown curls bounce as she shakes her head. "Three prefects, three additional passengers. Same number total."

Bajeri looks pointedly at Kirkling.

I explain helpfully, "Inspector Kirkling is decommissioned."

"Proctor," Kirkling snips.

Bajeri glances up to me, a nigh-imperceptible gleam of amusement in his eyes. His voice rises a hair. "And I am to do this for free, you tell me?"

"No, no, definitely not, sir," Emeric sputters.

"Because this is no small thing you ask for." Bajeri *sounds* mildly affronted. "I must make space in the wagons, so I must sell things here at a cheaper price than what Rammelbeck will offer."

Emeric nods. "We can cover that loss and pay fare up front, and we are happy to contribute as well to your food and travel supplies."

Before Bajeri can speak, Kirkling interjects, "And Schmidt will pay her own way."

Bajeri rubs his chin again, thinking, and shoots another look to me. Then he waves a hand. "I have no need of your coin. The way to Rammelbeck is rotten with bandits. If the three prefects will guard us, that will cover the cost of all six of you riding with the caravan. Have we a deal?"

"More than fair," Mathilde says quickly. "Thank you. I wasn't sure I'd get home in time otherwise."

Emeric nods. "Yes, sir, I'd be happy to help in any way I can. I'm sure we all would."

"Hmph." Kirkling is, unsurprisingly, frowning. "Schmidt will still benefit from the work of the prefects. That may be seen as improper."

Bajeri shuts his eyes. "We have a saying in Sahali: 'An ant does not concern itself with the weight of a mountain.'"

An awkward pause falls, as neither Mathilde, Emeric, nor Kirkling seem to know how to parse that. I fight down a laugh. This is one of Joniza's favorite negotiation tactics.

". . . Understood," Kirkling clearly lies, standing. "I will begin arranging for our departure. Please excuse me."

"We will leave at eight in the morning on Tuesday," Bajeri calls after her, "with or without you."

Mathilde leaves to pass word to Vikram as Joniza helps her father get to his feet. I can see why she wouldn't want him alone on the road; he always huffed and groaned when sitting and standing, but now he moves with a stiffness that wasn't there years ago.

Emeric clears away a neglected tea service, clearly wrestling with a question. His curiosity finally puts his restraint in a headlock long enough for him to get out: "Excuse me, sir?"

"Eh?" Bajeri squints at him.

"Could . . . could you explain a little more about that saying?"

Bajeri looks to Joniza. She gives a *go ahead* nod.

"I already know," I chime in. "Joniza told me after a bottle of wine."

Bajeri lets out a belly laugh as Joniza swats my arm. Then he puts a hand on Emeric's shoulder, his face turning deadly serious.

"Young man," he intones, "it means, 'When you want white people to stop arguing with you, make up a proverb.'" He gives Emeric a little shake and lets go, his agbada swishing as he heads for the door. "We will leave at nine sharp."

"Not eight?" I ask.

"That proctor woman knows if she makes you late, we will leave without you," he says dryly. "Of course I told her eight."

✤

Bajeri's instincts are spot-on. Kirkling winds up conveniently running behind on Tuesday morning, only to be swiftly escorted to the caravan the moment she emerges from the Book and Bell at a quarter past eight. I would find it funnier if I weren't already dozing in a wagonful of rolled-up rugs, curled around an ember-filled clay jar bundled in towels. Helga warned me that the root-bind could change my monthly bleeding, but I hadn't expected it to be early until I woke with cramps.

Even so, as the caravan pulls away from the inn, it's impossible to miss something that twists my stomach even more. The morning glories all over the façade have unfurled their round bells with the sun, and most blossoms are a plain snowy white. But a stain is spilling through them, dyeing the petals an unnaturally vivid scarlet. And from a distance, it's easy to see that one upstairs window is at the heart of the spread.

I don't need a map of the building to know that was our room's window. It must have happened so slowly, we didn't even notice.

I get to nap through most of our first day on the road. I need it; even without the drowsiness that usually plagues my first bleeding day,

I have to catch up on sleep from the two nights of privacy Emeric and I had. We didn't get swept up in another rush of passion in the past few days, just took our time getting comfortable with touching like we did in Hagendorn. There was something lovely about it, too—still new enough to steal my breath away, but familiar enough that I didn't have to worry about being a disappointment.

The Scarlet Maiden's mark still hasn't faded from Emeric's chest, but that's not a surprise. If touching alone counted as a claim to the Scarlet Maiden, the handprint would have vanished last week.

Still, there's a little hangnail of worry in the back of my skull now. I *probably* would have been ready for more by the summer solstice. Six weeks, though . . . It shouldn't feel that much sooner, but it does.

The rest of the trip couldn't be more different from the ride to Dänwik. Emeric, Mathilde, and Vikram divvy the days into a needlessly complex system of guard shifts, but it means that Emeric has a few hours every day to work on the case with Ambroszia's assistance, and that I get his nights. Once my cramps and bleeding slow, I join Helga in helping Joniza during the days. We tally inventory, inspect the tack for the mule teams pulling the brightly painted wagons, check in with the wagon drivers, make small repairs, and handle a thousand other little rolling bearings that keep the caravan in motion.

Joniza also shows me the caravan's little histories: Notches on Bajeri's wagon to mark his children's heights when he left, then when he returned. Fatatuma's berth, painted with maps of trading routes, murals of the stars, a city by a green-fringed lake that Joniza tells me is the family home. The jar of spices their mother packs to mix into the dough for the hard, sweet bread that lasts us from breakfast until dinner; it's a secret blend not even Joniza knows.

It's strange; the last time I felt this at ease in the company of others was in Minkja, before I left. I know it isn't the same as a family—I have no weathered notches in my life, and the only person to call me sister was chasing a mistake—but I do wonder, were I ever to find mine, if it might feel something like this.

We make it out of the thick forest by Friday night and camp on the plains under the open sky, the lights of Rammelbeck and Welkenrode on the horizon. After dinner, Emeric and I sit on the back of the wagon we sleep in, sharing a blanket and watching in silence as a streak of ephemeral mist, occasionally pierced by hooves, carves over the otherwise clear sky. Brunne must be leading the Wild Hunt through the stars.

Emeric lets out a soft huff after the Hunt has passed. "I completely forgot," he says. "I said I'd tell you what the prefect signa are right before we went into the library . . . and then I never did."

My brow furrows. "Oh, right. Vikram said he picked . . . an apothecary? Was that it?"

"The Alembic." Emeric shrugs off the blanket and, to my utter bewilderment, begins unbuttoning his shirt. "So prefects have two binding marks, right? One to bind us to the Low Gods' rules, the other to bind us to their power, like a warlock's bond."

"Right," I say, admittedly more than a little distracted.

"But a warlock carries a mark for every entity they're bound to, and not only are there too many Low Gods for that to be feasible, but that number also changes with region, time—you get the idea. So for the second mark . . ." He frowns. "To simplify the explanation, instead of us connecting directly to the Low Gods' powers, we route through a proxy of sorts. Something else innumerable, that changes with time and region. The—"

I make the connection. "The stars."

He grins, sheepish. "And here I was trying to impress you."

"I mean, 'I summon the powers of the gods through the stars' is pretty impressive on its own."

"I'll take it." Emeric lets the shirt fall to his elbows, then twists so I can see his upper back. Black lines are wrought between his shoulder blades, a complicated work of runes, rings, and strange symbols. I've seen it before on a dead man's skin, sewn into Adalbrecht von Reigenbach's back. Emeric's mark has a few conspicuous voids, though. "Do you see the part at the top? A circle with five stars?"

There are five tiny black stars arranged like a lopsided house: four crooked corners and one peak. I lay my fingertips on them and feel him tense. "Here?"

"Y-yes." This time he's the one who sounds distracted. "It's a constellation. Every prefect chooses one to be a part of their second mark, their signum. That becomes their link to the powers of the Low Gods. We only have a hundred constellations to pick from, and only one prefect can use a signum at a time, to keep our numbers in check. Hubert's was the Oak, and Vikram picked the Alembic."

"Damn, now I want a mystic code name too." I trace from star to star, enjoying the hitch in his breath.

"I should think yours obvious." He reaches over and taps his notebook, where a playing card's tip juts out. "Queen of Roses."

I huff a tickled laugh. "I can work with that. What did you choose for yourself?"

"The Lantern."

My hand goes still. For a moment, all I can see is my mother's lantern as she left me on that cold winter night thirteen years ago, the last flickers of it stealing into the dark. I choke out, "Why?"

"It stands for the eyes of Justice." His voice takes on the brutally earnest tone I remember from Minkja, when we sat by a fire and he told me his dream of holding the powerful to account. "Justice sees the entire story. There are no shadows to exploit. And that's what I want, to bring the whole truth to light in every case, not just what's convenient."

I can't say what I'm thinking; I can't ruin this for him. What I see in a lantern isn't what he sees, and that's that.

Instead, I force humor into my voice. "I have terrible news about who you're courting."

Emeric laughs then, and twists back around, only to draw me to the bedroll we share in the wagon. "I made my bed, Queen of Roses," he says wickedly, flicking a hand. The wagon's door closes, the curtains drawing shut with a silvery glimmer as he blows out the candle just beyond the pillow. "I'm more than happy to lie in it."

✤

"All right," Helga Ros says as she emerges from our Rammelbeck inn the next afternoon, "let's go find more of my horrible brothers."

I stand up from the bench by the inn door, where I've been enjoying the spring sunshine and secretly scoping out the flower boxes. We got out of Dänwik before the red morning glories could raise questions, but I'd rather not see how long we can push it. "They have room for everyone?"

Helga snorts. "This place is massive. Of *course* they have room."

She's not wrong. Rammelbeck spills down a mountainside like a landslide, and the mining town it used to be still shows in its rough edges. The higher the lanes climb, the rougher those edges get. But there was a time when Rammelbeck united with Welkenrode, its posh sibling on the opposite riverbank, to serve as the empire's capital for a dynasty or two. Our sprawling inn, the Jolly Magistrate, seems to be a relic from those days. Even though it's on the Rammelbeck side of the river, it takes up a long stretch of the street, with multiple courtyards and a large-enough stable to put up the caravan's mules.

When we arrived, Mathilde and Vikram split off to get Mathilde to her family before the Week of Barley festivities start. Kirkling insisted on checking in at the local prefect outpost to see if it had lodgings available— and on dragging Ambroszia and a slightly annoyed Emeric with her. That left Helga and me to carry on with the caravan and hope the inn Bajeri picked had room. I should have known better than to second-guess him.

"Let's start with Erwin," Helga says, adjusting the strap of her satchel with a wary eye to passersby. "Erwin and Dieter are twins, so you know what to expect. Henrik is across the river and the nicest of the lot, so we should save him for last, and Ozkar's . . . Well, let's just get Erwin first."

It's a quick walk to the riverside, but it takes longer to make it to the docks, where Erwin should be working. The Trench River runs deep and swift, branching from the Ilsza back in Hagendorn and threading all the way to the Night Sea in the north. It also ran lamentably narrow until the days of the imperial capital demanded wider banks; now the man-made canal walls accommodate all but the greatest of trade ships and barges. Rammelbeck and Welkenrode may no longer be the seat of imperial power, but controlling Almandy's greatest inland port is a decent consolation prize.

The Trench's waters are oddly deserted, though, especially for a day with clear skies and a calm current. Even more ominous: The closer we get to the shipping docks, the more Helga and I have to circumvent larger and larger crowds.

By the time we reach the docks, the problem is self-evident. A long cargo barge has somehow drifted askew, wedged diagonally across the entire width of the Trench. The words *Grace Unending* are painted in blocky white letters across the stern. It's large enough to make ants of the various crews working to dislodge it, and from the number of ships piling up downriver, I'd say it's been there at least a day.

"I swear to Brunne," Helga mutters under her breath, "if Erwin had anything to do with this . . ."

That seems improbable to me. "I thought you said he was a dockworker."

"I never said he was a good one." She leads us to the wharf, where teams of longshoremen are sitting around idly grumbling, and calls out, "Erwin Ros? Anyone seen Erwin Ros?"

More than a handful of dockworkers spit on the ground, and they all stay silent. Maybe Helga's theory isn't that outlandish after all. We follow a trail of jabbed thumbs and breadcrumb mutters past four different piers until we get a solid answer.

"Erwin's not reported for work today," grunts a burly woman leaning against a stack of crates. "But that usually means he's gone and blown his wages in the Sünderweg."

"Not just his wages, boss," cracks another longshoreman with a smirk. "He was on a proper tear last night." His face falls. "You're neither of you his wife, aye?"

"No," Helga says vehemently. "Sister, here on family business. Still don't want to hear about his bedtime adventures."

From context clues (chief among them the fact that *Sünderweg* means "way of sinners"), I feel like I'm getting a decent grasp on the situation. "Does he have a favorite brothel?"

"Think he's sweet on one of the *mietlingen* at the Green Sleeve," Boss muses, rubbing her chin.

The longshoreman who piped up does so again. "Aye, but last I saw him, he was headed into Madame Treasury's." He shakes his head. "Wouldn't be the first time some lout's gotten into trouble there."

"Thank you. One more question." Helga gestures to the *Grace Unending*, still wedged across the breadth of the Trench behind us. "Did Erwin do that?"

Boss barks a laugh. "Your brother may not be the sharpest mind in the empire, but no. High winds and a new hand at the helm, that's what I heard."

I don't miss the doubtful looks traded behind her back. I file that away for later.

"We'll send him down here if we find him," I lie.

"Don't bother." Boss sighs. "Until that damn barge is put to rights, whole port's shut down."

I wait until Helga and I have climbed up the bank to the street again, then ask under my breath, "So he definitely had something to do with it, right?"

"Told you so," Helga says dourly. She turns to the nearest bystander gawking at the *Grace Unending*. "Excuse me, how do you get to the Sünderweg from here?"

"Keep walking along the river," the man starts as he turns, only to pause as he sees us two. Sharpness darts through his face like the glint of steel between sheath and hilt. He swallows, touching his collar, where there's a faint pucker of something below the shirt. "Sorry, I, er. Anyway. Follow the river north until you hit the ropewalks, then you'll see it."

"Thanks," Helga says stiffly. We head north. After a minute of walking, she grits from the side of her mouth, "Is he following us?"

In answer, I twist to dig in the satchel at my side and don a frown as if hunting an elusive item. Out of the corner of my eye, I see the dark blond curls of the man we just spoke to trailing at a distance. "Yes."

"*Scheit.* I'm pretty sure I've seen him in Hagendorn. Is he the only one?"

"Hold up a second." I stop and keep rooting around as Helga obliges. Four people also come to an abrupt halt behind us, including the blond man. I pretend to find a little jar of balm in my satchel and start walking again. "Four."

"*Scheit-scheiter-scheiten.* All right, I guess we're going to Ozkar's first. His workshop's on the way to the ropewalks." Helga starts to pick up the pace.

I grab her elbow and wind my arm through hers, deliberately dragging. "Take it from someone who's made a lot of escapes," I say, terse. "There's one rule to getting out intact, and that rule is *don't panic.* Is Ozkar's workshop on this street?"

"I—I don't know, it's been a while. No. No, you can see the river only from the second floor. There's an apothecary on the street corner."

I keep an iron grip on Helga. "They think we're going all the way to the Sünderweg and that we don't know we're being followed. If we run, we give away both of those. So we keep walking, and when we get to the apothecary's corner, we'll sprint the rest of the way to the workshop. If we're lucky, they won't catch up fast enough to see us go in."

Helga huffs through her nose, still taut. "You *are* good at this."

"There's a reason it took a, well, an Emeric to catch me." I add, a bit self-consciously, "And even then, I was distracted with turning into jewels at the time."

"That's fair." Helga sneaks a look. "They're getting closer."

"Good for them," I say through clenched teeth. I'm putting on a stoic show for Helga, but my scars give a twinge as a prickle runs up my back. "Focus on looking for the apothecary."

Despite my calm, Helga's voice is pitching higher. "Do you have a way to—to call your prefect boy?"

"First of all: He is not my boy, he is a strong, independent young protractor," I reply tartly. "Second: We can handle this on our own. And third: I do not."

Helga tenses like she's about to bolt.

I tighten my grip. "Are you *sure* you can beat them to Ozkar's from here? Because once you run, they run."

"They're going to catch up——"

"Whatever they want, if they could do it in broad daylight with witnesses, they would have already. Do you see the apothecary yet?"

"I . . ." Helga cranes her neck a bit too obviously for my preferences. "I think it's coming up on the left. Green awning."

I spot the green canvas not far ahead, then scan the oncoming traffic. A bitter-looking nag is pulling a cart laden with pickle barrels down the street toward us. "We're going to cut in front of that cart at the last possible second, got it?" Helga nods. I wait, biting my lip, until we're lined up just so, and then——"*Go.*"

Startled shouts follow us across the street as we dash in front of the cart. The horse lets out a decaying whinny and shies to the side, making the cart tilt as its swearing driver grabs on to the bench for dear life. For a moment, the street behind us is nothing but chaos and yelling.

And we need that moment, because Helga has slowed her run, staring at a nearby storefront advertising a streetwitch's services. Then she blanches. "Oh, *damn*, that's right, Jakob said he moved over to Welkenrode——"

I see the feet of our pursuers as they try to find a route through the fracas, and make an executive decision. "Doesn't matter." I shove Helga into the shop and follow, whipping the door shut behind us.

A rather pinched-looking fellow looks up from the counter, wide-eyed. "Liebeskind's Pest Control, how can I help you?"

"Uh," says Helga.

I grab the back of her shirt and tug until she's out of sight of the storefront windows. There's a tattoo of footfalls, followed by confused, disgruntled accusations.

"We're looking for Ozkar Ros," I tell the man, partially to distract from the muffled voices outside.

His face falls. "Oh. Of course you are. Here, I'll write down his new address."

The voices are getting quieter, but I want to buy us more time. Besides, the least we can do is patronize our involuntary harbor. "*Aaaand* Helga here is looking for a cure for her bed lice."

"I—" Helga starts. I jab her with an elbow. She scowls at me, then finishes: ". . . would really appreciate that, yes."

"I just made a fresh batch today!" Liebeskind (I presume) brightens considerably as he turns to a wall of jars; the ingredients range from garden variety to deeply troubling. "Mine's the best in town, uses an extract from dead lice . . ."

He keeps chattering to a begrudgingly intrigued Helga. It's in the nick of time: A shadow has fallen over the storefront windows. A very cautious look tells me it's the blond man peering through the glass.

I blink. For a moment, I could have sworn I saw a strange— familiar?—glimmer of gold. But it's gone in a trice, and Blondie, too, seems inclined to leave, turning away.

By some miracle, he doesn't notice us all but pressed against the door, too busy thumbing a polished-bone amulet that I'm sure was beneath his shirt before. For a split second, I see the amulet's face—and go cold.

I've seen that mark before. I see it nearly every night.

Blood-red paint is smeared over the bone, making the crude shape of the hand of the Scarlet Maiden.

CHAPTER SIXTEEN

A Prefect's Time

HELGA AND I DON'T MAKE IT BACK TO OUR INN, THE JOLLY MAGISTRATE, until just after dark has fallen. While Helga managed well enough in Dänwik, I'm starting to realize that larger cities aren't her forte. Part of the reason we're so late is that she insisted on going to the nearest guard post. When that turned out to be a modest brick station right next to the Sünderweg with but a lone guardswoman puffing away on a pungent pipe at the front desk, I knew the best we'd get would be smoke in our faces. Helga, however, tried to file a report (declined), then elected to wait until enough guards returned from their rounds to escort us to the inn.

As one might suspect, the guards at this station take specific duties *very* seriously, such as preventing any outbreaks of embarrassing pests or sensitive diseases. This *naturally* requires them to spend quite a lot of time inspecting the brothels along the Sünderweg. Just about all of their time on duty, in fact—despite Rammelbeck having its own designated inspectors for this very purpose.

Eventually Helga accepted that we weren't getting an escort, but by then it was already sunset. And the rest of the reason we're so late is because she wanted to avoid walking along the river, which actually wasn't a terrible idea, except it meant finding our way back through Rammelbeck's labyrinth of side streets.

As we enter the Jolly Magistrate's main courtyard, I hear chair legs scraping on flagstone off to the right. Emeric bursts from a little waiting area, his face taut. "Are you all right? I thought you'd be back hours ago."

"There were some, uh, complications," I start, before a harsh laugh cuts me off.

Kirkling—I don't use this word lightly—*slinks* out of the same waiting area. "You mean you were concocting some new racket."

"We were chased by cultists," Helga snaps, "and the local guard was no help, and we had to figure out how to get back by a different route."

"*Cultists?*" Emeric puts a hand on my arm.

"I don't buy it," Kirkling says a little too loudly, moving even closer. I catch a faint whiff of *brandtwein* on her breath. "You really thought I wouldn't notice that Saint Willehalm's goblet *magically* returned to the library? How the guards in Dänwik were looking for a thief who left a red penny behind? And now you're making up stories about cultists—what kind of fool do you take me for?"

It's been a long day, and I am desperate for a plate of *spätzle* and a bath, and all in all that means I am pretty much done with Kirkling.

"The kind who's so obsessed with being a pain in my ass that she can't see she's preaching out her own," I spit back, "so yes, I *am* surprised you noticed. Give yourself a star. Now, if you'll excuse us, the adults are having a conversation."

Kirkling reels back. I'm pretty sure she's about to throw a punch (which I would find respectable, in all honesty).

Emeric seems to get that sense, too, because he swivels to subtly place himself between the two of us. "Let's just get some dinner—"

"Arrest her," Kirkling barks.

Emeric pauses. "Coming back late is not a crime," he says carefully, "and neither is being impolite—"

"She stole an artifact from royalty, damn you, and she's clearly planning some new scam." Kirkling just looks angrier. "She's only free because of *your* bias. If you weren't utterly besotted, you'd have already done your duty."

I know the nerve she's trying to hit with Emeric, but she just dropped a load of bricks on the absolute wrong one. Emeric draws himself up. I've only ever seen him this icily angry once: when I told him how the von Falbirgs expected me to bear the worst of Adalbrecht for them.

"My duty," he says frostily, "is to serve Justice. If you think Justice will be served by opening a new case into how a prince-elector stole a holy relic, exploited our legal system to reduce it to a trophy, and turned a critical public archive into a hazard so deadly, its patron saint had to ask a civilian for intervention, then I will be happy to do so— *after* we have resolved the Scarlet Maiden case. In the interim, if my bias means an innocent person stays out of jail, I believe that serves Justice far better than the alternative. If I'm wrong, on my head be it."

And without another word, he threads an arm through mine and leads me into the inn, leaving a red-faced Kirkling in our wake.

Helga follows a moment after. "I take it you're staying here?"

"Yes, if there's room," Emeric answers. "The local outpost's dormitories are all spoken for. Something about a shipping-fraud case."

"I figured you'd rather stay with Vanja." There's a flicker of humor under the weariness in Helga's voice. "I'm going to go take a bath and sleep for a day. Tell the nice people at the front desk that you're staying in the room for two under 'Helga Ros.'"

She disappears remarkably quickly for someone who's as tired as I am. It isn't until halfway through checking in that I start seeing hints of why. The clerk breaks into a bright smile when she finds the reservation. "Of course! We've already had your luggage sent up. Will you be taking dinner down in our tavern or in your room?"

Emeric looks to me. "I think I want to stay in tonight," I say.

The clerk winks. "Understood. I'll let our cook know to send up the special. Now, if you'll follow me . . ."

She leads us up not one but two flights of stairs; it gets considerably quieter the higher we go. "We're very proud of this suite," the clerk says peppily. "You'll find our finest in-room bath, with the latest in water-heating enchantments, and a variety of aromatic tinctures and lotions."

"Nice," I say, making a mental note to steal as much soap as possible.

"And, naturally"—as we reach the top of the stairs, she turns and unloads another wink—"we've provided the absolute best in sound-proofing enchantments as well, so you needn't worry about privacy."

The wheels begin turning, but by then it's too late. The hall's already lighting up with candles that burn magenta flames as the clerk unlocks a white door painted with garish pink roses.

"Congratulations, you two," she says, pushing the door open. "Enjoy your honeymoon."

Emeric and I walk in, both a little stunned. As soon as she shuts the door behind us, a shower of rose petals bursts from the ceiling, drifting artfully into a trail that leads to the bed, which is less a bed and more a fortress built to weather a sexy war. Its iron posts are bolted to the ceiling and the floor, softened only by red satin canopies. A matching canopy tents over the aforementioned bathtub. In fact, there's just a lot of red satin happening, everywhere.

I cough out a mouthful of rose petals as Emeric wanders into the middle of the room, looking like a man swept abruptly into a foreign land. Then he turns to me, raising a finger.

"I want to—to talk about . . . this." He waves vaguely at the entirety of the room. "But first . . . you *did* say 'cultists'?"

"It wasn't funny," I tell Helga the next morning. "All I wanted was *spätzle*! I don't even like oysters!"

Emeric tsks. After hearing the full story of Helga's and my afternoon, he couldn't be dissuaded from accompanying us to the docks today. (Not that I made more than a strictly procedural objection. It's a nice morning, and I am not above using cultists as an excuse to spend time with my favorite protractor.) "Someday we'll go to Rabenheim, and you can have real oysters fresh off the rocks."

"My Nibsi never was one for oysters," Lady Ambroszia muses from her post in my satchel. Since her personal motive for joining us was to see more of the empire, I figured the least we can do is take her out on the town. "Not that he ever needed them. Like a rabid boar in the bedroom, that man."

"That sounds . . ." I search for a word that isn't a synonym for *no wonder his first wife joined a convent* and come up with "bracing."

Helga grumbles as we draw near the piers.

I lean forward. "What's that?"

"I got the honeymoon suite so you two could have some alone time," she grouses. "And I just feel like you're not taking this seriously."

"I think I'm taking the blood-sacrifice-to-a-hellhound thing extremely seriously," I protest.

"Not that." Helga fusses with her russet braid as we pick our way down the rickety foot-traffic ramps to the wharf. "My bet with Jakob. He's going to be insufferable if he wins."

"Strong priorities," Emeric remarks from behind me. "We had to ask for new sheets this morning. Do you know how slippery satin is? I could barely even stay on the bed."

"Excuses," she calls back.

When we reach the piers, fewer crews are waiting around, but the *Grace Unending* is still lodged across the Trench River. Erwin's boss is there, though, and a handful of other dockworkers.

There are also new faces: a small cluster of city guards, one with a bailiff's sash. The bailiff is waving a piece of parchment at the boss, looking seriously peeved.

He sounds even more seriously peeved as we draw into earshot: ". . . someone has to pay the debt. If you can't tell me where to find Erwin Ros, then I suppose *you'll* have to round up a hundred *gilden*, won't you?"

Emeric slows, grabbing my sleeve and politely tapping Helga's shoulder. His voice drops to just above a whisper. "Lady Ambroszia, I'd keep out of sight; I don't know the local regulations for spirits that aren't bound to a warlock. And no one talk to the guards. Especially not you, Miss Ros. They're trying to collect a debt, and they'll use any relation as an excuse to pin it to you and be done."

But we've caught the bailiff's attention. Ambroszia quickly drops deeper into my satchel as his voice sails down the pier. "What brings a prefect among the wharf rats?"

"Just accompanying these ladies on their errands," Emeric answers.

The bailiff's eyes narrow as he looks from me to Helga. "And what are those?"

Helga stiffens. This calls for someone who's a lot better at threading truth through the eye of a liar's needle. I make a show of planting a hand on my hip and rolling my eyes, the picture of familiar exasperation. "From the sound of it, same as yours. Looking to collect from Erwin Ros. You seen him?"

"All I've seen is that he owes the Green Sleeve a hundred *gilden* for their services," the bailiff snaps, with enough venom that I suspect the Green Sleeve may be turning him away, too, until the matter's settled.

But that doesn't sound right to me. "Last I heard, he was at Madame Treasury's."

Three small, unusual things happen then.

First: The guards and the bailiff trade glances, and whatever fire and brimstone they've been mustering to intimidate Erwin's boss is abruptly snuffed.

Second: A young girl, maybe fourteen, steps forward from where she's been hovering nearby. "Excuse me—I work at—I mean, I *worked* for Madame. I think I can help."

And third: A dockworker who's been milling at the back of the pack slips away, jogging toward the ramps that lead up to the street.

"Very well," the bailiff says with wooden insincerity, "we'll go check Madame Treasury's." He makes a flicking gesture to the guards flanking him, and they head in the same direction as the running dockworker. Somehow I doubt they're going to do more than a cursory questioning, unless "questioning" has entered the arena as a euphemism.

Interesting. The guards are clearly on the take with Madame Treasury's . . . so why go the extra mile and pay the dockworker to spy too?

"Wait, please." The girl stumbles after them. "I need to report—"

"Go to the station," one guard laughs, then covers his mouth with a hand.

Emeric makes a noise of disgust.

"I didn't lie to them," I remind him.

"No, you were terrifyingly brilliant, as always," he says, then hastens after the young girl. "Excuse me, *frohlein?*"

I give an apologetic shrug to Erwin's boss, who waves us off. Helga and I catch up to Emeric in time to hear "What did you want to report?"

The girl's dark eyes get very large as she takes in the prefect insignia on Emeric's coat. She wrings her hands in front of her. They're mottled with lye burns old and new, but while her too-small dress and apron are certainly worn, they don't have the telltale pockmarks—so she usually wears a uniform when she handles lye. Expertly braided mousy brown hair peeps out from under a kerchief nearly as ragged as her clothing. "Oh no, sir, it's not worth a p-prefect's time."

"Then we're both in luck, because I'm not a full prefect yet." Emeric attempts a casual lean against a barrel, only to misjudge the edge and slip a little. Or at least, that's what it looks like. He's used that trick on me before, to get me to lower my guard. "Does it have to do with Madame Treasury's?"

The girl shrinks a little, hiding her hands behind her back. "I shouldn't say."

"Hmm. You don't have to say anything you don't want to. But I'm going to make a few guesses, and if you'd like to tell me I'm correct, you can, all right?" Emeric waits for her to nod. "You said 'worked' earlier. I'm guessing you don't work there anymore."

She nods again.

"I'm going to guess you have an older sibling who helps you with your hair."

The girl's eyes go even wider. She nods. "How did you know?"

"I used to help my little sisters with theirs," he says with a rueful grin. "Your sibling's plaits are much better than mine."

I decide to lend him a hand and pull a braid over my shoulder to show the ribbon. "He still ties my bows for me in the mornings."

The girl looks a little less on edge, a tentative smile unfurling. "My sister, Marien," she says softly. "She works at the Green Sleeve."

"But you worked for Madame Treasury's." Emeric's brow furrows.

Just saying the brothel's name makes her retreat a step. "I . . . really shouldn't . . . Madame won't . . ."

Emeric's voice turns firm but is still kind. "How many months of wages does she owe you?"

The girl's mouth drops open.

"He just does that," I say wryly. "What should we call you?"

She swallows and whispers, "Agnethe."

"My hands used to look like yours," I tell her. "A few weeks of salve and rest and they'll be right as rain."

Agnethe ducks her head. "Madame said . . ." Once the words start bubbling up, they boil over. "She called me a liar because I didn't tell her Marien is at the Green Sleeve. But I thought I did tell her! But Madame said I didn't, and she said she doesn't keep with liars and spies, and I've been cleaning for her for three months, but she said she wouldn't pay and I should feel lucky she didn't take me to the guards for spying, but I never!"

Emeric's voice stays friendly, but he links his own hands behind his back. I know he does that when he doesn't want people to see his knuckles turning white. "She hasn't paid you for three whole months?"

"The first month was supposed to be a trial, and I *thought* she said I'd be paid at the end, then she said it would be at the end of the second, but she said that month was a bad month and if she paid me it wouldn't be fair to the others, and then . . ." Agnethe's chin starts to wobble. "Marien's been stretching to feed us both, but we haven't paid the March rent, and if we miss another month . . ."

Emeric nods. "I see. Thank you for telling me. We'll get you your wages, *Frohlein* Agnethe."

"And in the meantime, if you want, you can wait for us in the Jolly Magistrate's tavern," I suggest. "Treat yourself to some apple cake. You can tell them to bill it to the room under 'Elske Kirk—'"

Emeric clears his throat.

". . . 'Helga Ros,'" I amend.

"You're paying me back," Helga tells me with a scowl.

"Um." Agnethe's hands twist in her apron. "The man you're looking for . . . I'm pretty sure I saw a bouncer take him to a private room two nights ago. He has hair like yours?"

"Yes," Helga confirms. "Loud, big googly blue eyes, a weakness for *brandtwein*. Bit of a sad sack."

Agnethe tries not to smile. "I'm pretty sure it was him."

"Thank you again, that's excellent information." Emeric tips a salute to her. "We'll see you at the Jolly Magistrate."

Once we climb the ramps and reach street level again, Helga turns to Emeric and me. "Ozkar might know something about whatever Erwin's into. Let me take Ambroszia to his new workshop while you two try the Sünderweg."

"Is that safe?" I ask. "There could be more cultists."

Before Helga can answer, Lady Ambroszia rises from the satchel, glowing. "I believe," she says haughtily, "I can handle a mere handful of scoundrels. You *do* recall what sweet Willi was able to do in the library when vexed."

"I do recall," Emeric says, "and would recommend keeping things nonlethal. But yes, that should suffice. We'll meet you back at the inn." He holds out a hand to me.

I take it. "Let's go see a madame about a dog."

THE FOURTH LIE

FAMILY

ONCE UPON A TIME, A MAID LEARNED TO LIE WITH HER HANDS.

She was only seven; she had lived in a castle for more than a year, and she wanted very much to leave. She wanted to go back to the cozy little hut where her godmothers had kept her safe and warm in a safe, quiet world. She did not like cold Sovabin, nor the mean cook, nor the name they called her by: *russmagdt*, soot-wench, for the scullery kept her covered in ashes more often than not.

She only liked the castle's magician, who had taken pity on her and was teaching her to lie. The magician believed that maybe, just maybe, if the *russmagdt* could impress the royalty of the castle, she might escape the scullery and find softer work in the halls above.

And so the cook found the magician and the soot-wench by the hearth fire of the great hall. "Your hands must always be moving," the magician was saying, showing the little girl how she'd tucked a bronze *sjilling* between her thumb and the side of her palm.

"Dishes aren't done," grunted the cook from the doorway to the kitchens.

The *russmagdt* shrank. She was supposed to do as he asked, but . . .

The magician frowned over her shoulder. "She did them. I saw the empty sink myself." The cook didn't answer, and her frown deepened. "Unless you made a new mess for her."

The cook swayed and braced himself against the doorframe. The girl could smell sour beer even from her seat by the fire; Yannec was his meanest like this. "It's no good, you daft . . . You're trying to make her more than she is. Her own family couldn't even find a use for her."

"You don't know that," the magician said coldly.

Godmother Fortune shook her head, vehement, her wreath of coin and bone jingling. "It's not true at all, Vanja dear. We have plenty of uses for you."

"We'd already kept you too long," said Godmother Death.

I was the only one who could hear them, see them, so all I said was a muted "They still left me."

"See!" Yannec crowed. "Blood doesn't turn on blood without damn good reason. You're wasting your time."

Joniza shot him a look of pure spite. "Go clean up your own mess."

He'd gotten what he wanted; I knew that, when I went to sleep, I wouldn't be able to keep his words out of my head any more than the rats I was meant to scare out of the pantry. He vanished back down to the kitchens, grumbling.

"Blood and family are not the same," Joniza said after a long moment. "Do you understand?"

I did and I did not. I scarcely remembered the faces of the family I left that cold midwinter night, nor the face of my mother, lit by a flickering lantern as she turned her back on me. My godmothers called me their daughter, but sometimes I thought they did not understand what a daughter was. Why else would they have sent me to Sovabin?

I was learning to lie with more than my hands, though. And so I said, "Yes."

CHAPTER SEVENTEEN

ℂOUPLES' 𝒜CTIVITIES

"ℒOOK!" I SHOW EMERIC THE BACK OF MY HAND AS HE PASSES THROUGH the gate into the Sünderweg. A wreath of green leaves has been stamped below my knuckles. "No bed lice!"

"What a relief," he says insincerely, wrinkling his nose at the same stamp on his own hand. "I suppose I should be happy they take hygiene so seriously."

Rammelbeck does, in fact, take hygiene seriously, at least in the Sünderweg. Like any decent brothel district, there are plenty of side alleys and narrow lanes for the client who likes a certain gritty ambience, but if you look carefully, they're all dead ends. Every street-level entry to the area is blocked by a gate. Each gateway lets visitors pass only after they submit to a brief and brusque exam from a streetwitch to detect bed lice, bed pox, bed warts, or any number of other stomach-turning ailments that start with *bed*. Even the bordellos we're passing flaunt weekly inspection placards just as boldly as their more carnal displays.

And displays there are aplenty, though it's not even noon. Not all are lurid—a crowd of uproariously drunk women enjoy a late breakfast outside one establishment, a damozel is tastefully arranged in the window of another—but nobody would mistake this for a temple district either. Every inch is a curated venue for carnal enterprise. Cosmetically "grungy" side alleys are being enthusiastically utilized by *mietlingen* and their clients, large signs advertise different services and rates with themed names, and a robust variety of . . . *sounds* drift through open windows.

I wish I knew what it was like for all this to be enjoyable, rather than uncomfortable. It's one thing when it's me and Emeric alone, fumbling a little, laughing more. Here I can't shake a squirming feeling, like I've accidentally walked into someone's private party and we all know I don't belong. The only consolation is that my misery has company, as Emeric, too, looks like he'd rather be doing his taxes. (Maybe that's not the strongest comparison; I think he does taxes to unwind after a long day.)

"I say we pose as newlyweds," I tell him, partially to distract us both.

He blinks at me. "What?"

"Well, if *I* were a shady brothel owner potentially involved in a kidnapping plot, I wouldn't let a prefect—*aspirant*, yes—conduct a scavenger hunt for the victim on my property."

"You're not wrong," Emeric says slowly. "However, we're in a bit of a gray area here. I'm supposed to remain in uniform while actively on duty, unless it calls for undercover work—"

"I mean, isn't all brothel work technically under covers?"

He lets out a sigh of pure suffering and carries on: "—which needs a stronger justification than what we have. Erwin Ros is connected to the Scarlet Maiden case, but we don't have reason to believe his *disappearance* is, so . . . just to be safe, let's do this by the book."

Madame Treasury's isn't hard to spot a few blocks into the main strip. Its commanding façade is painted black with golden trim to evoke its titular institution, and wrought iron railings frame a fan of slate steps that lead up to imposing polished-teak double doors. A very sturdy man is blockading the entrance as the brothel's very own on-call *Grace Unending*, his chin jutting like he's got several grudges on layaway and an itch to take them off the shelf.

"*Spintz*," he grunts as we walk up.

Emeric and I trade befuddled looks. I show the stamp on my hand. "I think we were screened for that already?" Then I lean to read the posted inspection placard. Apparently Madame Treasury's is due for a visit this time tomorrow. "Oh, is there an infection?"

"It's coin, not a disease, you—" The bouncer catches himself before he ends on an insult to prospective clientele. He jerks his chin at a little booth beside the stairs. "At the Treasury, you pay in *spintz*. No *spintz*, no entry."

"We're not here as customers," Emeric says. "We have some questions for the proprietress."

A beat passes as the bouncer eyeballs Emeric, specifically the prefect insignia on his coat. Then he asks, "You got a warrant?"

". . . No." Emeric's mouth flattens into a line.

The bouncer's gaze narrows to a slit. He points at the booth. "*Spintz*."

It's my turn for a long, theatrical sigh. We trudge over to the booth. The concept of apathy is manifested here as a woman a few years older than Helga, who shoves a wooden card over the counter and resumes gnawing on a strip of dried *wurst*. The card lists different, well, *acts* that can be purchased and the price of each . . . in *spintz*. It also lists the exchange rate, which seems to be about one *sjilling* for a *spintz*.

Once I do the math, I start to see why this place is trouble. Not because it's expensive, but the opposite: Every service they offer is steeply underselling the competition. That means the real income is from something else. The cheapest option listed is also the most foreboding: *SURPRISE ME (5 spintz)*.

"What's the surprise?" I ask warily.

"There's a wheel inside that you get to spin," the attendant rattles off, like she, too, would rather be doing her taxes. Her breath smells like the *wurst*. "You get whatever it lands on."

I hear the doors open and glance up. The bouncer is leaning inside, whispering furiously to someone and gesturing our way.

"One," Emeric grits through his teeth, "*surprise*, please." He slides five *sjilling* to the attendant, who trades it for five dull brass tokens. "We'll be back to cash these out shortly."

The attendant gnaws a bit of the dried meat off. "Mm-hm. You'll get four *sjilling* after the exchange tax."

"The exchange—?"

Her finger stabs at a small line of print at the very bottom of the wooden card. Sure enough, you can trade as much imperial coin as you want for *spintz*, but if you want your coin back, it's going to cost you. The only exception, conveniently enough, is for members of the city guard (and signed off with a perky *Thank you for your service!*).

"I see," Emeric says dourly.

As do I. There are flat fees for different brackets; no matter what, you lose at least 10 percent of what you pay for the *spintz*. It's a brilliant racket, I'll give the madame that, shaving money off every transaction, forcing customers to invest in the tokens up front and charging them to cash out. And at the massive scale Madame Treasury's runs on, all those little shavings add up quickly.

The bouncer doesn't stop scowling at us even as he lets us in.

I can see how the venue might roar to life at night; it's like a sultry bank lobby, all dark paint, black-and-white marble, and elegant brass fixtures. Twin winding staircases frame a round stage, where a wheel currently sits front and center. Galleries of doorways ring the upper levels, and matched bar counters unfurl on the ground floor. A trail of pungent smoke, half incense, half sense-dulling *kanab*, drifts toward the clear glass dome of the roof, cool morning light catching in the haze. It's not as rowdy as outside, but from murmurs, giggles, and the tempo of a distant staccato thudding, the Treasury is very much in business.

"You two." There's a snap of fingers a moment after we walk in. Emeric and I both look up. A woman is standing at the apex of the two staircases. I'd guess she's in her late thirties. Her striking white gown is only slightly lighter than her porcelain skin, but it's stark against the art-ful updo of her candy-red tresses. I hear a slight accent from the Deep North when she says, "Up here. Now."

"I was told I could spin the wheel," I say indignantly.

"Do you *want* to win anything?" Emeric says under his breath as we start toward the steps.

"It's the principle." I pout until we reach the top of the staircase and I get a better look at who I presume to be the infamous madame. There's a faint violet sheen to her curls that annoys me; I know some blonds choose to stain their hair that red hue with blueberries and beet juice, never mind *my* version of redhead involves gaining fifty more freckles anytime I think the word *sun*.

"Madame," Emeric says coolly.

"Prefect," she returns, batting unnaturally teal eyes at him, and that's when I decide I'm going to burn this place to the ground.

"Aspirant," I correct, glaring daggers.

"We will speak in my office," she states, and glides toward another large teak door recessed into the wall. A man I barely noticed opens it for her.

"Do you want us to call you 'Madame'?" I ask as we follow. "Or is it more of a *please, my mother was Madame Treasury, call me Gertie* situation?"

She ignores me entirely, sailing behind a monument of a wooden desk as enchanted lights blink on, then sinking into a white velvet chair so smoothly, it looks choreographed. The door shuts as soon as we cross the threshold. Despite an abundance of plush armchairs around the room, we are not invited to sit.

"I have no desire to waste *further* time on this foolishness," Madame dictates before we can say anything. "Nor to disturb the Treasury's clients—"

"Wait," I interrupt, "is it *the* Treasury? I thought Treasury was your last name. Or is it *your* treasury?"

"I think it's all of the above," Emeric says thoughtfully.

I'll give Madame credit; her chill doesn't crack. "The city guard was already here, and I'll tell you the same thing: I have no idea where Erwin Ros is. The last I heard, he'd been thrown out of the Green Sleeve across the street. No one here saw him the night he went missing. Are we done?"

Emeric's face stays carefully blank as we both approach the desk. "I'd like to take a look around the premises regardless."

"I'm sure you would." Madame leans back in her chair. "I'd no idea the prefects had this much time on their hands. Do let me know when you've got a warrant, and I'll accommodate."

It's clear what she's really saying: One man's disappearance isn't enough for the prefects to investigate, and the guards will stonewall anything concerning the Treasury. *(Thanks for their service!)*

"Not that it would do you any good," Madame adds with half a laugh. "The Treasury is cleaned thoroughly every day. Even if he were here, I doubt you'd find any trace."

I cross my arms. "Funny. I thought you fired your cleaning maid."

Madame glances up at me with a little flare of loathing. She doesn't respond.

"Yes, that's another matter to discuss," Emeric says after an awkward pause. "It's my understanding you withheld three months' wages from Agnethe and then dismissed her without pay."

"Mm. She signed a contract." Madame leans down to a drawer, making the most of the angle and her dress's neckline. She withdraws a slip of parchment and lays it on the desk, then slides it to her right. "You may read it if you wish."

Her fingertips keep the parchment glued pointedly in place. Emeric has to walk around to her side of the desk, which is exactly the point.

For a moment, all I can think of is the morning Irmgard called me to curl her hair after ruining my salve, how she let me hold a scalding iron inches from her throat because we both knew, much as I burned to, I couldn't hurt her.

No. Sovabin's behind me. And while Madame's attention is on Emeric, I can use this opening.

I scan her orderly desk for anything useful. *Purchase order: One (1) bushel strawberries (hothouse), ten (10) gross breadsticks . . .* Shopping list. Surprisingly boring. Next. *For your review: sketches of the new parlor layout.—Köhler.* I appreciate good interior design as much as the next scammer, but pass.

My eyes fall on a paper peeking out from an atypically untidy stack—a cover-up if I've ever seen one. *Offer for the Properties Herein, Being M.T.'s Inn and Brothel and Associated Properties—*

She wants to sell. Now *that's* interesting.

"Did you tell Agnethe she'd be paid in *spintz*?" Emeric's voice butts in. "That the 'exchange fee' would wipe out her earnings?"

"It's in the contract," Madame says evenly.

Emeric points to a line where a little wobbly *X* is drawn. "This isn't a signature."

"Poor thing was never taught her letters. But the signature below it is my witness, who will confirm I read Agnethe every word of this contract before she signed it."

"A witness you employ?"

Madame smiles. "I believe you met her working the *spintz* booth. It's not illegal to have a document witness on your payroll, is it?"

Emeric links his hands behind his back again, but that can't disguise the muscle jumping in his jaw. "It's not," he admits, returning to my side of the desk.

"Is this not a valid contract?" Madame pushes.

"It is," Emeric says through his teeth.

Then . . . we can't get Agnethe's wages after all.

I don't know how we're going to tell her.

"Perhaps your friend here could take over the cleaning job now that it's open," Madame suggests melodically. Then she purses her lips. "I'd have you work another position, dear, but I'm afraid you'd only make us money lying facedown."

The worst part isn't that I'm used to it. People always act like they're the first one to call you ugly, when you've been navigating a world that won't let you forget.

The worst part is that, even so, it rips at the scab every time. Part of me still chokes up. Will always choke up. Will flash through every single one of those searing reminders in a heartbeat. Will hear Irmgard cooing, *Now your back is as ugly as your front.*

Emeric swiftly plants his hands on the desk, blocking Madame's view of me. I can't see the look on his face, but I can hear the sudden switchblade edge in his voice, see the flicker of uncertainty in Madame. "I promise you," he says, with his deadly kind of calm, "for the rest of your life, you will look back on this moment and know *that* was the worst mistake you'll ever make."

"Is that a threat, Prefect?" Madame asks. Only—I blink, and it's Irmgard sitting there, toying with a quill, tilting her head at me.

Emeric doesn't move. "I don't threaten the inevitable."

"I would hate to report that I was threatened for upsetting you," she muses. "They'd ban you from the Sünderweg"—she sounds *just* like Irmgard—"and, given your company, it's clear you desperately need our assistance—"

The funny thing is, I remember how to deal with Irmgard.

"Oops," I say, and backhand Madame's inkpot right into her pristine white gown. She jumps to her feet with a screech.

Emeric straightens up and offers me his arm. "*I* have a code of conduct," he says mildly. "So the worst mistake of your life wasn't upsetting me. It was starting a fight with *her*."

"*GET OUT,*" Madame howls.

I bob a mocking curtsy and take Emeric's arm. "I'll be back for that wheel spin."

We aren't dragged from the brothel but rather forcefully *accompanied* out the doors and to the street. Emeric waits for the bouncer to resume his post beyond earshot, then says under his breath, "She absolutely is holding Erwin Ros in there."

"Well, if she wanted him dead, she's had plenty of time to do it and dump the body, so at least he's still alive." I rub the tip of my nose, thinking. "Did you see the offer on the table?"

Emeric reddens. "I was trying not to."

"No, you deviant, a *paper* offer. She's trying to sell the Treasury." I can't decide if I'm outraged or delighted that that's where his mind went for once.

"Oh." He only turns redder. "I. Er. *Anyway*. She tried to cast suspicion on the Green Sleeve, too, and I'd like to know w—"

"*TEMPTRESS!*"

The thunderous shout rolls down the street. A familiar head of blond curls is striding our way, and he's not alone but flanked by the other three cultists from yesterday. This time, the pendants with the Scarlet Maiden's hand hang openly around their necks. The blond man, who seems to be taking most of the initiative here, jabs a finger directly at me. "*Defiler!*"

I have been called many things in my life, but "temptress" is a new direction entirely. "Uh?"

"You betrayed the Scarlet Maiden!" he accuses as Emeric shifts in front of me. "You stole away her chosen servant, and now you've brought him here, *here*, to sully her sacrifice! Defiler! Heretic!"

Something tells me *excuse you, any sullying has been consensual* won't go over well with this crowd. Instead, I raise my hands and summon the collected, authoritative voice of the Scarlet Maiden's prophet. "You misunderstand. We are seeking out a—"

"You're *ruining* him!" shrieks one of the cultists.

"*Defiler!*"

Then the world explodes with rusty red. I gasp, and dust clogs my mouth, a mix of bitter metal and powdery clay. My eyes burn, trying to wash away a film of grit.

"Shove off, you lot, before I call the guard!" Someone grabs my arm. "This way, inside—"

"Emeric," I cough, blindly throwing out a hand. I won't leave him with them.

"Here." I feel his fingers catch mine. "Careful, here come some steps—one—two—three—done."

Then I feel wood under my feet instead of stone. A door shuts behind us. "I'll get rags and water," says the stranger. "She can sit on the bench."

Emeric helps me sit. "I think it's just chalk powder." He sounds surprisingly rattled. "I'm sorry, I didn't see until too late—"

There's a sloshing and a ceramic *thunk* on the bench beside me. A wet rag is pressed into my hand. The stranger's come back. "Wipe your face off first. Good." Unknown hands move mine to the edges of a large bowl. "Try to wash your eyes."

"What is this?" a new voice asks as I splash my face.

"Sorry, Jenneke, I'll clean up the mess. Those zealots from earlier threw chalk all over the poor girl."

"Nothing to be sorry for." The other voice—Jenneke—waits until I've dried my eyes. They still feel a bit crusty, patches of phlegm gunking up my vision, but at least I can see again. A tall woman about Helga's age comes into view at the foot of a wooden staircase that spirals up and out of sight. She's not the only person in the jade-toned hall, nor, I'd venture, the only *mietling*, but she's notably the only one wearing green, in the form of a long emerald robe of Gharese silk over a simple dress. A thick braid of deep brown curls crooks over one shoulder, and she's studying Emeric and me with hazel eyes set in a face of muted amber.

"If you'd like, a discreet exit is one of many services we provide at the Green Sleeve." Jenneke winks. "And given the circumstances, it'll be on the house."

We're in the Green Sleeve. Madame did say it was across the street. I'm not going to let a stroke of luck like this pass us by. I cough a wad of dust into a rag, attractively, then croak, "We're actually, uh, on our honeymoon. We were hoping . . ."

Jenneke raises an eyebrow. "Oh, congratulations," she says politely. "So you were looking for our couples' services?"

Emeric seems to be slowly perishing beside me. I shift angles, jostling an inconspicuous elbow into his ribs. "We thought we'd take a look around, see what we can—" My throat goes dry, but I make myself wheeze out, "explore."

. "Unfortunately we don't allow onlookers without prior consent from our clients, but I'm happy to discuss other options with you," Jenneke says briskly. "We provide couples' massages, *enhanced* couples' massages . . . or were you considering additional participants? Some of our staff are happy to join couples, whether that be all together or with one of you watching."

I think my brain packed up and walked into the sea somewhere around "*enhanced*." "Um."

"Or, if you're looking to improve certain skills in the bedroom or to try new things, we also offer hands-on tutorials."

"We should go," Emeric doesn't say so much as faintly emanate.

Jenneke's smile tightens. She pushes open a nearby door to reveal a parlor. "Why don't we discuss your needs somewhere private." She tips her head to the young woman who, I assume, brought the water and the rags for me. "Marien, I won't be long."

I glance sidelong at Marien. Going off family resemblance alone, she's Agnethe's sister, all right. I can't ask her directly why her little sister signed that scam of a contract, but maybe if I stick with this, we can get some answers later. "Thank you for your help," I say, and follow Jenneke into the parlor. Emeric slips in a moment later, looking uneasily at the sofas. I can't tell if he's got a dusting of red chalk over his face, too, or if it's a natural flush.

"Relax." Jenneke shuts the door. "This parlor's business-only. Now, what are you really here for? Because in my experience, newlyweds looking for adventure here are less"—she rolls a wrist—"squirrelly."

Emeric isn't willing to cede ground just yet. "Why do you think we're here?"

Jenneke gestures to a couch, flopping into one opposite it. "I'm no fool, Prefect. Erwin Ros went missing with an open tab the size of Dänwik. It looks bad for us. But I never would have let him rack up that bill if I didn't see he had the coin on hand." She frowns a bit sadly as Emeric and I sit. "And, frankly, Marien wouldn't have sent her sister to check with his boss if Erwin weren't a decent sort. Are the prefects also investigating, then?"

Emeric shakes his head. "Not officially. He's connected to a different matter. Is there a reason you think we should?"

Jenneke takes a moment to answer, tapping her fingers on the back of her sofa. "He's a decent sort," she says again, carefully. "But . . . he comes in here right after the *Grace Unending* stoppers up the Trench, with more money than most dockworkers see in their whole lives? And then he just *vanishes*?"

"Madame Treasury says you kicked him out," I say.

"Of course she did," Jenneke says with a look of disgust. "No, it was a rowdy night. He was at the bar one minute and gone the next. He owes us a hundred *gilden*; it'd be madness to just toss him into the street before he paid."

I lean forward. Maybe Erwin Ros is being held captive for another reason entirely. "I'm sensing some bad blood between you and the Treasury."

Jenneke scoffs. "Madame has been trying to strong-arm me into selling her the Green Sleeve for years. She wants to control both sides of the street, gate it off so people think they have to pay their way through in *spintz*. Did you know that's how she pays her workers, in *spintz*? They can use the tokens to pay board and upkeep at the Treasury and to buy cosmetics and dresses at the shops she owns. But if they want to cash out for Almanic coin—"

"It costs most of their paycheck," I say grimly. "We met Agnethe at the docks."

Jenneke sighs. "And Madame *only* hires girls who can't read her contract. Marien didn't tell me, or I would have warned her and her sister. If the girls lose their flat, I can let them both stay here, but that's all I can afford right now." She grimaces. "Being out a hundred *gilden* makes things tight."

At that, Emeric sits up a bit straighter. He fishes in his coat and pulls out a small card, then extends it to Jenneke. "I have a request. This is a prepaid courier token addressed to the local prefect outpost. If Madame approaches you again about selling the Green Sleeve, will you send this in?"

Jenneke takes the card. "You think she'd exploit the situation with Erwin?"

"I think it will help to know her next move," Emeric says nebulously. I suspect we're at the same hunch: Erwin Ros's disappearance has nothing to do with the *Grace Unending* and everything to do with Madame forcing a competitor's hand.

"You're welcome to look around anywhere that isn't, well, in use." Jenneke smirks. "Or, since that was a very unconvincing imitation of newlyweds, if you have any questions about *other* things . . ."

"We're good. It wouldn't hurt to check the place, though." I stand and head for the door, only to realize I'm on my own.

Emeric is still sitting on the couch, ears burning, eyes fixed on the coffee table. He seems to extract the words from somewhere below his sternum with an enormous amount of difficulty: "I . . . have a question."

There's a dreadful silence. I realize he's waiting for me to leave.

"Oh. I'll, uh. Go look. Looking for. Clues." I rush out, closing the door a little too hard behind me.

Is it me? Am I doing something wrong when we're together? I have to be. Why else would he not want me there?

Oh gods. All of a sudden I can't stop hearing Jenneke say *"hands-on tutorials."*

"Love me a man in uniform," Marien says. She's leaning on the staircase balustrade. "You're a lucky girl, you know that?"

"I do." I make myself push off the door, even though all I want is to rip it open and know what it is I'm ruining.

Ruining. That's right. "Before, you said those cultists had been by earlier?"

"Horrible wretches, all the way out from Hagendorn. Went and banged on every door in the Sünderweg, looking for a girl and . . ." She slows, catching on. "Oh. What do they want with you two?"

I peek around a curtain. The blond man is still outside with the others, glowering at the door. It doesn't make any sense; I told Hagendorn the Scarlet Maiden herself sent me on this trip. I don't know why Leni would tell them any different—or why they'd believe her over their god.

"I don't know," I say, "but I think we'll need that back exit after all."

CHAPTER EIGHTEEN

BEAUTIFUL

WHEN WE RETURN TO THE JOLLY MAGISTRATE IN THE EARLY AFTER-
noon, Joniza is lounging in the little garden partitioned off for tavern patrons who want to eat in the sunshine. She takes one look at the
red chalk splattered over us both and bursts into laughter. "What kind
of mess have you gotten yourselves into *now?*"

I figure Emeric and I can take a quick detour before we clean up and
figure out how to extract Erwin Ros. "Cultists," I tell Joniza by way of
explanation as I walk over. She nods sagely. "You look like you're having
a better day than we are."

Joniza raises a glass with a fancy little floral garnish. "Baba knows
a decorator here who always makes a big purchase. This time he's

apparently committed to a project large enough to clean out most of the caravan."

"So *Meister* Bajeri can start the return trip early?"

"*And* if we leave in the next few weeks, we can use the summer pass through the Alderbirgs down south, instead of going around." Joniza grins. "He'll make it to Sahali with plenty of time before Fatatuma's due date. We might even stop in Minkja so he can meet Bastiano."

I remember every long trip Bajeri made through Sovabin, every time he saw how we lived there but didn't say a word in judgment. "I think he'd like to see you happy."

"Hm." Joniza peels one finger from her glass to point at me. "You've gone and gotten insightful on me. Maybe this cult thing isn't so bad."

"No," Emeric says sourly, trying once again to brush red powder off his coat. "It is still extremely bad."

A head pokes around the doorway leading into the tavern: Agnethe. My stomach drops. We still haven't figured out how to get her paid.

"Please congratulate your father for me," I tell Joniza. "We've got to go handle something."

We head over to Agnethe. "Did you try the apple cake?" asks Emeric, pulling out a chair at an empty table. Agnethe nods as she sits across from him, fidgeting, but doesn't speak. "So," Emeric starts, "we went to see Madame Treasury."

I plop into the seat next to him. "She's *horrible*."

A flicker of relief darts through Agnethe's expression. I understand why; when you say a powerful person has wronged you, it's always a coin toss whether others will decide it's easier to pretend they didn't hear.

"When you signed the contract to work for her, what did she tell you it said?" Emeric asks.

Agnethe's face twists as she tries to recall. "That I'd earn a white penny every day I worked for her. Then she asked me to sign and said it was all right that I couldn't write my name."

"Was anyone else there?"

"No."

"Did she say anything about paying you in *spintz*? Or a fee to change them out?"

"Not until I asked for my wages. Then she said I was in . . ." Agnethe's brow wrinkles deeper. "Administration forfeit?"

"Administrative forfeiture?" Emeric's brow gets a matching divot as Agnethe nods. "That's not . . . I'm afraid that was a lie. Administrative forfeiture is what happens to someone's property while they're serving a prison sentence. Their assets belong to the local government until their sentence is over. In the meantime, they can be sold to anyone for the same amount as the most recent annual tax. But it has nothing to do with wages, or your contract." He leans back. "I have bad news and good news on that front. Part of your contract does say that if you're caught spying, you give up your right to any unpaid wages."

"But I wasn't spying," Agnethe protests. "I didn't know . . ."

"No one in their right mind would have agreed to that contract if they knew what was in it," he agrees. "Unfortunately, she claims someone witnessed her read it to you, which I don't believe, but it makes it your word against theirs. And the city guards like her quite a bit. That's the bad news. The good news is that this seems to be a pattern with her, and it's very illegal. If we can find others she's done this to, you can band together and file a civil petition, which I suspect you'd win. That would force her to pay you not just your wages but also fees for putting you through this."

"How long would it take?" Agnethe asks.

Emeric pauses, the cold hourglass of reality draining to clarity for him. The Godly Courts have the luxury of time—and the literal Low God Time, in fact—on their side; a trial can be summoned in a breath, the rulings dispensed in the next. The only delay is in preparing the case. Time, however, makes no exceptions for the courts of mortals.

"It could be weeks, maybe months," Emeric admits. "Miss Jenneke did say she could take in you and Marien—"

"But you won't need it." I put a hand on his arm, then reach for my satchel.

This was always going to be the best answer. I *know* how employer schemes work; they're a lock of their own kind. No one puts a lock on a door to keep it shut. They put the lock there to make it too hard, too time-consuming, for the wrong sort of people to get through. Madame waives her fees for the guards, she fakes her contracts, and she pays in her made-up money, all so she can draw out fights against girls like Agnethe until they can't afford another round.

I find a handkerchief by touch, then one of my larger rubies, and fold it into the cloth. Then I lower my voice. "Put your hands on the table, together, palms up." Agnethe does. I set the handkerchief in her open hands. "Listen very carefully. Do you feel that stone? Put this in your pocket like a normal hankie, and don't let that stone fall out."

"What is it?" she whispers as she obeys.

"The rent you owe," I say matter-of-factly. "Do you know where to find a jeweler in Welkenrode?" She nods. "Good. Go to them—not one in Rammelbeck—so no one here sees you. Tell the jeweler your uncle won that in a card game last night and wants it appraised. They will almost certainly make you an offer. Don't accept less than ten *gilden*—" Her eyes go very round until I frown. "I mean it, ten and not a *gelt* less. If the offer's too low, say you have to ask your uncle and start to leave, and they'll increase it. Put the money in the hankie so no one else sees, and take that straight to your landlord to pay your rent, then put what's left somewhere safe."

"B-but how will we pay you back?" Agnethe asks unevenly.

I give her a wry smile. "By learning your letters, so no one can get you into a contract like that again. Go now, so you'll be done with all this before dark."

Emeric waits until Agnethe's left the courtyard to say, "You shouldn't have to do that."

"Tell me something I don't know," I sigh. "But what am I supposed to do, let her get kicked out of her home?"

He puts an arm around my shoulders. "No. It's just . . . very generous. And you shouldn't have to be."

I lean my head on him. "I'm tired," I say quietly, "of watching the empire make a thousand more girls like me, every day." Then I stand. "I'm going to go wash off this mess."

Emeric pushes to his feet. "Same. I'll use the common baths. I think you more than deserve the tub in the room."

I do not bother with even a procedural objection on our way upstairs. I haven't had a private bath since I left Castle Reigenbach, and now that the prospect's on the table, I might knife-fight to keep it. Emeric seems to pick up on that, because he gathers a change of clothes and a towel and exits our room with *remarkable* expedience, shaking rose petals out of his hair as he goes. The petals dissolve after an hour anyway, or we'd be up to our ankles by now. We learned the hard way that they rain from the ceiling *every* time the door opens and closes.

I shuck my own clothes and wait in a towel while the tub fills up. The clerk was right to brag about the plumbing. Visually it may be a nightmare, but in terms of engineering, it's a triumph to have steaming hot water spill from a wall spigot shaped like a chubby-cheeked imp.

As I wait, I mull over the Treasury and whether I actually could burn the place to the ground without Emeric catching on. Or without getting

Erwin Ros killed. I might be taking this all too personally, considering I keep hearing echoes of Irmgard in it all.

There's a full-length mirror in our room, and an urge digs at me like a splinter. I walk closer, turn around, and look over my shoulder as I let the towel slide down my back.

The view is still as terrible as I remember. Once, I tried to romanticize the marks as thorns, like I might wield these scars and keep the world at knife's length. After Irmgard fouled the salve, they healed in knots of mottled gray and purple, not thorns but the barren fingers of a dead tree.

My own voice burns in my ears: *No one will ever want me.*

I throw the towel over a chair and climb into the tub before I have to look at myself a moment longer.

Irmgard I can't do anything about. I left her to rot in a dungeon in Minkja. Madame Treasury, on the other hand, is overdue a reckoning, and it's one I'm going to enjoy handing to her.

There's a shelf nearby laden with the tinctures, soaps, and perfumes the clerk promised yesterday. After I empty one bottle into the tub, rose-scented foam starts bubbling up. I shook off as much of the chalk as I could earlier, but I still go for a vigorous scrub. Too much of today has left me feeling dirty. When I'm done, I let myself slide down until the water comes up to just beneath my nose, and watch the red silk curtains of the tub's own canopy shiver in the draft.

It helps me to keep the metaphor going and think of these puzzles like locks. The Treasury is no different; I just have to be careful about choosing my picks. At the end of the day, I don't need revenge, I don't need money—I need Erwin Ros alive. And Madame knows we're looking for him. If I back her into a corner, she'll use that against me.

I'm toying absently with the edge of the canopy when the door opens and Emeric walks in. "I was just thinking—*OH.*"

"*SORRY,*" I yelp, yanking the curtain around the tub, but I'm very certain he got a complete and unabridged look at my frontal, well, everything.

His uneven voice carries through the fabric. "I thought you'd be done already, I'm so sorry, I'll go downstairs—"

"No, it's fine," I babble, "I took too long, I'm done now, you can stay."

"If—" His voice cracks. I hear the door shut, then a brief curse as rose petals spew from the ceiling. "Vanja, if you're not comfortable with me seeing you undressed, that's perfectly all right."

My toes curl in the bathwater. Part of me *does* want that, does want to feel his gaze go everywhere his hands already have. Almost everywhere. "That's not . . . exactly it."

There's a moment of quiet; the frenetic energy twists into something more pensive. Then he says, "May I make a guess?"

We were always going to have this conversation. I still want to sink under the water's surface. I make myself say, "Yes."

Careful footsteps approach the curtain, and then I hear him sit on the floor by the tub in a shuffle of fabric. Somehow his voice is grave and soft all the same. "I think you may be afraid . . . of me seeing your back."

My throat closes off. Of course he knows; of course he'd cut to the heart of the matter. I'm just wasting both of our time. Miserably, I draw the curtain back.

He's facing away, arms outstretched and propped on the knees he's pulled to his chest. Even if he were to look, from this angle, the walls of the tub are high enough to hide everything below my shoulders.

"There are so many girls out there," I tell him, my voice scratching on nearly every syllable. "Pretty ones, who aren't this—damaged. And they'll be better to you than me. I know what I am. You're too damn smart to not know it too."

Wordless, Emeric gets to his feet, picks up my towel from the chair.

He unfolds it, holding it lengthwise, his eyes averted as he returns to me, saying lowly, "Come here."

I'm too startled, too overwhelmed to second-guess. I stand and step into the towel, let him fold it around me—then hold in a squeak when he lifts me up and carries me to the bed. Butterflies practically erupt beneath my belly. "What are you . . . ?"

But Emeric only sets me on the edge of the bed. Then he sits beside me, taking my hands in his. "I'm—I need to say something. I'm going to try not to make a mess of it."

This is it, the part where we both pretend I'm passable the way I am, pretty enough with his spectacles off. Maybe I just wanted to hear that lie.

"We're not pretty people," Emeric says.

That I did not expect.

He's fighting off a grimace as he continues, "That sounds bad. I mean—there are people who you look at and immediately know, on a purely objective level, that they're beautiful. And I don't think that's either of us. In fact, I'm pretty sure anyone who meets me spends the first five minutes convinced they're being haunted by a census ledger. But . . ." His shoulders give an awkward little hitch. "You seem to like me nonetheless. I don't know why. But I have to believe you see something I don't."

I'd object, but I'm too busy trying to wrap my brain around the fact that Emeric feels this way in the first place.

"And if you were to ask me if I think you're beautiful . . ." He releases one of my hands to twist a damp lock of my hair between his fingers. "I'd say sometimes the sun hits your hair when I'm tying your ribbons, and it looks like it's burning, and I feel like I'm going to catch fire too. And sometimes, when you smile, it feels like my heart is going to explode—" I can't hold back a watery grin, and he exaggeratedly clutches his chest. "Enough, please, it can't handle this kind of strain—"

I shove him, but now we're both laughing. "*Stop.*"

His tentative grin sobers a little as his fingers trace over my shoulder. "In Minkja, when the pearls first worked on me, *really* worked, do you know what I wanted more than anything in the world? I wanted to snap the string so they'd never take your face away again, and—" Emeric's voice catches, turns throaty as his fingertips skim my collarbone. "I couldn't stop wondering if every one of your freckles tastes the same."

"Oh" is the best I can manage, because I think I want him to find out.

He lays a hand along my cheek. "I want you to see yourself the way I do, because there is beauty in every inch of you, Vanja. Just as you are. Whatever your back looks like, when you're ready, I'll find it there too."

I want to believe him, more than I've ever wanted anything. But there is nothing so terrifying as the thought of showing him the ugliest part of me.

For once I hear his words instead of Irmgard's: *I know bravery is real because I see you choose it every day.*

Maybe—maybe I can choose it, here and now, for him.

I take a deep, shaking breath. Then I shift my hips, turning away. For the second time today, I let the towel fall.

I hear his breath catch. Fingertips graze my spine, raising prickles on my skin. He doesn't speak for a long moment. When he does, his voice is tight with iron control. "Why did they heal like this?"

The scars are as bad as I said, as ugly as I knew they were. "Irmgard put soot and starch-root juice in my salve. We couldn't afford to replace it."

"Vanja . . ." There's a jagged edge to my name in his mouth. I don't know what to make of it, how to parse this, how to do anything but brace for the ghost of a whip.

This is the moment I have been building myself toward, when the worst truths are confirmed: that the damage goes too deep; that, at best, this part of me will always be something a lover must endure.

Instead, lips brush between my shoulder blades, over the thickest and most gnarled of my scars.

I go completely still.

Another kiss presses against the line of a scar, then another. Against the part of me that makes me remember *I am ugly, I do not deserve to be loved*, turning them into lies, breaking the memory like a curse.

I don't realize I'm crying until hot tracks spill down my cheeks. His hands steady my waist as I shudder, slide over my stomach, and I melt— there's no glamorous way to put it, I utterly melt—into his touch for once. Some part of me has always held back, clinging to the fear that I cannot be both known and wanted, that I will always have to surrender to one.

But he—he has found beauty, somehow, in the worst of me. This isn't a surrender; it's a release.

I turn to him, half laughing, half sobbing with relief, the last stones of a dam buckling in the rush as he gathers me up with only uncomplicated desire in his gaze. I didn't know I was starving for this, to be laid wholly bare and met with this divine hunger. I didn't know I could feel this way. I want more of this, more of him, more of it all.

We tumble to the sheets in a delirium, hands pulling at collars and hems until there is only skin sliding against skin, like we might strike a fire between us. I—I don't know where this is leading us, I just want to *feel*—

Then I remember this morning, in the Green Sleeve. "Wait," I gasp out, pulling back.

Emeric lets me go immediately, pushing himself away to give me room. "Sorry—that was—intense. Are you all right?"

I huff a feverish laugh, drying my face. "I'm—I'm amazing. I just want to know, am I doing something wrong?"

He stares at me like I've grown a second head. "What?"

"At the Green Sleeve. You didn't want me to hear your question. I thought maybe I'm not . . ."

"Oh. No, you're—" Emeric straightens his spectacles, contrite. "You said it yourself, you're amazing. It's the other way around. I thought *I* might not be . . ." He ducks his head, searching the linen for answers. (I have never been happier that we got rid of the satin.) "Saints and martyrs, this is embarrassing. I just want to make sure you're, er, enjoying yourself. And it's fairly evident when I've . . . had a good time? But I don't always know if . . . if-you-have? So that's—that's what I was asking about."

I blink. It's true: There's a definitive sort of conclusion for him, but I hadn't really considered how—that ought to happen for me. I thought it just felt good and that was all. "What did Jenneke say?"

"That everyone's different, so it's normal to take some time to figure out what works best." Emeric purses his lips. "But she said there's something we can try, that generally people, er . . . enjoy." At my quizzical look, he adds, "If I kiss you. Here."

His hand grazes my knee; then a fingertip traces a circle on the inside of my thigh.

It's my turn for a stilted "OH."

"But only if you want," he says quickly, "if you're not ready—"

"I think I—I do. Want that," I say just as quickly, surprising even myself. Then I consider the logistics, asking him to put his mouth—there. "Are you sure *you* want to, though?"

Emeric reaches for my chin, turns my face so I can look at him full on. "That," he says a bit raggedly, "is perhaps the silliest question I have ever heard."

The butterflies erupt with a vengeance as he catches me in one more deep, heady kiss, then starts easing himself toward the edge of the bed. "So that's a yes?" I squeeze out, still nervous. I mean, I know I just got out of the bath, but what if there's a *smell*, or if I—I look strange down there, or—

"I told you, Vanja." His lips move against the same spot on my thigh where his fingertip had been, and I find my hands already clutching the sheets for dear life. "Every inch."

Then he's moving up, closer—and then—and then—

For the first time in my life, I feel—

Beautiful.

✧

We spend the afternoon gloriously entangled, testing new waters, until we realize it's getting dark out. I wind up stealing his breeches and shirt to go put in a dinner order downstairs. (This is also how we find out that's a thing for Emeric, as he takes one look and promptly delays me for another ten minutes.)

I've just ordered our meals at the tavern bar when I feel an acute case of stink-eye burning into the back of my skull. Sure enough, Kirkling is scandalously close to a tipsy slump at the end of the bar, glowering at me like I pissed in her half-empty glass of *brandtwein*.

Maybe it's confidence from the afterglow, or maybe I'm just done waiting for her to invent a new pain in my ass. Either way, I find myself marching over to her. "Something wrong?"

Kirkling eyes me up and down, taking in the ill-fitting breeches and my haphazard braid, and swigs half her remaining liquor. "I see Aspirant Conrad's report today is going to be brief."

"Look." I plant my hands on my hips. "I get that you've decided to hate me. I can deal with that. But do you think, *maybe*, you can stop trying to wreck Emeric's case, since solving it is integral to *him not being fed to a hellhound*? If not for his sake, then for Klemens's."

"*Don't.*" The sneer drops off Kirkling's face, replaced by pure anger coiling like a viper. "Don't you *ever* invoke his name. Hubert Klemens was the best of us. He deserved better than to be fished out of a river like a common deadbeat."

I stand my ground. "You know I was framed for that."

"*Pff.*" Kirkling looks away, taking another sip from her glass. "He never should have been in Minkja. Hubert was supposed to retire when I did. Instead he stayed on another five years, just to look after Conrad. That boy is the best recruit the academy's seen in generations, but it's up to me to make sure he's worth the price." She snorts. "The only disrespect to Hubert is that Conrad's going to fail his Finding because he got distracted by a little two-penny charlatan with sheep eyes and a sob story."

I'm briefly speechless; I know she loathes me, but I wasn't prepared for her to break me off a chunk of uncut vitriol.

That doesn't mean I'm going to take it lying down.

"You waited for two months to assign Emeric an impossible Finding," I say coldly. "Let's just hope you don't drink yourself into an early grave. You'll need plenty of time to figure out how to explain *that* to Klemens when you see him."

Helga had the right of it: Trying to get through to Kirkling is like bouncing coins off a boulder. She just scoffs into her glass. I start to leave, then catch myself. Emeric said he wants me to see myself the way he does. That means I have one more point to settle.

"And for the record." My voice rises. "I did more to help a crime victim today than a prefect could. There's a statue of me in Minkja for a reason. If all you see in me is a two-penny charlatan, it's because that's what you want to see."

I turn to leave for real this time and indulge in a poisonous wink as I add over my shoulder, "I'm a hundred-*gelt* charlatan at *least*."

CHAPTER NINETEEN

The Waltz

"Well," Helga says shrewdly the next morning, "aren't *we* a ray of sunshine."

I swing my legs, perched on a bench in the courtyard of the Jolly Magistrate, waiting for Emeric. He has to go work at the prefect outpost today—something about logging progress on the case and doing research with Ambroszia—but before he sets off, he's insisted on getting us breakfast from a nearby bakery. I'm *aware* that I am beaming like a sap still. I think it would take an act of a Low God to dampen my mood. "Maybe I had a good night," I say cryptically. "Did you have any luck with Ozkar yesterday?"

Helga leans against the brick arch next to the bench. "Ugh, no. I told him Erwin got himself in some trouble, and all Ozkar said was 'Pass.' Then he kicked me out."

"Maybe I should try talking to him," I suggest.

"No," Helga says swiftly. "Not on your own or he may not even help you. Anyway, tell me about this night of yours. Have I won the bet?"

My beaming falters. It turns out it didn't take the act of a Low God after all, just one reminder. "I thought so . . . but the handprint is still there."

Helga's brow furrows. "Did you do what we talked about in Hagendorn? You know . . ." She forms a ring with her right hand's thumb and index finger, then extends the pointer finger of her left hand and makes a crude and unmistakable gesture.

I slap at her hands. "Can you *not?*" I check to make sure we're relatively out of earshot of anyone else. "We did . . . mouth . . . things. And it was really, uh, nice." (In fact, it was significantly nicer than what we've done before, and now I understand what he meant about . . . *conclusively* enjoying myself. But Helga doesn't need to know that.) "I thought that would count."

"Hmm." Helga's tone softens. "I mean, normally I'd say if it counts for you, that's all that matters, but you two have to work around the Scarlet Maiden's idea of a 'claim.' The main point of marriage in her time was to make children. To be purely clinical, she may consider him a virgin until he's had the kind of intercourse we talked about, the kind that can result in a pregnancy."

"But I can't get pregnant with the root-bind," I say, trying not to panic. "Would it still count? Or does that mean he has to—to—impregnate someone else? What if it doesn't happen the first time? What if—"

"Stop." Helga holds up a hand. "This is *exactly* why my rule is *what matters is what matters to you*. This is your relationship, even with . . .

extenuating circumstances. Focus on tracking down my ridiculous brothers, and don't let the Scarlet Maiden into your bedroom. Speaking of." She tilts her head to the courtyard's street entrance. Emeric's walked in with a greasy-bottomed paper bag and a grin that only widens when he sees me. Helga lets out a disgusted laugh. "Gods, you two are going to rot my teeth. Conrad! Where'd you get the pastries?"

She strides over to him for directions and tips a wave on her way out. Emeric sits on the bench beside me. There's an absolutely heavenly smell coming from the bag, but before I can plunge a hand in, he sets it on his other side. "Business first. I trust you remember how to use these?" He drops a round silver case into my palm.

"You got us message-mirrors!" I pop open the case and breathe on the mirror inside. There's a face engraved in the lid, and its eyes open as the glass fogs. Anything I trace onto the glass of my mirror will write itself onto the glass of his. To my surprise, there's a pulse of heat, which signals an incoming message.

My mirror's glass grays over. Then, to my even greater astonishment, lines scrawl across it in the undeniable shape of a pair of buttocks.

"Figured I'd get it out of the way," Emeric says mock-innocently.

I gaze up at him with pure adoration. "You complete me."

"And you haven't even tried these yet." He pulls two pastries from the bag and passes one to me. It's a still-warm double spiral of golden dough giving off a perfume of cinnamon and butter.

"Oh, we called these snail-shells in Sovabin," I say, like a fool, before taking a bite and realizing how incredibly wrong I am. Snail-shells are tasty, but this—*this* is a masterpiece of flaky layers and gooey filling.

"Do you?" Emeric asks, donning another innocent-but-not-really look.

I swallow my bite, wide-eyed. "Don't take this the wrong way . . . but this is almost better than last night."

"No, I concur." He downs a hearty bite of his own pastry, then glances sidelong at me. "Last night was . . . incredible, though. *You* were incredible."

I bump his shoulder with mine, an enormously goofy smile on my face. "You say that like you weren't the one making me nearly break the soundproofing."

Emeric chokes on the pastry. When he's done coughing, he says, "I suppose I can accept that. Do you remember . . . No, never mind."

"Do I remember what?"

He shifts with a bit of chagrin. "When we were in Minkja, and I caught you in Lähl, and you made a very cruel and hurtful remark about me looking like . . ."

"A schoolboy trying to buy his first *wurstkuss*?" I supply wryly. "Trust that the irony has not escaped me."

All his attempts to hide a smirk are failing. "I don't think either of us predicted this particular outcome at the time, to be fair." Then he sobers. "But I do mean it, you were incredible, and not just in—*that* way. I know it has to be terrifying to be so open with anyone, let alone me. Every time I think I've seen you at your bravest, you prove me wrong."

I can't tell if I'm blushing from head to toe or if this warmth, these bubbles, are just new constants in the way I feel around him. I finish another bite to buy myself time to think of an eloquent answer, but all I can come up with is unpolished truth: "Maybe I just like letting you in."

"Hm." He pulls two more pastries out of the bag, eyeballs them, and hands me the one with more cinnamon filling. "Then thank you for letting me stay."

I don't know what does it, exactly.

Maybe it's the way he leans just so and our shoulders fit together like they were designed to. Maybe it's how he knows to let the quiet rest between us because I need breathing room when we talk about these things. Maybe it's that he knew I'd like a pastry I've never heard of, knew which one I'd like better without me saying, somehow knows a thousand little things about me that I don't always know myself.

It's not an ornate bridge but an inn's courtyard bench. I'm not wildly successful or attractive, but I'm wearing his ribbons. There's no shower of petals, but there's a blue sky and a hint of warmth in the breeze. This is where it happens.

This is where I realize—accept—the clearest, most obvious truth of my world: I am disastrously, irrevocably, madly in love with Emeric Conrad.

It's not even a new feeling. It's like when we watched the stars ignite outside Rammelbeck: The first few were easy to catch, and then everywhere I looked, I found a new light blazing against the dark. If every star were a reason I care for him—that's how I feel, like I carry too many stars in me to count, like my skin might burst with the enormity of it all, like if I gather them all up, the only name I could give this is love.

I love his shyness and his cleverness and his laugh. I love how he twirls his charcoal sticks while he's brooding over his notes, how he genuinely cares about protecting people, how he makes me believe in something as fickle as justice. I love how he calls me his Queen of Roses, the *cheesiest* possible nickname, and how it makes me melt every time. I love his stupid spotless clothes and his stupid cute spectacles and his stupid brilliant face.

I think I understand, now, why they say you fall in love, because I don't think I could climb out of this feeling even if I wanted to. What a beautiful trap I've built for myself.

What a horror, what a delight, to find I've been caught.

"So," Emeric says conversationally, as if my own personal apocalypse has not unfolded beside him, "what are your plans today?"

I muster my senses as best I can. After all, this feeling isn't new, it's just the disaster of admitting it. Maybe, in time, I can even figure out how to say it aloud.

But for now, I just need to figure out how to phrase my reply so he has plausible deniability.

"I thought I'd go to the Sünderweg, have a chat or two," I give in mysterious answer. The clocktowers chime for eight. "I should get moving."

He, of course, grasps the gist of it in an instant. "Please be careful. Madame Treasury—gods, what a ridiculous name that is—she's not going to lose graciously. And . . . try not to break too many laws?"

I tap my chin, thinking, and say, with more than a little incredulity, "It might actually all be technically legal. How embarrassing."

"You are an unfathomable terror." He stands, helping me up. "I'd better get going too. Use the mirror if you need me. And . . ." Emeric plants a kiss on my cheek and murmurs in my ear, "Happy hunting."

⁓⁂⁓

One of my favorite dances is the waltz. You're familiar, I'm certain; the foundation is an easy box step—*one*-two-three, *one*-two-three—but the real magic is in where you take it.

Step one: Left foot forward. Direct.

It's a beautiful day, and one of the city's many couriers has arrived on the docks.

At least, she looks like a courier, wearing an official sort of uniform for an official sort of person. Someone from Dänwik might perhaps recognize elements of a royal coachman's stolen livery, but any insignias have been carefully cut away or covered. And besides, no one here is rich enough to be from Dänwik.

(Someone more observant might note the courier is short and slight and that something's off about the hat, like it doesn't quite sit right.

They might even realize braids are tucked under the brim, braids that don't match the soot-dusted thick black brows. No one here is that observant either.)

The courier reaches a burly woman nursing a bottle on the wharf. The barge is still gumming up the river, so instead of commanding a crew of dockworkers, the boss is commanding a strong drink, alone.

(Not completely alone—Madame Treasury's dockworker spy is still lounging nearby.)

"Erwin Ros," the courier says loudly. "I have an urgent message for Erwin Ros?"

"You and half the city, it seems," grunts Erwin's boss.

"He stopped by our clinic on Friday." The courier's voice doesn't bounce off the water so much as ricochet, angled to strike the spy. "It's very important we speak with him. He's carrying a new breed of bed lice, and the normal screening tests won't pick it up."

The spy doesn't move.

The courier decides to spell it out. "Any *houses of entertainment* Ros may have visited, even in the Sünderweg, are at risk."

That does the trick. The spy takes off, headed for Madame Treasury's.

"Please pass the message if you see him," the courier says blandly, not caring a whit either way. The real message is already in motion.

There's a pulse of heat from the mirror in her pocket. When she checks the glass, it's a simple confirmation: An hour earlier, Madame Treasury made another offer to buy the Green Sleeve.

⚬⚭⚬

Step two: Right foot up and over. A shift of the weight, moving at a diagonal.

The courier arrives at Liebeskind's Pest Control, checks the street for cultists, doffs her hat, and rubs the soot from her brows. Here, she *wants* to be recognized. The official-looking jacket is tucked under an arm, and suddenly she's just a girl on a stroll.

"Welcome back," Liebeskind the streetwitch says when she walks in. "How's your friend? Olga?"

"Helga, and much better. She was *so* mortified; she's a hedgewitch herself, but they don't get bed lice like that out in the backwater. I'm actually here to pick up a few ingredients for her."

Liebeskind bustles to his imposing wall of jars. "Of course! What do you need?"

The courier rattles off a few cheaper ingredients, then gets to the two key players: ". . . a scoop of dead bed lice, and a scoop of dried rose hip, freshly ground."

"I'll sieve the rose hip for you," offers Liebeskind. The courier is glad he's at least that savvy. Rose hips have plenty of uses, but they're full of nasty little hairs that cause all sorts of itchy misery on contact.

(Hopefully you're starting to see the shape of the box step now.)

He's not savvy enough to catch her a few minutes later, though, after he's bagged up the bed lice and the ground rose hips. While he's distracted, making change for the purchase, she sweeps the leftover pile of fine rose hip hairs into a leather pouch and stows it away in her satchel.

"Thank you for your business," Liebeskind says, holding out her change.

The courier wisely lets him drop it into her gloved palm. "No," she says, "thank you."

❧

Step three: The left foot moves to meet the right. The box closes.

The courier puts her braids back up under her hat but removes her gloves for the screening into the Sünderweg. The streetwitches look for only live infestations. The packet of dead bed lice hidden in the courier's satchel don't register so much as a warning.

The infestation of cultists, on the other hand, is making itself quite well-known. They've set up in the street between the Green Sleeve and Madame Treasury's. A small crowd is gathered around the blond man as he howls at the sky.

"*RISE UP! Rise up, children of the Haarzlands!* Heed the call of the almighty Scarlet Maiden, who brings a new day!"

How tiresome, thinks the courier as she pulls on her gloves. Then she moves through the crowd like a ghost, like a needle, leaving a pinch of dead bed lice in certain pockets, a dusting of rose hip hairs under certain collars. When she's done, she saunters over to the Treasury.

The bouncer is planted at the base of the stairs this morning. He doesn't have time to even grunt "*Spintz*" before she flashes one of the brass tokens from yesterday and breezes past, moving like a regular, too quick for him to see her face.

(They really should have let me spin the wheel.)

I pause at the top of the steps and don't go in just yet. Instead, I turn to stare at the blond zealot and wait until I catch his eye.

Then I sweep the hat off my head and let my vivid ginger braids fall free. As recognition dawns on the zealot's face, I slip another generous pinch of rose hip hairs from the leather pouch in my pocket and blow him a kiss.

Hundreds, maybe thousands, of tiny hairs drift in an invisible cloud toward the unsuspecting bouncer. When the cultists inevitably try to come after me, they're going to run right through it.

I step backward through the doorway and into the Treasury just as the hour-bells strike ten. It's time for the final step before my victory twirl.

When I turn, I find Madame sitting at one of the bars, wearing another impractical white gown. She hasn't noticed me yet; her eyes are fixed on the opposite staircase, her mouth twisting with impatience as she picks at a sleeve. I don't blame her for her nerves. By now, she ought to have had two very important visitors.

First: the city official who arrived an hour ago for the Treasury's weekly health inspection. If my guess is right, he's "spot-checking" his favorite *mietling*, on the house.

And second: the spy who arrived midway through the "spot-check" to tell Madame Treasury that, thanks to her kidnapping Erwin Ros, her brothel is about to be the epicenter of the latest innovation in bed-lice outbreaks.

If I were in her shoes, I wouldn't notice me either; I'd be focused solely on getting the health inspector off the premises as quickly as possible.

Somewhere in the gallery above, a door opens, and the creak of floorboards preempts a spurt of giggles. A formal-looking badge gleams on the health inspector's breast pocket as he starts down the stairs, good-naturedly cursing at the buttons of his breeches.

I *think* it's a trick of the light, but I could swear, for a moment, I see a glimmer of gold.

"Satisfied with your inspection, sir?" Madame trills tautly.

"*Quite*," he grunts.

Madame slides off her bar stool as he reaches the bottom of the stairs. "Same time next week, then. I'll walk you—"

She turns to find me waiting behind her and jumps.

"Madame Treasury," I intone seriously, once again raising my voice to ring across the floor and producing a folded snowy linen handkerchief, "I have a matter for you that requires utmost discretion."

"What are you doing back here, you horrible little troll?" she snarls.

I couldn't have written her a better line. Now every witness knows I've been in the Treasury before. Including the health inspector.

There is a beautiful moment when she registers the linen in my hand and has one heartbeat of perfect, ice-cold comprehension.

Then the doors of the Treasury burst open. The cultists storm in around the bouncer, shouting about defiling and ruin and other cheery topics; the customers start shouting about the rude interruption; Madame is shouting for the guards—everyone's just going all in on the shouting. Even better, some of the blond preacher's crowd has tagged along for the show.

Powder, meet spark: The bouncer shoulders in, pulls an untapped grudge off his layaway shelf, and funnels it into one hell of a swing at the preacher. A free-for-all melee breaks out. Through the open doorway, I see guards running up the street, but it's too late to stop the brawl.

I stitch my way through the chaos again, dispensing dead bed lice and rose hip hairs—with thought and care, of course. The jig will be up if everyone gets the same case of bed lice at the same time. Instead, I tag the first guards to arrive, a few of the patrons who were already here, and, most importantly, the health inspector. Never before have I been so grateful for faulty buttons, as his breeches are still flapping open and all I have to do is bang a fistful of lice and rose hip hairs against his belly as I fake-stumble past.

The havoc starts to lose steam as the cultists realize they're outnumbered. I wait for Madame to pull the health inspector from the fray, apologizing profusely and brushing him down. To my sheer glee, she even slips a hand below his waistband, whispering in his ear.

A strange look crosses both their faces as the invisible but potently irritating rose hip hairs start to take effect. Madame retracts her hand, staring in horror.

And that is when I deliberately trip and tumble to the floor in front of them both, letting my clean white handkerchief spill open at their feet. It is, of course, covered in bed lice. Just like Madame's hand.

The health inspector's own hand twitches toward his breeches, then flexes as he heroically resists scratching in front of a crowd. Others do not share his heroics, squirming in place. The inspector's face turns a mottled purple as he draws the connections I have so painstakingly laid out for him.

"You told me you kept them clean," he growls, and he doesn't give Madame a chance to answer before his bellow roars through every floor: *"GUARDS! SHUT THIS BROTHEL DOWN AT ONCE!"*

CHAPTER TWENTY

THE THIRTEENTH

THE SÜNDERWEG IS, AS I GUESSED, ABSOLUTELY RUTHLESS WHEN IT comes to venereal ailments.

Over the course of the next hour, I learn that Madame Treasury's is to be completely shut down for the next two weeks, which is the full life cycle of bed lice. Madame herself will be, by law, responsible for the room, board, and treatment of all her workers—she tried unsuccessfully to claim the *mietlingen* were only contractors—and the brothel subject to floor-to-ceiling inspections every day in its first week back, then every three days for the next month.

(It turns out the guards actually do take outbreaks seriously. At least, if the afflicted nethers belong to their own.)

All this would put a dent in any brothel's business, but the real damage is cutting off Madame's *spintz* scheme for a fortnight. She could undersell her competition only because the exchange tax funneled money right into her coffers. Now that spigot's been cut off.

I know the two-week shutdown is meant to starve out the bed lice, but I'm not sure the Treasury will survive either. At least, not with Madame at the helm.

And since city officials *will* be scouring every inch of the brothel to make sure, *very* sure, that it's completely devoid of occupants, it's just a matter of time before the Treasury dispenses with Erwin Ros.

The front door is wide-open, guards and official streetwitches trooping in and out, so I loop around to the staged seedy alleyway behind the brothel, curated for the client who prefers a certain ambience but none of the communicable disease. I post up by a pile of crates, leaning against the artificially grimy plaster and hoping no one pops by with a customer. The wait isn't long.

The Treasury's back door swings open, and a very mopey version of Dieter Ros is summarily punted into the alleyway before the door slams shut again. He staggers a few steps, then urps up mostly liquid all over a pile of aesthetic trash.

Considering what a pain in the ass this has been, I decide to cut to the chase. I whip the bone awl from my satchel. "Erwin Ros?"

He looks up blearily, wiping his mouth, and nods. I grab his free hand. He stares, befuddled. "Who're y—*OW.*"

"Don't be a baby." I shove his bleeding finger onto the cambric square, shaking off the awl, then let him go.

"Must be Vanja," he mumbles. "Helga told me . . . I—I'm gonna be—"

He is promptly sick all over the trash again. I suppose it adds to the atmosphere.

"Were you drugged?" I ask shortly. "I can take you to a streetwitch if they hurt you."

He teeters, straightens, then reconsiders and plants a hand on the wall. "I," Erwin declares, "'m verrrrry drunk. Listen. *Listen.* They have *so much brandtwein.*"

I knock on the back door of the Treasury. And keep knocking. And knocking.

"*Noooo,*" Erwin whines, covering his ears.

Finally a harried-looking server opens the door. "*What.*"

"Can we get some water over here?" I jerk my thumb at Erwin. He helpfully coughs up another splat of vomit.

A moment later a cheap *sjoppen* is thrust into my hands. I shove it at Erwin in turn as the door slams shut again, wishing I had some of Helga's hangover cure. "Drink up."

"Sound like Helga too," Erwin says sullenly.

As he works on his water, I start to fold up the cambric—then stop.

I haven't looked at it in a while, not since we left Dänwik. Udo's, Jakob's, and Dieter's drops of blood haven't faded or browned at all; they're still as fresh a red as Erwin's. And, even more unsettlingly, they're . . . branching. No, *branching* isn't quite it. It's as if blood is creeping along invisible lines that connect the drops. As I watch, Erwin's blood spot sprouts tiny tendrils of its own, thread by thread, stretching for the others.

"Gross," I say, mystified.

"What?"

"I said, what happened to you?" I stow the awl and cambric away. Four down, three to go; we're more than halfway now. If this keeps up, we'll meet the Scarlet Maiden's mid-May deadline with time to spare. "From what I gathered, you got bribed for something with the *Grace Unending,* you spent most of your bribe at the Green Sleeve, and before you could pay, you got kidnapped by some goons from the Treasury. Is that about right?"

Erwin seems marginally more coherent. At least, he's competent enough to step away from his own sick and sit on a crate, head in his hands. "I've been at the *Treasury?* That place is way too nice for me."

"Evidently not."

He rubs his eyes. "Well, you got most of it. We have to give helmsmen directions for navigating the Trench, stuff like depth, current, wind, bunch of numbers. I dunno. Someone paid me to switch out the directions for the *Grace*. That crew's pricks anyway. That night, all I remember is buying rounds at the Green Sleeve, then I woke up in jail. I thought it was jail. There were shackles." He considers. "And whips. Maybe . . . sexy jail."

"Not words that go together," I say dryly.

"I don't know what they wanted with that. They kept giving me food and booze and saying I had to wait. Then they just dumped me out." He pats himself down. "Oh, *scheit*. The money's gone. It's gonna take *forever* to pay the Green Sleeve. *Nggghhhhh*." Erwin hangs his head. "At least I can sleep this off before my shift on Sunday."

This is perhaps the first time I pity the fool. I say, not unkindly, "It's Monday."

Erwin slumps over into an agonized groan. "*Nooooooooo*."

I make a mental note to see if I can recover the bribe money from Madame, perhaps with a little bespoke burglary. At the very least, the Green Sleeve shouldn't be left on the hook. (I may be biased. Jenneke's advice for Emeric was clearly priceless.)

"The prefects are investigating this, you know," I say. "If you tell them what you know, they may get you clemency."

Erwin shakes his head. "Or they could put me back in jail—*real* jail, not sexy jail. I can't leave the Green Sleeve in the lurch."

It's hard to argue with that. I trust Emeric to be fair, but what if the prefects on this case are more like Kirkling? "I'm . . . friendly with a prefect," I massively understate. "He might be able to help. If you change your mind, I'm at the Jolly Magistrate, Helga and I both."

"Enh," he sighs noncommittally. "Sorry to be such a disappointment. And that we had to meet this way. Are you going to Sånnik's wedding next week? You can meet most of the others."

"I've already met Dieter, Udo, Jakob, and Helga," I say, brow furrowing. With Erwin, that ought to constitute the majority of the siblings Ros.

"I mean, not everyone will show, but it's as close as you'll get to all twelve of us in the same place." He blinks up at me. "Thirteen, I s'pose."

I stare back.

I—

It's like a puzzle, the annoying kind from street vendors, where they've twisted old horseshoe nails together and swear that, with just the right angle, they'll break apart. And you don't believe them until you're distractedly bending and turning the iron and without even trying—

The link splits.

I don't speak for a moment. When I do, the words come out forced: "I thought there were seven brothers and Helga."

But why would I think that? I hear it as soon as I say it aloud. Why didn't I ask?

Why didn't I see?

"There's seven of us boys, and then Katrin Little, Luisa, Eida, and Helga for the girls, and Jörgi's neither, and they make twelve, and then . . ." Erwin looks up at me. "Helga hasn't told you yet?"

"Told me what," I scrape out, but it's pointless. I already know.

"Ohhh I did it again," Erwin says softly. "Fouled it up. *Scheit, scheiter, scheiten.*" He reels to his feet and pushes past me. "Gonna go lie low until this all blows over with the *Grace.* Thanks for the water."

"Wait—"

But he's already gone.

My ears are roaring. Numbness starts in my belly and rolls down my legs. I sit hard on a crate. The message-mirror trembles in my hand as I pull it from a pocket, flick it open. I need to tell Emeric—

What, exactly?

A drunk might be my brother?

A drunk, and a minstrel, and a weaverwitch, and a shepherd, and the others—

Helga lied about—Saints and martyrs, *Eida.* I knew her because I saw her in Udo and Jakob and—

The mirror. I see her in the mirror, in my bloodless face, my wild black eyes.

I snap it shut, heart racing.

I don't know what to say. I don't know what to do. I could be wrong, this could be wrong, what are the odds that I would wander into a town in the middle of nowhere and land in my brothers' home—

I need the truth.

I don't trust Helga. Erwin is gone.

But there's one brother Ros still in reach.

Five minutes later, I'm standing in Liebeskind's Pest Control once more. "Sorry to bother you," I choke out, "but I need directions to the workshop of Ozkar Ros."

⁂

Welkenrode is—well, I'd like it a lot more if I weren't walking in a single-purposed fog. I register that the buildings are newer on this side of the Trench, the streets smooth cobblestone instead of hard-packed dirt. Even the food stalls look cleaner. The Konstanzian Imperial Abbey surveys it all from the crest of a shallow hill, and I suppose I could try going to Henrik Ros there, but—Helga's steered me away from Ozkar, again and again, for a reason. Now I think I know why.

It's an hour or so past noon. I should be starving. Instead my stomach is a knot too tight for anything but air. A glut of questions is screaming through my head:

Do you remember me?

How long have you known?

Above all: *Does she regret it, my—our—mother, leaving me in the woods?*

Ozkar's workshop doesn't immediately stand out, one more gray stone façade along a long lane. Then I see the iron bars over the windows. They're not just for human intruders: Runes and bones are wrought into the metal, glowing a faint yellow.

A soft bell chimes as I push the iron door open. The interior is lit by the steady colorless lights I've seen only with the prefects, burning in glass fixtures along the walls. There's something that seems like it ought to be a shop front counter, if a counter moonlighted as a kitchen table, had a side gig as a workbench, and freelanced as a garbage bin. Shelves are bolted to nigh every wall and overflowing with glass jars, wooden boxes that have persisted through five different label regimes, miscellaneous tools, and other inventive paraphernalia. Any empty wall space is crammed with tacked-up notes and a strange miscellany of pinned objects: a little wooden doll, a worn charm from a temple, dice, folded letters, a rat skull with a pin through its eye socket. Even what look like tiny milky stones, until I realize they're finger bones.

"Damn you, Betze." I didn't even notice the man standing at a long workbench in the far corner, his back to me. Not until his voice cracked across the room like glass. "I needed that filament twenty minutes . . ." He trails off as he turns and sees me.

Ozkar Ros looks to be in his midtwenties, with the same narrow build as Dieter and Erwin. He has Eida's narrow face, a dusting of freckles, vivid ginger hair cropped efficiently short. The leather apron covering his shirt and trousers has a rich topography of stains and singes, as do his buckskin gloves. A spectral mantle clings to him, twin round yellow eyes burning over his head. I make out the faint ghostly lines of striated primary feathers and the great disc of an owl's face, much larger than life.

Ozkar snaps his fingers, and the phantasm vanishes. Yellow lights ignite in Ozkar's pupils as he blinks at me, strolling around a defeated-looking arcane apparatus to dock himself by the front counter. "Ah. You must be Vanja. My word, you *are* just like her."

I ask, "Who?" not because I don't know but because I need someone to say it.

"Why, dear old Marthe, of course." Ozkar strips the gloves from his hands and lets them fall to the countertop, airing a bleak little chuckle. "Our mother."

THE THIRD LIE

HOME

ONCE UPON A TIME, THERE WAS A HELPFUL LITTLE GIRL.

Her first mother told her she was bad luck walking, the thirteenth child of a thirteenth child, that whatever she touched would turn to ruin. And then her first mother left her.

So the girl insisted on helping her second mothers, her godmothers, because she did not want to be sent away again.

Her godmothers, Death and Fortune, found this very confusing.

They were gods, after all, and the girl wanted for nothing. The three lived in a little cottage that was somehow always clean and big enough, in the heart of a yew thicket, and the world beyond the thicket changed every morning. Some days, a great empty seashore stretched and roared beyond the trees and the little girl could play in the waves. Others, they were planted atop a snowy mountain, or nestled deep in a forest of oak and ash, or rooted in a courtyard in a strange city, one empty of people but full of voices, where yews grew straight from the stone.

At first their only guest was Time. His gown would change each visit, sometimes shimmering, sometimes a waterfall of lace, once dazzling gold like the rays of the sun. He would sit with the girl and ask how she liked her home, if her godmothers were kind, her favorite food—little measuring questions to gauge how she'd grown. And then he would speak with Death and Fortune outside, bid the girl farewell, and vanish like color shifting through a prism.

The girl had as much to eat as she wished, as much to drink, soft and sturdy clothes, toys and books and bedtime stories. But she wanted to be helpful so she could stay.

At first it was just a game: Fortune gave her coins to flip, dice to roll, bones to throw, and laughed at how they fell. Fortune grew to like it very much, *tsk*ing or clapping and never telling the girl that she was casting lots for crowns and calamities, riches and ruin. Fortune said it was much more interesting this way.

Then Death, too, found a way for the girl to be helpful: She brought children to the cottage to play. They were sleepy and weeping, or wide-eyed and fearful, or sometimes screaming, and those were the worst of all. The little girl would tell them stories or show them her toys or teach them a clapping game she'd learned from her sister long ago. When the children had calmed down, cheered up, or simply had their fill of games, Death would take them away.

The little girl never saw them again. After a few months, she understood why. Once, she asked Death if the ghost children could linger a little longer, and Death only shook her head.

"Humans are not meant to stay after they are cut free of your world." She ruffled the girl's braids. "Be proud. You're making their passage much easier."

The girl, of course, was happy to be helpful.

One day, Time came to the cottage. He did not sit with her. The girl listened at the door as he spoke with Death and Fortune instead.

". . . too long," he was saying. "She's already changing. If you don't return her soon, it will be too late."

"She's happy here," Fortune insisted. "She's useful."

"She's a mortal girl with a full *mortal* life to live. If you love her, you won't take that away."

The girl did not understand.

At least, not until the next day, when Death and Fortune came to her. They had no ghosts, no coins or bones, only deepest sadness when they said the girl would have to leave.

The girl understood, suddenly, why some ghosts arrived screaming.

She asked what she'd done wrong. She asked if she hadn't helped enough. She said she would do anything, anything at all, if she didn't have to leave and be left again. She promised she would be good—not just good, *better*—if she didn't have to go, she would work twice as hard.

But Death and Fortune promised her a home in a castle, with a warm fire and a place to be helpful. They said they would still be with her, even if no one else could see, like a special game.

She still didn't understand. If she hadn't done anything wrong, why didn't they want her anymore?

The night before that awful morning, Death tucked me into bed, looking a little sadder than usual. Sometimes I liked to imagine that my birth mother looked that way when she remembered me. Other times I wondered if she was happy to be free of me. Me and the ruin that followed.

"Death," I asked, "what happened to my first mother?"

Death smoothed my blankets and didn't answer for a long, long moment. Death cannot lie, you see, so she had to pick her words carefully so as not to upset me.

"It is as I said." She kissed the top of my head and blew out the candle by my bed. "After she left the crossroads, one of you went home."

CHAPTER TWENTY-ONE

ꝒEADWEIGHT

"You'd be marthe's spitting image if she was still alive," ozkar says blithely. "Let's hope the resemblance ends there."

Dead.

My mother is dead.

All I wanted was to hear her say it was a mistake, that she never should have abandoned me, that I haunt her like she haunts me.

And now I never will.

There's a flat buzzing in my ears, punctured only by the hardscrabble clatter of Ozkar's metal tools on the counter. I don't even have a crate to sit on this time; the one seat in the workshop is a stool in the back, by the workbench. My knees lock up as I fight to breathe through this.

Marthe. I thought—I thought I picked that name by chance—

What a fool I've been, this whole time.

"Don't tell me that's news." Ozkar tilts his head in disbelief.

There's a chime from the back workbench. Ozkar starts, then snaps his fingers. The massive ghostly owl reappears over him as the yellow lights in his eyes extinguish. "Grandfather, the balance fork's done. Bring it here."

The owl shifts its weight, eyes trained on me. Its beak clacks open. "*Van . . . ja?*"

"*Now*," Ozkar orders. The owl flaps across the room as he sighs. "Don't mind Grandfather. Great-Great-Grandfather, technically. You were too young to remember, but you're named for his wife."

It's like—like a pin is being stuck through parts of me, fixing me to a wall I've never seen. The name I was given is not my own. The name I made into a mask—stolen from a long-dead memory.

Grandfather alights on a shelf and drops a small steel bar from his beak into Ozkar's outstretched hand. Then he resumes staring at me.

Ozkar snaps his fingers again. As Grandfather disappears and the yellow light kindles in Ozkar's eyes, more magic gathers around the counter, pulling bits and pieces from under crumpled papers and out of tiny glass jars.

He's a warlock, I realize. For some reason I assumed he was a witch, like Jakob or Helga, whose raw power is limited to the witch-ash they ingest. But warlocks draw their power directly through a contract bond with a supernatural entity. Their only limits are the spirit's strength and the price their contract extracts.

"What happened to . . . ?" I croak out, but can't finish.

"Grandfather? Don't feel bad for him. Old bastard's why our great-great-grandmother had to come south to the empire back in the day. He wouldn't stop moving his neighbor's boundary stones, got himself killed over it, and wound up one of the Deep North's *deildegasts*. Our blood tie makes the warlock bond vastly more potent, so it was worth the hassle to seek him out. Besides . . ." Ozkar squints at a configuration of tiny metal parts dancing between his hands. "Innovation demands a certain disregard for boundaries." He glances at me. "Or did you mean Marthe? Do you know anything about our family at *all*?"

It's the same tone Dame von Falbirg used to take with me when she'd demand to know why I hadn't finished a task she'd never asked me to do. All I can think to stammer out is "I—I was four."

Ozkar doesn't look to be softening so much as recalculating. "Right," he mutters. "Betze is late, and I'm not getting anything important done until that useless girl gets me my filaments, so I may as well, *yet again*, make up for everyone else's shortcomings. No interruptions. And I'm only going to say this once."

I nod, still numb, still utterly adrift, still famished for answers. I don't even realize I'm clinging to one of my ribbons until I feel the bumps in the weave beneath my thumb.

Ozkar twitches two fingers at a collection of pinned items on one wall. They lift free, wheeling around him. For all the emotion in his voice, he may as well be sifting through someone else's rubbish. "Both our parents are gone. Father drank himself to death a year after Marthe died. Marthe took you away the night before my twelfth birthday and didn't come back. In fact, that was my birthday present: helping Father track down her frozen corpse in the woods. Her lantern wasn't far away. We think she dropped it, lost the trail without a light, and tried to wait until morning. There was no sign of what happened to you." He shrugs and selects a folded piece of paper. "Personally, I thought . . . Well. There's plenty of hunger in the dark."

The note crumbles to ash in his hand. For a moment, Grandfather appears behind Ozkar, ablaze in yellow fire, beak open in a shriek. Then he's gone again. Ozkar's hands ignite with power.

"Don't feel bad for Marthe either," he says harshly. "All she ever wanted was attention. She did nothing for any of us, just kept dumping out babies so Father and the village would fuss over her. Nothing was ever good enough for her, and nothing was ever her fault."

"She said I was unlucky." The words escape before I can stop myself.

Ozkar's nostrils flare. "Last warning, and only because I heard that horseshit from her myself: Interrupt again and we're done. Marthe blamed everything on Luisa until Erwin came along, and then she blamed him for everything until you came along, and the midwife said she wouldn't survive another birth, so *you* got stuck with the short straw."

He goes quiet, staring intently at the cluster of metal pieces. They spin into a hypnotic whirl—then hitch, falter, and fall into his palm. With a scowl, Ozkar slashes a hand through the open air to his right. A bright yellow line carves in its wake, then pops like a seam, revealing an endless void of star-studded dark. He flings the pieces into it and, with another flick, stitches reality neatly back together.

I have stayed silent the entire time, still winching the ribbon around my finger, so tight it's digging into flesh.

"Get that kicked-dog look off your face," Ozkar snaps. "There's nothing worth sulking about, especially not in our family. In fact, if you're smart, you'll get far enough away that they can't off-load their deadweight on you. Now, let's settle the other business. Helga told me of this ludicrous . . . blood drop thing. That's going to be a pass from me, *thanks*."

A thrust of alarm finally pierces the cold haze. "B-but," I say cleverly, "we need it."

"What you *need*," he sneers, "is one single person with an ounce of sense in their empty skull to ask, *What can you do with a drop of someone's blood?* Or perhaps, *Why does it have to be seven brothers?* Or—here's a wild one—*What will it cost?*"

"It—it's to save a whole town," I force out. "People are going to die. Udo and Jakob—"

"People die every day," Ozkar says, unimpressed. He picks a glass jar off a shelf and shakes it, frowning. "If Udo and Jakob let themselves be at risk, that's their concern. I've had enough of picking up my family's slack, and just because you're late to the party doesn't mean you get a handout. Where *is* that Betze?"

I swallow. One last card to lay on the table. "The boy I . . . I love," I confess. "It's to save him too. Please. I'll give you anything."

A half-fogged memory stirs, too distant, too deep to make out the edges: Me, pleading a lifetime ago, begging, *I'll do anything, just let me stay.*

Ozkar looks at me as if sizing me up for the first time. His gaze falls to my hand, still anchored in ribbon, and I remember there are finger bones on these walls. "'Anything' is a dangerous promise, Vanja."

"I have money," I sputter, "I can—I can pay you in rubies—"

He points. "Your ribbon."

I take a step back without thinking. ". . . What?"

"It's from him, isn't it?" Ozkar doesn't ask so much as appraise. "It's important to you. Important things can hold a great deal of power. Nearly as much as a drop of blood."

Suddenly, horribly, I realize what every last pinned thing is in this workshop. Hopes, dreams, little treasures and memories. Things that matter to someone.

And he burns them for power.

That is Ozkar's price.

"I told you to stop the kicked-dog look," he scolds. "I want only the one. You can keep the other."

It's just a bit of ribbon.

It's the first gift Emeric gave me simply because he felt like it. He'll give me other ribbons, he'll understand.

When he ties my bows each morning, he's saying,

As long as you'll have me.

A ribbon doesn't matter more than his life.

But it matters to me.

And that's why Ozkar wants it.

It's for Emeric, I tell myself. Weighed against the staggering magnitude of what he is to me, I can give up this one small, priceless thing for him.

Hands shaking, I untie the ribbon.

After I hand it over, Ozkar makes me wait while he folds it, chooses a pin, chooses a place on the wall. I can't stop looking at it, even as he impartially jabs a finger on the bone awl, stamps his blood drop on my cambric.

The bell above the door chimes just as he lifts his hand away, and a frantic feminine voice rises behind me. "I'm so sorry, Weber's was out of the right fibers, and I had to try three different—"

"Excuses, Betze," Ozkar scoffs as I fumble with the leather bag where I keep the awl and the cambric. "Vanja . . . I believe our business is done."

I want to say something scathing and pithy, but I have nothing, nothing but the overwhelming sense that I am a disappointment to him, a fool, a failure for giving up the ribbon. I nod wordlessly. There's a jagged rock in my throat, and I may bleed if I try to speak.

I push past a round-faced, harried-looking young woman and stumble out the door, shoving the leather bag into my satchel, only to nearly collide with a man who snarls, "Watch it."

"Sorry," I gasp, jumping to the side. I make it a few steps up the street before realizing I'm going the wrong way. I double back, keep it together as I pass Ozkar's workshop again.

Start to dissolve a few buildings down.

At the end of the block, I crumple.

I slump against a plain slate wall and slide to the ground. The sun glares mercilessly, but all I feel is icy cold.

I'm such a fool. They have to think I'm the biggest fool in the empire, missing what was right in front of my face. Udo *had his reasons*, Dieter *did it for family*. Helga . . .

Helga, she's my—my sister—she knew, and she kept this from me—

My next breath knifes through my chest.

They didn't want me to know. Of course, they didn't want a useless little fool like me hanging around.

Exhalation is only a faint relief. Inhaling hurts more.

It wasn't supposed to be like this. I was supposed to be more than a thief and a liar when I found my family. I was supposed to be worth something. And I ruined it.

I didn't even ask Ozkar the one question that mattered, the *one* thing, I'm so stupid.

I didn't ask why she did it, what made our mother take me into the woods.

I didn't ask what I did wrong.

Someone curses as they nearly step on my feet, and I shrink against the wall even further. There's a metallic clink against stone. I look down. The message-mirror has fallen out of my pocket.

I reach for it. I don't know what to say. It hurts to breathe, hurts to think. I just want it not to hurt, I just don't want to be alone—

In the end, all I write is:

Can you
come get me

and

I'm sorry

No, no, that's stupid, useless—
The mirror pulses with heat.

On my way.
Where are you?

I don't know how long it takes before a shadow falls over me and stays there. Emeric is crouching by me, turning my face to look at his. His voice is a veneer of calm masking dismay. "Roses," he says softly, "what happened?"

My chin is shaking. I don't know where to start.

"I lost my ribbon," I say helplessly, and shatter.

He pulls me to him, strokes my hair as I bury my face in his shoulder, slowly rocks in place. Fragmented words spill out in the flood of my ugly sobs, the same ones again and again, starving for the answer I needed today, the one that may always be out of reach:

"What did I do wrong?"

～✟～

Emeric gleans the story out of me in tatters and gets us to the Jolly Magistrate somehow. I'm back in the fog, choosing a tourniquet over peeling off the bandages. I know that I keep telling him I'm sorry. Every time, he just holds my hands a little tighter and tells me it's fine.

"Vanja——" I hear Helga call from down the hall as Emeric steers me to the stairs. "Wait, Erwin came and told me, this wasn't supposed to——"

Emeric pauses, shifting to block the stairwell. "Can you make it the rest of the way up to our room?" I nod. "I'll be there in a moment. Miss Ros and I need to have a word."

I'm sitting on the bed when Emeric walks in, swearing under his breath as the rose-petal cascade is set off once more. I was in the middle of unlacing my boots when I just——I stopped, I guess. He takes over for me, kneeling and working at the laces without a second thought. "Miss Ros will give you space until you want to talk."

"Thank you," I whisper unsteadily as one boot slides free. "I'm sorry."

"You have nothing to be sorry for." He starts on the next boot. "I . . . I've heard other stories like this, from people whose birth parents gave them up. It's never, *ever* anything you did wrong. Sometimes the parents know they can't care for their child. Or they want to give their child a better life. Or they're sick and need help that they aren't getting. But it was never you or anything you did."

I want to believe him. I wish I could.

He drops my other boot on the floor, kicks off his own, and climbs into bed with me. I curl up beside him and lay my head on his chest. As his arms settle around me, I mumble, "Tell me about your family. Please."

"Of course." His hand moves in slow circles over my back, and I wonder if he feels the ridges of my scars like I felt the threads of his ribbon. "I . . . I think you'd like them. My mother, Clara, still runs a book-bindery in Helligbrücke. She named it Anselm's, after my father . . ."

He tells me of his sister Hester, newly seventeen as of mid-March, who helps their mother with the bindery. His younger brother, Lukas, who is quiet but devastatingly insightful, just like their father. His baby sister, Elieze, who can make anyone laugh and, to Emeric's horror, has recently discovered romance.

He tells me about the time Lukas accidentally upended paste all over his own hair and decided the only remedy was to cut it off. How Hester is working on a special printing type that can be read by touch for blind readers like her. About his mother's recent suitor, who endured a three-hour interrogation from the sisters Conrad before he was allowed to call upon Clara a second time. How, once a year, they all travel to Rabenheim to visit their father's grave on his birthday.

I drift off, hearing the warmth, the love, in Emeric's voice, and wonder if any of my siblings will ever speak of me that way.

He wakes me a few hours later, to coax some soup into me and help me into a nightshirt before I pass out again, grateful for oblivion. The ache has dulled its teeth on sleep, but it gnaws at me all the same.

The next time I half wake, it's to the sound of lowered voices outside the door. The bed is empty. I hear Emeric in the hall.

". . . nothing new to report."

"You were meant to work the case today. Distraction is no excuse." That's Kirkling.

"I *did*—" Emeric pauses. When he speaks again, his voice has leveled out. "I spent the morning and the first part of the afternoon reviewing records with Lady Ambroszia. I could continue that work here if it were . . . permitted."

"I'm not your babysitter, Aspirant; you are permitted to do as you please. This is a test of your impartiality, and I have only advised you of the consequences of letting Schmidt contaminate your case."

"When I told you the Scarlet Maiden cut her off from—" A strange tangle blurs his words. "—you said that didn't prove her innocence.

When I told you the Red Maid was a real, well-documented god, not Vanja's fabrication, you said she could still be complicit. Now we know the Scarlet Maiden coerced Vanja into obtaining a blood sacrifice from *her own family*, and that's not enough?"

Kirkling only ratchets out, "I find it convenient that none of those things have directly harmed Schmidt, only those around her."

"*Her name isn't Schmidt.*" Emeric's composure is slipping. "We have one month before the Scarlet Maiden collects her sacrifice. It's a waste of time we *don't have* to keep shutting Vanja out of this case. Her insight could be the key."

"Then I suggest you learn to solve your own cases, Aspirant," Kirkling says icily. "She can't argue *this* one to the Godly Courts for you either."

There's a deadly quiet. Then Emeric says, just as cold, "I have nothing further to report."

He steps back into our room and closes the door. Then he pushes his spectacles up into his hair and slides a hand over his eyes as a dissonant burst of rose petals showers down.

I slide out of bed and walk over to Emeric while Kirkling's footsteps stomp down the hall. It's my turn to wrap my arms around him. "Don't lose your Finding for me," I say into his shirt. "You've wanted to be a prefect for more than half your life."

"That's just it," he sighs, blowing a petal off his shoulder. "This *isn't* what I want. I want to help people who feel like . . . like how I felt when my father died. Like no one was listening, and nothing would change. I thought being a prefect would let me do that, but I couldn't do anything for Agnethe, and I can barely help you."

I take a deep breath, weighing my words. "You listen," I say with some difficulty. "You care, and you listen when you don't have to. You could have just written me off in Minkja, but you wanted my story, you said it mattered, you believed me. Don't ever say you didn't help me." I look up at him. "If more prefects were like you . . . I think the empire would make fewer girls like me."

Emeric is making the strangest face, blinking rapidly. "Well," he says, hoarse, "*I think that would be a terrible loss.*" He grimaces. "The . . . fewer-people-like-you part. Not the reduction of gross societal injustice."

That gets an uneven laugh out of me, the first since I sank the Treasury. "I'm glad you think so. Do you need a hankie?"

"No," he lies, terribly. "I'm supposed to be taking care of *you* anyway."

"Hold on." My satchel's on the floor nearby. I pick it up and dig out one of the few kerchiefs that isn't covered in dead bed lice, itching rose hip hairs, or my brothers' blood. (What a life I lead.) "Here." I turn around to hand it to him.

And then I freeze.

Emeric's standing ramrod-stiff. His face is turned to me, but his expression is unsettlingly slack.

Violent crimson light burns from his eyes, whites and all. His shirt is charring over the handprint.

"*Hello, little prophet,*" the Scarlet Maiden sings through him.

"Scarlet Maiden." Smoke stings my tongue. "What is this?"

"*Am I not allowed to speak to my prophet?*" she croons. "*Am I not allowed to use my servant as I wish?*"

This feels volatile, like a game of Find the Lady with razor-edged cards. "I don't think he likes being used."

"*How unfortunate for him.*" A patch of blazing red emerges as her handprint sears through the shirt.

"Why are people from Hagendorn attacking us in your name?" I ask.

Emeric's shoulder jerks in an awkward shrug. "*They claim my name in vain. I know nothing of them. You are taking too long to fetch my sacrifice, little prophet.*"

One of Emeric's glistening eyes spills over, a tear tracking down his cheek. I have to end this, fast.

"I already have five blood drops," I protest. "I just need—"

The Scarlet Maiden abruptly propels Emeric's body across the room to me. His hands lock around my wrists, unshakable. A terrible heat radiates from his chest. He wrestles me into a backward stumble.

"*I will have my sacrifice,*" she hisses, "*on the eve of the May-Saint Feast.*"

"Let go—" I squeeze out, trying to catch my balance only to hit the edge of the bed. Then it registers: The May-Saint Feast is on the first of May.

That's just over two weeks. I'll never make it in time.

The Scarlet Maiden shoves me onto the bed, still gripping my wrists so hard the bones grate as I thrash. A horrid animal panic screams to life. Suddenly I'm in Castle Falbirg, pinned against unrelenting stone, Adalbrecht von Reigenbach forcing my hands back just like this—no, *no,* this is Emeric—no, it's not him—I have to breathe, have to keep breathing—"Let me go—let me—*please*—"

Something hot lands on my cheek. Another tear has fallen from Emeric's otherwise blank face. It's wrenched into a horrible smile.

"*Two weeks, Prophet. Then, one way or another, I will have my sacrifice.*"

The crimson light flickers as an awful sound claws from Emeric's throat.

"*Ngh—NO—*" He releases me and staggers away, gasping. I scrabble back from him still, that feral terror lashing out even as my limbs tangle in the blankets.

Then the red subsides, leaving us both in the dark.

Emeric is staring at his hands like they're covered in blood. "Vanja—Vanja, no, I'm so sorry, I couldn't stop her, I tried—" He reaches for me only to freeze, aghast, when I flinch.

"I know," I say distantly. "Just . . . give me a moment."

He sinks to the floor, wraps his arms around himself as if to hide the now-dulled handprint, though the stench of burnt linen lingers. "I would never hurt you," he says, almost more to himself than to me. "I'm—I'm so sorry."

Half of me wants to agree, to hold him, to cling to the one anchor I have in this damned crumbling world.

The other half is afraid to turn my back to him.

And he can feel it. Even as I crawl off the bed and sit by him, he knows. Even as I make myself put one shaking hand on his shoulder . . . he knows.

"It wasn't you," I say, now more to myself than to him.

"But she used me to hurt you. She can use me again." His head drops.

I flinch back at his sudden movement, braced for more red light, for teeth snapping at my fingers.

I think that's when we both realize the scale of this new horror between us.

He asks wretchedly, "How are you supposed to even sleep next to me? How can you feel safe?"

He leaves the worst question unspoken: If the intimacy of last night wasn't enough to break the Scarlet Maiden's claim . . . how are we supposed to keep trying like this?

And that's when *I* decide I have had enough.

I lost my ribbon, I lost my hope of meeting my family when I was ready, and I have two weeks now to somehow put this all to rights. I'm not letting the Scarlet Maiden take Emeric from me too.

I look at the bed. Then I look at him.

"This isn't how I thought we'd have this conversation," I start, "but . . . what is your stance on manacles?"

CHAPTER TWENTY-TWO

VILLANELLE

I MAKE ONE MISTAKE AS WE WALK INTO THE INN'S TAVERN FOR BREAK-
fast the next morning, and that is forgetting to mind my sleeves.

Ugly purple bars of finger-shaped bruises circle my wrists, and
judging by the miserable night we just had, if Emeric sees them, he's
going to immediately go looking for a hair shirt and a moor to wander.
I've made sure to keep the sleeves of my shift rolled down accordingly.

However, what I didn't account for was encountering Helga, who's
finishing off a plate of herring and eggs in the tavern when we arrive.
She spots me and looks away, quickly shoveling the last of her herring
into her face with a piece of toast. But then, as she scoots her chair back
to scarper . . . her gaze lands on my wrist.

I realize too late that I'm nervously fiddling with my sleeve. And as I, too, look at my wrist, I see the bruise peeking out.

"*You son of a*——" Helga all but flies over her table and shoves between Emeric and me. "If you touch her again, I will peel you to the *bone*——"

"Wait, Helga, *stop*." I grab her arm. My sleeve, unfortunately, slides farther, betraying even more of the bruise.

Emeric goes white as a sheet. "You didn't say anything," he says, dismayed, stretching a hand to me. "I can——"

Helga smacks him away as other patrons gawk, whispering. "What part of '*to the bone*' was unclear?"

I yank on her arm until she looks at me. "The Scarlet Maiden possessed him," I hiss, "and it wasn't fun for anyone, and he had to sleep manacled to the bed, so good instincts, but let's take this down from a ten to a four."

Helga simmers to a grudging seven. "Has that happened before?"

"*No*," Emeric says emphatically. He makes a hangdog motion toward my wrists. "Please, let me handle those."

I relent and hold out my arms. Helga shifts in place, still scowling. "Well . . . don't get possessed again."

"It's not in my ten-year plan," Emeric grumbles back.

There's a stilted lull. Then Helga says, "If you want to, Vanja . . . can we speak later?"

I swallow as Emeric's fingers slide from my wrists. The bruises are shrinking. I'd be lying if I said it's not a relief.

I'd also be lying if I said I don't have questions for her, about us, about the family, about—everything. I just don't know if *those* bruises are still too fresh.

"Maybe," I answer, splitting the difference. She shrugs. As she heads for the door, I call after her, "One . . . one thing." Helga turns. "Did you ever wonder what happened to me?"

Her face falls. After a pained pause, she says, "December thirteenth."

"What?"

"Your birthday is December thirteenth," Helga says. "We looked for you nearly every day, all through the winter and the thaw and up to midsummer. By then any remnants would've been . . . gone. We lit a candle on your birthday every year after. Katrin Little still does, at the farm in Kerzenthal."

I can't speak for a moment. I didn't know how much I needed to hear that until it was in the air between us.

Emeric's knuckles brush mine. I anchor my hand in his and ask, "Dinner?"

"Here, six o'clock?" Helga waits for my nod, then ducks out.

Emeric and I have a rather subdued breakfast together, at least compared to yesterday's. Kirkling, the incredible human canker sore, stops by as we're finishing up to deposit Lady Ambroszia on the table. "Aspirant Conrad," she says stiffly. "Let us hope today is more productive. What are your plans?"

Emeric's face turns blank, his tone polite but detached. "Once we're done here, I will be accompanying Vanja to the Welkenrode outpost—"

Kirkling's notebook is out in a flash. "'Disregarding clear jeopardy to Finding integrity . . .'"

"—so that," Emeric continues through his teeth, "we may find a way to protect her from me. Last night the Scarlet Maiden seized control of me long enough to physically assault Vanja. It can't happen again."

Kirkling herself said only hours ago that it was convenient the Scarlet Maiden hadn't harmed me directly. Maybe this will finally convince her that Emeric's faith in me isn't misplaced.

"Hm." Kirkling pauses her note-taking. "I would like to see you make the most of your limited time, Aspirant Conrad."

. . . Or not.

"The Scarlet Maiden also moved her deadline up again," I add. "Now it's the eve of the May-Saint Feast."

Kirkling regards me a wordless moment, then closes her notes and inclines her head to Emeric. "Good day."

It's just like Madame Treasury, her tacit disrespect. She doesn't answer me because she doesn't have to, and she wants me to know.

(For a moment, I contemplate solving Kirkling with bed lice too.)

"Well," Lady Ambroszia says before I can pursue that fun thought, dusting herself off. "Godly possession? That sounds atrocious. Take heart, young man, my evening was much more fruitful. I made it all the way through 300 Blessed Era in those records." The glowing light in her empty eye socket blinks off a moment, then reignites. I realize that's her attempt at a wink. "But I'll keep those findings to myself around the young lady, hm?"

Emeric stares at his plate, mouth flexing like a bow resisting the string.

And then—it snaps.

"No," he says shortly. "Vanja is a consultant for the Scarlet Maiden case. It's time for her to consult. We're bringing her into the loop. Once we get to the outpost, we'll go over what we know."

An enormous weight lifts from my throat even as I grip my fork a bit tighter. "Are you sure?"

He takes a deep breath. When he speaks, he sounds almost . . . sad. "There was a time when I looked up to Elske Kirkling a great deal. She and Hubert made sure my father's killer faced justice, and she even helped me in the training academy, almost as much as Hubert did. But *every* time you meet her criterion to establish your innocence, she finds a new one. I have tried to compensate for my own bias in your regard. If she cannot do the same, then I can no longer trust her to objectively advise me on the best course of action." He lets out the rest of his breath.

"And, to be honest, we don't have *time*. It's going to take, what, four days to get to Kerzenthal from here?"

I think of Jakob's map. "At least. And then another four days minimum to Hagendorn."

"So if we leave tomorrow, spend one day in Kerzenthal, and proceed straight to Hagendorn, we'll have . . ." He prods the table, frowning. "Ten days to solve this, *if* everything goes right. And there's still one more blood drop to collect in Welkenrode beforehand."

"Right. Henrik, at the Imperial Abbey." I wash down my last bite of rye toast with a swig of coffee. "If we hurry, maybe we can go after we're done at your outpost."

Emeric puts a cautious hand on mine. "You don't have to . . . be ready for that yet."

I grasp what he's getting at. Ozkar was only a suspicion; Henrik is the first of my brothers who I will meet as—

As a sister.

The very idea feels alien, disorienting, like when I steal Emeric's spectacles to look through. It curves the world into a new form.

"No," I say, a bit bewildered at the buzz in my chest. It's close to the feeling when Saint Willehalm asked me for help. "I think I want to go."

Since time is short, we decide to take a carriage to the Welkenrode prefect outpost instead of going on foot. I wait by the courtyard's street gate while Emeric goes to call a coach. I'm studying a flower box, dismally noting the new distinct red-orange cast of the previously yellow daffodils, when I hear Bajeri's baritone rumbling over the stones. I can't understand the fluid Sahalian words, but he doesn't sound happy, and neither does Joniza when she answers back.

I turn. They're headed my way, still deep in what looks like debate, judging from Joniza's rapid gestures. She sees me and jabs a thumb at her father. "Vanja! Tell this stubborn old man to go home."

I know better than to do any such thing, so instead I say diplomatically, "Wasn't that the plan?"

Bajeri rubs at a line in his brow. "So it was. Köhler, my decorator contact, he was to buy most of my wares, but he sent a message last night that he must cancel our deal."

I feel like I've seen that name before, and not somewhere good. "At the last minute? That scumbag."

"*She* gets it," Joniza mutters.

"No, no, Köhler is a fair man." Bajeri sighs. "He had a major project fall through suddenly, and now he is also in a bad spot. At least *I* can continue on the rest of my route. My merchant friends here tell me Köhler has to get rid of enough green furnishings to cover half the Sünderweg."

Green.

The note on Madame Treasury's desk, the one about a parlor, it was signed *Köhler*. And she was going to buy the Green Sleeve . . .

. . . until I put her out of business.

"I am telling you, go *home* and let me finish your route," Joniza insists. "You should be there for Fatatuma!"

Bajeri shakes his head. "And I am telling you, these empire merchants don't know you. You will have to fight for a fair price every time, if they even let you in the door. No, it will be fine. I have decided." He tips his head. "I must go speak with my other contacts here, see what they will take. Good luck to us all today."

"Good luck," I manage, trying to muffle my guilt as he sets off down the street. Apparently I don't do a very good job of it, though. When I turn back to Joniza, her eyes are narrowed at me.

"What do you know?" she asks, suspicious.

"It's. Um." I swallow hard. "It's complicated."

"*Vanja*," she says blisteringly.

I open my mouth, then close it, mind racing. Maybe I can find another buyer? Or maybe I can exploit the shortages from the *Grace Unending* somehow? "I can fix it," I start. "I didn't know——"

"*Enough.*" She holds up a finger, her eyes squeezed shut, mouth twisting. After a long, long moment, she grates out, "I know you wouldn't try to hurt us, but . . . this is my family."

"I'm sorry. I swear I'll fix it."

Joniza just crosses her arms, jerking her chin as carriage wheels clatter to a halt behind me. "Your ride's here."

I turn and find Emeric opening the coach door from the inside. When I look back, Joniza's already on her way out.

ᴥ♔ᴥ

". . . but I didn't do any of that on purpose," I tell Emeric as we walk into the Welkenrode outpost of the Order of Prefects of the Godly Courts. "So technically none of it's my fault. Right?"

"I'd rather not answer that," he says tactfully, then turns to address the clerk sitting at the tidy front desk. "Good morning. Is Vikram Mistry in yet?"

"*Conrad!*" Vikram's voice carries in from a back room. "Did you bring any of those cinnamon delights?"

"Never mind," Emeric deadpans.

"Also, Yeshe Ghendt and Jander Dursyn are working in the east study, if you want their input or have anything for the *Grace Unending* case," the clerk says. "Do you need a guest badge?"

"Vanja is a registered consultant, thank you."

"*Vanja!*" I hear Vikram call. "My favorite criminal mastermind!"

"*Do you mind?*" another voice—either Ghendt's or Dursyn's, I'd wager—grouses from what I'd similarly guess to be the east study.

Emeric leads me down the narrow hall behind the front desk,

pointing out a privy and the east study and winding up in a large work-room of sorts. It's not unlike Ozkar's, with its shelves and apparatuses, but it seems geared toward a wider range of work, with everything from apothecarial studies to a tiny forge. Vikram's perched on a stool near the door, hunching over a tiny glowing orb that he seems to be meticulously sanding into powder.

"Please tell me you have a distraction," he says, his voice lodged in his nasal passages as he screws up his face in concentration. "I'm stuck making alloys while Mathilde's out, and it's the most tedious thing I've done since my family reunion."

"You're in luck," I say grimly.

We summarize the events of the previous night as impersonally as possible. Emeric is nonetheless shamefaced when we're done. Vikram, however, is decisively intrigued.

"Now *this* is a puzzle," he says, taking his hair down and finger-combing it in thought. "An antipossession charm, perhaps? But would it be strong enough?"

"Can it even be done?" Emeric asks bleakly. "She's a god."

Vikram goes still, eyes darting as if chasing invisible formulas. He taps a finger to his lips and says, "Nope. It can't. We can't block her from you. But not for the reason you think." He pushes off his stool and goes to a large cabinet in a corner, tying his hair back up excitedly. "If we cut you off from her, we cut you off from the rest of the Low Gods too. You'd have to go back to just using witch-ash for magic, which sounds like a bad move when you're contending with a hostile god."

Emeric and I trade looks as Vikram pulls jars off shelves. I say, "That would not be ideal."

Vikram starts tipping powder onto a scale. "So if we can't incapaci-tate the god . . . we incapacitate the vessel."

"A signal-activated sedative." Emeric straightens up so fast I'd almost swear he bounced on his toes. "Of course."

"And with a combination of paralytic and soporific elements, you'd be immobilized *and* unconscious," Vikram says around a vial's cork, which he just pulled out with his teeth. He empties the vial into a small mortar, the pestle in his other hand.

"If, hypothetically, your local criminal mastermind did not understand any of that . . ." I start.

Vikram spits the cork at a rubbish bin. It hits the rim and misses, to all our disappointment. "We can bind different spells to a substance that stays in the bloodstream for up to a week, and set them so they're activated at a specific word from a specific person. For example, you can assign it general healing magic and activate it if ambushed." He pulls a cast-iron mold off another shelf. "And for Conrad here, I can combine spells to both paralyze him and knock him out for five minutes, which should be long enough to restrain him if the Scarlet Maiden returns."

"And we'll both have the activation word," Emeric says firmly.

"Good thinking." Vikram funnels the contents of the mortar into the iron mold, then casually draws a complex wheel of runes and symbols in silvery fire, mumbling under his breath. When the mold clamps shut, a puff of steam swallows the runes. He uses a rag to pry the mold open once more, revealing a dozen pale blue tablets the size of my pinkie nail waiting inside. Using a spoon, he scoops eleven into a small glass jar that he stoppers and passes to Emeric. Then he hands Emeric the remaining pill. "There's a pitcher and cups behind you. Your activation word is *villanelle*. You know, like the poem."

Emeric gives him a dirty look as I hand him a cup. "Of course it is."

"You're welcome!" Vikram starts putting away the equipment. "You know, half your verses weren't that bad—"

"*Aaaand* we're going." Emeric ushers me out.

"Take one each week!" Vikram shouts after us. "Don't let him forget, Vanja!"

An aggrieved-looking woman pops her head out of the study across the way. "For the gods' sakes, Mistry, *WE LIVE IN A SOCIETY.*"

Emeric pauses as good-natured bickering boils up behind us. "One moment." He ducks back down the hall to confer with the prefect. Her glossy dark hair's braided up in the Gharese fashion for married women, and "Yeshe" is a Gharese given name, so I'm guessing this is Prefect Ghendt. When she eyes me and lowers her voice, I make a show of looking elsewhere, still shamelessly eavesdropping.

". . . see Holdings," Ghendt's saying. "They own a lot of businesses that *should* be profiting off the port being blocked. The money's just not there." Emeric asks something I don't catch. "We're looking for one, but so far, their own businesses' books are clean. If you hear anything else about that bribe, let us know."

"I will," Emeric says. "Good luck."

I wait until we're out of earshot to ask, under my breath, "Bribe?"

"I let them know one of my most trustworthy contacts heard a dockworker was bribed to give bad directions to the *Grace Unending*," Emeric says calmly, "but didn't have any identifying details. If you hear anything to the contrary, of course, they'd welcome the insight."

He opens a door to another workroom of sorts. One wall is slate, the others dotted with tacks and hundreds of tiny holes. The table and chairs in the middle of the room look like they've endured lifetimes of thoughtful mutilation at the hands of prefects mulling over puzzles. I set my satchel on the table, helping Lady Ambroszia out. She plops herself down on the tabletop, arranging her skirts as Emeric shuts the door.

"All right," he says slowly, picking up a piece of chalk from a tin bolted to the slate wall. "Here's what we have with the Scarlet Maiden.

First, I always start with Hubert's five motives, to see if we can identify a pattern in the behavior." He writes five words on the far left of the slate wall:

GREED

LOVE

HATE

FEAR

REVENGE

"I never really got why *love* is an option," I muse aloud. "It seems like the opposite of a crime."

Before Emeric can answer, Lady Ambroszia tuts at me. "It's not the crime, dear; it's the motive. Take it from a former kept woman."

I suppose that does make her the resident expert. "Fair enough."

Emeric draws a line through *LOVE* anyway. "We know the Red Maid of the River lost her lover to a hellhound; that much is documented in the song and the recorded legends. I looked to see if it's possible the sacrifice ritual might resurrect the lover, but that didn't turn up anything."

"Could the hellhound be trapping his ghost down there?" I ask. "Or maybe he won't rest until it's defeated?"

"We've looked into that possibility as well, but . . ." This time Emeric nods to Lady Ambroszia.

"Ghosts don't precisely work like that," she picks up. "A person's connection to the mortal world is severed at the moment of passing. To remain, we need something theoreticians call a material anchor—a supplementary connection that keeps us tethered here in the same way enchantments must be anchored to the material world. It's customarily the site of one's demise, but strong attachment to a person or an object suffices too. If we choose not to leave with Death, only the material anchor keeps us stable, and those degrade over time." She adjusts her hems. "If not for sweet Willi's help, I would have left this world decades ago. And if the Red Maid's lover yet remains . . . he would be a fearsome thing. We would know he was there."

"Any chance *he's* actually the hellhound, not the dead giant?" I ask.

"Boderad and Brunne predate the Red Maid, so no." Emeric crosses out *FEAR* next. "Initially I thought this might be it, but speaking of the hellhound . . . There is *nothing* to support the Scarlet Maiden's claim that he will go on a rampage, or that the sacrifices were to appease him somehow. Especially given his inactivity during her dormancy. The records only mention Brunne's bridal crown."

He writes *crown* beside *GREED.*

"Helga said something about a crown when she took us to Felsengruft," I say slowly. "And in all the murals, there's a crown at the bottom of the Kronenkessel."

Emeric sucks his teeth. "Good points. I forgot about both of those. And the hellhound guards the crown, so if that's what she's after . . ." He purses his lips and writes *Prior sacrifices?* next to *REVENGE.* "My other theory is that the Red Maid's past sacrifices were . . . pathological in nature. Reenacting her tragedy, but with her in control."

"It was always the same type of victim," chimes in Lady Ambroszia. "The few records we found on them, that is. Each one was an unmarried young man."

"So when I woke her, she just picked back up where she left off?" I sit on the edge of the table.

Emeric tilts his head. "Do you remember when I had to give you a very vague metaphor about painted devils and walls?"

"The one I did not understand in the slightest?"

He rubs the back of his head. "Yes. That one. What I was trying to say is that there are a lot of things she's *telling* us to fear—the hellhound, her wrath, and so on. She's been painting the devil on the wall and hoping we won't know it from the real thing."

"So . . . a misdirect." I frown. "Then what is she distracting us from?"

"There's the question." He steps to the middle of the slate wall and starts scribbling. "We know she manifested only when prefects came to Hagendorn, and she claimed one immediately as a sacrifice." *Prefect.* "We know she asked for blood from seven brothers—something *extremely* specific." *Blood + brothers.* "We know now that the most obvious candidates were your own brothers." *Family?* "And, loath as I am to concur with Ozkar Ros . . . we don't know what she'll do if she gets it." *Cost?*

I gnaw on a thumb tip, turning the pieces over and over in my head. "She picked you first," I say slowly. "And then only gave the alternative after we pushed her for one."

"And it's an alternative that targets *your* brothers," Emeric adds. "One that ultimately may harm them. I doubt *any* of that is coincidence."

The shape of the scam is starting to emerge. "So . . . I was never supposed to go through with it. She thought I'd find out they're my brothers and . . . let her take you instead. But why the pageantry, then? Why even offer the option?"

Emeric adds one word to the list: *Cult.*

"You said it yourself," he says. "Cults are wildly profitable. But they're profitable because they're infectious and *compliant.* Cultists don't ask where their money is going, they don't ask what their work is for; they just follow orders because an authority figure tells them it's right and their community reinforces it."

"I remember one from *my* youth," Lady Ambroszia chimes in. "Impoverished a whole region when it all fell apart. And young Conrad here and I have established quite a pattern of cults that did the same."

"But the Scarlet Maiden doesn't want money," I object.

Emeric *does* bounce on his toes this time. "And neither did you," he says with a tinge of triumph. "At the rate the Red Blessed grew, you could have been defrauding them for ludicrous amounts of money. But you knew it started as a scam, and you were trying to get out. The one thing you did have . . ."

"Was authority," I finish, connecting the dots and feeling like a fool. "So she got me to leave."

Emeric nods. "You've been gone two weeks, and there are already violent devotees chasing us all the way to Rammelbeck. I'd say there's been a change in doctrine."

"Udo and Jakob." I grip the table. "Would they . . . ?"

"Every use we've found for the seven blood drops requires your brothers to be among the living," Lady Ambroszia states. "They may not be pleased with the circumstances, but they ought to survive them."

"But I thought the Scarlet Maiden doesn't really want my brothers."

"We don't know," Emeric says slowly, "if they're a diversion or a true alternative. This is where I'm stuck, to be honest. Sacrificing me, using the blood drops—either could grant her power, perhaps enough to take on the hellhound? But she's a Low God with a growing cult to feed from—she should *have* that power. And she's already strong enough to outmuscle your gerblemers, which . . ." He sees the baffled look on my face. "Your glorbos," he tries again, but there's a strange mismatch between what I hear and the movements of his mouth. "Scrimblo and Glup."

"*What are you saying,*" I wheeze.

He looks helplessly at Lady Ambroszia, who just offers an awkward shrug. "I've no comprehension issues, my boy."

Emeric pinches the bridge of his nose. "Right. It's time to talk about this too. Vanja, hold this." He flicks open his message-mirror and hands it to me. "Your memories are being tampered with when it comes to . . . your parents."

I gawk at him. "I think I would *notice?*"

He gestures. "Look in the mirror and tell me your first memory of Castle Falbirg."

I see my brow wrinkle in the glass. "Being left there by my mother."

"How old were you?"

"Four."

Something—shifts. I blink.

"Four is very young to be taken in as a servant," he says carefully. "Do you remember anything from when you were five? Or six?"

"I remember . . ." I shut my eyes, then recall I'm supposed to be watching my reflection and open them again. If I think back, *really* think . . . "There were . . . other children. I remember playing with them in . . . the yard? Castle Falbirg doesn't have a yard like . . ."

But I can see it in my mind: a ring of grass and spongy moss, hemmed in by spicy-smelling yews.

And I can *feel* a bizarre petal-soft pressure steering my thoughts away, like too many blooms blocking out daylight.

"Your family lived in Kerzenthal." Emeric's voice is steady, measured. "How could your mother take you all the way to Sovabin?"

I see her lantern on that cold winter night, a dark forest shrouded in snow—no, I can *feel* the stones of Castle Falbirg—

"Look in the mirror."

In the glass, I see a red light flickering deep in my pupils.

Emeric says something, and it's as if the words are broken to pieces, shaken up in a bag, and emptied into my ears. That red burns even brighter. In the ensuing silence, it starts to fade.

She's in my head. The Scarlet Maiden is in my head.

"Fix it." My voice wobbles. Something about this—about my own memories being turned on me—scares me, in a way I've never felt fear. "Please—get her out—"

"I've been trying," Emeric admits, running a hand through his hair. "We've been looking, but every counterspell, every restoration charm, they've all failed. I don't know if anyone *can* break it."

A sick silence falls. I just—have to live with this? Not knowing what memories I can trust?

Someone knocks on the door.

"Come in," Emeric calls.

The clerk from the front desk pushes it open. "Excuse me, Aspirant Conrad, Miss Vanja. There's a carriage here from the Imperial Abbey. The High Augur, Abbess Sibylle von Eisz, says you wish to speak with her."

CHAPTER TWENTY-THREE

Augur's Tears

"You wouldn't happen to know a Henrik Ros, would you?" I ask the friar driving the open carriage as we roll through the gates of the Konstanzian Imperial Abbey. It was already imposing from a distance; up close, it's even more massive than I thought. The great domed temple of the augurs observes from a hilltop, but it's shored up by workshops, stables, infirmaries, refectories, long stretches of dormitories, towering scriptoriums, and other buildings I can't identify but would bet also end in *-orium*. Everywhere I look, there are friars, nuns, laypeople. All sport heavy silver pendants wrought like single staring eyes.

The friar glances over his shoulder. "Brother Henrik is part of why you're here. He went missing last night."

"Are you serious?" I demand. "I thought he was the nice one! First

Erwin gets himself held hostage for three days, now Henrik runs off? What is *with* this family?"

"We don't think he ran off," the driver says tensely. "His room was locked from the inside. Mother Superior can tell you more; I'm not an augur."

Thankfully we don't have long to wait before we're hustled to Abbess Sibylle, the Mother Superior herself. She's waiting at the end of a long walkway that stretches from a temple, her deep gold face in high contrast to the starched white headdress that covers her head and falls behind her shoulders, nearly all the way to the ground. Against the sky's blanket of flat clouds, her nacreous dove-gray vestments gleam like mother-of-pearl, nearly as bright as the ceremonial halo-like headdress of wrought silver eyes affixed to the back of her head. Another heavy silver eye hangs from a chain around her neck, and strings of clear glass prayer beads dangle from her crossed wrists.

"I'll just, er, be in here." Lady Ambroszia climbs into my satchel as the carriage slows to a halt, pulling a kerchief over herself.

"There's no need for that," Abbess Sibylle calls as Emeric helps me out of the carriage. "I have no quarrel with the dead." She bows her head. "Greetings in the blessed works of the Low Gods and in the eyes of Truth, Brother Conrad. Greetings to you as well, God Daughter. And to you, Lady Ambroszia."

Emeric bows, and I duck a curtsy. Lady Ambroszia pokes her head out. "Considering my . . . *involvement* with Nibs—Nibelungus von Wälft, I did not expect so gracious a welcome from House Eisz."

The corner of the abbess's mouth twitches. "All abbesses here are inducted into House Eisz only upon election. And even if I were descended from the first imperial abbess, I would not care particularly about her ex-husband's affairs." Before I can decipher if that was a backhanded snub, she fixes her soft slate-gray eyes on me. "I do not believe we have time to waste. Your brother is missing, and your feral god grows stronger by the hour. Please come with me to the martyrium."

She turns and sets off down the walkway at a startlingly brisk pace for a woman in heavy robes, headed to the temple. I half jog to catch up. "Your—Your Reverence, could you please elaborate on 'martyrium'? It's not still actively producing martyrs, is it?"

Abbess Sibylle regards me with a half-lidded stare before saying, with an absolute deficit of inflection, "That's the first time anyone's made that joke."

"A martyrium is a shrine built over the tomb of a martyr," Emeric clarifies. "I believe this abbey's is Saint Konstanzia, the first augur?"

"That is correct, Brother Conrad. She guides our visions." Abbess Sibylle's jaw tightens. "Which is why mine, as of late, have been so troubling. You, God Daughter, have taken Augur's Tears before, correct?"

Augur's Tears are collected directly from the eyes of the Low God Truth and taken in small doses to see the world as they do. The first and last time I took the Tears, Adalbrecht von Reigenbach was trying to poison me. To call the experience "troubling" would be like locking someone in a closet with an angry wolverine and calling it "a bonding exercise."

"I did," I answer. "I spent an hour tasting seasons and staring at tapestries until I fell off a waterfall."

Abbess Sibylle only sounds faintly judgmental when she says, "You experienced the vastness of Truth. An . . . *untrained* mind can see only fragments at a time, like single facets of a snowflake in a blizzard. Augury acts as a lens through which to focus those fragments into a clear vision." She trades the judgment for consideration. "Truth also sends me warnings of threats rising in the region. If the threat is significant and complex, though, Truth will share it in pieces. For example, shortly before Winterfast, I had a vision of the margrave of Bóern riding dead horses through Alt-Aschel, as the night sky burned with blue eyes instead of stars. In another, he strangled the empress with an iron crown."

"I mean, he was planning a *nachtmären*-fueled coup, so those pretty much sum it up," I say.

We reach the great doors of the temple; they're bracketed by stern-faced nuns, who haul them open in a cacophony of hinges. "Indeed," the abbess says a bit testily. "And that was no small threat. So you may comprehend my alarm over the past week as visions came to me in mere scattered fragments, even with Saint Konstanzia's help. I saw a mountain dyed red, a bleeding tomb, a flood of thorns eating Rammelbeck whole—dozens of pieces. And with every one, I saw you two. Sometimes Brother Conrad; sometimes you, God Daughter; sometimes both."

She leads us in. The exterior of the martyrium was austerity defined, its towering walls grudgingly allowing only a modest clerestory of narrow windows to break the stone monotony. Inside, it's made a few reluctant concessions to architectural splendor: Simple adornments on the limestone columns ringing the nave. A suggestion of a flourish on the sparsely populated stone pews' armrests. A divot of sorts depresses the floor in the room's center, where it shifts to black glass.

But the real glory is above, in the domed ceiling. A spectacular honeycomb of rainbow stained glass is further multiplied by mirrors spinning on wires and spraying color everywhere, turning the subdued stone of the martyrium into a canvas for infinite hues.

"I would have sent for you anyway, when we learned Brother Henrik was missing," the abbess continues, "but Truth had advised me to wait for their signal as well. They said it would be of no use until you could understand what you saw."

Emeric brightens. "When I filled Vanja in on the case."

"Oh," I say, barely keeping a lid on the sheer vindication boiling from my every pore. "I should let Proctor Kirkling know how wrong she was."

"Please don't," Emeric sighs.

"I should let her know five times," I say, beatific, "every minute of every hour of every day until she dies."

Abbess Sibylle motions to the handful of people in the pews, who begin clearing out. "I'm certain that will make her hate you less," she says in that flat voice again, the one that makes it impossible to tell for certain if I'm being roasted.

"How do you *know* so much about me?" I ask incredulously. She just points to the eye pendant. I add a defeated "Never mind."

"Now, the problem at hand," the abbess says. "The scale of this threat is too enormous for Truth to show it to me all at once—it would be like pouring a barrel of wine straight into a pitcher. But between the three of us, if we each focus on different elements, we may see as close to the whole picture as possible." She sees Emeric open his mouth and holds up a hand. "Bringing in more augurs won't change anything, as this is my vision, not theirs. You two, however, are very much a part of it."

"Never mind," he says appreciatively.

Abbess Sibylle just points to her pendant again in explanation. Then she adds, "And yes, before you ask: This should help God Daughter Vanja's particular . . . *situation* as well."

"Why do people keep calling me that?" I ask. "First Saint Willehalm, now you. I think I would know if you were my godparent."

"I wouldn't bet the farm on that," Ambroszia mumbles from my satchel.

The abbess snaps three clear beads off the string at her wrist and hands one each to Emeric and me. I'd thought they were glass, but now I see flickers of gold leaf moving in a slow spiral within: Augur's Tears. "On my signal, we will take these. I will meditate upon Brother Henrik's disappearance and how it connects to this calamity. God Daughter, I suggest you focus on what you have lost to this Scarlet Maiden."

Emeric rolls the bead across his palm. "And I'll try to see what she's really after."

"Am I supposed to swallow it or bite down?" I ask. "Or does it pop? The last time I did this, it was just murder juice."

"It will dissolve," Abbess Sibylle says, with a patience usually reserved for small children and orange cats. "Lady Ambroszia, you will be more comfortable in the pews."

"On it." I set my satchel on a pew to make it easier for her.

When I turn back, the abbess is pointing to where I should stand on the dark glass disc; Emeric is already posted up, facing away from us both. "You'll want to look at the wall," she advises. "At least, once you take the Tears. It's seldom best to see someone in the full light of Truth."

"Don't I know it," I say under my breath, taking my place. Adalbrecht von Reigenbach appeared to me as a horse-headed monstrosity right before I was sucked into his debatably tragic backstory. I'd rather not roll those dice again.

But there's nothing to worry about until the Tears kick in. I pinch the bead between my finger and thumb, still nervous. "Ready?" calls the abbess from where she stands at the peak of the perfect triangle we form. At an assent from both Emeric and me, she lifts her arms and face to the ceiling.

There's a chime and the whisper of glass slicing through air. The colors drenching the temple begin to shift, the mirrors and panes above us wheeling into a deliberate dance. Shafts of light spear down, vanish, cross, and merge. The glass beneath my feet pulses.

Suddenly the light is catching on invisible prisms, like we're at the heart of an incorporeal diamond, gathering and splintering in wild patterns. I look back at Abbess Sibylle. Her ornamental halo has transfigured, the silver eyes now burning molten white and slowly spinning behind her head. Her eyes, too, are blazing prismatic white, every color in the universe.

"Now," she orders, and tips her bead between her lips.

I brace myself and follow suit, then remember I'm supposed to face the wall. I slip one last glance at Emeric as the Augur's Tears touch my tongue. My mouth burns with salt and copper, my eyes watering—

And then, abruptly, he is etched against the shadows like a saint. A wave of terrible adoration drowns me, the heart, the truth of how I feel for him, and I cannot tear my eyes away. The red handprint burns before him, but it is not *of* him, not the way the lines of his prefect marks are. They've grown to a massive incandescent ring, tethering him to the stars in infinite threads. One constellation weaves into focus, its lights drawing into sharp focus: the Lantern.

The lantern. My mother's lantern. That's what I'm searching for, the memories I've somehow lost. I force my gaze away—

But the lantern is still there, hanging before me now, a sputtering flame in the dark.

Focus.

Silently, I ask Truth, *What is it I've lost?*

The lantern shrinks—or the world does, I cannot say. I see Castle Falbirg beyond the weak flame. Then the castle dissolves like smoke, leaving darkness behind. No—not just darkness—

Towering evergreens draped in snow. The lantern clutched in my mother's left hand. My mitten gripped in her right.

And before us, resplendent against the night, are my godmothers, Death and Fortune.

It all floods back in, all at once: Our cottage. Our life together. Our family.

Our separation when I was thirteen and they claimed me as a servant.

Our reconciliation when I was seventeen and they claimed me as a daughter.

In the Library of the Divine, it was Death holding back the *poltergeist*. In Rammelbeck, it was Fortune's work I saw in every golden gleam of luck. They've been with me this entire time.

The Scarlet Maiden took them from me, my mothers, she *took them—*

The crossroads go dark, but Death and Fortune still stand before me. Their mouths move. I can't make out even a single word.

Tears sting my eyes. "I can't hear you," I say unsteadily. "Can you hear me?"

My godmothers look at each other. Then they reach for me and fold me into their embrace. For a beautiful moment, I smell the yews, the cottage, I feel their arms around me, and that is enough.

Then we are rising.

I lift my head. The world shrinks below, the dome of the martyrium a flashing rainbow jewel, Welkenrode and Rammelbeck unfolding like Jakob's map. Crimson threads like those I saw stitched to Emeric spill from me; I touch one that runs far to the south and see Ragne's ever-shifting face. Another leads down into the martyrium and, when I brush it, conjures Udo amid a cluster of five red stars. A thread of shadows binds me to Death; a thread of mingled gold, bone, copper, and coal leads to Fortune.

My godmothers draw me over the hills to the southeast, following another strange thread, this one knotted in thorns. It isn't difficult to guess whose that is. Forests, villages—they fly by in the blink of an eye, the roads growing more and more crowded the closer we get to Boderad's Gorge—

And then we're before the stave church in Hagendorn's town square.

Leni stands atop a wooden scaffold beside the Scarlet Maiden's statue. Red still drips from the tip of the statue's spindle, as well as from the hole in her palm; smoke rises from the iron crown of roses. Leni, too, holds a crude brass spindle aloft like a scepter, and a red diamond is painted on the palm of her other hand. More red diamonds are painted over her cheeks, like the ones I used to daub on, but she's added a head-dress to the outfit. A polished brass disc with cutouts like burning roses now sits behind her head like a sunrise, like a farce of the abbess's halo.

She's addressing a crowd that stands below. I lived in Hagendorn two months, I've been gone two weeks, and I barely recognize a single person in the throng. The cult is growing out of control.

". . . pleased to grant Sister Walpurg the place of honor at tonight's feast! The Scarlet Maiden has seen her hard work and dedication and the shining example she sets for us all!" Leni bestows a wreath of strange crimson flowers—cornflowers forced to bloom red—upon a blushing, beaming young woman I've never seen before. Cheers ring through the square.

Then Leni raises the spindle. A hush falls.

"And now," she says sorrowfully, "it is time to reckon with our shortcomings. Who has failed the Scarlet Maiden today?"

A red mist gathers behind Leni. No one else seems to notice. It hisses once, and she points her brass spindle at . . . Sonja the farmer.

"*Sonja-a-a*," Leni half sings, in the same nauseatingly playful tone the Scarlet Maiden last used to greet me. "Confess your failures. You were to offer your finest calf to the glory of the Scarlet Maiden, but you chose the weaker of the two, did you not?"

"I needed to keep the one who will give milk," Sonja protests. "My family—"

"Your family enjoys the blessings of the Scarlet Maiden!" Leni cries. "And this treachery is how you repay Her? You will fast for three days, allowed only water. Anyone seen giving you food will be cast from the grace and love of our Lady and driven from Hagendorn."

Whispers and scorn follow Sonja as she pushes her way out of the square.

Leni sentences the innkeeper to a night in the stocks for doubting the Scarlet Maiden. The smith is made to forfeit his tools for a week for providing horseshoes to a passing outsider. Then the spindle is drawn on Auntie Gerke.

"Gerke, you have failed the Scarlet Maiden most of all. Multiple witnesses have heard you spreading dangerous heresy."

Auntie Gerke draws herself up, leaning on the arm of Sonja's eldest child, the one who wished to apprentice for the old midwife. Then my stomach drops as Gerke spits in the dirt.

"Isn't heresy if it's true," she says, loudly enough to reach every soul in the square. "You lot of ninnies don't want a god; you want someone to tell you you're special. You've sold our home to a demon."

Outraged gasps sweep the masses.

"You hear her sacrilege for yourselves," Leni says sweetly. "She wishes to be a scourge, then our answer will be the scourge. Gerke, your punishment is lashing, until either you recant, or you pass from this world and into the judgment of the Scarlet Maiden."

Iron silence locks around the congregation. There are a few—only a meager few—uneasy faces. The rest burn with righteous pride.

I am grateful only that Udo and Jakob are nowhere to be seen, that they're not here, quiet in the face of this horror.

Then the red mist behind Leni refines, collapsing into the silhouette I know—the long flowing hair, the cut-glass face, the ethereal robes.

The statue's wreath of roses bursts into flame.

". . . Mercy," Leni says with an air of surprise. "Gerke, for now you will be spared. Give thanks to the Scarlet Maiden, by whose intervention alone you have been saved." Then her voice rises. "Rejoice, friends, for here you are loved, here you are strong, here you are one with the power of the Scarlet Maiden! The false prophet has been sent away! Be strong in your faith, follow my word, and the Defiler will be kept from our doors!"

The red mist should stop at the Scarlet Maiden's visage, as I've known her. But it peels back even more, stripping away the layers of beauty, divinity, until all that's left is—

Me.

My face, swimming in blood-red miasma.

She looks right at me, and an inhuman smile stretches too far, too wide. "Hello, *Prophet*."

Death and Fortune haul me back, but it's too late. We're fleeing Hagendorn over hill and dale and treetop and tower, but a crackling red lightning bolt is giving wicked chase. I hear her horrible laugh—red flowers erupt from the mountain that overlooks Rammelbeck, familiar rooftops speeding by, then the Trench, then Grandfather's gleaming yellow eyes—

I slam into my own skin, staggering in the refracting maze of light. I'm here. I made it. I remember.

My eyes land on the pews. A regal elderly woman is sitting beside my satchel, where a cluster of red stars nests. Ambroszia and the blood drops. The Augur's Tears haven't burned out completely, not yet.

A hand locks onto my shoulder.

"*Rude to leave*," the Scarlet Maiden croons from Emeric, "*without saying goodbye.*"

His fingers dig into my collarbone so hard, there will be no hiding the bruise. I can see the Scarlet Maiden on him like a mantle, her claws sunk deep. One hand is steering for my throat.

For a moment I panic—and then I remember. "*Villanelle*," I gasp, "villanelle villanelle villa—"

Emeric's face stays blank, but there's a sense of bewilderment and fury from the Scarlet Maiden before his knees give out. I slide my arms around his chest as he crumples, his eyes shuttering, and ease us both to the floor. After a moment, the red glow dissipates like a breath in the cold.

"That was certainly educational," remarks the abbess from behind me.

I whip around to make sure she's not the new host of the Scarlet Maiden. Thankfully, any sign of godly possession is absent. Even her halo of eyes has reverted to stationary mundane silver.

My next breath escapes as a borderline hysterical laugh as I slump with relief. It worked. I stopped her, for now.

I don't know if I'll feel completely safe with Emeric until we've broken her hold on him, but maybe—maybe I can feel safe enough.

The ceiling has stilled again, settling the martyrium in a stable wash of color. I stretch my legs out and prop Emeric's head in my lap. "He should come around in about five minutes. I'm going to shackle him, just to be safe."

"Prudent," Abbess Sibylle says dryly. "That—*presence*—it was the Scarlet Maiden?"

"In the awful transcendent not-flesh flesh." I clamp a manacle around Emeric's wrist. "What did you learn about Henrik?"

To my surprise, Abbess Sibylle sits on the floor with me, leaning against a column. "I saw a great deal, beyond Brother Henrik, even. He's not in any immediate danger and is out of the reach of the Scarlet Maiden in his current company. Unfortunately . . . that company is Brunne the Huntress and the Wild Hunt."

I stare at her, disbelieving. "Not to cast any aspersions here, Your Reverence—I'm sure your augury is top-notch—but from what I've heard of Henrik, he's—"

"A poet," she sighs. "None aspersions cast. Brunne kidnaps them sometimes. She likes to have them sing her praises for a fortnight or so, then drops them back off with a blessing for their reward."

I snap the other manacle around Emeric's opposite wrist. "I don't have a fortnight," I say, "I have—well, two weeks, but considering where things are at with the cult *now*, we need it shut down yesterday. The more worshippers the Scarlet Maiden collects, the more powerful a god she'll become."

"Not," Emeric murmurs, "entirely true."

"Junior?" I fall into the old nickname out of anxiety-compounded habit, taking his face in my hands.

His eyes crack open. They are beautifully human, if a bit groggy, as they take in the surroundings. He slurs, "Oh, your lap is . . . very nice."

"I don't think the sleeping spell has completely worn off," Abbess Sibylle says, stating the obvious simply for propriety's sake.

"How are you feeling?" I try not to laugh. "Do you need help?"

He shakes his head in an ardent *no*. And then he declares, "You're so pretty. Prettiest . . . prettiest girl in the empire."

"Incredible," I tell the abbess. "He's completely lucid."

She ignores me. "We're going to help you sit up now, Brother Conrad."

Emeric makes a noise like a stubborn hinge as we do, but the change in altitude does seem to help clear his head. After a moment upright, he says, slightly mortified, "That was unseemly. Please excuse me, Your Reverence."

"Never mind that," she says, "what did you see? Why wouldn't a Low God gain strength from her followers?"

Emeric ventures a look at me, guilt and apprehension in his face. "Because we got it wrong. The Scarlet Maiden isn't a real Low God."

My heart crashes to the floor.

Kirkling was right about me. And Emeric will have to convict me before the Godly Courts himself.

Then he adds the last words I expect, dark as my outlook:

"Not yet."

PART THREE:

HARVEST
MOTHERS

OFFICIAL BUSINESS

"THE GOOD NEWS," EMERIC SAYS, WRITING FURIOUSLY IN HIS NOTE-book, "is that she's probably an immensely powerful demon."

"We need to discuss your standards for good news," I say darkly as I pace the carpet of the library study.

The convenient thing about having an imperial abbess for an escort is that, after going on a hallucinatory journey of self-discovery in her giant kaleidoscopic observatory, she can walk you around the abbey's library while you talk at the top of your lungs and not even *one* surly librarian can shush you. Even better, if you want a nice private study to yourself, like the one we're in now? People will just *clear out*. If I make it through this, I might see if the augurs are hiring.

Granted, the odds of survival without a conviction or five from the Godly Courts seem to be getting slimmer.

Emeric underlines something with a burst of zeal at the desk he's claimed. "It's good news because she's not a god, she's trying to *become* one, and that means"—he punctuates his sentence so hard, the entire notebook jolts—"she's not as unstoppable as we thought."

"And it also means I committed, and am extremely guilty of, profane fraud," I say, a bit waspish, "so again, standards."

"But it *doesn't*," he all but buzzes, speaking faster with every word, "because you *didn't*, because at best you would be an accessory and even *then* there is a lack-of-direct-culpability-due-to-the-difference-inscopeandintent—"

Abbess Sibylle clears her throat from an armchair solidly planted out of the midday sun, where she sits with her head tipped back, a damp cloth over her eyes. Apparently the greater visions leave her with headaches, and Truth keeps sending more glimpses her way; periodically she'll fall silent and unresponsive, a single eye in her halo burning white. "Brother Conrad, perhaps you could tell us now what you saw in the martyrium."

"Of course, Your Reverence." Emeric closes his notes with a snap. His chair creaks as he rotates it to face us in a series of excruciating scoots. "I was concentrating on what the Scarlet Maiden is trying to achieve, and in retrospect, Truth couldn't properly tell me without some context. I saw a weak entity, probably a *grimling*, in Hagendorn when Vanja arrived. Vanja, whenever you were asked to perform rites like blessings or omen readings in the Scarlet Maiden's name, that entity manifested what you said. She also did things other people prayed for *without* your knowledge. Essentially, she played the role of the Scarlet Maiden until enough people believed she *was* the Scarlet Maiden."

"Do you know what manner of *grimling* it was?" Lady Ambroszia asks. She's also been pacing like me, albeit over a much smaller area.

Emeric shakes his head. "I have a few theories, but my best guess is she was a diminished Rye Mother, given her association with flora and how she tried to claim she influenced the harvest."

I pull a face. One of my siblings—probably Ozkar, now that I think about it—used to promise a ghoulish Rye Mother, all in white, would come from the woods and steal me away for being too noisy. Rye Mothers are said to inflict a number of creative punishments, from mashing up children in an iron butter churn to making them suckle at a red-hot iron—Well. Let's just say Rye Mothers are very committed to a theme, and that theme is "Nasty Iron." The only good thing about them is that they supposedly foretell a good harvest.

"Doesn't that still mean I'm guilty, though?" I ask. "Since I created those openings for her."

Emeric leans back in his chair. "No. Think of it like this: If you set up a game of Find the Lady, people participate only of their own volition, even if they suspect it's a scam. But you can't reasonably be held responsible for a stranger pickpocketing one of your onlookers. You're only at fault if you know a criminal will exploit your actions, or if you witness the criminal in the act and intentionally continue facilitating the circumstances that enable them."

There's a faint gargle. The Mother Superior has gone limp in her armchair, mouth ajar. One of the eyes in her halo has lit up; she's having another vision. (I'll admit, I expected the process to be a mite more elegant.)

Emeric lowers his voice. "You should know . . . I'm leaving the not-a-god part out of my report to Kirkling to be safe. I'll just say we got more insight into the Scarlet Maiden. I don't trust her not to use this as an excuse for drastic action against you."

I slow my pacing until I stop a few feet from him. Bright noon light glares from the window nearby, making me hold up a hand to shield the side of my face. "It's not that I disagree," I say, hesitant, "but . . . I don't want you to compromise your case. Or yourself. Would you protect *any* other suspect like you're protecting me?"

He reaches for my hands, and our fingers link. "If you were any other suspect, Kirkling wouldn't be treating you like this," Emeric says, running his thumbs over my knuckles. "I chose the Lantern as my signum for a reason. I want light shed on every part of this case. I want the whole picture, and if that means keeping Kirkling from interfering until I have all the facts, so be it. If I'm wrong, I'll answer for it to the Godly Courts."

I still shift in place. "I thought that was the entire point of prefects, that you have all these rules and ethics and nonsense that you have to play by. So why does she get to ignore them?"

"Because she's decommissioned." Emeric scowls out the window. "Active prefects have to account for their questionable choices with Justice herself every year, and *she* decides if they're allowed to stay on the job. If Kirkling had to answer for even half of what she's put you through, she'd be stripped of her marks. She's only being allowed to proctor my Finding out of respect for Hubert."

I can't help but wonder, then, when Emeric has to answer for his choices with me, whether protecting me from Kirkling will be enough of an alibi.

The abbess sits up with a sharp inhalation as the glowing eye in her halo fades. She pulls the damp cloth off her face. "What did I miss?"

"Boring law stuff," I say quickly. Emeric makes a noise of indignation at the proximity of *boring* and *law*. "See anything good?"

Abbess Sibylle folds the cloth and sets it on a side table. "I saw horses."

("*Damn it,*" Emeric incants like a charm against evil.)

The abbess pretends she didn't hear that. "You, God Daughter, were riding through the night sky on a dark horse. In your hand you held a cluster of red comets, and their tails stretched too far to see their ends." She pauses, thinking.

"I saw the blood drops as red stars," I offer, pulling the cambric from my satchel. "But . . . I didn't think we'd keep pursuing them. Not if they'll help the Scarlet Maiden."

"That was the final part of my vision," Emeric confirms. "What the Scarlet Maiden wants. She has enough ardent followers to be a true threat to Almandy as a fully-fledged Low God. But gods that arise organically, from mortal beliefs, have an inherent link to the mortal world and the power of that belief. She doesn't. She can tap only a fraction of her cult's potential power. So she can sacrifice me, as a bridge between the mortal and the divine, to make that link. Or . . ." Emeric picks up the cambric. Immediately the blood drops abruptly retract, shrinking to the size of their original blots, turning a rusty aged brown. His line of thinking takes a sudden detour. "*Fascinating.*"

"She can make a link using blood ties," Ambroszia picks up for him, "between seven brothers."

"Blood ties?" I ask, taking the cambric back. The five drops turn bright, newly red again, branching into a crimson cobweb.

"The connection between birth relatives, however close or estranged, by virtue of shared blood," Emeric explains. His fingertip traces the lines, hovering an inch or so above the fabric in my hands. "It's one of the oldest forms of power, because we're born with those connections and they're very hard to sever. And the power magnifies the more contributors there are. See how there's only one line between two brothers, but six lines between four, and ten between five?"

"And seven is a sacred number," the abbess adds.

"Indeed." Ambroszia tugs on one faded horsehair curl. "So sacrifice seven brothers instead of one prefect, and the power of those cumulative blood ties will forge a comparable bond to the mortal world."

I've only barely met most of my brothers, and already I carry their lives in my hands.

Whatever she touches falls to ruin. My mother's voice thunders in my memory.

Emeric runs a hand over his mouth. "Wait . . . *Wait.* Lady Ambroszia, the Saxbern Treatise of 343. Verwinus the Elder's theory on bonding reciprocity. And Guodila's—"

"Sacred Factorials," Ambroszia finishes excitedly. "Of course! It would need further refining to be certain, but . . . that would explain why the Mother Superior saw the blood ties in her vision."

"*Does* it, though?" I ask a bit plaintively.

Emeric has mercy on me. "They're called blood *ties* for a reason. They could hypothetically be, well, *repurposed* to bind the Scarlet Maiden. And since they wouldn't be destroyed in a sacrifice, they wouldn't harm your brothers."

"So Truth put them in the vision because they want me to gather the last two blood drops." I run a hand over my braids. "Did Truth also conveniently find time-management skills, because ScarMad—"

"*ScarMad?*" Emeric splutters.

"Half the syllables, all the awful. Point being, ScarMad's planning to boot you into the jaws of a hellhound in two weeks, and Henrik is apparently *otherwise engaged* until then. So . . ." I trail off, connecting the dots. "I have to get Henrik back from Brunne." I sit in a chair and put my head in my hands. "Your Reverence saw me riding in the night sky. It's the Wild Hunt."

"That would fit with what I saw, yes," Abbess Sibylle confirms.

There's an odd twinge to her voice, like she's leaving something out. "I'm not sure how you would accomplish such a task, but perhaps Truth will afford me some clarity later."

I let a breath hiss through my teeth, racking my brain. Time was already going to be tight, and now I have to reclaim Henrik from a Low God *and* fix the mess I caused with the Ardîm family before we can even leave Rammelbeck.

"Brother Conrad, you are welcome to use our library as you please," the abbess is saying. "We may have some volumes of interest to you."

"Thank you, I would appreciate that."

Well, there's one person who might know how to get Brunne to give up my brother. I just have to . . . multitask, I suppose.

I get to my feet. "Your Reverence, can I get a ride back to our inn? I need to tell Helga our dinner plans have changed." Emeric raises an eyebrow. I say smoothly, "It's fine. Don't worry about it."

"Notably, every time you say that, it turns out I should, in fact, worry a lot."

"I will help you secure a carriage," the abbess says, also standing. "Brother Conrad, Lady Ambroszia, I shall return momentarily."

She accompanies me out of the library and down to the abbey's main drive, deep in thought. To my surprise, a coach is already waiting. I turn to ask. The abbess just points at her eye pendant once more.

"God Daughter," she says, "I did not wish to say this in the company of the others. But in my vision . . ." Abbess Sibylle purses her lips. "Bear in mind that this was an abstract fragment of Truth, that not everything can be interpreted at face value."

"What did you see?"

"For example, you couldn't possibly hold comets in your bare hand—"

The driver scoots to hop down and open the coach door, but I wave him off, yanking at the handle. "Look, I have a lot to do today and not a lot of time, so please just spit it out."

The Mother Superior looks directly at me, and for the first time, she seems—sad. "You were weeping," she admits. "And, somehow, I knew . . . you were *alone*."

⚜

"When you said you wanted company on errands tonight," Helga grumbles, "this was not what I had in mind."

I shift the lockpicks clenched in my teeth as I work on the back door of the Treasury. "Yeah, well, I had to introduce manacles in the bedroom last night, and it wasn't what I had in mind either, so we're all broadening our horizons in Rammelbeck. Just keep a lookout."

Madame Treasury gets this much credit from me, however grudging: This is *not* an easy lock to pick. I'll admit, I expected her to cut corners everywhere, but she's invested in decent-enough hardware that it takes a minute or two before the pins smooth into place and let the cylinder turn.

I ease the door open and peer in. It's dark and silent inside, with only the faint glow of the half-moon streaming in through the domed glass ceiling to anoint a few surfaces in smears of silver. I slip inside, motion for Helga to follow, and lock the door behind us. (It's a good lock. It deserves to be used.)

"What are we doing, exactly?" she asks as I wait for my eyes to fully adjust.

"Finding Erwin's bribe money so we can pay the Green Sleeve. And anything we can use to fix the deal the Ardîms had." I start picking my way to the empty main floor, listening for any signs of life and coming up empty. It's well-known the Treasury's been shut for bed lice, which ought to keep out most intruders. "You're here because the money's probably still here and this place is too big to search on my own. Madame got Erwin Friday night and kicked him out Monday morning. Unless she could think of an excuse for a hundred-*gilden* spike in sales—"

"Five hundred," Helga corrects. I gawk at her, and she grimaces. "Erwin told me he didn't spend it all at the Green Sleeve."

I find myself chewing my thumbnail nearly ragged at that. "Then it's *definitely* still here. Madame wouldn't have time to launder that through the brothel . . . or . . . the *spintz* booth . . . hm."

There might be more to the picture than I realized. A bribe that big means *very* deep pockets. Someone invested in shutting down the port for days, like the prefects were saying earlier. And the structure of the *spintz* scheme makes for a perfect way to launder money—that exchange tax is impossible to track.

I pull out my message-mirror.

> *Where do*
> *you usually find*
> *evidence of math*
> *crimes*
> *?*

I look around while I wait for Emeric's answer. "Five hundred *gilden* . . . If I were an absurd amount of money, where would I be . . . ?"

There's a creak and a glimmer of gold. I see a flicker of movement out of the corner of my eye.

Fortune's still with me, even if I can't hear her, can't see her, without Truth's help.

The wheel on the stage slowly rotates through a rogues' gallery of sexy enterprises until it lands on a wedge labeled *OFFICIAL BUSINESS* and illustrated with figures making very unsanitary use of a desk.

Looks like our first search should be Madame's office, then. There's just one hang-up:

"*I* wanted to spin the wheel," I pout.

In response, the wheel wobbles a bit, as if to say, *Go on then.* I give it a spin. It stops, once more, on *OFFICIAL BUSINESS.*

I beam. "Thank you for humoring me."

The wheel creaks over to *IN FOR A PENNY.*

Now I just need Emeric to tell me *where* in Madame's office to look for the math crimes. My mirror pulses with his answer.

In a graph.
They're always used
for plotting.

I only barely resist the urge to throw the mirror across the room.

No you ass
I mean ACTUAL MONEY
LAUNDERING

"Come on, we're checking the office first," I tell Helga, and start climbing one of the double sets of stairs.

Emeric's follow-up comes almost immediately:

There's money
laundering? And you
didn't invite me?

"You know what, ScarMad can have him," I mutter. I should know better than to ask about financial offenses unless I'm trying to seduce him.

"You say that," Helga pipes up as we reach the top of the stairs, "but you're grinning like an absolute buffoon right now."

We have to go through another lock to get into Madame's office, but at least the enchantment for the lights still functions, kindling as we enter. Emeric apparently has decided to be helpful in the interim, because when I check my mirror, he's added:

Recurring large transactions
for generic goods or services
that don't have a fixed price,
like art.
If you don't find them
in an obvious ledger,
look for a hidden one.

I write back:

All hypothetical.

In a moment, I get:

Hypothetically, if Madame
has ties to the Grace Unending

after all, Ghendt and Dursyn
would like to know.

The insufferable beanstalk. I didn't even tell him where I was going tonight. I shove the mirror in my pocket. "We're looking for a ledger," I tell Helga.

"I thought we were looking for Erwin's bribe money."

"Call it a hunch," I say, heading for a marble bust, "but I bet where we find one, we'll find the other. Start with the bookcase. Check all the books for a hollow."

Helga obliges, sliding a look my way. "Since we're doing this instead of dinner . . . can we still . . . talk?"

My stomach twists as I run my hands over the marble in search of a hidden lever or the like. I fixate on the base of the bust and say tonelessly, "Might as well."

All I hear is the shuffle of books as Helga pulls them off shelves, one by one, on the other side of the room. "First of all, we weren't trying to hide it from you—"

"Bullshit," I say tightly. "Eida came all the way to Dänwik and you let me think she was delusional."

Helga doesn't answer for a moment. "You said you wanted to decide when you would be ready to find your family. By that point, we were . . . pretty sure of who you are, so my options were to wait and let you figure it out on your own or to disrespect the first boundary you'd given me."

I find a small circular dent in the pedestal. When I press it, though, it ejects a drawer far too small for either a secret ledger or a minor fortune; instead it holds packets of burgundy powder. Madame's hair dye. I snort in disgust and close the drawer, then move to the desk. "Or you could have told me the truth in Dänwik."

"Eida did, and you looked like someone cut your puppet strings," Helga says bluntly. Then her voice softens. "I *am* sorry I didn't tell you sooner, or better, I just couldn't think of . . . how."

I skip the papers on the desk for now and kneel to look at its under-belly. There don't seem to be any signs of a false bottom or a secret panel, not even in the drawers I pull out. "You said 'we.' How long did you all know?"

"Jakob and Udo thought there was a chance from day one. After all, you have the name, you're the right age, and, if you haven't noticed, you look a hell of a lot like us. I wasn't so sure. And then when we learned your *real* story . . . we knew." Her voice thickens. "We just didn't want to scare you away. Not after all—If I'd thought you were ready, I—Vanja, we've been wondering what happened to you for *thirteen years*."

Her voice breaks on "*thirteen*." I stand and finally look at Helga, try-ing and failing to blink back the tears in my own eyes. "So," I rasp, "even with—everything—y-you all . . . still want me?"

There's a thud as Helga drops a book onto a shelf and stomps over to me. An awkward beat passes, then I half stumble to her, half let myself be yanked into a hug.

"We *never* stopped wanting you, you absolute donkey of a miracle," Helga blubbers. "*Never*."

I have thought about a moment like this for a long, long time. And now, here, with my older sister saying the words, I know it's nothing like what I'd dreamed. I can only squeeze my eyes shut and let myself be held.

After another long pause, she lets me go, dabbing at her eyes. "Congrats, I guess. They're not my terrible brothers; they're *our* terrible brothers. Let's find Erwin's money and get out of here."

"Yeah. I, uh. I need a minute." I teeter over to the sofa next to the bookcase and flop down.

There's a creak, and I'd swear I hear a jingle.

I shift my weight. There's no noise, but . . . there's not nearly enough padding for the size of the cushion.

"I think I've got something," I tell Helga, sliding off the couch. She starts for me, and I wave a hand. "No, focus on the paperwork on the desk. Last time I was in here, I saw an offer to buy the Treasury. I want to know who she'd sell to when she's making such a profit here." I begin feeling around the base of the cushion. "Oh, and I need your advice on something." I see her perk up from the corner of my eye and say, dour, "It has nothing to do with your bet. Which, by the way, *ew*."

"We bet on how fast you would break the Scarlet Maiden's claim," she says primly, "not how. I'm just helping with the most-direct option."

"Zero percent better," I grouse. "Anyway. I need to figure out how to get Henrik back from Brunne the Huntress."

Helga whistles low. Not in surprise—I told her about Brunne on the way over—but in apprehension. "That won't be easy. You could win a favor from her if you best her in a challenge, and there are any number of challenges she'll take you up on. The problem is she doesn't accept any she won't win."

"Remind me of her backstory again?" My fingertips catch on a latch. I flip it, and the sofa cushion pops up like the lid of an oversized jewelry case. There's a hollowed-out compartment lined in velvet. Inside, a plain canvas-bound book rests on top of a broad, shallow wooden box.

"Betrothed to a giant against her will, fooled him into letting her ride his special horse. While she was running away, the horse kicked the top off a mountain, and she turned into a god."

"Poetic." I flip through the book. There are rows and rows of daily deposits and withdrawals—Madame's real ledger. I stow it in my satchel and crack open the box. There's a *lot* of gold inside. I don't have time to count all five hundred, but, having once been in possession of a thousand *gilden*, I'd say the amount looks to be about half. I grab a pillow off the sofa, cut it open with my boot knife, yank out the stuffing, and start shoveling *gilden* inside. Something turns in my mind as I do: Abbess Sibylle saw me riding through the night. "Do you think Brunne would accept a race?"

Helga lets out a disbelieving laugh. "Yes, but again, because she would *definitely win*. Special horse and all."

I think of a black feather in my rucksack, back at the Jolly Magistrate. "Maybe, maybe not. I might know a horse."

Helga, surprisingly, doesn't question that. When I look up from shoving money into the pillowcase, I find her frowning at a piece of paper. "Get this," she says, then reads: "'Prefects called in. Change in plans. Hold the cash and keep the deliveryman on-site until things cool off. Once he's handled, we'll go forward with the sale.'"

"So they weren't keeping Erwin just to hurt the Green Sleeve." I sit back on my heels. "He knows the helmsmen of the *Grace Unending* were given bad directions on purpose. The bribers were going to kill him to shut him up and then take back their money. I hope he's lying low."

"He was planning on it, but . . . I'll let him know it's worse than we thought." Helga keeps flipping through the papers on the desk. "There're plans here for the Green Sleeve too."

I finish stuffing the pillowcase with all the *gilden*, knot it shut, close up the sofa, and go to look at the paperwork. The offer to buy the Treasury is still stuck under the same stack. I pull it out and find *Wälftsee Holdings* listed as the buyer.

When Emeric spoke earlier with Prefect Ghendt, she said, ". . . see Holdings." This could be it, where all those suspicious missing profits are getting laundered. But more importantly . . . Wälftsee is the lake in Dänwik. The one named for Prince Ludwig's family. And Emeric said art purchases can be a cover for money laundering.

Just like Ludwig's beloved gallery.

This isn't enough to make any hasty decisions on, not yet. But when I compare the letter Helga found to a scrawled note on the offer, the handwriting looks too similar to be chance. Flipping through the ledger, I find regular payments: fifty *gilden* three times a week to Wälftsee Holdings. All it says in the note beside each is a generic *Appraisals.*

My eyes fall to the plans for the Green Sleeve, where the name *Köhler* is printed on the corner of each page. It's one more reminder of what I have to put to rights in the next few days.

Then, slowly, the troubles twist in my mind—not burdens, but ties. Threads.

For the prefects, justice is an axe that can strike only once. Extraordinary power to be used against extraordinary wrongs. But the prefects are only as good as the laws of the empire; they can only cut back the overgrowth.

They can't shape the boughs to grow into something new.

Saint Willehalm said justice requires mending, sometimes. A needle, not an axe. Someone to close the tears, who knows how to pass without a trace.

Someone to pull the threads where they need to go.

The Green Sleeve. The sale of the Treasury. The bribe money. The *spintz.* Each one a stitch waiting to be drawn through the weave.

"I think we're just about done here," I tell Helga, "but we need to go settle Erwin's debt with the Green Sleeve. And then . . . I have business to discuss with Jenneke."

CHAPTER TWENTY-FIVE

Old Friends

Emeric is still awake when I return to the Jolly Magistrate, sitting up in bed and reading one hefty tome from a new stack on the nightstand. He smiles at me through the obligatory shower of roses as I close the door. "How was the money laundering?"

"Hypothetically, enlightening." I go to my rucksack and excavate the black feather. "And I have a plan for getting Henrik back tomorrow night. Bad news: It involves horses. Good news: You have to sit it out anyway."

"If you're sure," he says, sounding faintly relieved.

"I am." I take the feather over to a candle on the nightstand and let it catch the flame. It dissolves into red smoke instantly. "Don't worry, I'm going to have backup."

⚜ 356 ⚜

"Is that for who I think it's for?" Emeric gestures to the smoke trailing through my fingers. I nod, and he smiles. "That's something. But I'm definitely still going to worry."

"I know." I sit at the foot of the bed to start working on my boots. "On a different note, I need to ask you about tax law."

"O-oh." Emeric sounds vaguely sucker punched. "You . . . you do?"

"Well, it may be a bit more complicated than that." I yank the laces.

"I'm listening," he says.

"It's partially tax law"—I kick off one boot and start on the next— "partially property law, maybe some asset forfeiture . . ." He's oddly quiet. I glance over, working at my lace knot.

His face is so rigid and composed, for a heartbeat I fear he's about to be possessed. Then I realize he's shifted the book over his lap. Specifically.

"*Prefect Aspirant Conrad*," I gasp, scandalized. He buries his face in his hands. "You utter *reprobate*."

His ears might as well be giving off steam. "I'm *sorry*, I just—this may have been the start of . . . a dream I had once."

"'Once'?" I say skeptically.

"I don't want to talk about it."

I yank off my other boot, trying not to laugh. "Ooh, Prefect Conrad, I think this subclause is wildly overreaching, and look at this *huge* loophole—"

"*Can you just ask about the taxes*," he growls into his hands.

"Fine, fine. It—I promise I'm not messing with you—it has to do with the money laundering."

Emeric makes a sound like he's been kicked in the solar plexus.

"But it also depends on the declared property value—" I cut myself off; I'm pretty sure turning that shade of red is a sign of distress in most breeds of uncooked noodle. "Do you need a minute?"

"No," he says miserably. "Yes. No. This is *staggeringly* unprofessional of me."

I climb up on the bed, grinning. "Then let's get this out of the way, and we can be even more unprofessional after."

He lifts his head far enough to look at me clearly. "I wasn't certain if . . . That is, I don't want to rush you after last night."

I curl up next to him, letting the familiar whiff of juniper put at least a dent in my nerves. "I don't know," I admit. "The knockout thing helps. I just worry about her interrupting anything you're . . . doing for me. Especially if she really does want to keep us from breaking her claim."

"That's more than fair," he says. "I can keep sleeping in manacles, too, just in case."

I wiggle my eyebrows, or at least attempt to. It probably looks as though a stinging insect's gone after my forehead. "Well. I'm worried about her interrupting what *you're* doing for me. Not what *I'm* doing for you." I see comprehension dawn on his face. "So one last bit of business, and then we can talk about all the binding legal obligations and obscure bylaws you want."

"You have," he croaks between his fingers, "my undivided attention."

I peel the nearest hand fully from his face. "How much would you expect an establishment like Madame Treasury's to pay in taxes?"

"I would think—" Emeric starts, then catches himself. "Oh. Of course. The *spintz*."

"Mm-hm," I say smugly.

He starts laughing. "You unparalleled *terror*. Are you leaving her with anything?"

"Clothes on her back, maybe. If I'm feeling generous. So it should work?"

Emeric's faltering professionalism has reached its limits. He shoves the book off his lap, reaching for me. "I told her," he murmurs against a spot below my ear that makes my toes curl. "Worst mistake she ever made."

⚜

"So to reiterate," Joniza tells me the next morning, steely, "I am only helping you on three conditions. One: I am not, at any point, going to commit a crime. Two: This *will* get Baba home in time. And three: I am only doing this *three times*. After that, you're on your own."

"If this works out, you should be—" I start.

"*If*," Joniza snaps, jabbing a ring-heavy finger my way, "better be a *when*, Vanja."

The gold and satin of her regalia flash in the sun. She's not bedecked in her full stage costume but enough of it to look the part I need her to play: wealthy and bored. For my role, I've repurposed pieces of the footman livery once again, this time to masquerade as a wealthy and bored woman's personal secretary. I've also done an atrocity to my face with a cheap cosmetics kit I scrounged up, because I'd rather look ridiculous than be recognized.

"It'll be a *when*," I say hastily, making sure my braids are fully tucked under my sensible cap. "If everything goes mostly to plan, it'll be by tomorrow afternoon, in fact."

Joniza's mouth twists with doubt as we approach one of the Sünderweg's hygiene checkpoints, and she doesn't speak again until we're a couple of blocks deep into the district. She points to the Treasury. "Is that it?"

"That's the one," I say out of the side of my mouth. There's a figure in the *spintz* booth—the same woman as before—who's sulking as she turns away a disappointed-looking fellow. "Do you remember—"

Joniza gives me a withering look, then struts across the street, her head held high. I scurry after her. It only helps sell the illusion as Joniza plants herself a couple of yards away from the Treasury's front steps, hands on her hips, eyes narrowed. I hop the steps, extract a long measuring tape from my satchel, and stretch it across the doorway. "Seventy-two," I call back.

"Excuse me," I hear the *spintz* booth worker, who I've mentally dubbed "Spintzi," call.

Joniza ignores her, gesturing languidly at the railings. "And those?"

I make a show of laying the measuring tape along a rail. I don't get to make up a number before the booth door squawks on its hinges. Spintzi blusters out.

"*Excuse* me," she huffs, "what do you think you're doing?"

Joniza regards her like an eagle watching a sparrow hop around a pile of seed. "You work for Madame's Treasury," she observes rather than asks. I have to turn my face away so I don't blow the game with a snort. I know she got the name wrong just to be irritating.

"I do," Spintzi confirms stiffly. "We're closed. We'll be——"

"My father works with *Meister* Köhler." Joniza thumbs one of her many, many golden rings. "We have heard there may be . . . investment opportunities opening up."

Her eyes dart, just for a second, to the Green Sleeve across the street.

I take the opportunity to return to her side, jotting things down in a tidy little notepad that I may have stolen from the prefect outpost. My voice pitches reedier. "Three stories. I would estimate the upper floors are for the *mietlingen*. If we may look inside——"

"You may not," Spintzi says, indignant. "Madame *Treasury's* will reopen next Monday."

I have been on the receiving end of the kind of slow blink Joniza is issuing now. It was one of the most harrowing experiences of my life. "Hm" is all she says.

"Madame isn't selling," Spintzi insists.

Joniza draws herself up, face inscrutable. "'An ant,'" she intones, in exactly the way Bajeri did, "'does not concern itself with the weight of a mountain.'"

She turns on a heel and sashays over to look at the Green Sleeve. I hand Spintzi a card. "If Madame changes her mind, she can reach us at the Three Swans Inn."

Spintzi's face screws up like she's swigged vinegar, but she swipes the card from my hand. I see her squint at the letters a moment. There's no register in her stare, as I suspected. Jenneke said Madame only hires illiterate girls; Spintzi likely knows enough math to run the booth, and no more.

I catch up to Joniza in front of the Green Sleeve just as three health inspectors are allowed inside. Jenneke leans out, looking up and down the street, a troubled furrow in her brow. She's a decent actress. I suppose that comes with the *mietling* territory. Her eyes skim right over us as she shuts the door behind the inspectors.

If she's followed my instructions to the letter, this ought to be the second inspection this morning. And after the inspectors leave, the Green Sleeve is going to quietly close down for the rest of the day.

Of course, knowing Madame, she left Spintzi at the booth specifically to watch for this opportunity. After all, Erwin Ros, alleged bed-lice patient zero, was in the Green Sleeve long, long before he was taken captive in the Treasury.

Joniza and I need to linger a moment and look deep in discussion anyway, so I decide to tackle something that's been on my mind. "So, the proverb trick . . ."

"What about it?"

"When you paid for the salve after I was whipped, I kept trying to figure out how to pay you back, and you said something about my name not being in your ledger. Did you just say that so I'd stop arguing?"

Her mouth twists, not with doubt this time but reminiscence. She mumbles, "You were a little kid." Then she stalks away, heading for the checkpoint we came in through. Her hand whips for the sky, stabbing up three fingers. One definitely curls. "One down. Two left. Use them wisely."

⚜

The Three Swans isn't the most expensive inn in Welkenrode, but it's pretty damn close. I chose it for three reasons.

One: the occupants. If Madame has somehow figured out that I'm at the Jolly Magistrate, the *last* thing I want is her to use it to link me with Joniza—or worse, me with Emeric. On the flip side, per Emeric, there is one very specific guest staying at the Three Swans. One who's about to have an *actual* vested interest in Madame's dealings.

Two: Staying at the Three Swans is a good indicator that your disposable income exceeds most people's annual income. Considering the bed-lice outbreak and the fact that she released Erwin against her buyer's orders, Madame's deal to sell the Treasury is almost certainly dead in the water. (Unlike the *Grace Unending*, which has finally been maneuvered to open the Trench to traffic once more.) She needs a new buyer. One with disposable income to burn.

And the third reason I picked the Three Swans: It's right on the large round Sanktplatt. No matter which direction you're coming from, you have to navigate around not just the enormous fountain in the middle commemorating Saint Konstanzia, but also the rest of the broad busy plaza ringing it, before you catch even a *glimpse* of the entrance to the inn.

And when Spintzi shows up a few hours later, I'm already lurking in wait on a street corner.

Spintzi puts a hand to a pocket in her kirtle, as good as broadcasting where she's keeping Madame's message. She sizes up the hectic plaza a moment, looking for the best route. All involve squeezing around a crowd or three.

When she sets off, it's child's play to fall into step behind her, wait until the pinch-point arrives, and then——

Years of running (and assiduously cheating at) games of Find the Lady mean that when I switch the envelopes, there's not so much as a crinkle.

The only trick is getting ahead of Spintzi now, because I need to beat her to the Three Swans. "Hey, Fortune?" I whisper. I alone see the answering puff of bad-luck coal dust.

There's a creak from the fountain. It goes silent, its various jets gurgling and sputtering like Emeric presented with an immaculately cataloged anthropological archive. Then, with an enormous *BANG*, Saint Konstanzia's head pops off her statue like a cork. Another splintering *crack* rings through the air as the head lands in the pool, and a moment later a geyser of water discharges from the statue's gaping neck.

"Overkill," I say under my breath, "but I'm into it."

I squeeze through the highly distracted and likely traumatized crowd and slip into the Three Swans. An elegant restaurant fans across most of the ground floor, but I'm looking for somewhere out of sight . . .

There. Near the front desk is a little waiting area, tastefully screened off to let unkempt travelers gather themselves with dignity after a long journey while their rooms are readied. I slip into it and sit, watching the front desk through the screen.

After a minute or two, Spintzi makes her entrance. She fishes out the envelope and hands it to the clerk at the front desk, and I catch something about a message and waiting for a response.

If Madame wasn't dead set on hiring girls she can scam into contracts they can't read, she'd have a messenger who could see that the name on the envelope has changed; it no longer reads *Joniza Ardîm* but *Yeshe Ghendt*. Unfortunately Spintzi doesn't know the difference any more than she's aware the contents have changed. To her credit, I *did* steal an envelope from Madame's personal stationery to seal the deal.

But instead of Madame's message, Spintzi's just passed along the letter asking Madame to keep Erwin captive, as well as Wälftsee Holdings' offer for the Treasury.

And now both are going straight to Prefect Ghendt's room.

The clerk heads down the hall to hand off the envelope while Spintzi hovers by the door. Madame wants an immediate reply. I furtively open Madame's real message and find what I expected: an invitation to a dinner meeting tonight. I make a note to cash out another ruby in case Joniza feels like picking up the tab. Then I tuck the message into a pocket, whip out my notepad, slip out of the waiting area, and head straight for Spintzi, all the while scribbling down nonsense.

"There you are," I say, nebbish, as I nearly walk into her. "My mistress wishes me to convey that she accepts Madame's invitation. She looks forward to discussing matters further this evening. Good day to you." I bob a short bow and stride away before Spintzi can ask any follow-ups, and then I hole up in the waiting area once more.

I give Spintzi a ten-minute head start before I leave the Three Swans, going back to the Rammelbeck side of the Trench. I need to call in the second round of Joniza's assistance tonight, and then if—no, *when*—all goes well, tomorrow morning should be the end.

Poor headless Saint Konstanzia is still gushing water as I cross the plaza, all the while trying to hold in my snickering. Then, as I reach one of the main bridges spanning the river, I hear a falcon's shrill cry. A shadow falls over me, once, twice, and I look up, heart rising.

After all, Joniza isn't the only old friend I'm calling on today.

A black falcon swoops for me, banking at the last moment and landing on my outstretched wrist. She shudders, feathers rippling, and suddenly where once was a falcon there now sits a raven, blinking a red eye merrily at me.

"Hello!" Ragne croaks. "I would like a ride. I have flown here from Minkja, and goodness, my arms are tired."

CHAPTER TWENTY-SIX

THE HUNTRESS

"I UNDERSTAND NONE OF THIS," RAGNE SAYS AROUND A MOUTHFUL OF asparagus. She's sitting cross-legged on the bed in the honeymoon suite, wearing one of my nightshirts.

We're having a late dinner. Having flown across half the empire, Ragne needed a long nap to rest up for tonight, especially since her power swells and fades with the moon. It'll be closer to a crescent than a half-moon tonight, so she's been awake only for the past hour or so. Emeric's been at the Imperial Abbey's library all day, so it's been just the two of us catching up the best we can over (vegetarian) food.

When it comes to my current predicament, though, it seems I've fallen short in a few places.

"I need your help to win a race against Brunne the Huntress," I say, ticking off fingers, "so I can get back the brother she kidnapped, so I can get him to contribute a blood drop toward binding the monster that stole my cult by pretending to be a god I borrowed from a folk song."

"No, that makes sense," Ragne says, incredibly. Then she makes a face. "It is this '*claim*' you said. I do not like it. I am probably married to the Gisele, but I do not *own* her. No more does she own me because we have mated. You have mated with the Emeric, yes? But that was not enough?"

I try not to squirm, but this is even worse than talking about it with Helga. "We have, kind of, but not . . . That is, it's been using . . . hands. And mouths."

"So you have mated," Ragne says plainly. "Is that not a claim?"

Now I'm definitely squirming. "We think the Scarlet Maiden will only count it as a claim if—if it could make a child."

"She counts it only if there is a penis and a womb?" Ragne tilts her head, considering, as I try and fail not to spit out a swig of water. "I could grow a penis. I do not think the Gisele would like it if we made a child so soon, though. She has not asked me to grow a penis."

"Please stop saying 'penis,'" I wheeze.

"But you just said it," Ragne objects. She looks increasingly worried. "I thought our mating was fine, but we have not needed a penis." Then she shakes her head. "But why does it have to make a child? Does it still count if you do not get with child? Or if he does not leave seed inside you? Sometimes it can be almost a week before seed takes root in the womb. Does it count *then* or when the seed is—"

"I'm adding 'seed' to the list of things I would like you to stop saying."

Ragne hunches, cheeks puffing. "I do not understand this '*claim*' at all."

"It's weird *grimling* logic," I tell her. "That's it. We think she's secretly a Rye Mother."

Ragne looks as baffled as ever as she stuffs a roll into her face. "Perhaps. I do not like the Rye Mothers either. I will be happy to help you squash one."

There's a knock at the door before Emeric walks in. Thankfully he doesn't seem to have overheard much; he's grinning broadly. "I thought I knew that voice."

Ragne screeches and launches herself across the room through the flurry of rose petals, turning into a cat as she does. He catches her, and she promptly claws to his shoulders, rubbing her head on his temple and knocking his spectacles askew. "You have been far away for very long," she half yowls, half scolds. "It has made me very sad."

"It's good to see you too." He laughs. "I'm glad Vanja called you for help. She told you about the . . ." He waves a hand. "Everything?"

"I know about the everything," Ragne confirms. "It makes no sense to me."

Emeric carefully sits on the bed, holding himself stiff so Ragne won't lose balance. "We may still be missing some pieces. Speaking of . . . Vanja, darling, you wouldn't happen to have scared Erwin Ros into coming to the prefects, would you?"

I try not to preen too much at being called "darling." "Someone may have let him know he's in over his head with some bad people," I obfuscate, and by "someone," I mean Helga. I doubt she had to bully him too hard, seeing as his debt to the Green Sleeve is settled and he can hardly go back to the docks with the Wälftsee Holdings group wanting him dead. "Did Helga go with him?"

Emeric nods as Ragne jumps off his shoulder. "She wouldn't let Ghendt or Dursyn even see him until they agreed to clemency. At worst, he ought to have a year of community service, and any bribe money that's recovered will be distributed to people who lost money from the *Grace Unending* blockade."

"Good," I say blithely, knowing none of that bribe money will be recovered. It's gone to a better purpose anyway.

Suddenly Ragne sits up, whiskers twitching. "Oh! The Joniza is here! I smell her!"

"I need to go check in with her," I say, pushing off the bed. "Then I'll . . . not think about the fact that you can smell us that accurately, and come back up here, and we can get ready to go."

"Already?" Emeric asks.

I don't bother putting on my boots properly, just shove my feet in for now and knot the laces. "We need to be out of Rammelbeck well before midnight."

I duck out, hoping Ragne does not take it upon herself to get Emeric's thoughts on claims, and hurtle down the stairs. If I'm lucky, I can catch Joniza before she gets too far into the inn. Fortunately she's waiting for me by the entrance to the tavern.

I stagger to a halt in front of her. "How did it go?"

"I would like to remind you, I have no interest in owning one brothel, let alone two," Joniza says sternly as she hands me a slip of paper. A time and location are written on it: the final meeting. "So this *better* work out like you say."

"She agreed to sell them both, then?"

"The Treasury *and* the Green Sleeve. She wanted more time, but I told her I'm leaving town so it has to be tomorrow morning at the Three Swans." Joniza's stony expression cracks with a twitch at the corner of her mouth. "She was *so* annoyed I kept calling it 'Madame's Treasury.' And she couldn't say anything."

"You're a genius," I breathe.

"Flattery will get you nowhere," she grumbles, but that corner of her mouth is betraying her. "She's really going to sell me a property she doesn't own?"

"As far as she knows, you're about to hit the road again, and that gives her time to either win over the Green Sleeve or get very, very far from Rammelbeck before you find out."

"So what happens tomorrow morning?" Joniza asks. "Because I don't have four hundred *gilden* for the down payment."

I know firsthand how prefects work long hours, but I'm hoping that, by now, Prefect Ghendt has returned to her room at the Three Swans and had a moment for a little light reading. Specifically, the documents tying Madame and Wälftsee Holdings to the *Grace Unending*. "I'm going to tell Emeric exactly when and where your meeting is, and he will pass it on to some interested parties . . . and then you might have some surprise visitors tomorrow."

Joniza's fingers ruffle a staccato above her elbow as she thinks, arms crossed. Finally she asks, "Why go to all this effort? You could just turn over what you found in her office and let the Godly Courts handle her."

"Remember how they handled Irmgard?" I say a bit bitterly. "She was in almost as deep as Adalbrecht, and *he* wound up an embarrassing statue, and *she* got a trial by Bóernische court. I know Madame buys off officials, and I know she's just an accessory to the *Grace* fiasco. I'm giving the prefects everything they need to add this to her charges and get an actual conviction."

Joniza sighs. "None of this would be necessary if the city officials actually did their jobs, like in a civilized society."

"That's why I'm doing the job for them," I say grimly. "And Madame called me ugly in front of Emeric, so I'm doing it *my* way."

At that, Joniza's entire demeanor frosts over. "*Did she now*," she muses. "I see. Then tomorrow morning is your last assist from me." She heads for the door but tosses me a wink on her way out. "I'll make sure it counts."

⚜

"When I run my fastest," Ragne tells me, shaking her ink-black mane, "remember, you must push yourself up in the stirrups so you do not bounce."

"I stayed on just fine during the wedding hunt," I remind her, my breath fogging a little in the near-midnight chill as we trot down the hard road. Gisele always loved a good hunt in the woods when we were younger, and she made sure I was competent enough a rider to keep up most of the time.

Ragne whickers her jitters. "I was not running my fastest then."

I don't blame her for nerves. There's a shift in the world at midnight: Everything seems sharper, truer, like the raw young day hasn't dulled its edges just yet. The night turns more dangerous. More potent. Sometimes those mean the same thing.

On the outskirts of Rammelbeck, as we pass one last lonely farm, midnight means the mists rising from the Trench curl a little more wickedly, the stars above glint like shattered glass, the thick crescent moon bites a razor-toothed grin in the sky. I've dressed for the cold *and* for the ride, with an extra shift *and* breeches under my gown and a cloak over it all. Just because we're two weeks from May doesn't mean April has caught up yet.

"Is the saddle all right?" I ask. I may have bribed a groomsman to let us borrow tack from the stable for the night. "Not too tight?"

"It should be very tight, so you do not fall off."

"I'm *not* going to fall off!"

Ragne's trot slows. "I hear the Hunt. Get ready."

I look up. At the very hem of the night sky, over the rooftops of distant Rammelbeck and Welkenrode, a faint glow ripples. Then it hones to a point, like waves trailing a boat on still water. The nearer it gets, the more it coalesces to haze, and the more I can spy hooves piercing through.

"Hold on," Ragne warns, and, with a jolt, shifts into a canter.

We take off in a spray of dirt, the moon flashing along a waterlogged ditch carved between the road and the grassy heath. After a few seconds, Ragne clears the ditch in a leap, then pounds through the scrub toward the crest of a hill. We weave around thickets as the chorus of hoofbeats grows even louder, that ethereal glow casting an ever-brightening shine. I hear singing, laughter, even howls. A miasma unfurls across the ground, bright and shimmering, until we may as well be running on clouds spun from moonlight.

The Hunt is upon us.

"Hail, God Daughters!"

The call thunders through the night, ringing like a horn's call off stone, as a rider draws even with us. I look up and find what can be only Brunne the Huntress.

She's taller than any woman I've ever seen, and if her silver steed was once a giant's horse, she's grown to match. Ancient, slightly tattered bridal regalia billow beneath the white pelt of a frost bear clasped over her broad shoulders. Ornate leather bracers wrap around burly wrists, though they pale in comparison to biceps like hams fighting under a blanket. She wears no shoes, gripping the sides of her mount with only her equally as muscular thighs. A dusting of tiny lights gleams on her tanned face and shoulders like freckles made from stars; they nearly drown in the cascade of cinnamon-brown curls that reaches nearly to her horse's tail. A bow is strapped to her back, a quiverful of moonlight arrows at her hip.

Behind her streams a tumult of the otherworldly: baying spectral hounds, wraithlike *vila* dancing hand in hand, ghostly hunters cheering the game, shrouded *idisi* shepherding souls of long-dead soldiers who ride like hell itself gives chase. Among them is one note of mortal dissonance: a stout, soft-faced young man of about nineteen in friar's robes, with a shocking thatch of strawberry blond hair and gray eyes just like Udo's. He's clinging to the neck of a phantasmal elk for dear life, but when he sees me, his whole face lights up.

Henrik knows me. He *knows* me, and—he's happy to see me.

"Hail, Brunne the Huntress!" I finally call back, the wind whipping loose hair into my eyes. I can't help a toothy grin as I'm swept up in the rush, the feeling of riding on the bleeding edge of legend. "I have a challenge for you!"

Brunne's laugh booms so loud, I see trees shiver below. *Below.*

This is when I realize the haze has carried us into the sky.

I gulp and cling to Ragne's mane even tighter.

"You wish to challenge *me*?" Brunne roars. "Ha! Ha ha! What a jest! You are like a little doll to me!"

"You have—"

"You are as a little stick doll, so tiny! I must squint to see you! And, you, Eiswald's daughter, you are but a half god! Ha!"

The rest of Brunne's horde bursts into laughter with her. I wait until the jeering quiets, swallowing a thousand cutting retorts. Better to be underestimated when it comes to dealing with gods. Once the ruckus dies down, I point to Henrik.

"You have my brother," I shout over the riot of the Wild Hunt, "and I will race you for him."

Brunne looks over her shoulder, eyebrows raised, then turns again to me. "Oh, I see! Ha! What a surprise! But, teeny little doll girl, I have not lost a race once, not even against the giant Boderad himself! What chance do you have?"

"I need Henrik," I say firmly, "so I'm willing to find out."

Brunne throws her head back, laughing once more but with delight instead of ridicule. "Very well! I will race you to the Broken Peak. If you win, you shall have three favors of me. But if *I* win . . . I will still give you my praise poet. I do not think he is enjoying himself."

"I," Henrik says, looking a bit seasick on the back of his elk, "am not."

"But *you* must take his place in my Hunt for a full fortnight. No less." Brunne holds out a hand. "Is it a wager?"

I shake on it. It's like immersing my hand in a leather-encased pillow. "We have a wager. I need to speak with Henrik before we start, though."

"I will allow it," Brunne says. "But make haste! I do not care for waiting!"

Ragne veers toward Henrik's elk as I lean over her withers. "How are you holding up? Do you need a rest?"

She turns so I can see the red flaring in her eye; when her mouth stretches into a grin, I see it's full of distinctly un-horsey fangs. "I am ready. I will show the Brunne what to make of a half god."

"Saints and martyrs, I missed you," I say happily.

"Vanja?"

When I look up, Henrik is gaping at me. "Hi," I say, abruptly nervous. "Nice to meet you. Or . . . remeet you, I guess?"

"I got Helga's letter," he babbles, "I'm so excited—I was so little when Mother took you away, but you're just like I remember, I mean, you're not, you're all grown up and *amazing* and I want to hear everything—"

"Hurry, God Daughters," Brunne calls.

I grimace and pull my satchel over my head. "Here, I need you to take this. I don't plan on losing, but if I do . . . it'll be bad timing, let's put it that way. Take my satchel to Emeric Conrad at the Jolly Magistrate. He'll know what to do."

"That's your"—Henrik takes the satchel—"roommate?"

"That's what Udo called him," I laugh. It—it's so strange, to laugh like this, to talk about my *brother* like this, with *my other brother.*

I have to win. I have to get Henrik back.

Then Henrik reaches out once again, this time for me. I take his hand, and his fingers squeeze mine. "Thank you for this," he says fervently, "and good luck."

I shoot him a grin. "Remind me to tell you about my godmothers after this."

Then I let go and ride to the front of the drove. Once there, Brunne gives me a look. "It is no great victory to defeat a swaddling babe. I wish for a true challenge, little bitty God Daughters. Can you offer that without Fortune or Death? For this race is between us alone."

I hesitate. That does skew things a bit. But Ragne is the one who answers, fiercely: "I can."

Brunne unleashes another calamitous laugh. "Then we shall begin!" She produces a hunting horn from somewhere beneath the frost-bear pelt and blasts a signal that seems to mean *halt*, because the whole Hunt slows to a stop. I'm pretty sure she sneaks in a few arm flexes as she trots ahead and turns her mount to face the crowd. "These God Daughters have issued a challenge! We will race to the Broken Peak, and the first to touch the summit wins! Do not try to keep up, but ride at your own pace, and we will meet you there!" She blasts her horn again. This time, at the far, far edge of the horizon, a single star kindles over a jagged hill. That has to be Broken Peak.

I draw even with Brunne as she waves a *vila* over to us. The *vila* bares her teeth at me, then plants herself between us, holding her veil aloft. "When my veil falls," she hisses.

"May the best of us win," Brunne says. I nod silently, stomach in knots. I *may* have counted on Fortune weighing the scales.

But I trust Ragne with my life. I called on her for a reason.

In a flicker of moonlight, the veil drops—

And we're gone.

CHAPTER TWENTY-SEVEN

FAVORS

RAGNE EXPLODES INTO MOTION.

I lurch back and scramble to seize the saddle horn, Brunne's laugh ringing in my ears. The seat drops out from under me, then slams up again, making my teeth bang together so suddenly that there's a sting in my mouth and the taste of blood.

I repeat this cycle too many times within the space of a second before remembering to stand in the stirrups, lifting myself out of the thrashing saddle. Then it's all a matter of shifting my weight again and again, matching the pulse of Ragne's hooves on a road made of clouds. Brunne is ahead of us, her horse's enormous strides eating up the distance as copse-studded hillsides roll by below.

Ragne snorts and lowers her head.

The tattoo of her hoofbeats picks up. I keep as tight a hold on the saddle as I can and hunch to catch as little wind as possible. The world narrows to the mane whipping my face, the air whistling in my teeth, the star still far—too far—on the horizon.

Then the gap between us and Brunne begins to close. Measure by measure, inch by inch, we pull even with her horse's quicksilver tail. Then its flanks. Then the saddle. Then—

"Ha! Ha! Do you give up yet, little God—" Brunne twists to look behind her. Her jaw drops when she finds us keeping pace.

"We do not," I gloat. Then I mock-salute her as Ragne starts edging ahead.

Pure joy breaks across Brunne's face. She claps her heels against her steed's sides with a whoop.

Then I pitch forward as the cloud road begins to tilt.

"I said we would race to Broken Peak!" Brunne laughs. "I never said it would be by sky alone!"

I lean back, clutching the rear of the seat for balance as we hurtle into a steep decline. The ground meets us all too quick with a bone-shuddering jolt. Ragne throws her head up in a whinny, careening to avoid a stand of trees that suddenly looms out of the dark. Then we're plunged into the heart of a forest, weaving around towering evergreens and ripping through thin dead scrub, the smell of mulch and crushed pine needles and cold midnight thick in every breath.

I see the silvery specter of Brunne whisking through—*literally* through—the trees ahead. She has no need to swerve around the trunks. Every time we do, she widens her lead.

Then the forest wanes to a soggy grass-mottled fen. Ragne stumbles even more here, trying to pick her way through tuffets and still, dark pools. The star over the Broken Peak is closer now, much closer. The magic of the Wild Hunt has to be carrying us faster than I thought; it's the only way we could cover a week's ride this quickly.

But I don't think it will be enough. Like the forest, the fen isn't slowing Brunne at all. The only place we can match her is in—

The sky.

A wild idea, probably one of the worst I've had, pops off in my head like a firework. Before I can overthink it (or arguably think about it at all, even a little), I push my face closer to Ragne's ears. "Hey," I say, loud enough to reach her but not for Brunne to hear, "can you do wings?"

Ragne tosses her head again, but a shiver runs down her spine. "*Yes.*"

There's a feral susurrus. Midnight feathers burst from Ragne's shoulders like a wave breaking on a rock, growing and shifting and crackling as she tilts toward an open stretch of moor. For some reason I'd expected the wings to sprout from her sides, but they're rooted just above each foreleg, and when she spreads them to their full length, I understand why she needed open ground. Each black falcon wing has to be at least twice as long as a man, perhaps more. I feel the wind catch beneath them, tugging us up. Then Ragne leaps, flapping once—twice—

And we're airborne again, soaring over wetlands. The moon's reflection below chases us through a thousand watery eyes as we climb, streaking straight for the star at the crest of Broken Peak. Beneath us, Brunne falls away in a blur of silver. We've overtaken her again, and this time, there's no bringing us down.

I see little flares of towns. Ragne's massive shadow swallows houses all at once. Few people are out this late, but a handful of faces turn up in wonder, and for a moment—I understand.

I can see the threads streaming from me, black and gold and red and a thousand unnamed colors. I can see the threads of Ragne and the moon and the stars, the stories we tell ourselves to explain the mysteries of this world.

I know this, the power that spins from the mortal world and weaves itself into Low Gods. I understand how a bride fleeing an unwanted wedding becomes the huntress on our heels. I understand how a girl stained in her lover's blood could weep the flood that washed her world away. Somewhere down there, someone is telling a story to explain what they've seen of me tonight.

If I'm lucky, it will be the story of the girl who outran the Hunt.

But Brunne hasn't conceded yet. Her laugh reverberates through the swell of forest under Ragne's hooves, and I see the cloud road coalescing once more. Broken Peak is close, so close—the ribbon of the river Ilsza weaves through stone and moss, and beyond the gorge, I can see the lights of Hagendorn—Ragne's sides are flecked with sweat, her wings beating furiously—the granite mountaintop is moments away, seconds, heartbeats—Brunne is just below, sailing up the cloud road, nearly even, but she can't catch us in time—

I stretch out a hand for the summit—

And blood-red thorns surge over the rock, lashing for us.

Ragne banks, screaming.

And Brunne's hand slaps against the stone.

I lost.

I cling to Ragne's back, stunned.

I lost, and—and—I don't know what I'll do. I've failed. I've let everyone down.

"*You've brought me guests, Prophet,*" the Scarlet Maiden's voice shrills. The thorns weave into a giant squirming mockery of a face. "*Why don't you stay awhile?*"

Brunne shoves between us and the thorns. "*BEGONE, VERMIN.*"

She draws an arrow and swings her bow around in one smooth motion, then lets fly. A spear of moonlight pierces straight through the vines. They dissolve into red mist, just like the one that gored Emeric through the throat in Felsengruft.

Brunne takes my reins, looping them over Ragne's ears. "This way, quickly." All the cheer is gone from her face.

She leads us away from Broken Peak, following the Ilsza upstream until we reach a smooth grassy section of level bank. Then she dismounts. "We may rest here while we wait for the Hunt."

I swing down from Ragne's back as fast as I can. She immediately shrinks down to a cat and flops onto a spongy pad of moss. "Good night."

Brunne is pacing around her horse, scowling. "This race was not rightly won. It would dishonor me to claim it as a victory. But neither did I lose. But neither did I win! If not for that wretch, you would have won!"

My own legs give out on me, and I sit in the grass, hard. "I made a wager," I say heavily, because you don't cheat Low Gods. "I'll pay what I owe."

"Perhaps I can reward you nonetheless," she ponders. "You are clearly my equal. Would you like to be my wife? We will ride through the skies together until the memory of memory fades, a glory and a terror to all who behold us."

"That's very flattering," I say delicately, "but I'm not looking for a relationship right now."

"Fairly spoken!" She turns to Ragne. "Would *you* like to be my wife? We will ride through the skies togeth—"

"I have a wife, probably," Ragne yowls.

"Would you like another?"

I elect to steer things away from matrimony before Brunne proposes again. "I lost, I can deal with the consequences. Just . . . can I wait to join the Hunt until May? I'm trying to get rid of"—I flap a hand downriver, toward Broken Peak—"*that* thing by the end of the month, and I need Henrik to do it."

Brunne spins on a heel, triumph dawning on her face. "Aha! I have solved it. We have both won and both lost. We will *both* honor our wager. Sometime in the next three months, you must ride with me for a fortnight. And in exchange, I will grant you your three favors—so long as you do not ask to be free of your ride. Is this fair?"

I almost start crying with relief right then and there. I'm sure Emeric won't love my two-week sabbatical, but he'll come around. "Yes," I say, "agreed. Thank you."

"No, God Daughters, thank *you* for the best race I have run since Boderad!" Brunne also sits, crossing her legs. Her horse drops next to her with an earthshaking thud and lays its head in her lap like a hound. She starts scratching its ears, grinning. "It was foolish of me to underestimate a half god. I will not make that mistake again."

Ragne yawns, tail flicking. "I hope you will not."

Brunne chuckles. "What favors shall I grant you, then?"

"Ragne, do you want anything?" I ask, since she did the bulk of the work.

"*Nyaw*," she says, which I take as a *no* spliced with another yawn. "I have all I want."

"Then first, Brunne, I would like you to leave Henrik, Ragne, and me, all together, at my inn in Rammelbeck as soon as possible and no later than the next sunrise," I say, being *extremely* specific because I was raised by two Low Gods and know better than to leave things open to their interpretation.

"It shall be done."

I think for a moment. My goal was just to get Henrik. But there's one thing Brunne can do for us, something better than any history book or bestiary: "Second . . . can you tell me what you know of the Scarlet Maiden and the Red Maid of the River?"

Brunne's face darkens. "Of this Scarlet Maiden, I know little. She is not a Low God, only a pretender, and all I see is her cruelty and pollution when the Hunt passes by." Then a strangely regretful look steals over her. "The Red Maid . . . She is my fault, somewhat. It is true that my golden bridal crown rests at the bottom of what is now the Kronenkessel. When Boderad fell chasing me, he wounded the ground so deeply, a spring welled up and swallowed him and the crown both."

"Is he really the hellhound?"

Brunne nods. "Many of the world's monsters are born from those who die in great wrath, great sorrow, great greed. Boderad jealously guards my fallen bridal crown, as it is the only prize he will ever win from me. Long, long after us, though, there was a princess who lived in a castle near here. She was betrothed to her great love, but he left to fight for glory and honor in her father's name. Word came that he died in battle, and the king pushed for his daughter to wed despite her sorrows. He filled their great hall with strong and wealthy suitors, but she had no desire to marry another. So she named an impossible quest; she swore she would marry only the one who brought her my bridal crown to wear."

Something about that strikes a chord in me, like I know that game, that ruse. Still, I can't place it.

"Of course, none of her suitors were willing to face a hellhound. They lingered only in hopes she would relent. Then her original betrothed, her great love, returned, alive after all. The princess wished to marry him, but the angry suitors demanded she honor her oath and marry the one who brought her the crown. Her betrothed did not wish to cause strife among the kingdom's great lords, and so he went to the Kronenkessel and met his fate."

"He couldn't defeat Boderad?" I ask, trying not to think of what that may mean for Emeric.

Brunne doesn't help matters, laughing in disbelief. "Ha! Ha ha! No! No, God Daughter, there was so much blood! The water looked like blueberry wine, so much blood! I had forgotten how much blood a tiny human body contains!"

"Oh," I say, a bit queasy.

She thankfully sobers. "That was how the princess became the Maid Painted Red, for she was watching from the shore, and her dress was stained so. She wept and she wept and she wept, and her tears became a torrent, and that torrent became the river, and that river became the waterfall of the Kronenkessel. One cannot do such things and stay a mere mortal. For a time, she did bring abundance and protection to the people of the gorge and became known as the Red Maid of the River. Still, she desired my crown above all else and knew no peace without it. Once a year, she would allow one person, unwed and unpromised, to try to fetch it from the Kronenkessel. And every single one died."

So the origins of the claim have nothing to do with—with sex, or virginity, or anything other than making sure the sacrifice didn't leave a brokenhearted survivor behind. The real Red Maid wasn't reenacting her tragedy; she was trying to prevent its repeat. "Why did she go dormant?"

Brunne sighs and starts braiding her giant horse's forelock. "Even gods grow weary. One cannot live the same cycle again and again, failing each time, without longing for escape. Too many died for that crown, and nothing, nothing changed. So she withdrew, inch by inch, root by root, name by name. Something keeps the heart of her here still, lingering in Felsengruft. But all that leaves the tomb is her river of tears." A brief quiet falls. Then Brunne lifts her hands, wiggling her fingers, and goes "*Woo-ooo-oooo.*"

I pretend I did not see that. "Thank you for telling me."

"It is not entirely my fault, of course," Brunne huffs. "Yes, they all sought my bridal crown, but many choices led to this. Her father could have said the betrothal preceded her oath and let them wed. Or the suitors could have honored the princess's wishes above their own greed. Or perhaps the princess could have been given time to grieve and, someday, allowed another into her heart . . . but instead she made an oath as a wall between herself and the world. An impossible standard that none might satisfy. And it has cost many, many lives since." Brunne stretches out her arms. "There you have it. That is what I know. What is your third favor, God Daughter?"

Ragne rolls over and stands, stretching. "I hear the Hunt."

"Then think quickly," Brunne chuckles, shoving her horse's head off her lap. It whuffs crossly and lumbers to its feet, then grabs Brunne's bear pelt in its teeth and hauls her up as well.

"Can I save it for now?" I ask, dusting myself off as I also get up. "I, uh, didn't plan on three."

Brunne gives me a shrewd look. "I will suggest that you ask to call on me one time for aid, should you have need. I do not know this Scarlet Maiden, but I like not what she has done to my gorge."

"For my third favor, I would like to be able to call on you once for aid," I say with a straight face.

"Such wisdom! Such prudence!" Brunne booms loud enough that her horse rolls its eyes, tail swishing. "Death and Fortune are blessed with such a clever daughter. It will be done. You need only say, 'Brunne, come to my aid,' and I will race to your side." Then she beckons to Ragne and me both. "Come, God Daughters, it seems you will need a ride. Let us join the Hunt!"

The return ride is a blur, and not just because I witness it from the back of a giant horse, clutching a frost-bear pelt; Ragne's fully passed out, and the night is catching up to me as well. Brunne mercifully drops us off well before dawn, though the hour is still wee enough that few are around to marvel at her.

"Do not forget your favor, God Daughter," she reminds me as I help an unsteady Henrik off his elk, then lift a sleeping cat-Ragne off Brunne's saddle. "Once, and only once, will I come to your aid. And when it is time to fulfill *your* end of the bargain, go to the road in the dark of night, call me by name, and say you are ready to pay your debt, and I shall collect."

Windows rattle with her laughter all up and down the street, and then she's gone. The Wild Hunt is a giant misty curl spooling away, far, far into the night.

"What bargain?" Henrik asks, voice rising as he steadies himself against a stucco wall. We didn't exactly have time to talk while cantering to Rammelbeck.

"The race was a draw," I say, "so we both agreed to honor the terms of the other's prize. She granted me three favors, and sometime in the next three months, I'll ride with her for a fortnight."

Henrik's shoulders slump. "I'm sorry you have to do that for me."

I shrug. "I lived with Death and Fortune for two years, I can handle two weeks with the Wild Hunt. Besides, I couldn't just let her keep my—my brother." My awkward laugh comes out in a puff of fog. "Sorry, it's still a little strange."

Henrik bites his lip. "It's not your fault—you were so young, I'm sure you only remember me as . . ." He slows, an odd look crossing his face. "Did they tell you about me?"

I cock my head as Ragne yawns. "That you're a poet and a brother at the abbey?"

"You—" he starts haltingly, "you may not remember me . . . like this. I, er." He runs a hand through his wavy ginger hair. "I never really felt like I *fit* at the farm in Kerzenthal. I always thought it was because I liked sonnets and reading and philosophy instead of, you know, farm things. Ozkar was like that, and he left, and I didn't want to be a burden, so a few years ago I decided to run off to the Imperial Abbey. But it wasn't safe traveling alone as—as I was . . . so . . ." He takes a deep breath. "I cut my hair like a boy's, wrapped my chest, and put on some of Sånnik's old clothes, and when I looked in the mirror . . . I saw *me* for the first time. Does that make sense?"

Suddenly it does: I remember red-gold braids and hand-me-down dresses, the sibling closest to me in age, who always wove grand stories around our toys as we played together. "It does," I say. "How did the others react?"

Henrik grimaces with chagrin. "So . . . I *may* have panicked and run out of Kerzenthal on the spot. I mean, I was already packed to go, and I thought maybe I was just overwhelmed, but I figured if I got to Welkenrode and didn't want to change anything . . . I'd know for sure. And after a few days, I knew: This is who I am. I just had to send everyone letters after, once I got to the abbey, saying, *Sorry about that, I'm a friar now, also I'm actually a boy and my name is Henrik.* And that was that. I mean, Katrin Little and Helga came to the abbey in person to yell and make sure I was fine, but everyone got used to it by Winterfast."

"Well," I say with a tired smile, "when I said it was strange, I meant having brothers, period. And so far I like you a lot better than Ozkar."

"*Whew.*" Henrik presses a hand to his heart. "It's a low bar to clear, but I'm glad I do. Um . . . do you know where I can get a ride to the abbey?"

I shift Ragne in my arms. "At this hour? I'm getting you a room here, and if you try to argue, I'll tell Brunne you want to rejoin the Hunt."

He laughs and scratches the back of his neck. "That would be amazing. I haven't changed my chest binding in two days, so . . . I can repay you?"

I wink at him and head into the courtyard. "What's a little money between family?"

There's an exhausted clerk at the front desk, and after I shove a respectable stack of white pennies his way, he shuffles off to show Henrik to a room. I, too, feel the drag of the long night as I trudge up the stairs to the honeymoon suite. I can sneak in a few hours of sleep, but then I'll have to wake up to close the jaws of the trap I set for Madame.

When I push the door open, to my surprise, candles are still burning inside the suite. Emeric is huddled over the room's meager desk, snoring outrageously in a partial fortress of bookstacks. "At this rate, he's going to empty out the Imperial Abbey's library," I mumble under my breath.

"That's what I told him," creaks Lady Ambroszia's voice from behind a pile of books.

I set Ragne (also snoring outrageously and somehow *in harmony* with Emeric) on the bed, then walk quietly to the desk. Ambroszia's sitting with a book across her lap. "He didn't have to try to wait up for me," I sigh.

"Oh, he paced around for the first hour solid," Ambroszia says. "Then he sat down here and started reading like Death herself would give him an exam in the morning . . . until he keeled right over. Was your gambit successful? Did you reclaim your brother?"

"I did," I say with a half smile, and set about liberating Emeric's arms from a small mountain of notes. "Hey, Junior."

"*Hmphrgh,*" he retorts, blowing a few pages of notes off the desk.

"Come on, you can't sleep here." I decide to borrow one of his own tactics and pepper obnoxious smooches on the side of his face until he sits up with the groan of a martyr.

"You're back," he wheezes. "Did you win?"

I decide now isn't the time for the *winning's not everything, it's how you play the game* speech. "We got Henrik."

"Knew you could do it," he says with a bleary grin, rubbing his eyes. "While you were out . . ." His face ignites with some urgent recollection. He twists in his seat to look at me. "I found it" is all he says before he whirls to face the desk, scrambling through the papers and emerging with a weathered and positively macabre-looking grimoire splayed open.

"Found what?" I ask cautiously.

He jabs a finger into the page. There's an illustration of a ring of crude figures with their hands outstretched. Each one is tethered to a rusty red line, the lines converging on a single writhing silhouette in the middle of the circle.

No, not converging.

Binding.

"I know," Emeric says raggedly, "how to stop the Scarlet Maiden."

CHAPTER TWENTY-EIGHT

ENTRAPMENT

I SQUINT AT THE PAGE, THEN AT EMERIC, AND SAY FINALLY, "I'M GOING TO need you to explain this in the smallest words possible. Five syllables maximum, go."

"Lucky for you, I'm too tired for big words," he says in an impressive display of brevity that I don't believe for a second. He fumbles around in the papers and extracts his notebook. It falls open to a page with a narrow column of text.

"'You are,'" I read aloud over his shoulder, "'my fire, the one desire—'"

"*IGNORE THAT.*" Emeric hastily flips to a blank page, then launches another fishing expedition into the cluttered desk.

"Was that one of your poems?" I demand, delighted. "Can I read it? Can I read all of them? Can we send them to a printer and make pamphlets?"

He emerges with a charcoal stick, and I think even his knuckles are blushing. "*Absolutely* not to all of the above. Now, let's go over the basic theory. And I do mean *theory*; the field of magic is all but defined by its inability to be tangibly quantified—"

"Small words."

Emeric rolls his eyes. "I know *you* know all those words, but fine. This is our best guess at how magic works, but it's not true all the time. So. You can divide our reality into two worlds, as it were. There's the mortal world, populated by humans, plants, mundane animals, and so on. It has limits and rules that seem relatively consistent." He draws a lopsided circle on the page, then, inside it, adds a stick figure, a tree, and a somewhat-challenging scribble I take to represent animals. "Concurrent but *separate* from that is the world transcendent." He adds sloppy whorls around the edge of the circle. "The world of High Gods and Low, demons, *grimlingen*, spirits, and so on, which is where magic is drawn from. It exists in the same space as the mortal world and is shaped and empowered by the beliefs of mortals. In turn, *they* can influence and interact with our world in limited ways. So, for example, Fortune exists because mortals believe in an entity that controls luck. That belief gives her power *over* luck in the mortal world—but only over luck. Any questions so far?"

I frown, thinking. "That makes sense for all the gods and spirits . . . but what about creatures like the *nachtmären*? They exist in the mortal world."

"That," he says excitedly, "is *exactly* what you should ask. If our worlds were allowed to fully intersect, it would be disastrous. Any human could harness godlike power and then probably die from the strain, *grimlingen* could devour entire towns and then probably die because they killed the source of their power . . ."

"A lot of probably dying," Ambroszia adds dryly.

"So at present," Emeric continues, "the only way to channel significant enduring power from transcendent to mortal is through a material anchor. It's an object of our world that is transformed into a sort of conduit for magic."

"Like Gisele's pearls," I say. Dame von Falbirg had to empty Sovabin's coffers to pay a warlock to craft them.

He nods. "And the iron horseshoe von Reigenbach used to bind himself to the *nachtmären* in Minkja. Even the pigment of my prefect marks is technically a material anchor, though it's complicated because it's highly concentrated witch-ash, and that's its own thing . . . but you get the idea."

"Weren't you saying something about this, Lady Ambroszia?" I ask. "At the prefect outpost yesterday."

"Indeed." She stands, brushing her skirts, and walks over to Emeric's diagram to look. "My material anchor *used* to be the site of my tragic and untimely demise. As a mere ghost, I was able to possess a vessel for only a few moments. Willi made this journey possible by transferring my material anchor to this doll, allowing me to engage with the mortal world more extensively. But if it is destroyed, I fear I must, at long last, take my leave of this realm."

"And many *grimlingen*, like *nachtmären*, are similar—their body is the material anchor to the mortal world, but if it's destroyed, so are they." Emeric draws a smaller circle overlapping both the mortal sphere and the transcendent and draws an *X* inside. "They can, however, claim additional anchors to grow stronger, just as the *nachtmären* displayed new powers once von Reigenbach bound himself and them to the horseshoe. The puzzle we've had this entire time is the Scarlet Maiden's inconsistency. Her abilities don't match those of any *grimling* I know—a Rye Mother may be tied to vegetation, like she is, but she shouldn't be able to force visions on anyone."

"So you think she bound herself to an additional anchor to expand her powers," I connect.

"Exactly. If we can find that anchor in Hagendorn, *this*"—he taps the grimoire page—"can be cast to imprison her in it, using the blood ties. And then the anchor can be destroyed. The only catch is that the binding is meant to be cast by siblings working in concert, but I believe I can cast it with your help, using the blood drops as proxies. And a lot of witch-ash."

"And it won't hurt my brothers?" It feels like a load of bricks spills out of my gut when he shakes his head *no*.

We have a way out. We can turn her own tools against her.

We're going to make it out.

I start at the distant peal of an hour-bell. "This is amazing, *you're* amazing, and if I don't go to bed right now, *I* will also probably die or at least sleep through all the fun tomorrow. Are Ghendt and Dursyn ready?"

"I may have sent word that an acquaintance is concerned Madame is trying to sell property she doesn't own, and where exactly they're meeting tomorrow to sign the deal." Emeric passes Joniza's appointment card back to me. "And there's a surprise for you."

"I hate surprises."

"We both know that's not true." He gets up and starts moving around the room, blowing out the candles. "I promise, this one you'll like."

❧

Rain rolls in by morning, but it doesn't dampen my spirits in the slightest as I accompany Joniza into the Three Swans Inn, passing the newly re-headed Saint Konstanzia fountain on the way across the Sanktplatt. We're early to the meeting, partially so Madame doesn't see us walk into the inn where Joniza's supposedly staying, and partially so I can make sure Joniza gets a seat near Ghendt and Dursyn.

The restaurant of the Three Swans is busy with breakfast service, but I still spot the two prefects at a table tucked in a discreet corner as I take Joniza's waterlogged cloak. "Northwest corner."

"I see them," she says, brushing a few errant droplets from her hair. "Where are you sitting?"

If Madame recognizes me, the ruse is up, but I'm too paranoid to just trust this will all play out as I hope. I also can't risk the prefects trying to detain me. "Couple tables away, pretending I don't know anything. Just remember: If I'm right, they'll summon the Godly Court, and you may have to testify."

"*Pff.* I did that at Winterfast. At this rate I'll feel like they're just looking for excuses to call me." Joniza sets off for a table within earshot of the prefects, and I triangulate accordingly, plopping down at a table along the wall where I can hide behind a menu if Madame looks my way.

We don't have to wait long before she shows up in yet *another* impractical and elaborate white gown, hair as elegantly put up as ever, but with a grimy damp ring at her hem that almost makes up for my lost sleep. She sits across from Joniza, fidgeting, a very businesslike satchel at her side. It's clear she's eager to get this over with.

Joniza, on the other hand, insists on waiting until she's ordered breakfast. Then she takes her time ordering, thoughtfully asking the server for recommendations and inquiring about substitutes. Madame's foot taps faster and faster.

Finally, once a towering stack of apple pancakes has been delivered, Joniza allows business to proceed. ". . . contracts?" I catch.

I duck behind the menu as Madame turns to her satchel, putting me within her line of sight. When I look again, she's sliding a sheaf of parchment across the table.

Joniza riffles through the pages, face unreadable. Her voice, however, is crystal clear with the quiet precision of a trained singer who knows *exactly* how to project: "And this contract covers both the Treasury and the Green Sleeve?"

"It does," I hear Madame say.

And the first trap is officially sprung.

Joniza turns and looks directly at Ghendt and Dursyn, as if to say, *Anytime now.* They're already pushing away from their table. Neither are in uniform, but I remember Emeric saying something about getting clearance to operate undercover.

"Gertrud Kintzler," Prefect Ghendt says as I stifle a gasp, "you are under arrest for attempted property sale fraud and for your participation in import fraud . . ."

Her real name *is* Gertie. Emeric's right; I do love a good surprise.

I catch Joniza's eye to make sure she's fine. She smiles and helps herself to a big bite of pancake, subtly extending a finger toward the exit. That's my cue to start phase two.

I slip out of the Three Swans as quick as I can, then take off at a run for the city administration building, which I tracked down while scoping out inns earlier. It's a few blocks away, and the streets are clearer than usual thanks to the rain, so I arrive soon enough—I hope. When prefects call the Godly Court, time itself will stop to let the trial proceed. It may have already happened.

But I don't need to worry about the trial. What matters, terribly enough, is the paperwork.

My first stop is the regional tax archives, where the front office is staffed by a little old lady who has the air of one in possession of an undefeatable dumpling recipe and a willingness to use it. "Excuse me," I say crisply, channeling my best Emeric, "I'm assisting with a property purchase, and my client would like to know what to expect in terms of annual commerce and property taxes."

"Oh, of course, dear." The archivist begins the ten-step process of getting to her feet. "What property?"

"Madame Treasury's." I pause. There was a different name on the purchase offer from Wälftsee Holdings. "It may be under 'M. T.'s Inn and Brothel.'"

"And the owner's name?"

I fight down a smirk. That one I'm not about to forget. "Gertrud Kintzler."

"One moment." She shuffles into the back. Now, I'm not sure about the state of the archives, so I can't *say* that it takes an *unusual* amount of time for her to return, but it feels like it takes longer than expected. The rather puzzled look on the archivist's face when she emerges seems to ratify this.

"It's very odd," she says, peering into a folder. "I did find records for M. T.'s Inn and Brothel, and associated properties, under 'Gertrud Kintzler' . . . but . . . well, see for yourself."

She hands me a record of tax payments from the past year. I know what the hang-up is, but it's still stark to see in person.

Madame Treasury's entire business enterprise reported a total profit of a single *gelt* last year, for which it paid property taxes amounting to a single white penny.

It's because she doesn't report *any* transaction paid in *spintz*—not the brothel work, not the workers' wages, not their board and upkeep, and neither the food nor the drink served on-site. (And I'm sure the gratuitous greasing of administrative wheels is a factor, if "wheels" has been in the arena of euphemisms long enough to have a championship belt.)

"Very curious," I lie. "Would you mind issuing an official declaration of record for value and taxes paid? I'm not sure my client will believe me without documentation."

She's more than happy to fill out and sign the form for me, and to stamp it with the official archives seal. Once that's in hand, I head to the opposite end of the administrative building: the magistrates' complex. Most high-level magistrates have holding cells specifically for criminals of particular interest—such as a businesswoman tied up in a scheme to blockade a port for days—and, as a special present just for me, the prison intake area seems to be adjacent to the financial-services window.

Madame Gertie and the prefects arrive as I'm lurking out of sight by a stanchion. Madame's trying to maintain a superior façade, a tight smile clinging to her raised chin, even as she's marched over to a stone-faced booking officer.

Still I wait. I need the timing to be *just* right.

"Gertrud Kintzler," Prefect Dursyn rattles off, "you have been tried before the Court of the Low Gods and found guilty of currency fraud, conspiracy to commit mass fraud against various citizens and businesses of Rammelbeck and Welkenrode, and assistance in said fraud. You are being formally remanded to the custody of the Konstanzian Imperial Abbey Administrative District Magistrate for sentencing."

And there it is. I mince over to the financial-services window right next to them as Madame sneers, "You know this is nothing, don't you? I'll be out in a week, and I'll be *fine*. I'll be running the Sünderweg long after you're gone."

I'm not as good at projecting my voice as Joniza, but everyone hears me clear as day when I say to the window clerk, "Hello. I'd like to purchase some property in administrative forfeiture."

You remember that ugly little legal pretzel, after all? The one Madame deliberately misrepresents to threaten her staff? The one that, now she's been convicted, allows anyone to buy her property for the same price as the annual tax?

Well, today, I'm using it for one hell of a bargain.

I slide the stamped and signed declaration across the counter. The clerk reads it, eyebrows shooting up into his hairline, and I feel Madame Gertie's eyes burning on me as she does what must be truly appalling math. The clerk brings the tax archives seal up to his nose, but it's as authentic as they come.

Finally he asks, "Everything?"

"Everything," I confirm.

"No," Madame Gertie sputters, "that's not—She isn't even from here—you *little*—"

It's *extremely* satisfying to ignore her, to remind her that she doesn't merit my acknowledgment.

"Given the scale of the purchase, we'll need some time to fully pre-pare the paperwork," the clerk says, "but I can enter you into the general record as the owner now if you pay up front."

"And how much will that cost?" I ask calmly, not because I don't know, but because I want Madame Gertie to hear exactly how her own shitty scheme has bitten her in the ass.

The clerk swallows. "One," he says haltingly, "white penny."

"You don't even know who you're dealing with, you miserable bitch," Madame snarls, "you are in *so* far over your head, you have no idea who you've crossed—"

"Oh, I've already met Prince Ludwig," I tell her, fishing in my pocket. "Great host. Terribly sticky fingers."

That gets her to shut up a moment as Dursyn and Ghendt trade looks. But once she's recovered, she hisses, "I can get my property back. And I won't even need revenge, because I can't do anything worse to you than what your own mirror does every day."

I do look at Madame then, shedding all arrogance, all pretention, and mustering only the hard, hard ice I grew in Sovabin. I set a white penny on the counter, and I make sure she can hear the silver ring on the stone as I push it across.

I want her to remember how one moment of casual cruelty became the worst mistake of her life.

And I want her to remember this moment when, after years of getting rich at the cost of girls like me, one of us took *everything* from her.

I say, cold as the crossroads that made me, "You were warned."

In the end, a bailiff has to physically pick up and drag her, thrashing and screaming, off to her cell. I watch her go with a smile as the clerk finishes writing my receipt.

I could get used to this, slipping through the cracks to set things right. Not just taking, but mending.

"It feels like this should be illegal," Prefect Ghendt says under her breath, eyeing me.

"Hmm," I say blithely, collecting my receipt. "Someone really ought to fix that. Now if you'll excuse me, I believe I've earned a nap."

CHAPTER TWENTY-NINE

RAINFALL

"THIS SHOULD BE EVERYTHING," I SAY A FEW HOURS LATER, STACKING what is hopefully the last heap of paperwork I'll see for a week or five. Jenneke, Joniza, and I are sharing a table in the tavern of the Jolly Magistrate, wrapping up what I suppose can be called a business lunch. "So let's review the terms of our agreement."

"Yes, please," Jenneke says politely, drawing her embroidered green robe a bit tighter. This one's a bit sturdier than the one she wears at the Green Sleeve. "Not that I don't trust you, but . . . this is not the hour for surprises."

Joniza snorts into her cider. "I can see why Vanja brought you on."

"The property formerly known as the Treasury, as well as its associated businesses, will remain under my ownership but be managed by you, Jenneke," I start, running my finger over that part of the contract. "All after-tax profits will be reinvested into wages and upkeep. All transactions will be made in standard coin. If anyone even *thinks* the word *spintz*, they're out."

"So far, so good," Jenneke says. "And Marien took the offer, so I'll be training her to eventually run the . . . well, not the 'Treasury' anymore."

"I still say it should also be the Green Sleeve, so you're collectively the Green Sleeves," Joniza says. "Your customers will walk down the street and right into their lovers' arms."

"I'll consider it," Jenneke says diplomatically.

I steer us back on track. "Point being, Marien and Agnethe will be taken care of. And"—I move to the next clause—"there will be at least five rooms open on the premises for people who need free short-term housing."

"Yes, let's nail that down, please," Jenneke says. "Just for *mietlingen* who want to transition out of brothel work?"

"Or for people who've wound up in a situation like Agnethe's, where they've been cheated out of wages, or who've just fell on hard luck. And they can stay up to three months. I'd rather ask fewer questions and help more people, to be honest." I shrug. "Better to deal with a cheat or two than shut out the dozens who need help."

"Agreed." Jenneke folds her arms. "And the terms of the buyout?"

"Once the Other Green Sleeve has turned a profit for a solid year under Marien's management, she can buy it from me for the same price I paid." I tap the final clause. "One white penny."

"I'll drink to that." Joniza raises her *sjoppen*. We toast, and then, when the mugs hit the table, she asks, "And Köhler will be hired on to redecorate the Not-Treasury?"

This is the part I've been waiting for.

Jenneke looks at me, then at Joniza, a small grin breaking across her face. "Actually," she says, wiggling a little as she tosses her braid over a shoulder, "we went over some numbers with our bookkeeper. The, er, *mystery money* that arrived at our door . . . it'll cover Köhler, but there's plenty left over. And we want to *completely* redecorate the place. So we're still going to hire Köhler to execute the project, but we'd like to buy the décor directly from your family. And we'd like to buy everything."

Joniza's eyes nearly fall out of her head, which is a rare sight. "All the décor?"

"And fabric, spices, perfumes, jewelry . . . I mean *everything.* The rest of the caravan merchandise." Jenneke lifts her arm to show a mended patch on her sleeve. "We have so much in need of updating, and anything we don't use, we can sell through Madame's former side businesses. Of course, we're happy to honor Köhler's previous deal as well, if you'd like to sell the rest of your goods elsewhere."

"No," Joniza says a bit foggily, "I think my father will take your offer."

"Wonderful." Jenneke beams. "Now where do we sign?"

Jenneke handles her signatures quickly, then takes her leave, heading back to the Green Sleeve to start putting things into motion on her end. I, on the other hand, have a bit of an unexpected dilemma when we get to my own signature—specifically thc last part.

Schmidt is a name I picked because I needed something and, as far as I knew, my father is—*was*, I recall with a pang—a blacksmith.

But my family's name is Ros.

I . . . just don't know if I'm ready for it to be mine.

Considering I just pulled a completely legal scam against one of Prince Ludwig's business lackeys, it might not be the best for my family's name to go into public record. I'm busy signing *Vanja Schmidt* on the papers when Joniza's voice breaks into my thoughts: "Congratulations."

"For what?"

"You actually fixed it," she says, leaning back in her chair. "More than fixed it. This should be Baba's last trade circuit before Fatatuma takes over, so . . . I don't know how often I'm going to see him after this. But if we can leave *this* early, I might be able to go all the way to Sahali with him and maybe even stay until Fatatuma's baby comes. I haven't been back in . . ." Her voice scratches. "Too long. I owe you."

I'm getting dangerously emotional myself, so I just say, "How did you put it? 'I don't keep your name in my ledger'?"

Joniza coughs a laugh at that, crooking a bittersweet smile. "I suppose I should come clean about that. Sahalian doesn't have a word like *family*, exactly. We have one word for blood kin, and another for people who share a home, and another for the people who care for you, and so on. To say someone isn't in your ledger means you don't have to track what they owe you, because you trust them to make it right. You can depend on them whether or not you share blood. That's what I meant in Sovabin. That's what you are."

"Well," I say soggily, "same."

Joniza passes me a hankie and pushes her chair back. "I'm going to go tell Baba. Don't leave town without saying goodbye, or I *will* put your name in my ledger. How much do I owe you for lunch?"

"Don't worry, I think the government pays for my meals now if they're business-related," I sniffle.

Joniza gives me a long look. "Get an accountant," she advises before heading out.

I keep sipping my cider, turning over a troublesome little pebble of thought that's stuck in my emotional boot. This past week has proven something terribly inconvenient and just as terribly undeniable.

I *like* solving problems. Or rather, I like solving problems for good people by *causing* problems for bad people. A saint asked me to steal for him. I helped people here in Rammelbeck thanks to a lot of ill-begotten cash and a flagrant disregard for a veritable cornucopia of laws.

The empire needs people like Emeric, people who are willing to hold the powerful to account and to the same laws everyone else follows. But justice can't just be an axe; it can't just be about punishment.

Someone has to close the distance between the letter of the law and its execution. Someone has to find where people are falling through the cracks and mend the gaps.

And *someone* has a rucksack full of rubies, a knack for causing problems, and, at best, a mutual disdain for the law.

I just . . . know Emeric's life is his work with the prefects. I don't know how this will work for us, if I'll always have to hide the one thing I'm actually good at.

But that's a problem for Future Vanja, one contingent on my getting us out of ScarMad's clutches first. I don't have time to dwell. I settle my tab and am about to head upstairs when I hear familiar voices in the courtyard—voices raised in anger.

". . . not worried about this?" Vikram is demanding. He and Emeric are standing near the tavern's entrance, under a ledge, to keep out of the rain. "How much longer are you going to have to protect her?"

"It's—" Emeric cuts himself off, running a hand through his hair as I pop out into the open. There's a weary resignation to him that alarms me. "It's fine."

"Is it?" I have a fairly solid hunch that I'm the "her" Vikram's talking about.

"Proctor Kirkling figured out the Scarlet Maiden isn't a real god," Emeric says, "and—"

"She came to the prefect outpost today," Vikram fumes, "to get materials to submit an amicus finding."

I squint, confused. "I thought you do math on those."

"*Amicus*, not *abacus*," Emeric sighs. "When two prefects work the same case but reach different conclusions, the one who *isn't* presenting to the Godly Court may submit an amicus finding for Justice's and Truth's consideration."

My stomach drops at the implication, and Vikram confirms it: "Which means Kirkling is going to try to get them to convict you, Vanja, even if it blows up Emeric's own Finding."

"*But*," Emeric says, steely, "she hasn't been an active prefect for years. I doubt she'll be allowed to submit it, and even if she is, we all know it won't have the same standing. Proctor Kirkling is just trying to intimidate us. I won't give her the satisfaction. Now if you'll excuse me, I'm going upstairs to pack. Thank you for the walk, Vikram, and I'll see you at dinner tonight."

Vikram makes a noise like a particularly aggravated iron stove as Emeric ducks inside. "You're also invited," he says grumpily. "We would love to have you. Mathilde can only stay until sunset, but she wants to hear all about how you ruined Madame Treasury's life."

"I didn't, the law did," I say with a straight face. "I'll be there."

Vikram is still scowling at the doorway Emeric went through. "In case I don't get a chance to say this later . . . I've known Conrad since he was ten. I can count on three fingers how many people I've seen him moon over. And I've never seen him with anyone the way I've seen him with you."

I push a nonexistent hair strand behind my ear, bashful. "Thanks."

"I'm not telling you this to be nice," Vikram says with a startling bluntness. "I like you, and I can tell you care—really care—about him. Despite that smug know-it-all act, he's not nearly as invincible as he'd like us all to think." Vikram's gaze pins me dead-on. "And he looks at you like an addiction."

That knocks any cheeky retort off my tongue.

"So take care with him." Vikram steps back, toward the courtyard's exit. "Please."

❧❦❧

The rain is still coming down by the time we leave for Kerzenthal the next morning, pouring hard enough to strip the petals from flowers in every window box up and down the street. They float down the gutters as we load the carriages: a stream of daisy, daffodil, crocus, cornflower, all a vivid forced red against the dismal gray.

It's *carriages*, plural, because our party has grown to six—seven if you count Lady Ambroszia. Ragne's using the impending new moon as an excuse to join us, but I can tell she's worried how things will play out. And when Henrik mentioned he was going to ride to Kerzenthal for the wedding on his own, it was all the excuse I needed to lobby for an additional carriage. At this point, cramming Helga, Emeric, Ragne, Henrik, Kirkling, Ambroszia, and me all in a single carriage for a four-day ride is a recipe for a personal hell.

The first day is fine. Emeric opts to give Helga, Henrik, and me some privacy, and Ragne spends most of the day napping on the carriage seat as a squirrel. After adding his drop of blood to the cambric, Henrik and I get to catch up. He and Helga fill me in a little more about our family: Udo and Jakob are actually two of three triplets, and their—*our*—sister Luisa is married and living near Eida, just north of Welkenrode. Sånnik is third youngest and the final brother I haven't met, and our eldest sibling, Katrin "Little," is training him to help manage his bride-to-be's farm. (Katrin was named for our aunt Katrin "Elder," who took over when our parents passed away.) Even though Katrin's married with children, everyone still calls her Little. Jörgi, my second-eldest sibling, has been content to stay and help on the farm as well.

They all know who I am. They all remember me.

They're all waiting to meet me in Kerzenthal.

Excitement transmutes to anxiety over the next few days. It doesn't help that the rain only pours harder and harder, until the lowland fields look like mirrors with stubble. Or that each successive sunset dyes the sky a deeper scarlet, even though Kerzenthal is but halfway to Hagendorn. Or that the roads flood badly enough that, more than once, Ragne has to get out, turn into a bear, and jolt the carriages free of the muck.

Even with her help, it takes us longer than it should to reach Kerzenthal. We finally arrive on Wednesday, the day before Sånnik's wedding, in the late afternoon. It drizzled occasionally in the weeks before now, but there's no doubt that this downpour is also the Scarlet Maiden's doing. If anything, it's just further proof that I was never meant to collect the blood drops in time. She's wanted Emeric all along.

Rolling into Kerzenthal, even in the rain, is a very unsettling experience. The town is bigger than Hagendorn, smaller than Dänwik, and halfway between a memory and a discovery. It feels like—like looking at my siblings' faces, seeing echoes of myself and the others, even as every one is strange and new to me. I don't know the tannery near the town square's entrance, or the apothecary next to the inn. But I *do* recognize the inn, even though the paint on the plaster's the wrong color and the oak tree beside it is too big. I know the little chapel down the lane because I remember sitting on someone's lap as we passed by in a wagon; I know the bakery not by sight but by *smell*, because no one else bakes their rolls with a pinch of cardamom.

Each one is a little blister of memory, bursting at first touch, pained relief surging every time.

Kirkling is surprisingly helpful when we disembark. She offers to get a room at the inn and wait with Lady Ambroszia while the rest of us continue on foot to the Ros family farm. While we're off-loading the luggage, the innkeeper comes out to merrily berate Helga and Henrik for staying away so long, only to spot me and plunge into furious whispers.

I don't realize my hands are in fists until Emeric takes one and carefully unfolds it enough to twine our fingers, shifting to stand between the innkeeper and me. "Are you doing all right?"

I nod, but I can feel my breath shaking, so I just tip forward to lean on his sternum and mumble, "I'm glad you're here."

The innkeeper insists on sending us out with ribbed oilcloth rain canopies, which I appreciate, even if she does keep eyeballing me uncomfortably. "I take it she remembers me," I say once we've cleared her earshot.

"She said you still have braids like the ones you used to wear," Ragne supplies. She's trotting along as a hound with a coat so thick, the rain rolls right off. Henrik and Helga both look at her, startled, and she yips a laugh. "My ears are very good like this."

"Incredible," Henrik breathes.

"Isn't it?" Emeric has gotten along with Henrik perhaps the best of all my siblings. I even suspect Henrik got to see a poem or two in one of the intervals when they shared a carriage.

We round a bend in the dirt road, avoiding ruts and puddles as best we can. I'm figuring out how to both juggle the oilcloth canopy and hoist my skirt out of the way when Helga says, "There's the gate."

I look up. Far down the road, there's a fenced paddock around grazing horses. A tall arched gateway crowns a smaller dirt lane that leads to a barn and a sprawling farmhouse. An anvil is ringing from a little roadside half shack to the left of the gate. A garland of horseshoes swings from the gate's top beam, and in the middle is a flat iron horsehead with *ROS* punched out.

It's another little blister of a moment but even more dizzying, almost like holding a tracing up to the light and aligning it with a drawing beneath. The barn is in the same place, but the build is different, and it's sprouted a stable I've never seen. The heart of the farmhouse is as small as I remember, but the walls have grown outward, the roof's been raised to a second story, and I even spot chimneys for outdoor ovens around a back corner.

My father wasn't a smith. He was a farrier, shoeing horses for locals and passing travelers. My aunt helped breed and train horses. My family runs a *horse* farm.

I start laughing, albeit with no small degree of hysteria. Then Emeric sees it and starts laughing in disbelief, too, just saying, over and over again, "Of course it is. Of course."

"The Emeric does not like horses at all," I hear Ragne explain to an utterly flummoxed Henrik, "unless the horse is me."

"Oh dear. Well, yes, *Ros* comes from the old Deep North word for 'steed,' *hros*. Our family's been in the business . . ." Henrik dives into what would be a fascinating family history if his voice weren't being slowly drowned out by the riot of my own heartbeat.

This is the rest of my family. What if—

What if they think I'm just a good-for-nothing thief? What if I'm a disappointment? All these years lighting candles for a memory of me . . . What if they don't want the girl I've become?

What if they don't want me?

If not for the anchor of Emeric's hand, I would run all the way to Hagendorn now and not look back.

Then we reach the gate, and the anvil goes quiet. I can hear laughter, murmurs drifting from inside the farmhouse.

A soot-smudged person in a blacksmith's apron ducks out from the roadside stand, tongs in hand, wiping their brow. They have Udo's and Jakob's deep brown hair pulled into a serviceable bun, black eyes like Eida's—like mine. Those eyes widen when they land on me.

I remember sitting on a stool in a corner of that stand, counting riders that passed by while our father taught Jörgi the proper way to hold the hammer. I remember this dirt road, the smell of the rain and the mud.

I see my mother, my father, my siblings. I see the Ros family. I see me.

"Vanja?" Jörgi asks unsteadily, and I have no words, I can only nod. The tongs fall to the ground as they race to the gate, shouting, "*VANJA!*"

The farmhouse goes quiet. Then the doors burst open. Eida is first out, then a woman I don't know—*no*, I do, it's Katrin, she used to sing me a song about *strietzel* to stop my crying—Jörgi's reaching for me, Katrin is flying down the road—everything is streaked with tears—

And I stumble through the gate, into their embrace.

My name is being called like a victory cry, and there are so many arms wrapped around me—around one another—I barely feel the rain. I can barely understand what they're saying through their own tears and over each other, can hear only the joy, the joy, the joy.

But Katrin's voice I piece together word by word. She's saying the same thing again and again, like a prayer that is finally answered:

"I knew, I knew, *I knew* someday you would find us," she's weeping. "I knew if I lit the candle, you would find your way back home."

THE SECOND LIE

TRUST

ONCE UPON A TIME, THERE WAS A VERY LITTLE GIRL WHO RUINED everything she touched.

That was what her mother said, at least, and all good little children trust their mothers.

(Her mother said that too.)

One cold morning, the little girl was eating breakfast with her siblings when she tried to pick up the milk pitcher. It was much too heavy for her, and so—*crash!* It spilled all over the table. Her mother shouted, "Now look what you've done! You've wasted our milk!"

"It was an accident, Mama," one of her sisters said softly.

Their mother huffed and puffed as she fetched a rag. "Trust me," she said, bitter, "she did it to be a problem."

Later that morning, the little girl was helping comb flax for her mother's weaving. Since it was so cold that winter day, she sat by the fireplace. But a lonely spark flew out and into her basket of floss, and— *crackle!* All the flax vanished in a puff of flame.

Her mother threw the still-burning basket out into the snow. "You've done it again! All that flax, gone!"

One of her brothers looked up from his book, rolling his eyes. "She can't control fire, Mother."

"Trust me," their mother said, "she sat near the hearth on purpose."

The little girl played quietly in a corner the rest of the morning; even her rag doll made barely a sound. There was no *crash* nor *crackle*; she was sure to stay out of her mother's way and not make noise, not make trouble.

Still, her mother's thread tangled on the spindle again and again, knotting itself into a mess.

"You were distracting me," her mother accused. "I can always tell."

The little girl had nothing to say, because she had done her best to be good.

At noon her father came in from the cold, though the fire of the forge had kept him warm. The little girl's family ate lunch all together, smiling and laughing, and she thought perhaps she hadn't ruined that much, at least.

Then, before her father went back out, the little girl heard him speaking with her mother.

"No more, Marthe," he was saying. "I'm going to take the midwife's draught until you're past bearing age."

"Please," her mother wheedled. "You need more hands to help the farm. We're barely scraping by as it is."

"And another mouth to feed, that would help?" her father said, not unkindly. "Even if it would . . . I was *there*, I saw how you bled. The midwife told you what will happen if you try to carry another babe. Vanja's our last. I won't let myself be your death."

The front door closed.

The little girl did not know what it was, exactly, but she knew she had ruined that too.

⌁

When I look back on that night, I know Marthe waited until after dinner for a reason. My older siblings were out with my father, making sure the horses and pigs and goats were all shut up and warm in the barn. The only children left inside were the ones too little to stop her.

She bundled me up in no more than she had to, and still, my siblings noticed. When they asked where she was taking me, she answered, "To seek her fortune."

"Her hands will get cold," Dieter said. "She doesn't have any mittens."

My mother grudgingly shoved my hands into the oldest, most-threadbare mittens we had.

"Doesn't she need boots?" Ozkar asked skeptically. "Those slippers are too thin."

Marthe's frown only darkened as she yanked boots onto my feet.

"She's too little to go," Helga said. Our mother had no answer for that. "She's too little! Please don't take her away!"

My siblings crowded Marthe, begging and pleading. I didn't understand. She had promised that, where I was going, I would be warm and safe and happy, that we would see each other whenever we wished.

"Be quiet," Marthe snapped suddenly, in a voice that blasted through the room worse than the cold as she yanked open the door. One of her hands seized mine. The other took a battered old lantern off the wall, its candle sputtering. "I'm taking her somewhere better and coming right back. Don't you trust your mother?"

She led me into the midwinter night, and only one of us made it home.

My father would blame himself, believing there must have been a curse, that one way or another, he was destined to be the death of Marthe. My older siblings would blame themselves for not seeing, the younger ones would blame themselves for not stopping her, and all would blame themselves when they found no trace of me.

But I alone knew the truth, because I trusted my mother.

Everything I touched would fall to ruin. Starting with her.

CHAPTER THIRTY

HOMECOMING

W E'RE NOT BROUGHT INTO THE FARMHOUSE SO MUCH AS INGESTED. IT might as well be a living, breathing creature unto itself, every room teeming with faces strange and familiar, uncles and aunts and cousins who I've never met, or who I met once a year at Winterfast, or who saw me once when I was a baby. Hands reach for me, patting my braids, my freckles, my cheeks.

More than once I hear "*Marthe, just like Marthe*" through the huddle. But Katrin Little is careful not to let that knot around our ankles, tact-fully moving us forward anytime the whispers grow too loud.

I lose Emeric to the inspection of my uncles, Ragne to a gang of raucous children; I notice only as I'm being towed through doors and into another chorus of delighted shouts. Round-faced Aunt Katrin we find commanding legions in the kitchen. She looks so much like Udo that I'm immediately more at ease, even more so when she gasps, bursts into tears, and crushes me in a hug that smells of nutmeg.

She abandons her post to carry on with us, ushering us into a room of adults drinking, laughing, and playing cards while being serenaded by Dieter Ros. He sulks when they neglect his performance to crowd around us, even plays a few notes of "The Red Maid of the River" until Helga stomps on his foot, but he gives me a lazy wave on my way out. In a large room crowded with beds and sleeping pallets, we find Sånnik up to his elbows in fresh flowers, making garlands with a crew of cousins too young to help in the kitchen but too old to play upstairs. He knocks over a basket of posies in his haste to reach me, laughing and crying, "You made it! You made it!"

"I'm sorry," I babble, "I don't want to distract from the wedding—"

"Hush now, none of that," Aunt Katrin says. "Weddings are nothing *but* distractions." As if to prove her point, one of the garland-weavers slaps another with a bunch of fern fronds.

"I—" I smack my forehead. "I should have brought a gift, I just came from Rammelbeck too—"

Sånnik grabs my shoulders. He has the same eyes as Jörgi's and mine, and they crinkle with his bittersweet smile. "Vanja, you're *here* with us, you're back. *Thirteen years* you've been gone. We don't need a gift when we have a miracle." A squabble breaks out behind us, and he grimaces. "I've got to get back to it, but will you stay for the ceremony? Helga's letter said you have until midsummer, right?"

"It got shortened, I have a week now, but—well—I'll try," I say. "Let me talk to the others."

He lets go, looking wistful. "And the roads are terrible right now, so I understand. Whatever you need. I'm just . . . so happy you're here."

"We're going to show her the sitting room," Katrin Little says, steering me onward. She adds to me, "It'll be quieter in there, and you can breathe a moment."

It *is* quieter, red sunset light filtering in through the windows, illuminating the work of a seamstress as she makes final adjustments on the regalia for the fidgeting bride.

"You must be Vanja," the bride says as soon as she sees me.

"I'm sorry," I say again, automatically, "I promise we came as soon as we could, I don't want to take attention away—"

"Nonsense," the bride says, flapping a hand. "Sånnik's been so excited since he got the letter—we're going to be sisters, and—You don't remember me, do you? I'm Anna, and this is my mother." She gestures to the woman perched on a stool behind her. "Your mother used to sell us thread."

The woman takes the pins out of her mouth, eyeing me over. "Oh, *ja*, you certainly look the picture of Marthe, but never fear. I can tell already you're your own woman." She cackles. "Marthe would never pass up a chance to make someone else's party her stage."

"*Mother*," Anna hisses.

"No, she's not wrong," Aunt Katrin sighs. "Vanja, we thought you ought to see your corner."

"My . . . ?"

The Katrins lead me farther into the room. It takes a moment, seeing past the new whitewash on the walls and the different woven rug over the old boards, but . . . the fireplace, the wreath above the mantel, the lantern hook on the wall—I know them. This was the main room of our home, where, at the end of each day, all thirteen of us would roll out straw ticks and sleep crammed together. In the winters, they'd make sure I slept closest to the hearth.

In a corner by a window, a little shelf is fastened to the wall. It holds a candle, a dried rose bleached dusty peach by the sun, a faded rag doll, and a clay disc painted with the words *Vanja Ros.*

"We light the candle on your birthday," Katrin Little says, and I already know, but it feels like a dream that she's saying it and I'm here. When I don't answer right away, she adds, a little nervously, "We didn't have much else to remember you by. The rose was from the *komtessin* down the way. She remembered how you liked them whenever Papa brought you along to shoe her horse."

"It's——" I can hardly speak around the knot in my throat. I've lived so long without these roots, with my family as a question and emptiness for its answer. I left Kerzenthal, left Death and Fortune's home, left Sovabin, left Minkja, left Hagendorn. I left them all changed, but this is the first time my aftermath calls me by name. "It's perfect."

Katrin Little wraps an arm around my shoulders, blinking back tears in her own hazel eyes. "All we ever found was that lantern with Mama, but we kept hoping for so long . . ."

"What was she like?" I scratch out. "I barely remember her, and Ozkar said——"

"Ozkar says a lot of things he shouldn't," Katrin Little mutters darkly as Anna's mother *tsks*.

Aunt Katrin shakes her head. "But it's usually closer to the truth than not, I'll give him that. Your mother was the weaver's daughter, youngest of thirteen, like you. She liked being the baby a bit too much, and whenever things didn't go her way, she'd cry and fuss about being the thirteenth and say she was unlucky until she got what she wanted. Her parents couldn't say anything nice to her siblings either, not without her *accidentally* breaking things or interrupting to boast about herself."

"But when she was in a fine mood, she lit up a room," Anna's mother adds. "The whole town knew it was easier to keep Marthe sunny than deal with her rain, and she and Helmut—that's your father, Vanja—they were like summer together. I thought maybe that'd put her to rights, wanting to make someone else happy for a change, or when she had Katrin Little. And it seemed like she was content . . . for a bit."

"For a bit," agrees Aunt Katrin. "Then she started moping about how my brother had to work all the time and came home too tired to dote on her, and suddenly Jörgi was on the way. The midwife offered her charms to keep from getting with child, but she'd have none of it. When she acted out after Jörgi came, we all thought it was the cradle sorrows—I got them myself for a few months after my second babe, after all. But when the triplets were born, half the town was here, bringing her food and gifts, keeping the house clean, watching Katrin and Jörgi, and still she'd say the gifts were cheap, the cleaning was shoddy, Katrin and Jörgi were being spoiled . . ."

"Nothing was ever good enough," Katrin Little says. There's a hollowness to her voice that reminds me: She was only a year or two younger than I am now when Marthe died. "Nothing was ever her fault."

"Do you remember when she announced she was pregnant again in the middle of Jost's wedding?" Aunt Katrin asks. A snort from Anna's mother comes through a renewed mouthful of pins. "And when she made Ozkar show off his reading at her father's funeral?"

"Ozkar used to get so angry when she'd say he got his wits from her," Katrin Little says, "and that Dieter could play so well only because she sang to him, and that Jakob wove so well only because she taught him. The only time anything was good enough was when she could say it was her doing."

Aunt Katrin picks up the rag doll, running her hands over the plain, repeatedly mended dress. "We thought she'd stop after the triplets, then after the twins, but . . . she seemed to think the more children she bore, the more special *she* was, and the rest of the town tired of it. She bled badly when she birthed you, almost too much. The midwife said she'd die bearing another, and she cobbled this excuse in her head, that you were to blame. Then she found herself with thirteen children on her hands, and by then she'd burned too many bridges to look to us for help. And you know the rest."

I do; I was her ruin. "What happened to the lantern?" I ask stiffly, partially to buy myself a moment to take this in, partially because I can see it, even now, against the dark of the crossroads.

Katrin Little lets out a grim, sad laugh. "Papa kept using it. We couldn't afford a new one at the time. One of the triplets took it when they moved away, I can't remember which."

Aunt Katrin hands me the rag doll. *Strietzelina.* What a silly name, what a silly little girl I was. I wonder if I would have stayed silly had I stayed here, learned an honest trade instead of a liar's, fallen for some farmer's get and been content with the troubles of a small town. Or if I would have been like Marthe, with a hunger so terrible, no love could fill it.

Or if it was always going to be that way between a thirteenth child and her thirteenth child. If one of us was always going to be the other's ruin.

"A lot of folks have a lot of funny ideas about family," Aunt Katrin says. "That you don't get to choose family, that you stick by blood no matter what, that kin come first, on and on and on. Well, you've likely noticed ours is a big family, and you're wanted as much as any of us. But that doesn't mean you have to want us, or all of us, or any of us at all. Ozkar left and never looked back; Dieter still won't share a roof with him. Henrik had to leave to find himself. Helga, Udo, Jakob—they wanted something different, but not too far from home. You've been on your own these thirteen years. You're free to decide what this family is to you."

I'm gripping the rag doll so hard, I fear I may tear the worn fabric.

I think I want this, but—but I want them to know what they're inviting in. "I'm a thief," I say hoarsely, "and a liar. Hagendorn is suffering because of me. I don't know how to—to train horses or care for children or treat the sick. I don't know how to make anything but trouble."

"Erwin would tell you she saved his life after he crossed the wrong people." Helga's voice is calm, but it fills the room from where she's leaning against the doorjamb. "Henrik *will* tell you how she challenged Brunne the Huntress herself to win his freedom just last week, while also taking down a brothel that abused its workers. And . . ."

She shifts in the doorway so we can see Emeric in the other room. He's deep in conversation with my uncles. I expected him to rigidly answer a barrage of questions with the precise measurement of optimal decorum; instead he's gesturing wildly as he speaks, face shining. It's the way he gets when he speaks of his family, his dreams, what drives him to serve Justice.

I can't hear the words, but I know the shape of my name on his lips, the spark of wonder in one uncle's eyes as he sneaks a look at me.

"I have it on good authority," Helga says, "that there's a statue of her in Minkja."

"Good thing Marthe's not here to hear about it, or she'd not rest until she had two for herself," Anna's mother mumbles around her pins.

"Like Auntie said, you're free to make of this family what you will," Katrin Little tells me, squeezing my shoulders tighter. "But it sounds to me like you make the right sort of trouble."

❧

And so we stay.

I let Emeric decide, since the risk is mostly his. We have a week to make it to Hagendorn, and in normal weather it's a four-day trip. I'm not sure if he's swayed by my aunts stuffing him full of butter cakes or by the rain coming down harder than ever. Either way, he just says, "We'd be staying overnight anyway, and the ceremony's at midday. We won't lose much time."

It's a rowdy night, like they usually are before a wedding: Old pottery is smashed on the floor to scare off *grimlingen*, and Anna and Sånnik have to sweep it up together before she's sent to one end of the house and he to another, to stay separated until the ceremony. There's a minor kerfuffle over scrounging up beds, one slightly ameliorated when I say Emeric and I can share, albeit at the cost of a spike in raised eyebrows and auntie whispers. I get barely any sleep as it is, staying up long into the night with my siblings. Even after hours of catching up, by the time I pick my way across a sea of cousins on sleeping pallets to crawl into bed, I know we've only brushed fragments of the past thirteen years.

On the way, I pass Helga, who's peering out the window, a furrow in her brow. "Ragne's fine," I say, "she just wanted to stretch her legs after being in the carriages so long."

She shakes her head. "Your friend is a half god who turns into a bear. I know she's fine. Udo and Jakob should have made it by now."

"Didn't they say they'd be held up with shearing?"

Her mouth purses. "They say that every time, and they still make it every time."

They aren't here in the morning either, but there's too much to do to fret. I'm caught up in a whirlwind of final preparations, helping set up the barn for the ceremony since the rain is still pounding down. Ragne and Emeric are drawn into it, too, helping clear the barn, hang flower garlands, put up arches, place stools for the elders, set up the feasting table—everything. The town's innkeeper even drags in Kirkling, and, astonishingly enough, she gets right to work, helping shuttle hot dishes to the table.

Then, an hour or so before noon, I'm abducted by Luisa, my

second-eldest sister. She has the same strawberry blond hair as Henrik, but Udo's gray eyes, and easily the best fashion sense of the family. "I have a dress that will fit you," she says firmly, steering me into one of the upstairs parlors, "and how do you feel about cosmetics?"

"Um." I swallow. I wore them while masquerading as Gisele, but that was with a face enchanted to be lovely. "I haven't . . . It always seemed like a waste for a plain—"

Luisa cuts me off with a suck to her teeth like a winter gale. "Ohhh I am adding this to the list of big-sister talks you never got. Sit." She half pushes me onto a stool. "*Everyone* is plain. Sure, there are a few naturally beautiful people in the world, but the rest of us get by with a little powder, a little stain, and knowing which goes where, and there's no shame in that. Why don't I do your face, and anything you don't like, you can wipe off?"

I'd be lying if I said it isn't a daunting prospect . . . but she clearly knows what she's talking about. "All right."

"Change first," Eida says, handing me a fern-green gown to go over my shift. "Then we'll do your hair at the same time."

An idea strikes, and I fish out the lonely ribbon from Emeric, the one Ozkar let me keep. I still carry it with me, just to feel the bumps below my fingers when I need to settle my nerves. "Can you use this?"

The next half hour is a flurry of fabric, combs, and tiny sponges. When Eida and Luisa are done with me, they lead me to the mirror, and—

I don't know what I expected, exactly; perhaps a transformation like with the pearls, but this isn't like that. It's better somehow, because it's *me*. It's still my face, my freckles, my chin, but it's as if my face was a dull pebble, and whatever sorcery Luisa has done is the water that draws bold stripes and glittering flecks from the stone. Eida's managed the same with my hair, weaving the top half into braids but letting the bottom hang loose, the ribbon fluttering artfully where the braids gather in the back. Somehow it looks more purposeful than when I do it. The green of the gown even works with my hair somehow, as if it were designed to. It's all me, just—polished.

I'm still no great beauty, but maybe . . . this is the beauty that Emeric sees in me.

There's a rustle. Helga is holding out a wreath of greenery dotted with wild yellow roses. In some parts of the empire, it's traditional for the parents and the siblings of a bride or a groom to wear garlands of the same flower, to mark the family. "You don't have to wear it . . . but we made one for you."

"I still say it should have been tansies. Roses for the Roses is tacky," Eida grumbles.

Katrin mutters back, "The bride picked tansies."

I take the wreath, hands shaking. If I wear it, everyone will know me for a Ros.

It hits me then, that all this is real. Or rather, it's been like descending a greased staircase, step by tentative step, only to slip up and topple to the landing. This is *real*. I have a family, one that wanted me, still wants me, even knowing what I am.

Maybe not *despite* what I am. Maybe—*just* as I am.

My throat closes off, my eyes welling with tears, and my instinct is to shut them and hide and stuff it all away so no one has to bother themselves with my mess.

"Oh, Vanja, you'll make *me* cry." Luisa wraps her arms around me from the side.

I feel a hankie dabbing my cheeks as Eida laughs. "Don't go undoing all Luisa's work now."

"Sorry," I sniffle again, only for Katrin to pat the back of my head.

"No more *sorrys* today, it's bad luck" is all she says.

Strains of lute music start below. It's the signal that the ceremony's close at hand, and the room explodes into motion as my sisters finish their own primping. Then we rush to the barn to meet the rest of the siblings. Half of Kerzenthal seems crowded in the barn, and I can't help scanning for Emeric among them, both dreading and desperate to know what he makes of how I look.

I don't find him, though, before Dieter's switched to a wedding march. We siblings cluster to one side of the barn's entrance, sheltered from the rain, just as Anna's family gathers on the other; the people inside split to open a path to the mayor, who's standing under the wedding arch. Sånnik stands with us, handsome in his best suit and a rose wreath, alternately wringing his hands and grinning like a fool. His grin blossoms into a teary smile when Anna's brothers walk her to the barn under an oilcloth canopy. Her own smile is dazzling as she takes his hand.

The families lead them to the mayor and then return to their respective sides as Dieter's lute goes quiet. The mayor keeps it short and sweet: First Sånnik and Anna trade wreaths to signify joining each other's families. Then, after a few quick and heartfelt vows, they exchange simple silver rings to signify joining their lives.

And just like that, with a ring and a wreath, I have a new sister-in-law. A new part of my family. They kiss as we all cheer, but something is stirring in my chest, like the charge of Saint Willehalm, the call to help Agnethe, the pull of threads as I raced through the night. It's the desire to find my way back from the crossroads and out of the woods, to find the place I once called home, and to see if I still could.

When I laid my head down in the pantry in Castle Falbirg, trying to shut out the rustles and squeaks of rats, I would fall asleep telling myself that my family was heroic and mighty and brave and they would come and rescue me someday. When I was older, more fearful, I ground those fantasies to bitter dust. We'd been so destitute that my mother left me to die rather than keep feeding me; no one was coming to save me. And after Irmgard took it upon herself to teach me what I was . . . I knew I wasn't worth saving.

But this is my family, living, flawed, loving. Not a fantasy, not a shackle. Real, reaching for me with open arms.

If Anna can join the Ros family so easily . . . can't I?

And the answer is in a wreath of wild roses, an old rag doll, the blood and the laughter and the tears of my siblings, the painted letters on a shelf by a hearth.

I am a thief, a liar, a daughter, a sister, trouble, wanted.

And my name is Vanja Ros.

✺

The barn erupts with music and dancing as a piper and drummer join Dieter in song. I know we have to leave soon, but for the moment I let myself be whirled around the room, exclaimed over by townspeople who still remember me, handed sweets and pastries until I feel like I may burst.

It's midafternoon before I know it, before I can even catch my breath away from the dancing. I'm watching from safe harbor near the hayloft ladder while an aunt reels a stilted Kirkling around the dance floor when a flicker of movement tugs my attention away. Emeric has finally found me. He stretches out a hand.

I lace our fingers. "Thank you."

"For what?" he asks, taken aback.

"For helping. For letting me stay for this. For being here."

His face softens into a well-worn smile. "If you could see how happy you look right now, you'd know it was never even a question."

There's that swell, that rush again. The words surge up, almost tear free before I catch them: *I love you.*

But they stay locked away, and even I can't break them out. I tell myself it's just that we're here, now, and I don't want to ruin this moment if he can't say them back.

I lie to myself that it has nothing to do with the sand drifting to the bottom of the hourglass. They say it's better to have loved and lost, but I don't know if I can stand finding out for myself.

"I was wondering . . ." He settles against the other side of the hayloft ladder with a swing of our joined hands. "After we sort things out in Hagendorn, do you want to come back here for a bit?"

I have, in fact, been staunchly avoiding the question of *after Hagendorn,* partially for the same reason I guard *I love you* like crown jewels. And partially because . . . I fear what that *after* looks like, not just as far as the Finding is concerned.

As ever, I opt for a smoke screen. "Assuming Kirkling doesn't have me thrown in jail?" I ask sardonically. "Don't you have paperwork that goes with all this?"

Emeric shifts, uneasy. "I . . . If I go through with the Finding, yes." When I gape at him, he ducks his head. "I don't know. I can't stop thinking about how prefects are supposed to have all this power and—and freedom, to help people . . . but in Rammelbeck, my hands were tied while *you* actually solved problems."

I think a moment, trying to figure out how to put this. "I solved a lot of problems with a lot of money," I say finally, "put in the right place, at the right time. And by breaking the law in the right place, at the right time, without getting caught. I got Madame Gertie out of the picture, but the law's what keeps her out. Without the prefects, she could have just moved her whole operation over to Lüdz and gone right back to exploiting desperate people and paying the city to look the other way."

"Hubert used to say laws are only as good as the people who uphold them," Emeric sighs. "It doesn't bother you that I'd be going after people who break the law?"

"It'd bother me if you were like the city guard, only following the law if you feel like it," I answer bluntly, "and going after people who need to break the law to survive, when that just means the empire failed them. But people like Prince Ludwig, like Adalbrecht—they have everything, more than everything. They *make* the laws. And then they break them, they hurt people, just so we know they can. I can help their victims; I *can't* stop them from making new ones. Prefects can. So you'd better pass your Finding and get to work."

Emeric's head tips back, eyes closing, and I'm briefly distracted by a very intriguing thing happening with his exposed throat. Between the lack of privacy during the past week and the threat of the Scarlet Maiden, I'm achingly aware of how long it's been since we could get lost in each other. "I needed that reminder. Thank you, Vanja."

I bite my lip. "How—how do you think 'Vanja Ros' sounds?"

That makes him open his eyes again, turning to search my face. Whatever he finds there softens his gaze as he answers, "Perfect." Then his smile crooks in the way it does right before he says something he *knows* is incredibly cheesy. "You already look like the Queen of Roses."

"I'm going to regret this, aren't I." My own sheepish grin betrays the lie as I twist a lock of hair around a finger. "My sisters wanted to dress me up. I don't know, it might be too much."

His free hand skims the side of my face, my ear, catching one tail of the ribbon. "I think," he says even softer, simmering, "should you choose it, you'll make a beautiful bride someday."

For a moment, the music, the crowd—it all fades away. It's just me and him and the storm in my heart, these feelings so vast and relentless, they might flatten every wall of the barn.

Then—I see red.

At first I think Emeric's bleeding. Crimson is seeping through his waistcoat, spreading from his chest. When I touch the fabric, though, it's bone-dry. The red continues unfurling until, stark and unmistakable, the handprint of the Scarlet Maiden stains his clothes.

"Vanja," Emeric says suddenly, voice spiking with alarm, and when I look up, I see he hasn't even noticed the handprint; his eyes are locked on me. He swiftly plucks a petal from the wreath on my head and shows it to me.

It's bright scarlet.

When I look down, red is spreading through my borrowed gown, climbing from every hem. It's overtaken Emeric, too, dyeing everything we wear the same vivid carmine.

There's a commotion and murmurs of shock and dismay at the barn's entrance. We turn to look.

Udo and Jakob are staggering through the doorway.

They're exhausted and soaked, like they've ridden through the night without stopping. Not even the rain could wash away what look like bloodstains. Udo has Jakob's arm slung over his neck, but Dieter and Sånnik rush to help them both as the music stops.

"What happened?" Helga pushes her way past the guests. "Are you hurt?"

"They took them," Udo says helplessly, collapsing into a chair.

"Took who?" Sånnik asks.

"My lambs. They took them all." Udo buries his face in his hands. "And they slaughtered every last one."

CHAPTER THIRTY-ONE

TRANSCENDENT

"LENI HAS COMPLETE CONTROL OF THE CULT," JAKOB SAYS WEARILY. "And it's overrun Hagendorn."

All of us siblings are gathered in the sitting room. Blankets are draped over Jakob's and Udo's shoulders and mugs of hot tea have been pressed into their hands. Some guests and family still linger in the barn, but Anna and Aunt Katrin are winding things down. Emeric and Kirkling hover at the doorway, Ragne perched on Emeric's shoulder as a black sparrow.

Udo shudders. "She was calling Vanja a false prophet, and I said the Scarlet Maiden followed her in to begin with. And Leni . . . she and her cult took all the lambs, even the newborns. She said I had to make it up to the Scarlet Maiden for doubting, but the way the ewes were screaming—" The words choke off. Sånnik rubs his back.

"What about the villagers?" Helga asks. "Can't they do anything? It's our town."

Jakob shakes his head. "They're outnumbered. Badly. Leni won't let anyone leave either."

"But Auntie Gerke alone—"

"Gerke's dead." Jakob's voice is distant, direct, like the sorrow's there but trampled flat. "I'm sorry, Helga. She got caught helping Sonja's family sneak out. She drank enough witch-ash tonic to kill anyone twice over and grew the forest so it closed off the road. It cost Gerke her life, but Sonja and her family got away."

Helga's hands are pressed to her mouth, her head shaking *no, no, no.*

"We left in the dead of night and cut through the forest until we were clear of Leni's guard. Just barely made it through the crossroads before Prince Ludwig shut those down too. Glockenberg, Hagendorn—they're both cut off now. No one goes in or out." Jakob stares into his mug. "Everything blooms red, all the way to the crossroads and growing."

"How much worse can it get?" Katrin Little asks. "Isn't this the god that asked for your blood?"

Emeric clears his throat. "It is. She's also claimed me for a human sacrifice." He tugs at his own collar to reveal the tips of the red fingers that nearly reach his collarbone. "She said the blood was an alternative, but now we think it was an excuse to get Vanja out of Hagendorn and install Leni in her place. Sacrificing the blood will kill anyone who's contributed, so we suspect she knew Vanja would discover your familial connection in the process and choose to let the Scarlet Maiden take me."

"But we can use the blood to stop her instead," I say, almost frantic. I did this, I brought the Scarlet Maiden to Hagendorn, but I can fix it, I can fix it, and—and I won't lose my family again. I need them to know I can fix it. "She wanted the blood because there's magic in the ties between us as blood relatives. Emeric found a way we can turn that magic on her, and we can do it without hurting any of you. We just need to get to Hagendorn."

A quiet falls over the room as my siblings all look at me. I brace myself for anger, blame, eviction; I've ruined Sånnik's wedding, I've ruined Udo and Jakob's home, I've ruined the lives of the people of Hagendorn.

They've learned what happens when I'm let in. There's no denying now the ruin that follows.

Sånnik draws himself up, steel in his brow. I brace for the worst.

"Then you've got to go," he says, "fast."

It's as if some great machine churns into motion. "We need the wagon," Katrin tells Jörgi, "the covered one, and the draft ponies—Eida, pack up leftovers for them—Luisa, go to the innkeeper and get their luggage ready—"

"I'll drive the wagon," Sånnik says around our siblings bustling out. A pause catches the room.

"You just got married, asshole," Dieter grouches. "*I'll* drive."

Kirkling's voice rises. "I can also drive. We'll trade off so we can ride through the night." Emeric and I both look at her, astonished, but there's no time to interrogate where this turn for the helpful is coming from before she turns to him. "Do you have the witch-ash you need for the binding spell? And your sedative?"

Everything comes together so fast, I don't even have a chance to pitch in before we're being bundled into the covered wagon along with blankets, waterskins, crates of food, a few changes of clothes, and a sack of horse feed that's probably the best pillow we'll get. "We'll follow as soon as we can," Jakob promises, voice rising to be heard above the rain. "You'll just have to hold on for a day or two."

"Wait!" Katrin grabs the edge of the wagon (wholly unnecessarily, as Dieter's just now climbing into the driver's bench). "Don't you need the last blood drop?"

My hand goes to the cambric and awl in my satchel. "I don't know," I admit. "If we add more, it gets stronger, and if the Scarlet Maiden manages to get it . . ."

"But it makes the binding stronger, too," Helga says, eyes burning, teeth bared, "and you need to end her for good."

Sånnik pushes his way forward as my sisters trade looks. "Then take it. Take us with you, Vanja, one way or another. And come back to us when you're done."

The cambric is heavy and damp when we've finished, an intricate knot of blots and lines. And as Dieter cracks the reins and pulls us into the sunset-drenched road, I pray it will be enough.

❧

The rain pours more than it doesn't over the next three days. It ought to have taken two at most to reach the crossroads, even with stopping each night, but the ponies have to plow through a week's worth of mud. The only upside is that the moon is waxing again, and the larger it swells, the stronger Ragne gets and the longer she can help. We stop only a few times a day, and then just for half an hour to trade out drivers and ponies, stretch stiff legs, and make unglamorous use of hedges off the roadside.

I'm starting to suspect Kirkling is one of those people who strongly commits to being a pain in the ass on a day-to-day basis, only to metamorphose into a decent and competent person in a crisis. When she's not driving or sleeping, she's checking supplies, reviewing the binding spell with Ambroszia and Emeric, even reminding Emeric to take his weekly sedative tablet the night before we reach the crossroads. Even though it's a few days early for another dose, we've all noticed the flowers blushing red the farther we go, and no one wants to wait until we're even farther into the Scarlet Maiden's domain. Especially after the first fresh kirtle I changed into turned a violent red on the spot. Emeric hasn't even bothered with a new shirt.

I try to help where I can, too, but there's only so much I can do, fixing meals for whoever's driving, keeping Ragne warm and dry while she recovers her strength, making Emeric walk me through the binding spell, too, so I know what part I will play. More often than not, though, the best he and I can do is huddle together, hand in hand, knowing the same queasy knot is growing in both our bellies as the road spooling out behind us turns an ever darker, deeper scarlet. My wreath of roses hangs from one of the wagon beams, and perhaps the eeriest thing is how the red petals haven't wilted, not even a little.

We drive all through the sabbath and reach the crossroads just after dawn on Monday morning. The first of May, the May-Saint Feast, is on Friday, so if we keep pushing on, we should make it to Hagendorn late on Wednesday, the day before the Scarlet Maiden wants her sacrifice.

Unfortunately, Prince Ludwig has other ideas.

I'm dozing on the half-depleted horse-feed sack when Kirkling's voice jolts me awake: "Prefect Emeritus Elske Kirkling and Prefect Aspirant Emeric Conrad, on official business of the Godly Courts. Let us pass."

I sit up and find Emeric and Kirkling in the driver's bench. Dieter's also waking from a nap as cat-Ragne stretches her paws. When I peek out, I see it's just as Udo and Jakob described: Soldiers have blocked off the western road to Glockenberg and Hagendorn, resolute in a sea of red foliage. Worse, Prince Ludwig is with them, sporting a ridiculous gold-plated suit of armor.

"By order of the *prinz-wahl*, this road is closed," one soldier calls.

Emeric and Kirkling trade looks. "I repeat," Kirkling replies, "we are on official business of the Godly Courts, whose authority exceeds the *prinz-wahl*'s."

Prince Ludwig trots his palfrey over to his soldier's side. "Oh, did I mishear?" His voice is jolly but wound taut in a way that makes me think of a bright-scaled viper coiling to strike. "A full prefect might have the authority, but I thought you said Prefects '*Emeritus*' and '*Aspirant*.'"

Under other circumstances, I might have enjoyed the thwarted look on Kirkling's face, but I'd rather she not be thwarted while her sense of human decency is still operational. "We are here to resolve the situation in Hagendorn on behalf of the Godly Courts. On what grounds do you deny our passage, Your Highness?"

Prince Ludwig flicks a hand like he's dismissing a maid. "I've already sent for Helligbrücke's high bishop. Your services are not necessary. Now be on your way, or my soldiers will send you on it."

Kirkling mutters, "We're not done," but only loud enough for us to hear. She snaps the reins and begins turning the ponies around.

"I could fly the Vanja and the Emeric past these soldiers," Ragne suggests.

Ambroszia pokes her head over the wagon's backboard, porcelain clinking against the wood. "There are archers. Although . . ." She stumps around to look at Kirkling. "Elske, I have an idea."

"As do I." Kirkling stops the horses on the side of the road. "*Meister* Ros, thank you for the ride, but we'll be carrying on from here on foot. Conrad, get down. Sch—Miss Ros, bag up enough food for you and Conrad. Miss Ragne, I assume you can handle your own provisions."

Ragne's tail switches. "What is this plan?"

"Lady Ambroszia will create a distraction while you three make a break for it," Kirkling says shortly. "I will slip by the guards on foot, carrying the doll so her material anchor remains protected, and follow you to Hagendorn as quickly as I can. No—Conrad, don't argue, just do as I say."

"If anything happens to you . . ." Emeric shakes his head. "Hubert would never—"

"Hubert Klemens wouldn't have blinked at letting me handle that clown prince," Kirkling says. "Certainly not to stop a monster like the Scarlet Maiden, and . . . certainly not to save you. Now get ready, we don't have time to lose."

Ragne leaps out of the wagon, shifting into a sturdy black mare as she does and landing in the mud with a splatter. She kneels to let Emeric and me climb onto her back, though Emeric looks wholly baffled, arms tightening around my waist as Ragne pushes to her feet. "I thought you said you'd fly us over."

"She will," I tell him. "You're going to hate it."

Dieter coughs from the driver's bench, then tosses something to me: the wreath of roses. "Don't die. I'll take Luisa's dress back. Bye." He flicks the reins and jolts the ponies into motion before I can reply.

"Definitely your brother," Emeric murmurs, and I jab him with an elbow.

"Ambroszia." It's a bit weird for me to address her while Kirkling's holding her, but we make do. "What should we expect?"

"Something quite monstrous," she answers, with a wicked flicker in her broken eye. "I am, after all, still part of the world transcendent. And that means I can become what they believe me to be. Now be a dear and, in about three seconds, scream."

Ephemeral mist starts radiating from the doll. Ragne melodramatically tosses her head and shies away. Then the acting gets less necessary as the haze carves itself into ragged hems, skeletal arms, a face contorted in torment—almost like Saint Willehalm's warped form when the goblet was missing. Suddenly I understand.

I draw an enormous breath and scream, at the top of my lungs, *"POLTERGEIST!"*

Shouts rise from the soldiers. They're buying it, and that makes it true: Ambroszia's appearance grows more twisted and nightmarish by the moment. Ragne dances down the road, seemingly no more than a skittish horse, but I know she's getting room for a running start.

Kirkling gives us a nod and steps back, off the road, vanishing into the red shrubbery.

"Hold on," Ragne warns as feathers spurt from her shoulders once more. I slip the rose wreath over my wrist, then gather fistfuls of mane and hope that'll be enough.

"Wh—no, *absolutely not*—" Emeric's grip on me tightens, but it's too late.

Ragne's wings unfurl, and she takes off at a canter, then a gallop. Ambroszia is cackling madly before her as rain whips my face. I hear screams of *"Poltergeist, demon!"* and see spears and arrows readied.

Ragne sweeps her wings once, twice, and we're airborne. Emeric is making a sound behind me like a ceramic lung being punctured by a fork. Steel glints below—a soldier looses a shot—

And in a blast of dust and cobweb, the ghoulish *poltergeist* of Lady Ambroszia catches it. And a spear. And the next dozen arrows that follow as we soar over the blockade. Ragne flies even higher through the rain, rising with the forest as the shallow hills bubble up. There's a strange tint on the horizon, as if red is seeping into the cloudy sky itself, bleeding from Hagendorn. As I take one final look back at Ambroszia, I see the stain spilling all through the thick forests of the lowlands.

Emeric clutches even tighter when I turn to face forward. "Can—can we just—hold very still?" he gasps.

"You should try this when there's a saddle, it's a lot better," I say apologetically.

"*Is* it?"

"It is much faster to travel this way," Ragne calls to us, tilting to head for the heart of the stain, "but I will get tired very quickly. If we can make it to this Glockenberg, then I can rest, and tonight—"

"*My little prodigal returns,*" the Scarlet Maiden hisses in my ear. Red blooms at the edge of my vision. Emeric's fingers dig painfully into my sides.

I scream for real this time, trying to jerk away, and spit out, "*Villanelle!*"

Then, as his grip slackens, I realize what I've done.

Emeric slumps over. I grab for him with one hand—the other is still hanging on to Ragne's mane—but only catch his upper arm. His weight drags me sideways as Ragne whinnies and beats her wings, trying to recover her own balance.

Then it's as if she slams into a wall of slush. It's not an impact so much as a brief absorption—then repulsion. We're thrown from her back. The world inverts, spins—I'm falling—I see Ragne as a raven but from behind a wall that shimmers like heat waves, unyielding no matter how she claws—I've lost my hold on Emeric, but we're both plummeting to the treetops—

A shockingly green gout of willowy branches bursts from the forest, slowing our fall, reinforced with thick springy vines. The wind is still knocked out of me when we land on a bed of spongy moss, but that's all.

I gaze up, dizzy, blinking away rain as a shadow falls over me. I make out snarls of white hair, a rust-streaked stone face, uncannily emerald eyes, Ragne wheeling in the sky above.

"God Daughter," the Briar Hag, queen of the Mossfolk, grates out, "you had better be here to fix this."

CHAPTER THIRTY-TWO

THE WAY OF BRIARS

"THAT'S THE IDEA," I WHEEZE TO THE BRIAR HAG. HER NOSTRILS FLARE, and she yanks on my collar until I'm sitting up, then stamps her crooked staff as if to say, *There better be more.* "We brought the blood the Scarlet Maiden asked for—"

"Not a good start," the Hag grunts in my face, her breath earthy and cool like moldy soil.

"—and are going to use the ties to bind her."

The Briar Hag's eyes narrow. "Bind her to what?"

"The material anchor, the thing she's using to be more powerful than a normal Rye Mother. It's somewhere in Hagendorn. We're going to find it, trap her, and destroy it with her inside." Looking around, I find a jarring sight: Not only are we in an island of rich green foliage among the burnished red, but dozens, maybe hundreds, of eyes are blinking from tree knots and budding on branches.

"*Hrmph.*" The Briar Hag waddles over to the unconscious Emeric and starts poking him in the side with her staff. "Ought to work. She's no Rye Mother, though. Get up, boy."

"Not a—what *is* she, then?" I demand.

The Hag shrugs. "Don't know. Doesn't matter. I want my forest back." She pokes Emeric again. "Is he dead?"

"He'll come around in a few minutes." I crane my head to look for Ragne. She's still clawing at the barrier above. "Are we trapped in here?"

"No 'we.'" The Briar Hag crooks a finger, and a long vine, just like the ones that caught us, climbs into the air. When the vine reaches Ragne, a flower blooms at its tip. An identical bloom sprouts at the base near us. "Eiswald's daughter, be still."

"Give me back the Vanja and the Emeric!" Ragne's raven-voice croaks through the quaking petals.

The Hag rumbles, "It's not my doing. The Scarlet Maiden is pushing all the Low Gods out, and you're close enough to count. You'll go no further. But I'm no god, and she can't budge *me* from my roots, so your friends are safe as I can keep them. Understand?"

"I do not like this," Ragne huffs.

"Me either," I say. "But we'll be all right. Can you help Kirkling?"

Ragne's disgruntled answer makes the flower shake even more. "I will. But *then* I will find a way in!"

There's a groan from Emeric as Ragne swoops away. He pushes himself up on an elbow. "What . . . happened?"

"We learned a very important lesson about gravity." I help him the rest of the way. "I think we have to continue on foot. Brunne owes me a favor still, but I don't know if she'll make it through."

The Briar Hag's staff thuds into the ground. "The closer you are to the gorge, the better odds Brunne will have, as that is where her legend was born and her strength is greatest. Save her favor until you face the Scarlet Maiden." The ground beneath us contorts, somewhere between a wave and the breath of a buried titan. "I will take you as close to Hagendorn as I can."

The moss carpet around us buckles and folds, forming the sides of a little cart, lifting us up on wheels made of gnarled root still mired in earth. It half rolls, half swims through the ground, gaining speed. Shrubs scurry out of the way; trees creak into bows and curtsies as we pass. We're moving fast, faster even than in the wagon.

"How will we repay you?" I ask, because Low God or no, I know the Hag's help must come with a price.

The Briar Hag is stirring the air with her staff as if it's a stew, and the trees churning past are no more than parsnip chunks, but she snaps her fingers, and a pure-gold comb appears in her stony grasp. "You will comb and braid my hair."

I gulp. A Briar Hag's hair is notoriously unpleasant to dress. But if that's the cost to save Emeric, to save my family, it's a small price to pay. I rise to my knees, take the comb in one hand, then find the end of her long knotted hair and begin. The hairs are fine and smooth like flax, though helplessly tangled. *It's just like combing flax*, I tell myself. I did that easily enough when I was four.

Then a spider crawls onto my hand.

I yelp and shake it off. Emeric's at my side instantly, reaching for the comb. "Let me."

"The God Daughter has to do it," growls the Briar Hag.

"It's fine," I tell him. "Just . . . handle the bugs."

"Start at the ends," the Briar Hag orders, "and work your way up."

I set the comb's golden teeth to a tangle and begin to work the hairs through. For a moment, as strands slip and unweave, I see a flicker of—

A girl stumbling over a bridge on a cold winter's night, clutching a fistful of rubies. Me.

I blink, and it's gone. In my hand sits a lock of sleek combed hair.

"Keep going," says the Briar Hag.

I pick up another knot as Emeric discreetly extracts a beetle. As the comb passes, I see a princess arguing with her father, red-eyed and hollow with grief. I see her standing on the edge of a cliff before Broken Peak, looking down into a dark pool, where a subtle golden star winks from the depths. The Red Maid of the River.

On the third pass, I see a bride riding through the night sky on a cloudy road. Her veil catches in the stars, pulling her shining bridal crown from her head.

Brunne.

As I comb and comb, I see the strands of our lives: Brunne, before she was a god, promised to a giant just to keep the peace. The Red Maid of the River, a god who will never be satisfied, who's watched life after life lost trying to bring her a golden crown. Me, spinning a lie because it was easy, staying in Hagendorn because I was wanted, raising not the ghost of a god but a monster in her image.

"Now make the braid," says the Hag.

The strands slip through my fingers and beyond. I see threads binding me to my siblings, to the bloodstained cambric at my side, to Emeric. I see crimson ties stretching from both him and me to Hagendorn: the chains of the Scarlet Maiden. She has claimed him as her sacrifice, but even before then, she claimed me as her prophet.

The strands weave, one linking and leading to another and another: A liar, a broken god, a bride. A crown, a river, a spindle. Heartbreak, hunger, freedom.

Just as Brunne led to the Red Maid, the Red Maid led to me. Even without blood or bond between us, our threads are woven together.

And the true Red Maid, just as Brunne said, still lingers.

In my hands sits a long, perfect, bone-white braid.

"She is no longer the Red Maid of the River," says the Hag. "Nor will she answer to 'Maid Painted Red.' But if you can call her by name, she will come. I think you, God Daughter, Daughter Ros, understand the power of that."

"I think you've helped me more than I've helped you here," I say slowly.

The Briar Hag's moss-covered shoulders stiffen. "The woodwives were soft for Gerke's dumplings," she says tersely, after a pause. "See to it that Helga sticks to the recipe."

She doesn't speak much for the rest of our strange ride, her scowl alleviated only by the occasional birdcall or flick of a squirrel's tail. They grow increasingly rarer, and the woods grow redder and redder the farther we get, as if even beasts know better than to be here. Finally, as slanting sunset light spears through the leaves, we come to a halt. I open my mouth, and the Hag holds a finger to her lips, shaking her head. She points with her other hand, and I take it to indicate Hagendorn's direction.

When I turn back to mouth *thank you*, the Briar Hag is already melting away, into the brush.

Emeric and I are on our own.

He catches my sleeve. His voice is barely above a whisper. "I need to borrow the awl. It's linked to the Scarlet Maiden, so I can use a tracking spell to locate any physical objects in the area with a similar link. That should lead us to the material anchor."

"How long will it take?" I pass him the bone awl and start picking my way forward.

"It depends on how far it is. My guess is it's somewhere near the bridge where she first manifested, though."

I begin to see a familiar shape emerge through the woods: Jakob and Udo's house. No smoke curls from the chimney now. "That's close."

"Then it should take only a minute or two." Emeric pauses, closing his eyes, and I wait too. He holds the awl in one hand and hovers his other over it. A wheel of silvery runes spins to life between his palms, rotating in mechanical increments before vanishing in tendrils of smoke. "Done. It's looking now."

"Udo and Jakob's house is up ahead," I tell him, settling my rose wreath on my head to free up my hands and taking the awl back. We resume our trudge through the underbrush. "We can probably hide there until dark—"

I step around a thick elm trunk and find myself staring into the rotting eyes of a lamb's head mounted on a pike.

Emeric's hand claps over my mouth, muffling my shriek. It's too late. Blistering red light kindles in the head's exposed sockets, maggots spilling as its jaw drops to let out a shattering scream.

"HERESY," it mewls in a horrible babylike pitch, "HERESY!"

The ground heaves again, but this time it has nothing to do with the Briar Hag. Cries of "Heresy, heresy!" rise in our ears, and then, suddenly, with a nauseating jolt—

We're out of the woods, standing in the main square of Hagendorn. All the old buildings remain, but they've been marked with crude red spindles over every window. The sweet reek of fresh-sawn wood radiates from new longhouses crammed into the gaps, repulsive against the stench of old blood coming from the iron statue beside Leni.

The roar of "Heresy!" pours from hundreds of throats in the crowd surrounding us. We've been afforded a wide berth, a ring of empty dirt between us and the seething masses, as if our very presence might taint them.

We have not been afforded an exit.

Leni surveys us from her scaffold, sunset light flashing off her tawdry brass halo, her spindle hoisted in the rain like a mace. She's dyed her blond hair a rusty red and stands framed between two more burning-eyed lamb heads that chant, *"Heresy, heresy, heresy."* She holds up her empty hand—the red diamond on her palm is stark even in the ubiquitous crimson haze—and silence falls.

"So," Leni sings, "the false prophet has returned. Have you defiled our sacrifice? Are you here to sow more ruin?"

The throng of strangers takes its cue, jeering, *"DEFILER! RUIN! FALSE!"*

Leni crows, "It is just as I promised! The Scarlet Maiden works through me and me alone! I will lead you into the age of plenty, I will lead you against our enemies, and though the unfaithful are in our midst, you need not fear!"

"How's that tracking spell?" I grit to Emeric through my teeth.

His brow is furrowed. "Nothing yet—but the anchor has to be here somewhere, she wouldn't have been strong enough to manifest from a distance—"

A familiar jangling murmur sweeps around the square, rising above the taunts and the fall of rain.

"REJOICE!"

Leni falters. "What?"

"Rejoice!" The Scarlet Maiden's command cracks through Hagendorn. Mist gathers in the open space before Emeric and me, spooling higher, higher, wisps twisting into definition like fibers spun from a distaff. With an eye-watering flash, she towers over us, smiling blissfully beneath her crown of burning roses. *"My prophet has returned to the flock."*

Leni's face pales. "But—I—I'm your proph—"

The Scarlet Maiden carries on over her: *"We feared you would stray, but we welcome you back with open arms, for you have done as I asked! You have delivered unto Hagendorn its salvation: two sacrifices, both worthy of me. And now, tell me: Which will you give, and which shall you keep?"*

It's my turn to go cold. "You said I had until the eve of the May-Saint Feast."

"You are here now," the Scarlet Maiden clangs, *"and I desire my sacrifice. I will have it by midnight tonight, one way or another."*

Of course. I'm so stupid, I should have expected, I should have *known* she'd just move the cutoff up again.

I shoot Emeric a look. He shakes his head slightly, wide-eyed. We still don't know where the material anchor is.

The Scarlet Maiden is here, we have the tools to bind her, and we have nothing to bind her to.

"Don't we need to arrange for—for a feast?" I try to stall. "That's why—"

The Scarlet Maiden bends so her terrible, lovely face is burning inches from mine. *"You will choose, Prophet, NOW."*

We need time. We need an opening. Maybe—maybe if I can weaken the cult's faith, I can put a dent in the Scarlet Maiden's power.

"I choose you," I say as loudly as I can, hoping that if any original Hagendorn villagers hear me, they can forgive me someday, "because I *am* a false prophet. In January, I got drunk, fell on the bridge, and spilled rubies I was carrying. I made up a lie about having a vision so I'd get help fishing them out of the brook, and then that lie kept growing. You're not the Red Maid of the River. You're not even a god. You're just a lie I tricked people into believing."

The Scarlet Maiden rears back. Wrath fouls her face—

Emeric says suddenly, "There—I've got it, I know—"

I play my final card: "Brunne, come to my aid!"

Only silence answers.

We're too deep into the Scarlet Maiden's domain.

The Scarlet Maiden laughs, a dissonant, musical sound. "*Oh, my foolish little prophet! Did you think I was not with you even then? Who do you think doused the fire before it swallowed the Ros brothers' house? Who do you think saved Leni's daughter from the* waldskrot? *My protection has been upon Hagendorn for months.*" Miasmatic tendrils coil toward us, bristling. "*And now it's time to pay the price.*"

The dirt shudders beneath our feet once again, this time writhing like great worms through dry silt. Roots squirm to the surface—no, not roots.

Briars.

They phase right through the intangible Scarlet Maiden, cutting a deep green road into the mob. "*GO*," the Briar Hag thunders.

I don't need to be told twice.

I grab Emeric's hand and run.

CHAPTER THIRTY-THREE

The Way Out

"Felsengruft," emeric pants behind me as we dash down the briar road. "The anchor's in Felsengruft, under the Broken Peak."

Sure enough, the thorn walls are steering us onto the footpath to Boderad's Gorge. There's no time to wonder why the anchor isn't in Hagendorn. I hear shouting and fury behind us but don't dare look back. "Did you see what it is?"

"No, only that it's in the rite hall." Emeric draws even with me. "She's—she's even stronger than I expected if she can move us like that. It takes an enormous amount of power to shift reality."

The briars wane around us as we reach the woods once more. Green eyes blossom in the trees, and this time, mouths split in the bark.

✣ 450 ✣

The Briar Hag's rasp comes from every side. "I'll keep the mortals locked down as long as I can. Make haste."

"It took us, what—two hours to hike there last time?" Emeric asks as the eyes shrink away. "If we hurry . . . maybe an hour."

The sunset is dyeing the already-russet forest an even deeper red, making rubies of the falling raindrops. I check my satchel to make sure the bloody cambric is still there. "How are you holding up, magic-wise?"

Emeric is rummaging through his own satchel, consternation on his face until he surfaces with an intact vial of witch-ash oil. I recognize the black cork: It's the highest concentration made by the Order of Prefects. "Phew. Survived the fall. And I'm fine, the tracking spell is very lightweight. The binding was always going to call for witch-ash anyway." He grimaces. "Not that we have a surplus of options. Did I hear right? We have until midnight before . . . ?"

Choking apprehension clogs my throat. "That's what ScarMad said, that she'd have a sacrifice by then, no matter what."

"If it comes to it"—Emeric's voice hitches—"destroy the blood drops and save your family. My life isn't worth—"

"It won't come to it, then," I say, furious he would even suggest such a thing. "All right? I'm not letting it happen."

He squeezes my hand but doesn't answer.

Neither of us can speak of the other way out for him. A scant handful of hours remains, enough that, if we're truly desperate—

No. We want to take our time, we want it to matter. I won't let her take that from us too.

The choice dangles between us, a razor pendulum, nonetheless.

I remember climbing past the beeches and hawthorns of this path just a month ago, yet—maybe it's the rain, maybe it's the dwindling sunset—something's different. We scramble along the trail until I see the striped hornfels walls of the gorge through the trees.

My stomach twists. That can't be right. We've been walking for barely half an hour.

When we break through, it's to a deafening roar.

I expected the long rope bridge that spanned the gorge, but it's nowhere in sight. Instead, great plumes of spray blow into our faces from where the Ilsza plummets into the rocky teeth of the Kronenkessel. We're at the waterfall's foot, not its head.

Emeric stops short. "It's the sacrificial bridge." His voice sounds numb.

I follow his gaze to a spindly bridge of ancient stone. It's the one we saw far below us when we first crossed the rope bridge. And, I realize, the one in every mural, mosaic, and memory I've seen of the Kronenkessel.

The one the sacrifice jumps from.

"We must have missed a turn," I insist, knowing full well I'm in denial. I turn to go up the trail—

The world judders. Suddenly it's not dirt beneath my feet but wet stone. In the final dregs of sundown, the water pooling on the surface looks like blood. We've been moved again, now to the middle of the ancient bridge. The Kronenkessel tosses and froths just beyond the edge, horrific, inevitable.

We're still in the Scarlet Maiden's trap. And she's hell-bent on forcing us into an end.

I sway in place, trying to think, clinging to Emeric's hand too tight. "We can—we can cross to the other side and find a way up to Felsengruft from there."

"She's just going to keep shifting us," he says, almost disbelieving. "She's not going to let us reach Broken Peak."

If we can't reach Felsengruft, can't reach the material anchor, then we have no way to destroy her.

"I'll call Brunne again," I say desperately, *Don't panic* beating in my mind like a drum.

Yet we both know how well that summons will work. The gorge is flooded in red haze, one not even Brunne the Huntress can pierce.

But the Briar Hag told me about Brunne for a reason, told me about the Red Maid for a reason, there has to be a way—

A faint golden gleam twinkles from the mad, foaming waters of the Kronenkessel.

A wild idea seizes me. I let go of Emeric's hand. Before he can even react, I've whipped my satchel over my head and dropped it on the bridge.

Then I hurl myself off the edge.

I hear Emeric scream my name just before I hit the water. If I can get the crown, maybe I can rouse the real Red Maid, maybe she can save us. Maybe that will be enough.

It's cold, bitterly cold, and the rush is dulled to a distant churn. I let myself be dragged down, then force my eyes open. The water stings, but I can make out great granite thorns, the inverted spume where the waterfall hits.

I cannot make out the bottom of the pool.

This is where the giant Boderad fell, where his fury turned him into a hellhound, and the wound is greater, darker, than I could have fathomed.

Still, a tiny ring of gold glitters against a spur of stone: Brunne's bridal crown.

I know instantly that it is too deep for me to reach. I'll never be able to dive that far, let alone make it back up. But I have to try, I have to fix this, somehow—

Something shifts in the depths. One milky glowing eye blinks at me from a deep beyond even the crown—then another.

My breath bubbles out. I thrash and kick, pushing toward the surface. I can *feel* the current change with the hellhound's rise, the current of the waterfall reversing, pulling me deeper as water rushes to fill the void Boderad leaves in his wake. The water even tastes different, like stale brine ice—no matter how I fight, I'm being dragged down—jaws open beneath me, each tooth as long as I am tall—

A body knifes into the pool and to my side. Arms wrap around me, and there's a flash of silver. It's as if the water itself repels us, shoving us to the rocky rim of the Kronenkessel.

I'm hauled halfway onto muddy stone just as an algae-stained snout breaks the surface. The crack of teeth is so loud, all sound buzzes out for a moment. I collapse, sputtering.

". . . you *thinking*?" Emeric's voice fades in.

The hellhound sinks below the water, and a wave surges in its wake, lifting us both all the way onto the bank before draining away. Emeric sinks to the ground beside me, winded and stricken. "You didn't—that thing would have torn you apart—"

"The crown," I cough out, my teeth chattering as I look around. We've washed up on the same side of the Kronenkessel that we came from, the Broken Peak looming impossibly high above the opposite shore. There's a meager crescent of pebble and dirt here, and a thin track leading to the sacrificial bridge. "Brunne's crown. I thought if I got it for the Red Maid . . ." I hang my head. "It's too far down."

"Never mind that, you could have *died*," Emeric says wretchedly.

I just give a hunched little shrug, because what is there to say? He's running out of time, and I don't know how to fix it. "Haven't you figured it out yet?" I ask, half laughing, half broken. "I'd do it again if it'd work. You absolute bastard, I'd do anything to save you."

He pulls me to him, shaking as he buries his face in my bedraggled wet hair. "Not for me, Vanja, please. Not for me."

For a long, sweet, awful moment, we stay this way: on the bank of the pool, wound together in the cold, holding on like the only warmth in the world is between us. But night is falling, the shadows creeping in.

We both know there's only one final way out.

It was always going to come to this, in the end.

I lean back and draw a breath, steeling myself. "We need more time," I start. "We can leave here, keep the blood drops away from the Scarlet Maiden, and regroup . . . but not if she'll take you in a few hours anyway. We have to break—"

"No," Emeric says swiftly.

"—the claim," I finish. There's a tortuous pause.

"Is that what you want?" he asks me, in a way that says we both know the answer is *no*.

My fists ball up in his sodden shirt. It's a testament to our mutual misery that we're clinging to each other, soaked to the bone, and it's doing nothing for either of us. "It doesn't matter." We both flinch at the lie. I try again. "We can take our time later, we can . . . make it special. But we need to get out of here first."

"This isn't right," he whispers. "I don't want to do this to you."

I shake my head. "If you're not ready either, I won't force you. I just . . . don't know what we'll do."

Emeric finally looks me in the eye. "I . . . I've been ready. But you deserve more than the least terrible of your choices." His shoulders slump as he confesses, "But I don't know what else we can do either."

"You said you would choose me every time, Emeric." I take his face in my hands, touch my forehead to his. "So please, this once—let me choose you."

A shuddering breath passes between us, crackling like lightning. Then a soft, almost feral noise breaks from his throat as I bring his lips to mine.

Ever since the Scarlet Maiden possessed him, each kiss has been short, sweet but fleeting for fear of interruption. For the first time in two weeks, I let myself—make myself—linger.

I can do this. Despite the knot in my stomach, I can do this for him.

He's clearly missed this, too, every stolen breath ragged, every touch of his hands, his mouth, almost reverent. When I move to plant a knee on either side of his hips, he sucks in a breath like he's witnessed a miracle, kisses me with a ferocity that should draw an answering wildness from me.

It does, and it does not.

Part of me is here, savoring the taste of his skin, reveling in his shiver when I peel his shirt away. Part of me would martyr myself to sanctify his hands ghosting under my shift, to bathe in the holy fire they leave in their wake. Part of me burns to wreck myself on him utterly.

But the rest . . .

The rest of me is ready to run.

Braced for the worst.

Fixated on the red handprint between us, throbbing on his bare chest like it's pushing me away, all but screaming, *Stop, wrong, mine, mine, mine.*

I can't let go, can't lose myself in him the way I want. I should be swept away, not annoyed with the jab of a pebble in my knee, not distracted by my wreath of roses bobbing against a rock in the water nearby. This should be about us.

It is, and it is not.

It didn't have to be sonnets and choreography and flower petals. It didn't even have to be planned. I just wanted more than a quick, performative rut in the mud. I wanted it to mean more than just—getting it out of the way.

But this has to be enough.

I want this to be right, I want it to be right *so* badly, I will do anything, even if it feels terribly wrong. I make my hands skim down his chest, working myself up to reach for the waistband of his breeches. I can do this, and it will be enough to save him.

Won't it?

This is how I'm supposed to *claim* him, right? But my mind will not be quiet.

What if—what if it doesn't count because I won't get with child? Or what if we're both supposed to finish and I can't? No, if it were that, we'd have claimed each other in Rammelbeck—but what makes this so different?

Is it really just letting him into me this way? His hands, his mouth, they didn't count?

Is this really the only way that's good enough?

And then—

The threads knot.

I go still, hands frozen on Emeric's stomach.

"Vanja?" he asks unevenly.

"It's not enough," I breathe, staring at the handprint as it pulsates on his chest. "We don't . . . we don't have to do this. It's not going to work."

"What?" Emeric stares at me, dazed and bewildered.

I don't blame him. "It doesn't matter what we do, none of it's going to be good enough, because it never *can* be," I say in a rush, thread after thread finally cinching into something like comprehension. "We're trying to—to do this right, but there *is* no right way, because she's always going to change the rules and say it doesn't count. We were never going to break her claim. She just wants us to feel like nothing we did was good enough. *We* were never good enough."

Emeric sits up, running a hand over his mouth. "Like how the Red Maid asked for the crown. We weren't supposed to—"

He cuts off, chin falling to his chest. Red light dances across his cheeks.

But I expected this, from the moment I saw this game for what it is. I'm ready.

I push myself off him, rolling to my knees, and bark out, "*Villanelle.*"

Emeric drops to the ground.

Then—his whole body jerks.

His eyes are forced open, blazing red, the handprint too bright to look at directly.

"*Thank you,*" the Scarlet Maiden warbles through him, slurring a bit as she works his jaw like a ventriloquist's dummy. He staggers to his feet, movements stilted and unnatural, a marionette with no strings. "*It's less elegant to puppet him myself, but so much easier when he doesn't fight.*"

It didn't work. The sedative didn't stop her this time.

Horror washes through me. "Let him go," I whisper, insensible.

That red glow spreads through Emeric until he's a lantern lit from within. She has him. She has him, she's going to take him, she can march him into the jaws of the hellhound herself—

I lunge in a blind panic, hoping to seize any part of him I can. Emeric's yanked backward, limbs dangling.

The Scarlet Maiden appears behind him in her full glory, a cutthroat smile bleeding triumph onto her face. She lifts Emeric into the air with a simple gesture. "*You have made your choice.*"

"I didn't choose shit!" I yell, stumbling toward her like I'm an infant again, full of fury I can express only in a senseless howl. "Give him back!"

But the Scarlet Maiden just drifts lazily higher, taking Emeric with her, out of reach. "*Time to pay, Vanja.*"

Bloody light convulses around them both, and then—

They're gone.

CHAPTER THIRTY-FOUR

A Crown of Gold

"*COME BACK!*" I SCREAM INTO THE NIGHT SKY. "*DAMN YOU, GIVE HIM BACK!*"

Of course, there is no answer.

I stand there on the muddy edge of the Kronenkessel, trembling, terrified of what is sure to follow: The Scarlet Maiden will sacrifice Emeric now, and there is nothing, nothing, I can do to stop it.

I stay that way, frozen for a minute that feels like an eternity. Then another. Still there is no sign of them. The rain hammers down, the waterfall howls in my ears, the mist rolls on, and beyond that—silence.

For a moment I'm back in Minkja, bruised and defeated in Emeric's room, knowing one wrong move and I'd lose him.

But I didn't. I found a way out—

I had Ragne and Joniza and Gisele and Barthl then, I have none of them now, there's nothing I can do and I *led him here*—

My breath gums in my lungs, making a sickly sobbing sound. Oddly enough, that gives me just enough to lock onto. This is panic, this is raw, open fear, just like I felt at that moment in Minkja. Just like then, I need to give it room to pass.

I had the tolls of a clock to guide me in midwinter. There's nothing of the sort in Boderad's Gorge, so instead I squeeze out a guttural "*One.*" Breathe. "Two." Breathing. "Three."

I did this, I ruined it, his blood is on my hands—

"*Four,*" I force out.

I count to thirteen, for luck. Then I open my eyes and make myself pull at the threads of this web.

Sunset has gone, purpling night seeping across the sky. The Scarlet Maiden is nowhere to be seen, nor Emeric. Maybe she's waiting for midnight.

I look around and see the two lumps of our satchels still on the bridge. I can—I can get those, see if I can use anything in there. I can try to make it to the other side. I can look for a way into Felsengruft, try to make it on my own.

It's not much of a plan, but I have to try something.

I pick my way up the short path to the bridge, barely holding myself together. By the time I step onto the narrow strip of stone, I know I'm wobbling too badly to keep going like this. Instead, I crawl on my hands and knees.

I'm halfway to the satchels when I notice the two unwavering pale lights keeping perfect pace with me below the surface of the Kronenkessel.

"Oh, come *on,*" I almost whimper. The hellhound doesn't blink. I nail my gaze to the stone and keep going.

Finally one satchel inches into view, then the other. I pause only to loop them awkwardly over my shoulders, then continue inching over the frigid, slick stone, hands and knees aching with chill. If I can at least make it across the bridge, I'll be on the correct side of the gorge.

When the stone under my palms subsides to dirt, I look up—

I'm back where I started, on the wrong side of the bridge.

A strangled cry worms from the bottom of my throat. I slam my fist onto the ground and runny mud spurts into my face. Panic wells up once more.

I grit my teeth so hard it hurts and make myself sit on my knees, ransacking my brain for an answer, *anything*. My hands are digging through Emeric's satchel, and I can't tell if I'm looking for something specific or just trying to hold on to something of his for an anchor, anything, anything. The message-mirror slips coolly through my fingers. His notebook can't help me now. The vial of witch-ash oil, with its black cork—

No, that's no good either. The last time I used even half a drop of the prefects' witch-ash oil, it nearly knocked me out on the spot. This power is useless if I'm barely conscious to wield it.

Maybe I can get this to Kirkling. I—I'll do that. Get out of Hagendorn as fast as I can, get the witch-ash oil to Kirkling, pray she can use it in time to stop this. I push myself to my feet and lurch for the trail to Hagendorn.

It's immediately swarmed with crimson thorns. Then the mud tilts under me—I'm sliding down—

I stumble and fall ass first onto the little curl of dirt that banks the Kronenkessel, landing in a puddle with a grotesque *squelch*. I don't let myself wallow, just force myself back up—only to watch the dirt track bristle over with slippery grass. When I lunge for it anyway, it's lifted out of reach beneath a sheet of unbroken granite. The other nearby cliffs turn smooth, like a great hot iron has pressed out any possible handholds.

She won't let me leave.

My mind scrambles for an answer the Scarlet Maiden can't block. The Kronenkessel feeds the river that cuts through the gorge—the hellhound is still watching me; if I go in the water, it'll be on me in a heartbeat, but maybe I can clamber around the edge and get to—

Granite teeth break through the place where the pool spills into the river, barring my path.

There's no way out.

She wants me here. Wants me to watch Emeric die.

And there is nothing I can do.

"Fortune?" I call brokenly, praying for one more miracle. "Death?"

But there's no answer.

The Scarlet Maiden has pushed them out.

For a long moment, I stand there, alone in the rain and the cold, staring at the billowing mists of the waterfall. I am numb enough to comprehend the full measure of what I'm about to lose; I am powerless to hold off this magnitude of despair.

So I do what any rational person would do on the edge of losing the boy they love to a horrific death, an end I led him to myself.

I give up.

I lie facedown on the muddy bank of the Kronenkessel and cry. I cry like an abandoned daughter. I cry like a liar caught in her web. I cry like the architect of my own undoing, knowing the price is so, so much more than mine to pay.

I've failed. I've failed my family. I've failed Emeric. I've failed Hagendorn.

Everything I touch is falling to ruin. My mother was right about me after all.

She was right to drive me out if this is what I bring down.

Between my sobs and the roar of the waterfall, it takes longer than it should for me to notice . . . the rain is slowing.

Slowly, agonizingly, I lift my snot-streaked face.

The persistent sludge of clouds above is thinning, the rain dwindling to a drizzle. A flash of yellow bobs in the water. I look over and see my wreath of roses from Sånnik's wedding.

But . . . it's sunny yellow, not bloody red.

My shoulder hitches until I can see the strap of my kirtle. It's a mottled brown, stained with mud. Beneath the stains, it's seeping to green.

Something's shifting.

One—one more time, I make myself sit up.

I'm still walled in on the bank of the Kronenkessel. I don't see the Scarlet Maiden or Emeric anywhere. I don't see *anyone* anywhere, in fact, which seems strange, considering—

How much ScarMad loves an audience.

That's what's taking so long. She doesn't just want to sacrifice Emeric. She doesn't just want me to watch. She's easing the rain and releasing her grip on me because she *got* what she wanted.

She wants all of Hagendorn, all of her adoring cult, to see my desolation, my defeat.

We thought she wanted godhood, that she was always after Emeric, but—

This is personal.

It's about me.

Slowly, the stitches gather. I stumble to my feet, mind reeling. I see the shape of the braid—I have to start at the ends, work my way up—it's not a web, but a tapestry—

Ambroszia's cobweb thread telling me, *I can become what they believe me to be.*

Nothing was ever good enough, my sister says, staring at an empty hook on a wall in Kerzenthal.

Brunne sprawling on the moss after the race, saying, *Those who die in great wrath, great sorrow, great greed.*

Ozkar in his workshop, Grandfather clouding the air behind him. *You were too young to remember, but you're named for his wife.*

Saint Willehalm in the library, recounting, *Her tears swept her own castle away . . .*

Jakob washing the Ros brothers' little statue the night the Scarlet Maiden first manifested, blood flickering in the lantern light as he mutters, *Won't stop bleeding.*

Nearly five months ago in Minkja, Prefect Hubert Klemens is dead, and Emeric is chasing me through the Göttermarkt. A vial of witch-ash oil has broken in his grasp. In a moment of desperation, I lick a drop from his bleeding palm.

And in that moment—a tie threads between us.

Not as potent as those between blood relatives, but a tie nonetheless. Like the one linking me to the Scarlet Maiden—and, through me, linking her to Emeric. Our own small, evil constellation.

She's not a god, not a Rye Mother; she's just a fraud like me, painting devils on the wall and hoping we fear the fangs too much for a closer look.

I know what her material anchor is. I know why it's in Felsengruft.

And as I pull my rose wreath from the water of the Kronenkessel, I see in the reflection of the night sky how I'm going to get there.

"Took you long enough," I say hoarsely, turning around as Brunne's horse lands on the bank, pawing at the mud. "No wonder our race was a draw."

Brunne laughs and throws out a shimmering hand. "Come now, God Daughter! Do you want my aid or not?"

Red briars have grown over Felsengruft, spreading from the stone door-way like streaks of fungus. They even squirm and pulse with a sickening, veinous red glow. Naturally, this gives me pause.

The Scarlet Maiden is gathering her audience, which means hiking them all up to the gorge. I doubt she'll waste power trying to shift reality for them. It's one thing to toy with two people you're already linked to, another to move the world for hundreds of strangers. I wasted at least half an hour bawling, so I don't have much more than an hour left, and that's not enough time to hack my way into the rite hall.

Brunne's lip curls as she swings me off her horse. "Fear not the thorns. They are but shade and spite, and"—she passes me one of her moonlight arrows—"you need a light anyway. I will wait here."

I give the arrow a curious twirl. "Can't trespass on another god's domain or something?"

She makes a face. "Saints and martyrs, no. I care not for caves."

"You're a *god*, Brunne."

"But what if it collapses and I'm trapped inside?"

"I'm going now." I straighten the wreath on my head, adjust both satchel straps (two feels excessive, but Emeric would never forgive my leaving his behind, and I intend to give it back), and stride toward Felsengruft.

The deep carmine vines contort even more wildly the closer I get, but I remember how Brunne turned them to mist before. I hold out her arrow and touch it to the nearest thorn. It dissolves.

The rest of the briars retreat, unravel into smoke, shrink away until the entrance is clear.

I step, once more, into Felsengruft.

This time I understand the murals on the walls. They're not just Brunne's tale but also that of the Red Maid of the River. Their stories unfold before me, lit by moonlight, sometimes framed in crimson vines.

I extinguish every thorn I see. Brunne's right; they're little more than dust.

Of course they are. I know a game of Find the Lady when I see one. It's always been about shifting power, seeding enough to sell the lie, making us look where the Scarlet Maiden wanted us to.

I reach the chamber where the stairs split: up for the rite hall, down for the barrow. I don't know how things will go in the barrow, so I opt for the rite hall first. If all else fails, I need the material anchor, at the least.

I find it exactly where I remember: sitting, forlorn, between two stone benches. I'd been distracted—we'd all been distracted—the last time we were here and left it behind.

I'm sure that only made her angrier, in the end.

It swings in my hand as I leave the rite hall and descend, finally, into the barrow, Brunne's shining arrow held aloft.

The thorns dared not usurp these walls; there's only the sound of rushing water and an unsettling honeycomb of grave niches arrayed around a thick, slow spiral of stairs. It's been a long, long time since anyone was interred within. Unless I'm mistaken, the last one to seal herself into a tomb was the Red Maid of the River herself.

The farther I go, the more my breath fogs in the light of the arrow, and the clearer I can hear it: the sound of heartbroken weeping.

Finally I reach a great iron door at the bottom of the spiral. There is no handle, no keyhole, just a heavy, permanent, unadorned slab in a stone wall—and a shallow river flowing out from under it, draining into the mountain's natural network of underground channels.

I set Brunne's arrow on the steps behind me, wade into the river, then reach out and pound on the iron door.

"Enough," I call. "It's time for you to come back."

The sobbing continues.

I take the wreath from my head. "I—I know what it's like, wanting something so badly, you're afraid of getting it. I know about—about being so scared to get it, you make it impossible to let anyone in, and then you lose everything. You never wanted Brunne's crown. You just—" My own voice chokes up. "You needed the obsession, so you wouldn't have to look at your pain. And by the time you knew better, too many people had died to let it go. But now there's a monster in the Haarzlands that's taken your name and hurt your people. I don't have a crown of gold. But I have brought a crown of my family's roses, from when I finally let myself come home. Maybe—maybe that can be enough."

For a moment, the weeping falters. The waters go still. I see them again, the threads of story and song, the power of belief and the shackle of expectation all in one.

The voice is so quiet, so fractured, I barely hear it: "I don't want to be the Red Maid anymore."

I lay the wreath in the water. "I know. You thought your sorrow trapped you here, didn't you? But it's not that. My name might have called me back; I think yours has kept you. Every river in the gorge starts here. With you. You don't have to be the Maid Painted Red or the Red Maid of the River." I swallow, praying I'm right, praying I will call and she will answer. "They want you as you are. Please, Ilsza. Come home."

There's only silence.

Then—the water reverses, drawing the wreath under the iron door.

And with a *crack* like a mountain splitting, it opens.

✿

I ghost down the trail from Felsengruft, the anchor in my left hand, Brunne's arrow still in my right to light my way through the dripping dark. The rain has ended, the skies clearing, but droplets still patter softly from every leaf and branch, breaking like stars upon the earth.

I pass the cabin where Emeric and I first painfully spoke of what the claim meant to us, what we meant to each other. I pass the toadstool-marked beech, still valiantly warding off the creep of red growth and flourishing its green moss like a shield. I pass the distant stones of the Witches' Dance and wonder if I'll ever learn their story.

Finally, I reach the rope bridge.

At the other end, hundreds of people cluster as close to the edge of the cliff as they dare. Some are even pushing out onto the planks of the bridge.

And, of course, the Scarlet Maiden is waiting, posed between her audience and me.

In this moment, we could not be more different. She's floating between the rim of the waterfall and the span of the rope bridge, Emeric's unconscious form cradled in her arms, but more than that—she's radiant, lustrous and inhuman, the image of a god in the prime of her power. Every angle is polished and precision-carved, every perfect ripple of impossibly red hair, every gentle undulation of her gauzy robes. The only ugly thing is the look on her face when she sees me.

Me, dirty, sodden, alone, hollow-eyed and full of fury. Not where I'm supposed to be, not where she left me. Me, making a problem. Me, ruining everything for her, one last time.

Me, battered and ugly as the old lantern swinging in my left hand, the one she carried to the crossroads those thirteen years ago.

I reach out, knock the bridge post for luck, and say coldly, "Hello, Mother."

CHAPTER THIRTY-FIVE

How I Met Your Mother

THE SCARLET MAIDEN'S——NO, *MARTHE'S*——VOICE RATTLES IN MY SKULL, for my ears alone; she doesn't want her congregation to hear. "*Your mother is dead.*"

"Marthe Ros abandoned me to Death and Fortune on a midwinter night," I respond, stepping onto the planks of the bridge. "And then she dropped her lantern and froze to death looking for it. You must have been *furious.* I bet you felt like a fool. Death warned you, didn't she? Only one of us would make it home. You never expected that to be me."

The ghost of Marthe Ros doesn't answer, her eyes on the lantern.

I heft it so she can see. "You died looking for this, and when your ghost found it, you wouldn't let go. But then you had to watch, hanging on the wall all those years, as Katrin and Jörgi and Eida——"

"*You don't get to say their names,*" she hisses, the mask cracking.

"—as they all cried and mourned and lit candles for *me*. As they prayed for *me* to come back and never once shed a tear over you." I let the lantern dangle precariously near the edge of the rope bridge. We both know what happens if I let go. "Then Udo and Jakob took your lantern with them to Hagendorn. Was your hate enough to keep you from Death? Or were you rooting yourself here, with blood ties to two—oh, Helga, *three*—of the children you resented so much? Ozkar told me that binding himself to an ancestor's ghost made them both more powerful. You just did it in reverse, making that bond little by little. You took your strength from us."

"*You think you're so smart,*" she snarls. "*I brought you here. I felt you on the edge of the Haarzlands, and I called to you with thirteen years of hate. You don't get to be wealthy, to be loved, to be* happy, *not after what you did to me. So I split you from your stupid little sweetheart, I made you drop all your rubies on that bridge, and then I let you do the rest. You always thought you were better than me. Don't blame me for ruining your own life.*"

"I thought I was better than you?" I repeat flatly. "I was *four*. I—You know what, never mind, I'm not arguing with you about this. Give me Emeric and I'll let you leave on your own terms." I jostle the lantern. "You know mine."

But Marthe just cocks her head. I can almost see it beneath the glamour and the façade: the lines of a face I know all too well. She in turn jostles Emeric, the garish handprint flaring on his bare chest. "*Go ahead. Drop it. Then I'll drop your boy, and we'll see which one smashes to bits first. You win, he dies. I win, he dies and I'm a god.*"

My eyes narrow. I suppose I should have expected her to bargain.

"*Or how about this?*" Marthe drifts closer to the rope bridge. "*You have your brothers' blood with you. You can pick what you keep: your lover or your family.*"

"Well, I know you're not a real god yet, because Low Gods can't go back on their word," I drawl. I'm almost to the middle of the rope bridge now.

Right where I told Brunne I'd be.

"*All I ever wanted you to do was choose. Don't you see? You don't get to have it all. You don't deserve to win.*" Marthe hovers just beyond my reach, nearly eye level, and wraps one hand around Emeric's neck, holding him out. "*Now choose, or I'll choose for you.*"

Then—the red fades, only a little, from Emeric's eyes. They drift, sharpen, widen as he takes in as much of the scene as he can.

"*Oh,*" sighs Marthe, "*and I thought your lover here should watch you decide.*"

That's a twist of the knife I didn't expect. I hold Emeric's gaze with mine, willing him to trust me one more time.

"And if I choose the blood?" I demand. "You'd kill your own children?"

(I'm stalling. I think, by now, we have sufficiently established that Marthe would in fact feed us all to the hellhound for a single pretzel.)

I see it, then: the head of the waterfall beginning to roil and foam.

Marthe's laugh is like stepping on broken glass; after all, I just told her which choice I'd make. "*You have to pay for what you did to me. It's what you deserve.*" She hoists Emeric, grinning horribly; after all, she will punish me by taking him instead. Even this far above the Kronenkessel, I see the twin lights of the hellhound's eyes circling in the water. "*And I deserve to be the god of Hagendorn.*"

A cool, resonant voice splits the air: "Hagendorn already has a god."

A figure swells above the waterfall.

She's robed in the shimmering rainbow of sunlight striking mist, translucent curtains of river-grass hair spilling like a torrent. She stands taller than the Scarlet Maiden, taller even than Brunne, born of the waters that feed the Haarzlands, beautiful as a drought ending, terrible as a flood.

My crown of yellow roses blooms on her brow above a face shining with divine wrath.

"I am Ilsza of the Rivers," she declares, voice shaking the gorge itself as the congregation on the bluff gasps and murmurs. "And you are not welcome in my home."

Ilsza lifts an arm. A startling quiet falls as the waterfall flexes and shudders. The cascade arcs away from the cliff, rising into the air, leaving the Kronenkessel as it curves up, up, up. In seconds the river is running in midair, just below the rope bridge.

Raucous cheers roll from upriver—cheers and a rising cacophony of hooves.

Ilsza has made the road.

Brunne charges over the crest of the waterfall, whooping, the rest of the Wild Hunt churning in her wake. Marthe gawks at them, even more aghast. While she's distracted, I set the lantern down on the rope bridge's planks, then brace myself.

And for the second time today, I take the leap.

(Thankfully, this time with a better plan.)

For a moment I'm airborne, the expanse of the gorge tilting beneath me, the abyss as vast as the sky above.

But the river flows under us, and I am not afraid to fall.

I know—I believe—I can be the person Emeric sees in me, the beauty and the terror, sister, God Daughter, more. And I can save us both.

I crash into him, wrap my arms around his chest as tightly as I can. We topple toward the river—

Brunne's hand seizes my satchel's straps, swinging me onto the saddled back of a silvery elk. She helps Emeric up behind me as the red haze sloughs off him. "We ride with you!" she bellows, and presses reins into my hand.

I wind them over my knuckles as Emeric wheezes, goes perfectly stiff, and then reaches to grab the saddle horn. "*WHY DOES THIS KEEP HAPPENING,*" he yells above the thunder of hooves and the river.

"No, look, it's a ghost elk, not a flying horse this time!" I shout in return. My eyes are tearing. It could be the wind in my face, but in my heart, I know it's relief—relief to hear his prickly voice, relief to feel his arms around me, relief that he's out of Marthe's grasp.

"The horse," he grinds out, "is not the issue here!"

"Yeah, about that." The river-road arcs around, wheeling us back to ScarMarthe (Scarthe?). The Wild Hunt is keeping her busy for us, jabbing her with spears, yanking her hair, firing arrows that pass right through her. "Emeric, meet my mother."

"Your—oh gods, your *mother?*"

"The lantern's her material anchor, there on the bridge." I dig in my satchel and surface with the cambric and awl. "She's haunted it for thirteen years. And she's been drawing power from our blood ties, including mine to you—remember when I licked your hand in Minkja?"

"One in a series of unfortunate awakenings," he mumbles into my shoulder. "So—she had an indirect link to me. That's how she was able to fake the claim of a god to a sacrifice."

"And how she's been able to possess us, move things, send visions—all that. She started as a ghost. She's been reserving her strength for the big things and using everything else to look more powerful than she really is." I swallow and pull the witch-ash oil from his satchel. "Like cutting me off from Death and Fortune. She used our blood connection to push them out first. So—I think I have to push back."

Emeric's hand lifts from the saddle horn to grip mine. Then he reaches for the reins. "As long as we're in this," he tells me. I know the rest: *We're in it together.*

I pull the cork out with my teeth, then swig a full mouthful of the vial. "Help me," I gasp as magic explodes down every vein, burnishing my breath in juniper and lightning. Emeric takes the vial and drinks the rest, and when I sway into him, I feel a thousand threads singing between us. It's too much—no, I won't let them down, I won't fail them again, I can fix this, I can be not a ruin but a mending—

His hands steady mine, guide me. I prick my finger on the bone awl and press it to the cambric—

And become the thirteenth star.

In Kerzenthal, Katrin Little goes still where she's standing in Jörgi's forge. Jörgi, too, lets their hammer sink slowly to the anvil, wordless. Luisa stops in the middle of drying her daughter's face. Udo, Jakob, Dieter, and Helga are sitting in a dining room at a roadhouse near Prince Ludwig's blockade; they fall silent. Ozkar fumbles a tool, the curse dying on his lips as he stares blankly at his workbench. Eida drops the chalk she's using to mark a bolt of linen. Erwin goes quiet at the bar in the Green Sleeve. Sånnik sinks onto the edge of his bed in his new home. Henrik, sitting by a window in an inn on his way back to Welkenrode, lets his quill fall into his notebook midverse.

The blood drops ignite—not just mine, nor just those of our seven brothers, but drops from all thirteen of us. Scattered across the Haarzlands, we are cardinal points, dozens of ties connecting each of us to the others. We are a web, a briar, spokes on a wheel, segments of a rose unfurling, our own constellation. We are thirteen red stars, and I carry them with me.

And raying out over hill and dale, river and gorge, are threads binding us to our mother. If we are a wheel, she is the axle.

"Do you see them?" Emeric's voice half whispers, half rings in my ear. Ilsza's stream bends our path, carving a ring around the Scarlet Maiden, who's still surrounded by the Wild Hunt.

In answer, I let the bone awl drop away. He presses the hilt of the silver knife into my empty hand.

"Don't sever yours yet," he says, "and hold on."

I feel his heels jab the elk's sides, far from me and pressing close all at once. The elk tosses its antlers and picks up its run. A scintillating red thread draws near—

And as I slash the knife through it, Eida gasps.

I don't have time to think before another of Marthe's ties rotates into sight. This time Jörgi puts a hand to their chest, blinking.

Henrik, Udo, Helga, Jakob—one by one I cut them free of our mother. I hear her shrieking with rage, clawing wildly at the Hunt, but we're halfway down the circle already. Ilsza watches us ride past from her waterfall throne, the silver knife slicing again and again. Dieter lets out a breath. A single tear rolls down Katrin's face. Luisa shivers. Erwin knocks over a *sjoppen*, swearing. Sånnik rocks back. Ozkar, when I break his tie, simply mutters, "*Finally*," and goes back to work.

When we've come nearly full circle, I see Emeric, too, has been busy. The ties between us siblings are deftly weaving into something like a reed cage that's closing in on Marthe.

"Brunne!" I call.

She lets out an ululating cry, and the Hunt bolts in every direction, darting through gaps in the cage's bars. One last *vila* slips through just as the threads contract around Marthe's thrashing form. She's reeled in toward the old lantern resting on its side on the planks of the rope bridge, the ties tightening, shrinking, shredding the pretense.

Her long red locks shrivel and dull to hanks of carrot-colored hair. Her unearthly beauty fades to something more bitter, more weary, more human: the face I saw through the Augur's Tears, uncannily like my own. The crown of burning roses becomes a thick woolen cap, the silken robes an old wadmal dress and cloak.

Marthe becomes as I remember her on that winter night, the one who has haunted us for thirteen years.

But it's time for us both to move on.

"Ready?" I ask Emeric, reaching for Marthe's final link to the siblings Ros.

"This won't change a thing!" Marthe screams at me. Her voice is no longer resonant with the charade of divinity. "You can't get rid of me, I'm already dead, I'll just keep finding you! You're cursed, you always were, you're always going to ruin—"

"That's enough of that," Emeric confirms.

With a swing of the silver knife, I cut my mother loose.

Gold and shadow explode on either side of me: Godmothers Death and Fortune in all their glory, radiating the coldest of wrath.

"Your luck," Death tells Marthe, "just ran out."

Emeric makes a wrenching motion. The blood ties converge on the lantern with a squalling *snap*, like metal twisting against glass, dragging Marthe into the old iron frame. It jumps and jolts, skittering over the planks, straining to keep her contained, but the ties hold—

And Fortune smiles.

With a gust of bad-luck coal dust, the lantern rolls off the bridge.

I watch it plummet, heart in my throat, head pounding with the agony of the witch-ash oil. With the waterfall flowing into the sky, the Kronenkessel's surface is smooth and clear, a perfect window into the deep.

And I'm not the only one watching the lantern fall.

The pool explodes, the great gray muzzle surging skyward. Water slings off fur matted and stained with years, centuries, of algae and muck and blood. The jaws open—

And slam shut on the lantern with a final burst of scarlet.

Far, far, far below, I see the tiny golden gleam of Brunne's crown in the half-empty Kronenkessel. Now—while the waterfall is still airborne, while the hellhound is retreating with its meal—now might be the time—

I look to Ilsza as our elk slows to a halt on the rope bridge. She's staring into the deep, transfixed on the sublime gold, the ghost of a dream that's always been just out of reach.

Then she looks to me, gives the softest of nods.

And she lets the waterfall go.

The Kronenkessel fills in as the hellhound sinks beneath the roaring froth once more. Within heartbeats, there's no sign of Boderad, the crown, or the lantern anymore.

It's over.

She's gone.

My mother is gone.

"Huh," I hiccup. Something hot streaks down my cheeks. I'm crying. I—I didn't think I would cry.

Maybe it was the final crumb of hope I had that she'd regret it, every way she hurt me. Maybe it's knowing that will always be out of reach. Maybe it's knowing I have to be the one to let go.

The night almost seems darker for it.

No—not *seems*. My sight is dimming, my heartbeat rising. The witch-ash is catching up to me. It's time to pay the price.

I feel myself falling one more time, but there are arms to catch me, the voice of the boy I love saying my name. It's the last thing I hear before I slip away, into the stars.

CHAPTER THIRTY-SIX

PENNY GHOST

THE FIRST OF MAY COMES BITTERSWEET IN HAGENDORN.

Less than a week earlier, the square was crowded with strangers calling themselves the Red Blessed, swearing fealty to an invading god, building colonies in longhouses, and swarming the older homes on the command of their queen.

It's a lot harder, it turns out, to stay trespassing without a god on your side. The longhouses are mostly empty, the square mostly locals. A few sheepish congregants have stuck around to help clean up the mess. Everyone else, drawn here by the promise that they are chosen and special, has either slunk away of their own volition . . . or found themselves encouraged to leave by a god less willing to feed their ego.

The town is recovering the best it can. Plenty of people have come from Glockenberg to lighten the workload. Ilsza, too, first visited with a river of trout to help renew their larders, and she's been happy to help pull up statues and tear down extra longhouses. Those remaining are being converted into a permanent lodge for travelers, a storehouse for harder times, and more.

Among the architectural survivors is the stave chapel. There's only one occupant, and now that I'm up and walking again, she's who I want to see.

Udo is standing by the chapel's double doors, arms crossed. He's on guard duty solely because he's been working around the clock to put Hagendorn to rights, and this is the closest thing to rest that we can trick him into. "You sure you're well enough?" he asks gruffly as I approach. The nearby innkeeper shoots me a side-eye, and Udo scowls until he moves on.

I'm getting used to it, those looks. And I can hardly blame them.

I just nod. "A bit of the wobbles, but breakfast helped."

Witch-ash hangovers are no joke. I've spent the past three days alternately delirious and unconscious. I'm told Helga and Emeric took turns nursing me through fevers, chills, and what was probably a very glamorous bout of half-awake vomiting.

But when I woke this morning and found Emeric asleep at my side, not a single trace of the red handprint left on his chest, it was more than worth it.

(As was the bath I took shortly after. Saints and martyrs, *the bath.*)

Udo pushes a door open. "Shout if you need help."

"I will." I step inside the chapel and take a moment to let my eyes adjust to the dim. They pick out a heap sitting on the dais, head bent, shackled hands clasped in prayer. She's still wearing her red robes, though the brass halo is nowhere to be seen.

Leni looks up at me and mutters, "The fraud."

I don't like standing over her like this. Instead I sit on one of the benches, close enough that I don't have to yell, far enough away that if she gets jumpy, I can get a decent head start. "I want to talk to you."

"About?"

About what happened after I left. About the choices she made.

About anything my mother said, any trace of her that's left, because, even in my delirium, I watched over and over as her lantern fell into oblivion and I did nothing to stop it.

I guess it's harder to let go than I thought.

I come at it from an angle. "Jakob says . . . you still believe the Scarlet Maiden's real."

"She saved my daughter," Leni snaps.

I try not to sound condescending. After all, I laid these foundations. "It was a ghost, Leni. My mother's ghost."

"She worked miracles through me," Leni insists. "I saw visions, heard voices."

"She wanted you to believe she was a god because it gave her power. She wanted that power to hurt me."

"You're the Defiler, of course you'd say that."

I grimace. "I bet she told you that right before she had you send those people after me in Rammelbeck."

Leni hesitates. Then she says, "This is a test. The Scarlet Maiden said we would be tested. Only the worthy may rise in the age of plenty, and I am among them. I am strong in my faith, I am Her chosen prophet and the shepherd of Her flock."

I have a lot of thoughts about shepherds who demand death of all the lambs. (For starters: terrible way to run a business.) But I'm not here to preach. I'm here for answers. "The Scarlet Maiden gave you power over the cult—"

"*Congregation.*"

"—and you used it to hurt people," I continue. "Why?"

Leni's face darkens. "I wasn't hurting them. I was guiding them, teaching them. They needed to follow Her truth."

I lean down so my eyes are level with Leni's. "I don't think," I say tonelessly, "you believe that."

For a moment, the look in her eye makes me glad she's in shackles and that Udo is at the door. "They wouldn't *listen*," she seethes with the same bile as Marthe, "I told them the truth, I told them what we—what the Scarlet Maiden wanted, and they wouldn't just *do* as they were told. They needed to be tested."

She says *tested*. What I hear is *punished*.

My Scarlet Maiden was a benevolent god in a hard land; she was a fleeting superstitious hope and little more, until Marthe made her real. Maybe it was different because I knew she was a lie.

Maybe my mother just gave Leni what she'd wanted all along.

I stand. "Well, you can keep waiting for the Scarlet Maiden, but Hagendorn's going to decide what to do with you in the meantime. I'd think of something better to tell them than 'I was just testing you.'"

I'm nearly at the door when Leni's voice catches me: "Who's taking care of my daughter?"

My heart gives a squeeze at that. At least she has one point up on Marthe. "Sonja," I say. "Your daughter will be going to your sister in Glockenberg."

Leni begins a prayer as I leave.

It's close to noon. I make my way around the square, where people are setting up modest decorations for the May-Saint Feast. There's been an abundance of flowers, and with Marthe gone, they're even blooming in colors other than red now, so garlands are in high supply *and* demand. The smell of roasting fires tells me the feast is going to be very trout-forward, but I don't think anyone minds.

I lend a hand where I can, where I'm allowed. Some distrust still lingers in my wake. Others saw me on the bridge; they may not have the full story, but they know enough.

Jakob eventually calls me in for lunch. He's already eaten, and he and Kirkling are on their way out as I walk in. I wish I could say Kirkling has thawed entirely, warming up to me as the daughter she never had, but for now she's settled for a slight improvement of casual indifference over outright antagonism. It's been enough that Jakob and Udo allowed her a sleeping pallet in the corner of their main room, instead of making her sleep with a handful of strangers in a slapdash longhouse. (They still aren't sure what to make of Lady Ambroszia, but I think they're coming around.)

Emeric is still inside at the long table, though, working on a bowl of soup and an intimidating stack of paperwork. He's more than happy to shove it aside as I ladle myself a bowl. "Miss Ragne said to tell you she will be very angry if you disappear on her for another three months."

"Funny, Joniza said the same thing." I sit across from him. Ragne stuck around until this morning, but she's been anxious to get back to Minkja and her probably-wife, and I'm sure it's been a long fortnight for Gisele as well. Helga, too, will be gone until the feast tonight, though she's just at Auntie Gerke's house in the woods. I don't know if she'll live there on her own or move into Hagendorn to be closer now that she's the only trained midwife.

"How are you feeling?" Emeric asks. "I can't imagine Leni was an enjoyable conversation partner."

"It cleared some things up for me." I poke at my soup. "But . . . it's hard, seeing how much damage Marthe did just—just to hurt me."

Emeric starts and scribbles something in his notebook. "That reminds me, I'll need to formally take your statement after lunch. But you shouldn't blame yourself. I—I know that's not easy—she trained you to feel responsible for her choices—but this isn't your fault."

I make myself swallow a spoonful of soup before I mumble, "I know."

It's harder to believe it.

It'll take time, slowly peeling each finger off my throat. I want to let her go. That doesn't mean she wants to release me.

"At least this should, incredibly, be a fairly cut-and-dry case after all," he says, tidying his paperwork. "I'm sending the documents off this afternoon to . . . in layman's terms, to officially declare that you are not complicit in the profane fraud. There will still be a ceremonial trial for the Finding, but you may not even need to testify."

A weight rolls off my back. "That's it? I'm in the clear?"

"You're in the clear," Emeric confirms. "So . . . have you considered what you want to do after the Finding?"

I swallow. "When the prefects say you're supposed to be single for a year?"

"And I remind them that's a terrible tradition?" He shakes his head. "No, that's my fight. I'm asking what *you* want. I know I've said it before, but I do think you could have quite the lucrative career consulting for the prefects. I'm personally going to see if we can open a case into Prince Ludwig, which you might enjoy."

My mouth twists. "I feel like I owe it to Hagendorn to help put things back together first, at least for a bit."

And—there's more to it.

We made it out, amazingly enough. We've made it past the day I thought might be our last. But that problem for Future Vanja has finally, like the witch-ash, caught up.

The law is supposed to help people. More often than not, it doesn't—because there are loopholes you could drive a cart through, because the powerful and privileged are held to different standards, even because of simple human mistakes. And maybe people like Gisele, like Abbess Sibylle, can right those problems over months and years. I can't write laws; I certainly don't have the diligence or integrity to enforce them without turning into a monster. (Can you imagine? Me, answering to Justice for all the rules I've broken in the span of a year? We'd both die of old age before I got to the end of the list.)

But the law is failing people now. They're hurting *now*. And those people—they're who I can help.

I just haven't figured out how that's supposed to work, exactly, with my cheerful, necessary, and absolute disregard for the law . . . and a prefect for a suitor.

But if anyone can figure it out, it's Emeric.

After everything, if anyone can make this work, it's us.

At least, that's what I'm telling myself: That this isn't a crown at the bottom of an old, deep wound. That we haven't spilled this much blood chasing something that will always be out of reach.

He rests his chin on his knuckles, elbow propped up on the table. "I think Hagendorn would appreciate your help," he says slowly. "What about your family? Do you want to spend time with them too?"

"I—I do—but I don't want to hold you up," I stumble. "We have to go to Helligbrücke for all the Finding ceremony stuff, right? And for them to finish your prefect mark?"

"*I* have to do that." He gives me a crooked smile. "And Helligbrücke is just a few days away. I can wait for you there, until you're ready."

My throat catches. We've been through a lot since I veered from the road we'd agreed to, but—"Even though that didn't go so well last time?"

Emeric just reaches across the table, takes my hand in his. "I trust you, Vanja." Then his smile tilts even more. "And if you're with your family, now I'll know where to look."

❧

The May-Saint Feast kicks off with a faint strain at sundown. Ordinarily the food is made in advance, the garlands hung and the ribbons tied the eve before, and the day is full of sweets and sweethearts, posies and prancing about elaborate Maypoles.

Tonight, everyone is tired from another day of work, the feast itself is a bit slapdash, and the flowers just remind us of the Scarlet Maiden.

But then someone from Glockenberg breaks out a pipe, and Sonja's eldest child produces a fiddle. The innkeeper rolls out a keg he managed to keep hidden from the cult, and it's officially a party. Sweet beer flows, a warm breeze stirs the oncoming night, and soon the square is full of dancers laughing and singing almost in defiance of the nightmare of the past month.

And Emeric and I have never been able to resist a dance.

He whirls me over the hard-packed dirt and through the fray, one hand clasping mine, the other firm at the small of my back. We laugh and spin as, one by one, stars pierce the deepening blue. Then—there's a moment in a lively reel when he lifts me by the waist into a giddy twirl, and—

I know.

It's the way he holds me, his laugh, the firelight gliding over his face, the safety and the thrill I feel in his arms. We're both cracking up, pressed close and winded, and before I can catch my breath the reel calls for another lift and twirl.

It hits me solidly this time, a rush in my blood, a hunger in my heart. I know what I want.

There is no deadline, no pressure, no embarrassing mark to erase, nothing to measure up to. There's only the love I have for him, uncomplicated desire.

The song winds down, and I tug Emeric out of the circle of dancers as he gives me a quizzical look.

I ask in the only way I know how: I open his hand and trace a circle in his palm.

His face turns earnest and solemn all at once, gaze locking on mine. I don't know whether firelight is catching in his dark eyes, or if he burns as I do.

Then he folds his fingers over mine and raises them to his lips, answering me in the way only he can.

Hand in hand, we quietly slip away to my lean-to room and shut the door.

We are ungainly, fumbling, overeager.

But we take our time, make this just for us.

And in all the ways I need it to be, it is perfect.

⚜

We find beauty and more in each other, again and again. When we are spent, we lie on the barren mattress, entwined in matched crescents of jumbled limbs and dizzy reverie, relishing even the strange new aches, the way my back still sticks to his chest as if denying even the slightest distance. It was a surprise to me, that it didn't hurt the way I'd been warned. But we took our time getting here. Maybe that's all I needed.

I know I should get up and find blankets for us before the room cools and a chill falls, but I don't want to leave this sweet, drowsy now, the rough pillow under my cheek contrasted with his arm curled over me, his lips resting—just resting—against the nape of my neck. The only thing that could be better is the prospect of the morning, when we've rested and can do this all again.

His murmur is so soft and low, I think at first that I'm dreaming: "Still awake?"

"Mm," I hum noncommittally, more asleep than not.

There's quiet, for so long I think he's passed out mid-query. Then he shifts. I feel his lips against the side of my throat.

"I love you, Vanja Ros," Emeric whispers. "I'll say it better in the morning."

He eases back down to the mattress, his breath evening out. In moments, he's dozed off.

I, on the other hand, am wide-awake, heart pounding.

He loves me.

It's not that I didn't know, really. It's that he said it first. Even if he thought I was sleeping, even if he thought I might not hear—

His heart is in my hands, by his own design. And what a fearful, resplendent thing it is. What a horror, what a delight.

What a terrible power to hold, even if I surrendered the same to him weeks ago.

I gave him the power to ruin me with a word.

Instead, he told me I'd make a beautiful bride.

Is this what it's like, to see a road before you and want it? To want the impossible and find—it's actually within reach?

Is this what Marthe believed when she married my father? Is this why she hated the idea that I might get it?

This bed is a haven, but the room beyond is colder. It's not all existential metaphor either—just because it's May doesn't mean nights in the north are balmy. Emeric lets out only a half-formed huff as I slip off the mattress to get us that blanket.

It's cooling in here faster than I thought. I opt for stronger measures and open the iron door set into the chimney.

Voices, hushed and furious, immediately carry over the embers. I have to lean to hear, but the words are clear enough.

"—can't believe you'd *still* push for this!" That's Helga. She must be back from Auntie Gerke's. "Does Conrad know you intercepted his paperwork?"

Kirkling's nonanswer is calm and dry. "If you weren't rummaging through my belongings like a thief—"

"You left it on the table."

"I wasn't expecting anyone but your brothers, and they're still at the feast. But I don't know why you're surprised."

"I'm surprised," Helga snaps, "because Vanja *isn't guilty*."

I bite my tongue so hard, I taste iron.

The axe was right in front of my face, and I still didn't see it fall.

Of course Kirkling didn't have some miraculous change of heart. She only started being helpful after she found out the Scarlet Maiden wasn't a real god, and for one reason alone:

She knew she'd already won.

"Aspirant Conrad *has* to try her as an accessory to profane fraud, at the least. He made the decision to give her critical details of the case, which any suspect could easily use to steer his conclusions. With the Scarlet Maiden's material anchor destroyed, the only evidence to Ros's innocence is her own testimony. Perhaps 'my mother tried to become a god to spite me thirteen years after her death' is enough for you, but the court has higher standards."

"I'm pretty sure that's why you lot have Truth attend the trials," Helga retorts.

"That's not the point," Kirkling says stonily. "It's a matter of impartiality—"

"You danced at our brother's *wedding*. You've had a month to see Vanja for who she really is. When is that enough?"

I hear parchment shuffle. "This isn't personal. It's merely how I am required, by duty, to advise the court. And now I ask you to leave, so I can return to my work."

"If this is your idea of duty, you should have stayed retired." Helga slams the door on her way out.

I look to the bed. Emeric is still asleep, his face almost heartbreaking in its peace.

And just for a breath, I think, maybe—one more time, we'll find a way out.

It's the two of us, after all, undefeated, still here. We'll find our way. As long as we're in this, we're in it together.

But I know, in my bones, that this isn't the end.

It was always going to come to this. This is what we've been shepherded to.

I am back on the shore of the Kronenkessel, the walls closing in.

I am on the low stone bridge, and this time I know I cannot leap. Not without dragging him with me.

It is as my mother said after all.

I could swear off crime right now, and it wouldn't change a thing. Not to anyone who wants to use me against him. Not to Kirkling, who will not stop until Emeric has to—

To choose.

All she wants him to do is choose. He doesn't get to have it all.

And even if we outmaneuver her, there's the next time. It might be another prefect who wants to knock Emeric down a peg. It might be the backlash from openly flouting the first-year rule. It might be a city official he's crossed, who decides to expose his double standards for the laws he held everyone to—everyone but me.

It might be Emeric himself. I never wanted him to choose between me and being a prefect. Before this month, it was because I was afraid he'd take the dream he's hunted for ten years.

Now I'm afraid he will keep his promise and choose me.

And there will be more girls like me, like Agnethe, made every day, because no one with the power to help them will listen.

I can be selfish, cruel, deceitful, untrustworthy. But even I know what the right choice is.

And—I can't let him choose me.

I don't know what I deserve, but that—that is too much to ask.

He will be the dream I drown, the one just beyond reach.

I have—

No—

I have to let him go.

I move in a fog about the darkened space, quiet, creeping, quick, while the numbness of this desolation holds me together. I pull on a shirt, stockings, a pair of breeches. I empty my satchel of the amnesty token, the message-mirror, anything from the prefects.

I know these will only haunt me, but I take the ribbon I have left, the luck charm from Minkja, the folded draft of a desperate letter, the notebook he gave me—still blank, because I've always been too afraid of spoiling it. I pack them all into my rucksack still heavy with rubies, and am wadding one more change of clothes at the top when he stirs.

"Roses?" Emeric's voice, fuddled and tender, rips my heart in two. "Come back to bed. It's cold."

I set the rucksack down, sit on the edge of the bed. Lay my hand along his cheek, trying not to cry. He senses something's wrong and frowns, reaching for his spectacles, mouth opening to ask—

"Villanelle," I say brokenly. Every syllable a betrayal he will not forgive.

He falls back, silent.

I bend down, shaking, and kiss him one last time.

"I love you, Emeric Conrad," I whisper, knowing he will never hear the words. "I won't let myself be your ruin."

Through my tears, I cover him with a blanket. I pull on my boots, my cloak. Sling the rucksack over my shoulder. I realize, as I touch the doorknob, he might try to rationalize this, somehow, as anything—anything else. A kidnapping, sleepwalking, even Brunne's debt—no, I never got around to telling him of that.

But I need him to know this was premeditated. Not greed, not revenge, not my mother's hate, not my own fear. Now I understand how a terrible crime can be done for love.

On the empty pillow, I lay a single red penny, crown-side up.

And I then leave Hagendorn the way I arrived: miserable, lost, alone. There is but one difference this time, and it is that I know I've made the right choice.

The clamor of ongoing festivities covers my exit, but not well enough. I've made it to the mouth of the road out of town when Kirkling's voice arrests me on the spot:

"So. Running away from the consequences."

"Sure," I say dully.

"Conrad told me how much witch-ash you drank." This isn't the angle I expected Kirkling to take. "That much should have killed you within the hour, yet here you stand."

"I have no idea what you're talking about." It's the truth.

"Don't trifle with me. What *are* you?"

I slough off a wretched half shrug. "Maybe Death just refused to take me."

"How long are you going to keep lying?" Kirkling spits. "How many lives are you going to—"

"*Don't* you fucking say 'ruin,'" I snarl through my tears, finally whipping around to face her. "You want to tell me about ruined lives? You know what I figured out? You don't give a single damn about me or anything I've done. Not a one." I hurl the words at her, a wild slash of a bitter knife. "This was never about me. You don't blame me for Klemens's murder. You blame *Emeric*. You were Klemens's partner; you were supposed to retire with the man you loved, and then he chose Emeric. And you've been using me to torture him for it. You won't rest until he loses either me or his future as a prefect. Until he suffers like you."

For once, there are no sneers from Kirkling, no denials, no deflects. She only gapes at me, cut to the bone.

"Congratulations," I half sob. "You win. *I'm* choosing for him. But even after everything, he still looks up to you. If you have any respect for me at all, then forget this conversation. Let him believe you were right, let him think I abandoned him out of my own mess, let him pass his Finding and move on. I'm giving up everything for him, for you. So just do that for me."

Kirkling takes a step toward me. "*Stop——*"

If I waver now, I will yank out the dagger pinning me to my own resolve. I can't. Not for him, I won't.

Instead, I look up to the night sky, find the stars I'm chasing. Five points, like a crooked home.

"Brunne," I say, eyes on the Lantern, "I'm ready to pay my debt."

In a flicker of moonlight, a glowing hand reaches for mine——

And we're gone.

THE FIRST LIE

RUIN

TART NOT FROM THE END, NOW. YOU START AT THE END TO UNTANGLE the threads.

To make the braid, you start at the beginning.

❦

Once upon a time, a mother sat in a bed painted red in a small, crowded home. The bloody sheets had been changed and washed, the other children banished from the room. In her arms, she held a tiny wriggling girl with eyes as black as her own, the last she would ever bear. And the mother spoke the words like a promise, like a curse:

"You ruined me. Everything you love, you'll ruin."

❦

Once upon a time, a girl fled into the night on a dark horse. The riot of the Wild Hunt leapt and sang all around, but no matter how they tried, she only clung to her mount, wordless, and could not be consoled. She had fled her greatest love, fled her family, fled the ghost of a curse she was desperate to break.

But the augur's promise had come to pass: The girl rode through the night sky, and despite the ghostly company, their rousing songs, their merry chases, she was weeping.

And she was alone.

❦

Once upon a time, a cruel maid came to the stone lanes of Welkenrode.

It was a bitter night, autumn leaves rattling across the cobbles, and no trace of moon lingered in the sky to shed any comforting glow.

That troubled the cruel maiden not one bit. She knew where she was going.

She passed a long-closed dress shop, a milliner's with the proprietress still bustling around within, but spared them not a glance. She only came to a stop at a store with windows barred in iron and simmering yellow, the better to keep its secrets inside.

The bell chimed as she pushed open the door. No one was at the counter, or anywhere in the sprawling disastrous workroom. So the maiden glided over to one wall, studying the collection of pitiful treasures, marveling at how such trash could carry scraps of power.

And then she found what she was looking for.

"Saints and martyrs, Betze," harped a man as he blustered into the workroom from the back. "I told you—*Excuse* me, hands off. What do you want?"

Irmgard von Hirsching did not take her hands off.

Instead she looked to Ozkar Ros, smiled her poisoned-sugar smile, and asked, "How much for the ribbon?"

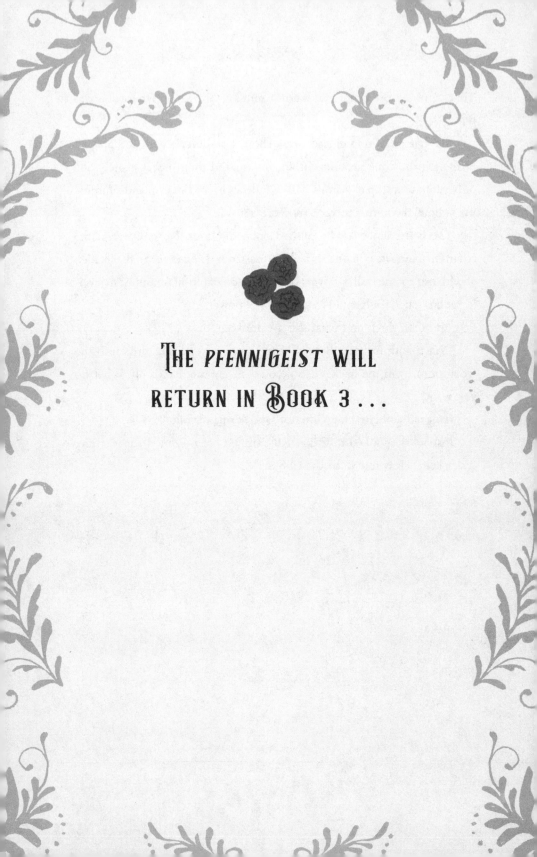

THE *PFENNIGEIST* WILL
RETURN IN BOOK 3 . . .

GLOSSARY

Noble Titles & Governing Bodies

Blessed Emperor: ruler of the Blessed Empire of Almandy. Elected from one
of the seven royal bloodlines by the Kronwähler.

komte / komtesse: count / countess; nobles who manage smaller territories
within margraviates and principalities, and serve as vassals to the higher-
ranked ruling families.

Kronwähler: the somewhat-inconsistent body of electors who can elect an
emperor. Comprised of the seven *prinzeps-wahl*, and up to twenty-seven
other cardinals and delegates representing various imperial interests and
factions.

markgraf / markgräfin: margrave / margravine; noble rank for rulers of the
border marches of the empire, which command the most powerful of
the empire's armies. In exchange for military strength, these noble families
have given up their eligibility for any member to be elected as Blessed
Emperor.

prinz-wahl / prinzessin-wahl / prinzeps-wahl: prince / princess / princeps-elector; a
noble descended from one of the seven royal bloodlines, who rule over
principalities in the empire. The royal houses vary in power and influence, but beyond a small security force, they cannot maintain their own
military. One designated member of the family is eligible to be elected
Blessed Emperor . . . if there's a job opening.

All Things Wicked and Godly

Briar Hag: leader of a region's Mossfolk, with command of the forest itself.

deildegast: a *grimling* of the Deep North, born from the ghost of someone
who tampers with boundaries.

grimling / grimlingen: lesser malevolent supernatural creatures.

kobold: hearth spirits who protect the home . . . so long as they're shown the
proper respect.

idisi: feminine spirits who shepherd the souls of dead soldiers. Sometimes found with regional Wild Hunts.

loreley / loreleyn: beautiful water-women with fish-like tails who lure fishers to their deaths.

Low Gods: manifestations of human beliefs, imbued with various powers. Unlike the unnamable and unknowable High Gods, Low Gods have specific names and roles, but these change regionally in response to local lore.

Mossfolk: various spirits of the forest, including dryad-like woodwives, impish *waldskrotchen,* and terrifying Rye Mothers.

nachtmahr / nachtmären: grimlingen that control and feed on bad dreams, occasionally stealing the dreamer and riding them through the night.

sakretwaren: Holy wares sold outside temples, such as prayer incense, luck charms, makeshift relics, pre-made offerings, ritual supplies, etc.

vila: capricious feminine wind spirits as fond of dancing as they are of hunting.

Wildejogt: The Wild Hunt, led by various Low Gods in the dead of night. Riders may be other spirits, local gods, human volunteers, or those who have displeased the leader.

Currency

gelt / gilden: gold coin, worth 10 white pennies, 50 *sjilling*, or 500 red pennies.

rotpfenni: red penny, made of copper. Lowest form of imperial currency.

sjilling: shilling, made of bronze. Worth 10 red pennies.

weysserpfenni: white penny, made of silver. Worth 5 sjilling.

Miscellaneous Terms & Expressions

damfnudeln: steamed sweet dumplings.

glohwein: sweetened spiced red wine, served warm in the winter.

brandtwein: strong liquor made from distilled wine.

mietling / mietlingen: Hireling, the polite-neutral term for a sex worker.

Pfennigeist: The Penny Phantom, and none of your business.

scheit: crap, crud. Strongly favored by discerning narrators.

sjoppen: mug, pint.

ACKNOWLEDGMENTS

I think I would like to first acknowledge a nap, honestly. And I fully support you acknowledging one as well. *Painted Devils* is my first book drafted, edited, and released during a global pandemic, and if there's anything I've learned from that, it's that we all really need a nap.

The thing they don't tell you about your fourth book is that you have to keep coming up with new material for acknowledgments without cannibalizing the previous three, and by this time, the list of names you owe a firstborn to is getting *extremely* long. (Which means if I ever slip up and have a kid, we'd all better buckle in for a wild remake of the Judgment of Solomon.) I don't think it would be possible to list everyone without pulping an acre of the Amazon, but I've assembled a sampling of the wonderful folks who made this book possible. And because I am an incurable Virgo, it's coming to you as a bullet list:

- My agent, Victoria Marini, who has gone to bat for me so many times now, and swung so hard, the Yankees are trying to lure her into the stadium with a set of brass knuckles and an Airtable under a propped-up box.
- My editor, Jess Harold, who has been graciously juggling a myriad of flaming chainsaws since stepping into the role, including one chainsaw for my typeface opinions and one for getting me to actually do my job.
- The Sales, Marketing, and Publicity teams at MacKids, who have taken on the unenviable task of pitching my feral girls, grumpy noodle boys, and viscerally upsetting magic systems, and somehow turned it into an art form. Morgan, Teresa, Molly, Allison, Mariel, Mary, all masters of the craft! And speaking of art: shout-out to

Mike Corley for continuing the streak of absurdly great covers, and Rich Deas and Maria Williams for once again designing a gorgeous book.

- My publishing teams abroad, who have put so much love and effort into bringing these books to places I can only dream of.
- My author community: Hanna, my partner in Petty Auntiehood; Elle, Claribel, Tara, Laura, Linsey, my fellow Margaret, and everyone who's put up with my Shakespearean monologues in the DMs; Ayana and Rosie, who let me traumatize them with the early draft and *still* haven't blocked me on everywhere; and every author who's taken the time to read and/or boost my nonsense. It takes a village, so thank you for putting up with this particular cat-lady-possible-witch.
- The booksellers who have been pushing my work so hard for a while I expected a visit from the DEA; your support has kept my career alive, which is? probably? a net positive? Time will tell. My gratitude, nonetheless, is eternal.
- The readers who have managed to restore my HP throughout 2021 and 2022 through their lovely and heartfelt reviews, emails, fan art, photos, playlists, *cosplays*—truly an embarrassment of riches. I'm so glad the book found you. You're probably very worried now after that ending, but have a little faith. (Just not enough to fake a god.)
- My friends and family outside of publishing, who are probably confused that I've kept at this for five years, but have been good sports about it overall. No, I still can't tell you confidential news. I still appreciate your enthusiasm. And to my parents in particular: This book definitely wasn't about you, and that's a good thing.
- Once again, my cats have merited an acknowledgment. Sadly, my dapperest of gentlemen made a very sudden departure from my

world last year, and I still miss his weird little self and his gloriously fluffy belly. My old grandpa cat and the two parkouring demon kittens have helped ease that quite a bit, as well as turning the apartment into a cat sitcom premise, and I am at least a little thankful for that. Less thankful for the damage to my houseplants.

• And as ever, to the awful girls: You are wanted as you are.